The Art of Impossibility

B WAHL

Raven Crest Books

ISBN-13: 978-1479292738
ISBN-10: 1479292737

DEDICATION

For my father, who showed me how to live with courage in the face of suffering.

The saint of yesterday spoke of truth with perfect conviction. The saint of today stammers as he or she tries to say something honest.

\- Unknown

PROLOGUE

The psychiatric profession doesn't have a name for whatever is wrong with Michael Wilson. This, in itself, seems improbable. After all, the Diagnostic and Statistical Manual of Mental Disorders lists two hundred and eighty-six conditions – that's two hundred and eighty-six reasons to lose sleep, stay under the bedcovers, or stare into space for prolonged periods – and yet none of these labels describes Michael. Some of those psychological problems seem especially popular at the moment, like Asperger's syndrome, OCD, or bipolar disorder, but they've got nothing to do with Michael.

Most people, at one time or another, have put their hand into a pocket and were surprised to discover an object. They feel the thing between their fingertips and thumb or squeeze the object against their palm, wondering what it is. They certainly don't recall putting anything into that pocket, but it must have got in there somehow. The object feels strangely familiar, but what the hell is it?

That's like Michael's problem.

PART ONE

CHAPTER 1

A Croatian man named Zlatko Grden discovered that his car would not start on a particularly cold morning. In order to warm the engine, Zlatko lit a fire under the engine of his Opel Kadett using newspapers. The engine ignited and then blew up, completely destroying his car. Zlatko explained the accident by saying that he believed he had used too many newspapers.

From the journals of Professor Charles Kidding, extract #190

Michael walked through the doors of the Pittsford Pub, scanned the clientele, and worked his way around to the bar. His entrance was never like that show Cheers where Norm walks in and everyone shouts "Norm", and then Norm grunts "Hey everybody," like he doesn't even care. In fact, his arrival at the pub on Thursday evenings was rarely acknowledged.

The customers who sat at the bar varied, but there were a few regulars he could usually rely on. Michael had come to know their first names. He spotted Mitch, who owned a barber shop, and Bob, a guy who sold timeshare. Luckily there was an empty seat next to Bob, and Michael sat down. Some Thursdays Michael might not get to sit next to one of the regulars, and attempting a conversation around the corner of the bar or over someone's head was hardly worth the effort.

"Evening Mitch… Bob. How's things?" Michael said.

"Can't complain," said Mitch, and Bob nodded in agreement.

Michael wondered about what to say. He'd read quite a few of those books about making friends and communicating. The first one had been *How to Win Friends and Influence People,* because that was popular. It had some tips about using a person's name a lot when you talked to them, how to talk about what other people are interested in, and about being careful not to argue with people. He'd found that book useful.

There was a pause and Bob took a long drink from his glass of Bud. Michael used to wonder if Mitch and Bob came together, but over time he had noticed that they arrived at different times. They were always in suits with ties loosened, so Michael figured the pub was a way-station between work and family life.

A waitress approached Michael, one of the college girls, and smiled perfunctorily. "What can I get you?" she asked.

Michael drank real ale at home. He special-ordered a variety of very good ales, mostly English, some European. He even had a separate fridge for them because you need to serve quality ale at about twelve degrees centigrade. Michael had a fine leather notebook he'd bought which he kept next to the ale fridge. When he tried a new ale, he'd make notes about it, commenting on the taste. But when he went out to the Pittsford Pub he didn't mind settling for the best microbrew on hand.

Michael made his order and the girl reached for the cooler cabinet behind her. She poured his ale in a manner which Michael always secretly resented. She poured it quickly and it built up too much of a head, but she was pretty and usually friendly and he didn't want to offend her.

"You guys get a weather report for the weekend?" said Bob.

"Perfect spring weather from what I read," said Michael.

"Yeah, it's gonna be great," said Mitch.

There was a pause, and Michael noticed the deep amber shade of his ale. He inhaled the brew and took a good mouthful, letting it rest on his tongue for a few moments. Bob was glancing up at a baseball game which was on and Michael noticed that the waitress was talking with some customers at the other end of the bar. When he read the papers in the morning he might try and remember an interesting story. The sort of piece they call a human interest story.

He caught Mitch's eye.

"Did you hear that story about the couple who were sailing out on Lake Ontario and got into trouble?

"Oh, yeah. I heard about it on the radio," Mitch said. Bob had some pretty strong views about the sailors, saying that they deserved to have their boat wrecked and were lucky not to have been killed, because big storms can come up on Lake Ontario in a minute.

"What actually happened?" asked Bob.

Michael told them the whole story with Mitch chipping in along the way. He'd read another book once called *How to Make Anyone Like You: Proven Ways to be a People Magnet.* It gave lots of advice about how to give an 'exclusive smile', how to give the killer complement, how to deliver effective empathizing. Things like that.

The conversation stalled and Michael could see that Bob wanted to get the attention of the waitress because he needed another gin and tonic. Bob frowned and then went to the other end of the bar to order.

"So how's the barbershop game these days?" Michael asked Mitch, smiling.

"Oh, same old thing. Hair grows, you know. Barbering is pretty recession-proof."

Bob smiled and so did Michael because the recession-proof comment was supposed to be funny. Michael had hoped Mitch would have more to say about what he did, but he didn't seem too interested in talking about it. He thought about asking Mitch whether people ever got upset about the haircuts you give them, because he imagined people were very sensitive about their appearance and might sometimes take it out on a barber. But then he recalled that he'd asked Mitch about that before.

He'd read another book once called *The Art of Talking to Anyone.* It was filled with real-life situations and sure-fire strategies, and it was an all-in-one handbook which provided you with everything you needed. Bob returned with his gin and tonic and climbed up on his stool. He looked up at the game and shook his head.

"The Cubs sure seem like they want to lose this one."

Mitch agreed that it looked like it was going that way. Michael reflected for a moment, but he didn't follow baseball and drew a blank. Bob stared at the TV and Mitch was looking at his beer bottle, reading something on the label. Laughter erupted suddenly from the other end of the bar, and Michael wondered what was so funny.

Those books are meant to be *life-changing*. It often says that on the back cover.

CHAPTER 2

A man named Delbert Buttrey kidnapped a stranger near Lexington, Kentucky and forced him at gun point to mow his lawn. The motive behind Delbert's kidnapping has not been determined.

From the journals of Professor Charles Kidding, extract #77

Mary Magellan had a particular way of looking at the objects of this world. She supposed that when most people looked at objects, they saw simple utilitarian value. Such as, *there is a spoon – it is used for spooning something, perhaps soup, into my mouth. There is a cashier – he will take my money in exchange for this kitchen appliance. There is a rock – it will probably just sit there and act rather rock-like.* Mary could of course see utilitarian value, but the objects of this world were, for her, imbued with artistic possibility. It was as if objects required an extra dimension, as if the normal parameters of height, length, and width placed unfair limitations upon their being.

And yet, Mary was surprised when she saw artistic merit in a 12-gauge shotgun. She had never particularly liked guns or even touched one before today. To her, guns were rather unreal objects which existed in movies, loud things that spat smoke when fired by some unfeeling hero or villain. An artistic revelation attached to a menacing chunk of blue-black metal and varnished oak had been both strange and exciting.

It was Burt Tasco who told her about the shotgun when she visited *Tasco's Odds and Ends*. Mary had strolled into *Tasco's*, noticed the shop was empty of customers, and absorbed Burt's image as he sat at the battered oak desk at the far end of the store. She ignored the tatty second-hand items on the shelves and made her way to Burt and the back room where the kettle was kept. Burt needed only to look up from his book momentarily as Mary passed, her slim hand patting his shoulder. There was never a need for convention between them.

"More coffee Burt?" she said.

"Sure."

Mary returned a few minutes later and placed the steaming mugs on Burt's desk, then propped herself on the stool in front of him. Burt would finish the paragraph he was reading, and then they would talk. This was how it worked. Mary gazed at Burt, taking in his image. The paperback was dog-eared and old, the title serious. There was a photo of a long, teetering Giacometti figure on the front cover, and Mary supposed it was philosophy. Burt's right hand absent-mindedly stroked his arthritic, deaf cat, who always sat on the desk while he read. Mary had known him for several years now. He lived above the shop with his wife, but felt happiest behind the desk.

Mary liked the fact that he read philosophy – Camus, Sartre, and others she didn't recognise. He read a lot of history too, usually searching for those great themes which seem to explain why humans do the things they do. She liked the smell of his cigar smoke and the way he listened very thoughtfully to what she said, which she knew was a rare enough thing. She had quickly seen beyond the sagging skin, the age spots, the dentures, and hairy ears in ways that allowed her to appreciate this learned, sensitive, and able man. And Mary was assured of Burt's fondness for her. An older man appreciates the attention of a pretty young woman, but it was more than that. Burt had explained it to her one day.

"I've thought enough about life to appreciate eccentricity," he'd said, "and you're eccentric. Of course there's eccentric-creepy and eccentric-interesting, and I'm pretty sure you're eccentric-interesting."

Mary had told him that she wanted to be eccentric-creepy instead. She even sat behind the desk for Burt when he had to be away. They had a way of being together. Mary had ideas, but Burt had read and thought about life in ways that allowed him to put the loosely arranged items of Mary's creativity into a useful context. In this land of discarded objects, they had become strange compatriots who could speak freely on matters mundane, comic, or absurd.

Burt put his bookmark carefully into his paperback with a practiced hand and smiled at Mary.

"Thanks for the coffee," he said, picking up the mug and taking an appreciative sniff.

Mary pointed to the book. "Any pearls of wisdom in that thing?"

"The ideas are mostly German and French, so that means plenty of angst and ennui."

"Those are great words, aren't they?" replied Mary.

"They're fabulous words," said Burt, "because they're serious and funny in equal measure – they make you think *and* crack-up." Burt and Mary shared a small laugh over Burt's observation, and they sat in silence for a few moments. Then Burt brought up the 12-gauge shotgun because it made for a good story.

"You wouldn't believe this old lady who came in yesterday. I look up from my desk and there's a silhouette in the doorway of this tiny woman holding this shotgun up across her chest, and it's so heavy she's straining to keep it up and she's even got this old lady's handbag hanging off one elbow and a plastic shopping bag clutched in one hand. So she starts wobbling down the isle towards me, legs out and stretching at her dress, just trying to stay upright, and she ambles along and I think I'm suddenly in some B-movie, you know, something like *The Night of the Deranged Old Folks*. Anyway, I didn't know whether to get up and help her, or duck and cover. So I'm just staring with my mouth hanging open until she finally makes it to my desk and sort of drops this gun on me. So I catch the gun and this plastic bag she's carrying and put it on my desk, and from the way she's huffing and blowing I think maybe she's gonna have a coronary, and now I'm feeling bad that I didn't help her because it's pretty obvious she wasn't gonna shoot me. I look in the plastic bag and there's a few boxes of shells."

Burt is grinning from ear to ear and he takes a drag on his cigar.

"So why was she bringing the gun in?"

"Well it takes me ages to figure that out because she starts telling me all about her husband – Hank or Henry, no wait a minute, it was Herb. Anyway she's telling me all about how Herb loved hunting and how he shot anything that was in season and how he skinned and boned everything in the garage and how most of that meat tasted different to what you buy in the shops and I really can't figure out why she's telling me all this. So finally I ask her why she's bringing me the gun. Well, Herb has apparently shot his last bunny because he dropped dead recently and the old lady wants to sell me Herb's gun and how much can I give her for it? I don't think I'm supposed to buy a second-hand gun and even if I could I certainly wouldn't want to, so I tell her I can't pay her for it."

He paused for effect, letting the story take hold, letting the tension build up a little.

"Go on then, what happened next?" asked Mary.

"Something dark sort of comes over this old woman. She seems to slump a bit and her eyes are far away and glassy and her arms go limp. And then these great big tears come down her cheeks, but she's not making a sound. 'Are you okay' I ask her, but it's like she doesn't hear me. And then she just turns and starts shuffling for the door, her shoes scraping along. I get up and try to give her the gun but she just shakes her head, and then she's out the door and I didn't really want to follow her into the street carrying a shotgun."

"Jesus, so she just walked off without the gun?"

"Yeah, I'm now the proud owner of a shotgun I don't know what to do with."

"Can I see it?"

"Sure, if you want," says Burt. The old man pushed himself out of the chair and disappeared into the back room. Burt returned and placed the gun and bag of shells on the desk, and Mary slowly took it in, an expression of incredulity sweeping over her face. She cautiously ran a thin white hand over the blue-black hardness of the barrel and the glossy wooden stock.

"God… it's so cold on my fingers," Mary said, a note of dreaminess in her voice, "but it's quite beautiful as well."

"I guess it is sort of attractive," Burt said. "It's really been looked after."

"Can I look at the bullets?"

Burt grinned. "They're called shells. Yeah – have a look."

Mary removed a single shell from a box and inspected it closely. "Do you know anything about the shell? I mean, what's in it – how it works?"

"I never fired a gun, but I know about the basic mechanics of one." This did not surprise Mary – Burt seemed to have some intuitive grasp of the mechanical world, a talent which came in very helpful concerning some of her more complicated artistic inspirations. "This red plastic part," Burt continued, "is called the casing. It's got shot in it, lots of small metal balls. This part on the bottom is called the brass head. At the very base of the brass head is the primer."

Burt turned the shell over and pointed to the primer, a small circle in the centre of the bottom of the shell.

"When you pull the trigger the firing pin on the gun hits the primer which ignites gun powder in the brass head. There's waterproofing called the wad which sits between the powder and the shot to make sure the powder always stays dry."

Burt held the shell up to the florescent overhead light and Mary could see the wad between the metal casing and the shot. "Anyway," Burt said, "when the firing pin ignites the powder, the powder burns really fast and produces gas which forces the shot out of the gun."

Mary's vision went soft and her mind emptied in the way it does when she allowed different realities to spill into one other. And then she was back, her bright eyes fixing Burt to the spot, leaving him wondering what she was up to.

"So if I took this plastic end bit off the shell I could get at those small metal balls you mentioned?"

"Yes…" Burt replied.

"And if a person wanted to, they could take the bb's out and put something else in there?"

"I guess it's possible," Burt said in a rather guarded way. "I mean I wouldn't try to put a toaster in there."

Mary smiled and then drifted away for another moment.

"I'm just thinking that a lot of art is very nice. I mean it's quite agreeable. Do you remember when we went to the Lilac Festival and looked at all those paintings? It was all very pleasant. Do you remember?"

"Yeah. It was mostly watercolors. Landscape paintings or maybe paintings of animals," replied Burt.

"The style of painting was very gentle and the people selling the paintings were lovely and everything was really pleasant – I mean it seemed pleasant. Even the weather was perfect. There wasn't any tension. I mean, no one was going to get killed looking at that art."

A sarcastic smile crawled over Burt's face. "No – I don't suppose anyone was going to die looking at those paintings."

She fashioned a knowing grin.

"What are you up to?" asked Burt.

"I need to borrow your gun."

CHAPTER 3

A woman auctioned her forehead for use as advertising space on eBay. The ad received twenty-seven thousand 'hits', and her forehead eventually sold for $10,000. An on-line casino has had their internet site URL tattooed onto the woman's head.

From the journals of Professor Charles Kidding, extract #47.

Michael woke and stared momentarily at the red numbering on his digital clock: 3:58 am. He sighed with weary acceptance. For many years now he had emerged from the warm forgetting of sleep sometime between 3:45 and 4:15 am, though 3:58 am was a strangely popular time. It was a perplexing rhythm – almost tidal in its obnoxious regularity. Michael lay as still as possible for two further hours, trying to keep his eyes closed, trying not to toss about. He'd read somewhere that if you can't sleep you should just lie quietly in bed and rest, as this gives you much of the rejuvenation offered by sleep. He didn't really believe it, but liked to recall the theory anyway. Sometimes he tried to remember how many years he'd had this problem for.

At 6:05 am Michael got out of bed, turned on the bathroom light, and stared at himself in the mirror. A familiar dilemma presented itself. He reasoned that the sort of men you see in magazines – models or sports stars – were the sort which were generally considered attractive or desirable. When he compared the image which stared back at him to these men he seemed to do quite well. He was tall, slim but fairly well-muscled, had the right sort of jaw, hair, lips, and so on. But at just that moment when he felt reassured, some part of him, maybe some irrational part, didn't believe it.

Michael undressed and showered slowly. Showers were a good way of managing time, so not something to rush through. Opening his closet, he scanned neat rows of trousers and shirts displayed on glossy wooden hangers. Michael read the *Crew* and *Land's End* catalogues he received with some interest, though he only bought his clothes from malls because malls were another way of moving through time, which the brevity of a catalogue purchase couldn't provide. He put on khaki trousers, a cotton blue oxford and a dark green V-neck cashmere sweater. With hardly a crease to his appearance, Michael left the house quietly through the back door at 7:00 am, not wanting to wake his landlady, Mrs. Deveroix, or Sam, her twenty-year-old grandson who lived with her.

The early spring grass was still damp beneath his leather loafers as he made his way to his car, which was parked in the second garage. Pulling out into the road he felt a peculiar need to stop outside the house, and found himself recalling the first time he'd seen the place. This was Sutherland Street, one of the oldest and best-regarded neighborhoods in Pittsford, NY, a well-to-do suburb of Rochester. Mature oaks and maples lined the wide quarter mile long road, which was boxed in at either side by Jefferson Street and Monroe Avenue. The houses were large and colonial in style, sturdy, very tasteful, expensive. Old Mr. and Mrs. Deveroix didn't like the emptiness of the big rooms and so had converted the second floor to a separate apartment. Michael had a living room, bedroom, kitchen/dining area, and bathroom to his own. The Deveroix's had needed the money really, and having spent most of their lives there, didn't want to move. The house itself was red brick with dark green wooden shutters and well manicured lawns and shrubbery – elegant, yet unpretentious. Michael was discriminating and he knew the value of objects, so the house appealed to him.

Mr. Deveroux had died last year and not long after, Sam, their grandson, had moved in. How many years had he lived here? Was it twelve? He'd thought of buying his own home, but never quite did. Money certainly wasn't the issue – hell, he could buy up half of Sutherland Street if he felt like it. He'd thought about getting a place on his own, but something just kept him moving in a straight line.

Michael shook off the reverie, put his BMW sedan in gear, and picked up his daily newspapers at the news shop in town – The Financial Times, Wall Street Journal, New York Times, and Investors Business Daily. He'd brought this month's magazines with him as well – Fortune, Harvard Business Review, Money, The Economist, and Forbes. Each morning meant researching the markets from about 7:30 am till 2:00 pm. Michael needed to be *doing* and to be *going somewhere next*, and that meant getting out of the house for a while each day.

Today he drove the fifteen miles out to the Penfield Starbucks, which is strange, he knew, because there is a Starbucks right in town – a Starbucks he could walk to in ten minutes. But there were a lot of Starbucks scattered about, and he liked to use them all. He never had any business meetings with anyone. Some years ago it had been a pretty high school girl who'd made his Grande House Blend for him at his local Starbucks. She'd smiled and seemed pleasant, but as he was taking his seat he thought she'd spoken to another staff member, saying something about "the man who'd moved in". He didn't really need people wondering why he spent so much time sitting alone in the same place every day.

Michael checked his watch as he entered the Penfield Starbucks: 7:41 am. He quickly scanned the staff and clientele, noting that Busty Redhead and Skinny Guy were behind the counter. They were okay. They didn't seem to have much interest in him. There was a short line, and Michael was relieved that there were three tables free.

Michael ordered house blend and found a seat in the corner. He inhaled the coffee deeply and slowly through his nose, his mind open to any nuances in the aroma. He'd read about that. *Fine wines, ales, and coffee should be taken with the nose first.* He liked that idea, and it was true. It's best to slow down and get absorbed into the aromas and flavors. It's a distraction and helps time move on somehow.

Michael read slowly through the papers. There was no need to rush. He had plenty of material to get through. His current futures contracts all looked pretty safe at the moment given world events, and he noted that the Chinese were not making any headway on dumping tons of cheap clothing onto Europe, and weren't likely to. So he decided to make a futures bet on the Chinese clothing industry stalling over the next three months.

Sometimes he thought about how he would respond if someone asked him what he did. *Private investor in the commodities market,* he'd say. Then the other person might say, *Oh really, how does that work*, and he'd explain how he researched the international money markets and made bids against the future value of various currencies or commodities. The imaginary person would be quite fascinated to learn more about it – maybe they even wanted to get into the commodities market themselves. Michael might have to warn them against some of the pitfalls. *Commodities are a loser's market for most players, to be honest. You do have to be careful.* Michael's knowledge would be rather substantial, although he'd talk about it in a casual way. But that conversation never quite happened.

The usual haze descended on him by about 11:00 am, which meant going for his third coffee. Trick is to get the caffeine level just right – high enough to stave off the lethargy, yet not so high that the caffeine jitters with the shaky hands takes hold. Michael had read international news for so long that not much interested him about it any more. It was a means to an end, though maybe the end wasn't as clear as it used to be. The same patterns recurring in somewhat different ways. People trying to get control of other people in ways that leads to conflict. Outrageous successes, falls from grace, and terrible tragedies. Different interest groups bumping up against one another. Claims and counter-claims and always lawyers and politicians and bankers wading in. Add some sports and that's the news for you. Lots of fuss about so many things and the world keeps going around. At noon he popped out for a Subway lunch, then back to Starbucks for more research, and he was home at 2:30 pm.

Michael warmed up his computer, went on line, and then to the website of the internet brokerage he used. He put in his password, hit return, and received the usual automated greeting from his personal online broker.

Hello user # 43666002371-L,

Welcome to Web Ventures Brokerage Service, provider of the largest range of financial instruments. Please click below to indicate the financial instrument you wish to use for investing, selling, or altering a financial contract (where possible). You may contact me directly via the email link below to ask any questions you may have, and I will be pleased to offer you my personal attention.

Yours Sincerely,

Broker LH884562

He could do a lot of trading electronically and only needed to email his personal broker occasionally. He bought a futures contract on the Chinese clothing industry going soft over the next three months and staked $80,000, which seemed a reasonable bet.

Michael heard the heavy stomp of Sam's footsteps coming up the stairs and he swiveled in his chair to face the open door to what was his living-room. Sam lent against the door jamb and put his hands in his pockets, a goofy grin crawling over his face.

"Hey Mr. W – how's it going."

Michael stared in a noncommittal manner at Mrs Deveroix's grandson. He was huffing from the stair climb and folds of fat pressed rhythmically at the fabric of his t-shirt which portrayed a picture promoting a band called *Human Sacrifice*. The shirt featured an image of a scantily dressed and shapely woman who was chained to a rock and looked like she was about to be devoured by a huge, purple, mythic beast. Michael noticed, as he always did, the greasy sheen reflecting off Sam's face, and the disorganized collection of angry pimples.

"Just fine Sam. What are you up to?"

"Oh, just hanging out, you know. Playing music and stuff."

When Sam had moved in with his grandmother, he took a room in the basement. He played a lot of death metal and the bass could be felt throbbing two floors up, until old Mrs. Deveroix would pound on his door and shout at him to turn it down.

There was a moment of frozen silence, Sam leaning and looking about the room, Michael smiling. Both had played out this routine before and there seemed to be unspoken rules about how it happened. Sam slouched into the room, hands in pockets. He wandered towards Michael's oak bookcase, running a finger absent-mindedly along the spines of some books.

"Man, you sure got a lot of books."

They both seemed willing to pretend that this was a new conversation they were having.

"Well, I suppose so."

"They're all like important novels aren't they? I recognize some of the titles."

Sam pulled out a hard-backed copy of Hemmingway's *The Old Man and the Sea* and opened it up. He wasn't too careful with it and one of the sleeves popped out as he thumbed the pages. Michael's stomach muscles tightened involuntarily.

"You read all these books then?" Sam asked.

"Oh, some of them. There's a lot of reading there."

Sam drifted around the couch and Michael wondered if he was going to look over his collection of CDs and ask about his stereo again. Michael was acutely aware that the large boy never sat down during his visits. Sometimes he thought about inviting him to have a seat, or even offering him a drink, but he never did. Michael didn't mind Sam's visits – he was company of a sort – but he didn't want him getting any more comfortable than he was.

And then Mrs. Deveroix's voice came from the stairwell.

"Sam – you're not bothering Michael, are you?"

"No," Sam called, a note of distain in his voice.

And then Mrs. Deveroix was in the doorway, thin bony hand on her hip.

"Go on Sam, you let Michael get on with his work."

Sam raised his eyes to the ceiling and slouched out. The old woman waited until Sam had made his way downstairs.

"I don't want that good-for-nothing bothering you."

"It's no bother, really."

"He won't get a job and he's on dope, and I'm not having him upset you Michael."

Michael smiled reassuringly. "Honestly, it's no problem."

Mrs. Deveroix's annoyance slipped for a moment, and she looked down. Michael noticed that her thin hands trembled, and he tried to recall if this had been the case before Mr. Deveroix had died. The old woman nodded and went down stairs.

Michael gazed beyond his computer monitor, through the window, and across the street to the Pittsford High School grounds. The final bell had rung and several groups of students made their way across the crisp green lawns. Spring sunlight was everywhere. Michael absorbed the bright green of the grass, the tennis courts, the architectural symmetry of the buildings, the fluffy cumulus offset by deep blue. Expensive faded jeans and snug shirts revealed muscular curves, and here and there couples made contact, fingers entwining, a hand resting against a hip, and Michael felt distinctly conscious that he was on *this* side of the window looking out at it all.

CHAPTER 4

An anxious thief ran into a bank in Florida brandishing a gun and screamed "freeze mother-stickers, this is a fuck-up". The bank staff laughed hysterically at his mistake, and the robber fled the scene in humiliation.

From the journals of Professor Charles Kidding, extract #47

Mary's vehicle, a converted bread van, was also her home. For over twenty years the van had trundled around the city and suburbs making deliveries, and then just got tired. Mary fell for the dented rectangular block of a vehicle the moment she walked past it and noticed the faded For Sale sign. For the past two years, home had been wherever she parked. But the bread van didn't have the space she needed for her studio work, which is why she rented a room in a dilapidated house on S. Clinton Avenue.

As she drove, she glanced over at the shotgun occasionally, which lay across the passenger seat. The gun was not going to be used for conventional purposes – the gun was about an idea. She recalled a billboard she'd seen once which advertised paintball, and smiled to herself. Paintball, that activity where middle-aged men, men who probably missed out on Korea and Vietnam and the Gulf, pretend to hunt and kill one another. Grown men running about and shooting each other with blobs of paint. A bit like grown men staring at internet pornography and whacking off – stimulating, and yet not the real thing. She couldn't imagine that any man who had ever known real war would ever want to chase others around and shoot a blob of paint at them. Where's the artistry in that? She'd thought about the shotgun a lot since borrowing it from Burt. She had an image of what she wanted to do, but the image was hazy at the edges. Still, the *process* might turn out to be more important than the *product*. It often was.

Mary turned left onto S. Clinton and gazed at the stretch of decrepit and worn road, shimmering in the mid-day sun. She liked having her art studio on S. Clinton. It was an area just outside of the city centre, yet had the worst signs of city decay and neglect. Plastic bags, empty pop cans, and other detritus wafted or clinked along the street when the wind blew. Grass grew up through cement cracks everywhere and the street hosted an odd assortment of dark drinking holes, beauty saloons catering for minority clientele, and convenience stores advertising the cheapest brands of beer in 44 oz brown bottles. All the shops had barred windows.

Mary managed to park the bread truck outside her studio. Once inside, she put the shotgun on a large table in the center of the room with great care, half expecting the unloaded weapon to go off just because she put it down. Mary looked around her studio. Different creative acts call for different moods, which call for just the right music. She popped a CD into her stereo: *The Innocence Mission,* singing *Surreal.* Those high, ethereal notes began to float around the bare white stone walls and ceiling, an echo reverberating, and she put the track on 'repeat'. She opened a new video tape, wrote *shot-gun 1* on it, and slid it into the camcorder which was already on its tripod in a corner. Mary checked to make-sure the camcorder was on wide-angle so it would take everything in, and pushed record.

The table was high and Mary sat on a stool as she carefully eased a shell from its box. She gently worked a craft knife around the edges of the perforated plastic circle at the tip of the shell and peeled it off. Inside were what looked like hundreds of little steel balls, just like Burt had said. Mary had an old coffee can ready, and she gently tapped the shell on the edge. Nothing came out, so she tapped harder and they tumbled out all at once in a clatter which made her jump so much she teetered on her stool. Peering into the shell, she made out a flower-shaped rubbery thing with plastic beneath it.

"The wad," Mary whispered, remembering the waterproofing which covered the powder that Burt had spoken of. She recalled how boys sometimes say 'shot my wad', and smiled, wondering if there was any connection.

She got up and surveyed a row of acrylic artist's paints she kept on a shelf. Without knowing why, she considered black or primary red. Black means mortality, decay, or the unknown. Red means blood, life, stop, or perhaps mortality as well – either color could quite easily have a relationship to a shotgun blast. Mary allowed her mind to drift and vision to soften as she gazed at the two bottles of paint, and then a decision happened within her for no recognizable reason, and she put the black paint away.

Mary slowly poured the red paint into the shell, filling it to the top. She cut a small piece of Serane Wrap off a roll she'd brought with her and placed it over the top of the shell, a sheen of scarlet pushing up against the plastic. Burt had showed her how to open the gun and put the shell in, and how to lock it down again. Lovely man – letting her use the gun and not asking pushy questions, even if he did the usual eye rolling and head shaking. Mary slid the shell in, being careful to keep the barrel up as far as possible. She wondered if it would go in with the wrap folded over the top edge, but it did, and it seemed to hold.

Mary locked the barrel and leaned the gun gently against her stool. She picked up a 3 x 3 foot canvassed frame and hung it up on the wall. The frame had been primed in white and almost disappeared into the white of the painted brick, except for short shadows beneath and to the side of it. The *Innocence Mission* swirled overhead and she knew it was right. She picked up the shotgun, climbed up onto her battered stool, and tried to site an aim down the barrel like she'd seen them do in the old TV Westerns. The gun was surprisingly heavy in her hands and the small metal site at the end of the barrel wavered around the centre of the canvas, the stock pressing tight into her arm pit. Just as her arms were growing critically weak with the weight, she squeezed the trigger.

The blast ripped the air about her and Mary felt the shock of suddenly flying backwards and for an instant she was looking at the ceiling moving past overhead and then the sense of crashing square on her back, head bumping. Her eyes were closed now and she lay still, aware first of pain at the back of her head and right shoulder and then of the acrid burnt smell in her nostrils. She lay there for some time, thinking that if she moved something might break. Finally, Mary opened her eyes and gingerly propped herself on an elbow, surveying the scene before her.

"Oh God", she whispered.

The stool was on its side and she saw that she'd blasted herself about three feet through the air. And then she saw the canvas, still hung on the wall.

Well, she was a good shot, at least.

The blast had ripped a jagged hole in the centre of the canvas, but where was all the paint she had expected? A lazy layer of smoke drifted slowly between her and the canvas. Carefully, she got herself onto her feet and moved in to get a closer look. She felt sore all over, but nothing seemed seriously wrong with her. She saw some paint against the wall in the hole and on the edges of the torn canvas, but the color had somehow transformed into a burnt blackish-red.

She stepped back from the painting and let her mind drift free. She knew immediately that the canvas could only be displayed where it had been shot – carrying it away and hanging it somewhere else would impoverish everything. She imagined doing another one, maybe for someone else. *Your painting comes with a personal, on-site shot gunning by the artist herself, ma'am.* Mary smiled through her soreness at the thought.

She rubbed her armpit and cocked her head, continuing to gaze through a layer of slowly drifting smoke. She recalled a chapter from one of her art books entitled *The Application of Paint.* It had not mentioned guns. She was aware of something gritty beneath a sneaker, and she noticed what looked like grey ash on the floor. She laughed. Was that what became of the missing paint? She'd have to ask Burt about all of this.

Mary liked working with the shotgun, but it wasn't right yet. She had a vague sense that there was a development she did not yet see. Mary walked to the camcorder, ejected the tape, popped the tape back into its plastic case, and placed the case on a shelf next to several others. She sensed an idea growing somewhere in the recesses of her mind. She'd need to keep the gun for a while and wait.

CHAPTER 5

Sixty-two year old farmer Leo Dobronogov needs to remember his passport every time he uses the toilet. This is because his house is in Russia but his outdoor lavatory is in the Ukraine. Dobronogov has been fined twice by boarder guards for failing to provide the proper documents.

From the journals of Professor Charles Kidding, extract #137.

At 8:45 pm Mary Magellan hopped into her converted bread truck and made the 8 mile trip to Michael's home. She was greeted quietly and courteously by Michael at the back door, something which had become a part of the ritual. Mary never needed to ring the bell, as Michael always seemed to know she was coming. He was very discrete, and Mary did her best to play her role, though she often had to suppress an impulse to do otherwise.

As usual, Michal led Mary up to his rooms and closed the door behind them. Two years ago, when Mary started coming, Mrs. Deveriox had made some small conversation when she met Mary. Mary had been cheerful and engaging, but Mrs. Deveroix sensed that Michael was disturbed by their chatter, so she decided to put herself out of the way whenever Mary arrived. It was the regular nature of the visits – once weekly and always the same time of evening – which eventually led Mrs. Deveroix to conclude that this was an *appointment*, not a visit.

"A vodka and orange juice then?" asked Michael.

"Yes please."

Michael mixed her drink and slowly poured himself an English ale, noticing that Mary had drifted over to the stereo and was looking through his CDs.

"I'll bet you haven't listened to the CD I made for you," she said.

"I'm looking forward to it," said Michael, his tone conciliatory, but formal. He didn't really like the fact that Mary had given him a CD. But she always seemed to be pushing at the boundaries, didn't she?

Mary pulled a CD from her purse, *Conjure One*, the band's first album, put it on and adjusted the volume. She knew the right volume by now – it had to be just loud enough to cover any sounds they may make together. This mattered to Mary largely because it mattered to Michael. He handed Mary her drink with a small smile, and they sat next to one another on the bed. They both took a long sip, Mary examining his expression. The lights were off, but pale moonlight flooded Michael's bedroom through muslin curtains.

"What does pecuniary mean?" asked Mary. "I heard it on the radio today. I hate not knowing what a word means. People use words to psych other people out. It bugs me."

"It means the same thing as the word financial."

"Why don't they just say financial then?" asked Mary.

"Well, it's probably like what you said about how people use language."

They sat in silence for a few moments, Mary sipping at her vodka and orange, Michael his ale. He wondered when she might start some new line of inquiry, some new means of exploring him or life or whatever. "Well then…" he said. *Well then* – the phrase meant nothing in itself, but a great deal in this context. It marked a moment of transition. Mary took his pint glass and put both drinks on the bedside table. She placed a thin hand against the soft cashmere of his sweater, and Michael undressed down to his briefs. He lay face down on the bed, making room so that Mary could sit next to him. She took a bottle of massage oil from her purse. She had prepared it herself, a mixture of almond oil, sandalwood, mandarin, and rose. She applied the oil carefully and slowly, working it evenly over the whole of his back.

For Mary, massage was not a mechanical or technical process – it was about developing a moment to moment understanding of the muscles, bones, tendons, and ligaments beneath her hands. It was like a conversation between her hands and Michael's back, and she lost herself in it. Sometimes a little knot of muscle asks for more attention, sometimes Michael emitted a barely audible groan which told her to work more on that area. During his first massage, Michael had tried to make small talk, but Mary never replied, so he stopped chatting. Eventually, he saw the sense in the silence.

Thirty minutes later, Mary wiped the excess oil away and stepped back from the bed. Michael sat up on the edge of the bed and for a few moments they stared at one another in silence. Michael's gaze moved slowly from her bare feet up to her dark hair and pale face. She wore a black cotton skirt which stopped just short of her knees, and a slack leather belt containing a long row of silver bullets. She held a thin hand against a jutting hip, elbow outward, head tilting. The form of her small breasts could just be made out through a loose fitting black t-shirt. Michael gazed at her pale face, dark eyes and dry full lips for as long as he could manage, then stared dumbly at a hipbone pressing at the fabric of her skirt.

Mary had once asked him what he liked, how she could make him happy, but Michael had been unable to answer – in truth, the question had stunned him, and he hadn't known what to say. And so she imagined it for herself, and, as it turned out, she had been accurate enough.

Mary reached down and slowly lifted her skirt until the space between her legs was revealed. Michael stared at silk white underpants and the smooth wide arc between her legs. Very slowly, Michael went to his knees and lifted her t-shirt up, pressing his lips against her warm belly. His hands came up behind her back and he pressed hard at the sinewy bands of muscle on either side of her spine, slowly pushing up and down her back. He cupped her bottom in his hands, pressing, massaging.

Mary slowly removed her skirt, belt, and t-shirt, and stood before him in her white panties. Still on his knees, Michael placed his fingers lightly against the outer edge of a knobby ankle. He moved his fingers slowly over the muscular curvature of leg and thigh. Unhurried and deliberate, he traced the jutting hip, the inner curvature of waist; his fingers moved now across to the small protrusion of warm and soft belly and then up, pressing harder against her breast bone. His fingers, touching lightly again, felt the rise of a collar bone, and moved across a bony shoulder, and now down the thin muscular shape of arm. At last, his fingers stopped at her wrist, and Michael gazed at the soft and subtle protuberance of Mary's tummy. In the bluish light and shadow which painted her form, Michael could just make out soft and tiny tawny hairs on her lower belly, hairs only a woman could have. He lowered his gaze and stared at that extraordinary one inch horizon between her legs, a horizon framed by the simple shape of white panties.

In the beginning, it had just been a massage. Michael had noticed a business card pinned to a cork board at the YMCA. In plain black lettering it had read, *Mary Magellan, Accredited Masseuse*, followed by a cell phone number. Michael had never had a massage and was curious, so he called. For the first few months, he had merely received his hour-long massage once a week, and he and Mary had fallen into a strange ritual. He had been discrete and proper in the extreme, and it was this rigidity of behavior which intrigued Mary. She felt an irresistible impulse to poke at his formality, if only to see what might happen. And so after the massage she would drop down onto his fine leather couch, slouching, arms spread out, making herself at home. Coquettish and presumptuous, she had prodded him with all manner of questions.

At first, Michael had not dared to sit down as he feared it would only encourage this strange masseuse, but he could not just stand there either, so he busied himself, cleaning up here, putting on a new CD, acting as normal as possible. They parried, Mary poking at him with over-familiar and absurd questions, Michael politely answering her and yet not telling her much at all. And before long, Mary had decided that Michael was a handsome man who invested his money successfully, that he had no girlfriend, and that he seemed uncomfortable in his own skin. Michael had felt annoyed, even angry, at Mary's unprofessional manner – on one occasion he cancelled a session and got as far as looking through the yellow pages for another massage therapist. It was as if against his own will that he reinstated their weekly appointments. During massage, Mary's hands always remained active. And then, one evening, Mary had asked a question, and in the silence that followed, her hands, strangely, came to rest against Michael's back.

Michael… don't you need a woman to be with?

"I'm sorry?" Michael replied.

"Don't you have physical needs? Needs to be with a woman?" A long pause followed and Michael felt an odd pain begin to throb in his chest and throat.

"Yes, I suppose so."

Mary had gently encouraged him to role over on his back and then she moved her hand lightly over his chest and down onto his stomach, staring into his eyes and smiling. Michael had appeared stunned, immobile. And then she held him, her face against his neck, breasts pressing against his chest. And so it happened without a word said. Previous to that evening, Michael had always left Mary thirty- five dollars in a tea cup by the door to his rooms to pay for the massage. Handing her money was something he found embarrassing. When Mary left that evening, she found two hundred dollars in the cup. It was always two hundred dollars in the cup thereafter.

Mary ran a hand through Michael's hair, another signal for transition. He stood up from his knees and waited, watching. Mary removed her panties and lay on his bed, legs open, knees bent – a bearing of complete receptiveness. Michael entered her slowly. He felt very hard, and when he was completely inside Mary he could feel the tip of his penis *just* touch the supple firmness of cervix. He rocked slowly, pubis pressed against pubis.

There is certainly a neurological relationship between the genitals, the eyes, and the toes. And so when Michael felt that exquisite release, his eyes shut tight and his toes curled up. When he opened his eyes Mary appeared to him as she always did at such moments; her eyes gazed at him but as if *she* was no longer there.

Michael withdrew from Mary and lay on his side, facing her but with eyes closed. He never knew how long Mary might stay – it seemed to be something she was entirely in control of. He opened his eyes and noticed that Mary was staring at the ceiling. There was just enough light for Michael to see that there was life again in her eyes. She was back.

"Michael," she said, "did you really lose your poetry or are you afraid I will want to read it?"

Michael frowned. "I wish I hadn't told about that."

"You're afraid I'll want to read it, aren't you?" she said.

Michael didn't respond. He glanced over at the wall, wondering what time it was, but he couldn't make out the clock. They lay in silence, the sound of crickets coming up from the lawn.

Mary blew out a long breath. "What do you think about the big bang, then?" she asked.

Michael didn't follow her. Was she talking about sex? "What big bang?" he asked.

"You know, the big one, at the beginning of everything?"

"Oh, that big bang," said Michael. "I guess it's alright."

Mary turned to look at him, a grin spreading across her face. "Yeah, that's what I was thinking too," she said.

Michael closed his eyes and Mary turned on her side, facing him. She stared at him for a while, and then closed her eyes. Mary reached out and placed her palm against his bare arm, and they lay in silence for fifteen minutes. Finally, Mary got out of bed, found her cloths, and made her way to the bathroom. She turned on the light, dressed herself, and ran her hands through her black hair. She turned the bathroom light off and made her way past the bed and to a shelf by the door to Michael's rooms. Mary reached into the cup on the shelf and retrieved the cash Michael had left for her. She walked quietly to the bedside and stared through the dim light at Michael.

"Michael – you still awake?" she whispered.

"Yeah," said Michael.

"I'm leaving now, okay?"

"Yeah," he said. "Thanks."

She placed her hand on his shoulder for a moment and then let herself out quietly.

CHAPTER 6

A New Zealand man was very angry about the requirement for all citizens to provide personal information on annual census forms. In order to get around this legal requirement, he floated above New Zealand airspace in a hot air balloon during census week.

From the journals of Professor Charles Kidding, extract #134

Michael left the YMCA at 4:05 pm because he needed to get to the down-town Department of Motor Vehicles to renew his driver's license before they closed at 5:00 pm. But as he got onto 490 westbound he wondered if he would need identification aside from the license, debit card, and other odds and ends in his wallet. Might want a birth certificate or social security card, he thought. He checked the time. 4:18 pm. He made it home at 4:32 pm, ran through the back door and up the stairs. Mrs. Deveroix's car wasn't in the garage and the heavy throbbing of bass indicated that Sam was buried deep in the recesses of the basement, so no need for social niceties. Michael jogged into his bedroom. He crouched in one corner and spun the numbered dial on a small metal safe. Opening it, he grabbed a black canvas multi-file.

He'd had the multi-file for many years and felt a strange regard for the order and tidiness which it offered. Unzip the canvas material and individual files fanned out, each with a separate tag onto which Michael had typed a heading: In HOME went his lease contract, in TAXES went his tax returns, in IMPORTANT PERSONAL DOCUMENTS went his birth certificate, passport, and Social Security card, in BANKING went his monthly bank statements, in AUTO went his car title, insurance certificate, and car servicing receipts, in INVESTMENTS went financial contracts he bought and sold, in MEDICAL went his medical insurance policy. He liked having all his important personal information organized and locked up in one place. There was safety in that. It was a little odd perhaps, but occasionally he would unzip the multi-file and gaze down, noting the headings. There might not be any particular need to open it up, but there was something strangely reassuring about all that categorization. He didn't keep anything in his wallet that he didn't need – just his Visa, library card, driver's license, and cash.

Michael began to unzip the multi-file but the zip snagged on the canvas material. He tugged forward and back, but it was truly jammed. He checked his watch: 4:36 pm. He'd have to sort the zip out at the DMV. Michael closed the safe, spun the dial, tucked the multi-file under his arm, and jogged for the car.

He nipped through the DMV entranceway at 4:58 pm, noticing a weary and obese woman in a DMV uniform shuffling past him with a big ring of keys. There were still five people in line, which gave him time to work the zip free. It had been four years since the last renewal and, not recalling what he might need, Michael pulled out his birth certificate, social security card, and health insurance card, and tucked the file under his right arm. He carefully removed his driver's license from his wallet and then decided to add his Monroe County library card to the collection of documentation in his left hand.

It was his turn next, and for reasons he couldn't fathom his heart was pounding and he was struggling for breath. He'd had time to settle down from the jog up the front steps, so why was his heart banging away? The single remaining DMV employee was an older, very thin black man who was moving at a pace which was all his own. The whole place had the smell and look of every inner-city municipal office – battered and tired. Michael was suddenly aware that he was gripping his documents with such force that his left hand ached, and then he wondered where his wallet was. It was normally kept in his left rear pocket, so he reached around with his document-stuffed hand and felt at his left buttock. Oh god, it's not there, he thought. Electricity shot up his abdomen and his mind went blank, but an instant later he was aware of the weight of his wallet in his right hand. He blew out a large breath of air, cheeks puffing, and wondered if anyone had noticed. When it was his turn, Michael approached the desk and tried to display his identification in some semblance of order, which was difficult as the desk space was minute.

"Hello," Michael said cheerily. "Just need to renew my license. Nothing too interesting for you, I'm afraid." The old man shook his head slowly and let out a tired laugh. He trained a yellowed eyed on Michael.

"Son, nothin' too intresting happened here since we had a hold-up in '78. So don't worry 'bout it." He glanced wearily at Michael's birth certificate and filled out some information on a form. Turning the form around, he slid it forward.

"Just sign here son."

Michael stared down at the rectangular box at the bottom of the form. The man had put an X next to it. He'd hoped he wouldn't have to sign anything, but there it was, a box with an X and a DMV man looking at him, waiting on him, probably just wanting to get home.

Michael detested having to sign his name in public. He was afraid that a comparison might be made to the signature on his license or visa, and somehow the signatures wouldn't match, and then someone might think he was a fake. Could he be publicly accused of being an impostor? He knew the fear was completely irrational. He had told himself that a hundred times. It's his signature – only he can do it right. How can *his* signature that *he* signs be wrong? In all these years of signing his name, no one had ever questioned it. It all made sense in theory, but he could never quite reassure himself. What if the surface under the new signature made the signature look different? What if the new pen he used made some sort of difference? Sometimes he told himself to relax when he did the signature, but what if he was too relaxed? Sometimes he told himself to just do the signature quickly without time to think about it, but could that make the signature wrong as well?

Michael accepted the pen the old gentleman held out for him and placed the point carefully in the top left side of the box. He held his breath and focused all his attention on that tiny point of steel and black ink, and began a slow arc of M. When he finished the signature, he looked it over carefully and it seemed close enough to his other signatures, but he couldn't be sure. The slope of writing might be too upright. And then Michael felt the flutter of something electric and awful right beneath his sternum – an anxiety like something trapped and wriggling, reckless in its need to escape. Michael pulled his lips tight, slowly drew a large breath through his nose and held it. He had read about the science of panic. Panic occurs when there is too much oxygen in the blood. A very old part of the brain named something he'd forgotten senses that there is a lot of oxygen in the blood and then interprets this to mean that a threat exists, and then this old part of the brain triggers a fight or flight response. Trouble is, there's never anything for Michael to fight against and he really didn't want to run out into the DMV parking lot just now. Sometimes there wasn't even anything to run away from. He watched the staff carefully, wondering if they knew he was about *lose it*, wondering if it was obvious that he was holding his breath in an attempt give his system a chance to turn oxygen into carbon dioxide, wondering if he would go POP before he could get out the door.

As slowly and quietly as possible, Michael let the air escape. He was aware of the old man staring at him and he offered him a forced smile.

"You okay son?"

"Yes, yes, of course," replied Michael, a spastic laugh escaping him.

Michael fell into his car seat and closed the door, a feeling of relief sweeping through him. He'd already put his visa, library card, and new driver's license back into his wallet, and now he carefully placed his other documents in the multi-file. He then scanned the innards of the multi-file for a moment, zipped it up, and placed it on the floor just in front of the passenger seat. Michael pulled out of the DMV parking lot and headed down West Main. He passed an automatic teller and recalled he only had about twenty bucks in his wallet. Michael liked to keep a few hundred on him, so he pulled in and made a withdrawal.

He carried on down West Main and entered the armpit of the city. Cheap liquor outlets, cut-rate convenience stores, Bennie's bail bonds, Adult Videos, the grimiest funereal parlor he'd ever seen.

Michael's ass was really sore. That new stack of twenties in his wallet was pressing into the muscle of his butt, producing a throbbing ache. At a traffic light he pulled the wallet out and put it on the passenger seat. He was thinking about what to do now. Friday evenings could be tough. He didn't feel like going home, but that's where he was heading. He could go to the City Library or a book store. The malls would be open for a while so he could do some shopping, maybe get a coffee.

His mind drifted as he kept on driving, heading home but maybe not heading home. He spotted a newsagent and wondered whether next month's magazines had come out yet. *Harvard Business Review* and *Fortune* hit the stores pretty early – they might be out. Michael pulled into a small side road and then into a parking lot behind the newsagent. He'd never been into this one before. Normally he picked up his magazines in one of the large suburban bookstores. But the shop was pretty large – maybe it would be interesting. It was something to do anyway. He climbed out of the car, pointed and pressed his key, and the door locks clicked in a rather meticulous and German way.

The Newsagent was brightly lit and strange to Michael in every way. It was crammed with many rows of magazines, but sold a lot of cigars, cigarettes, alcohol and other odd items he didn't expect. The first row of magazines were, to his surprise, all pornographic. Thousands of the things. He scanned the front covers and felt a tingle between his legs. He was amazed to see a few men standing around him, paging through these magazines. He walked carefully out of the isle and into the next one. Strangely, this isle was filled with women's magazines. *Hello*, *Cosmo*, and others. You might have thought they would put these magazines at the other end of the store. Michael heard a loud car alarm go off and he had a vague thought about how annoying it was these days that car alarms were going off all the time and about how it was mostly due to the fact that people didn't take the time to learn how to use them properly. The next isle was filled with a rather eclectic assortment of magazines – political, general world news, music and film… and there it was – the new *Fortune*. Michael picked up the copy and got in line. There was an older black man working the till. The black man accepted the magazine from Michael, punching at the till.

"Dat a be three senty five."

Michael smiled and reached for his wallet. He was stunned when all he felt was the material of his khaki trousers and the plain roundness of his own ass. An image of his wallet on the passenger seat flashed into his mind and his awareness of the piercing car alarm took on a radically different meaning. Bizarrely, in that instant of awareness, the sound of the alarm stopped. A powerful electric charge flew up his abdomen and down his arms and Michael felt his mouth drop open. He stared stupidly at the bored expression on the cashier's face.

"I… I… haven't got my wallet with me – I'm sorry, I have to go."

Michael wanted to run for the door but he strode briskly, squeezing between several people, gripped by a desperate need to see his car again. He was aware of the many prying eyes and inquisitive expressions around him. Through the front door, Michael sprinted around the building and then stopped abruptly. His legs trembled with adrenaline as he stared at the empty space where his car had been.

"Oh god, my wallet," whispered Michael.

And then he remembered the multi-file, and stood stock still, rendered immobile by the revelation.

PART TWO

CHAPTER 1

A woman pressed the high-pressure flush while seated during an airplane journey. She became stuck and was only freed when the Scandinavian flight landed in America.

From the journals of Professor Charles Kidding, extract #194

Julie Miller managed the Vital Records Section of the Department of Health. A Friday evening, she cleared away some stray paperwork which had accumulated from the last three appointments, and looked up at the clock: 5:13 pm. The secretaries had already said goodbye and it was quiet as cats outside her office, so she imagined most everyone had left for the weekend. A lot of nights she stayed late to tidy things up, but tonight the quiet felt oppressive and she determined to head off.

Opening the door to her car she imagined her empty apartment, an image which left her standing there, like a still life. Julie had a habit of freezing certain moments of her life and then wondering what that image might be called if it were an art piece. She saw herself for a moment from a distant and elevated angle, and entitled the image *Thirty-two-year-old woman stands in a Department of Health parking lot holding onto her door handle, unable to move as she imagines the innards of her apartment*. Despite herself, she smiled and then shut her car door a little harder than she intended. The Department of Health was downtown, straddling East Main Street. She could walk down East Main and have a drink at Bennigan's Bar and Grill. It was a pleasant enough evening.

Bennigan's was quite busy, but luckily there was a table available. Julie felt a little guilty sitting there on her own, in case some family or maybe a group of friends needed it. The college kid waitress didn't seem to mind though, and she ordered a glass of chardonnay which arrived almost instantly. Julie let the spicy tang of the wine rest on her tongue while she glanced around the room. It was probably the usual mix. Colleagues blowing off steam after a week of work, couples holding hands, friends confiding in each other. She wondered if people noticed her. Maybe they would imagine that she was waiting for someone to meet her. That was common enough – friends arrange to meet at bars, don't they? And sometimes one of them is late and the other just goes ahead and orders a drink.

The wine was so cold that condensation had run down the glass and formed a symmetrical ring on the napkin, which Julie examined as her mind wandered. She thought about her role as manager of the Vital Records Department, and about how the only other time she heard the word *vital* used was… as in vital organs. Vital records… vital organs. Vital organs certainly are vital. You really do need them most of the time. Vital records… birth certificate, marriage certificate, divorce certificate, death certificate. She supposed they were sort of vital. You aren't really born, married, divorced, or dead until one of her staff takes an inky stamp, raises it aloft, and then SPLAT. Yes sir, we offer the full range of services from getting you born to getting you dead, and everything vital in between.

Julie placed an index finger on her cold watery glass and drew a circle, very slowly arcing the line around until it met itself, completing a circuit. She took another drink. The wine went down the wrong way and she began to cough and gag loudly, conscious of how ridiculous she must appear, aware of her aloneness. She noticed several people looking up at her and the college girl waitress wavered, wondering if she should offer assistance. Julie waved her away with a little smile she managed to produce through more hacking. She would just have clear her lungs of the liquid, though it would be really helpful if someone would smack her on the back to start her breathing.

CHAPTER 2

A Japanese crew claimed that their trawler was sunk by a cow which had fallen from the sky. No one believed them until an explanation was offered by the pilot of a Russian military cargo jet. The pilot's attempt to take off had been repeatedly thwarted by a cow who kept wandering onto an isolated Russian airfield. The crew loaded the cow aboard as a means of solving the problem, and because they wanted the cow. While cruising at 30,000 feet, the terrified cow ran amuck. Fearing that their plane would be damaged, the crew expelled the cow from the plane.

From the journals of Professor Charles Kidding, extract #17

Burt stared across his desk at Mary, his forehead deeply furrowed. He looked down at the shotgun and bag of shells which lay across the desk, and then back to Mary's expectant expression. He couldn't decide if he wanted to scold or compliment her, so he just laughed in disbelief.

"Let me get this straight," he said. "You poured acrylic paint into a shell, covered it in Serane Wrap, and fired it at a canvas?"

"Yup."

"What made you think you could put paint into a shell and fire it?"

"You only said I shouldn't put a toaster in there – you didn't say anything about paint."

Burt shook his head and grinned. "How did it go?"

"It blasted a hole in the canvas and knocked me on my ass – I don't think you're supposed to sit on a stool when you shoot. Anyway, most of the paint seemed to disappear. I mean there wasn't much on the canvas or wall, which spoiled the effect a bit."

Burt laughed. "When gun powder is ignited, the heat inside a shell is something like 1,500 degrees Fahrenheit. Most of your paint was probably vaporized at that temperature."

"There was this grey ash on the floor of my studio."

"Yeah," said Burt. "That's your paint." Burt picked up the gun and peered down the barrel. He pulled his head back suddenly, eyeing Mary sternly. "You haven't loaded another round of artistic expression in there, have you?" Mary shook her head. Burt looked down the barrel again. "Paint that didn't get vaporized or turned into ash," he continued, "probably ended up on the inside of the barrel."

They stared at each other, a comfortable, even stare.

"Burt, I liked it. I mean using the gun in that way. It's a way of applying paint to canvas."

Burt smiled. "Yes, it certainly is a way of applying paint to canvas."

"But the project isn't finished," Mary continued. "I'm not sure exactly where it's going. I liked the violence of the shot, but I lost too much of my paint. And I'm not even sure I'm shooting at the right target."

Burt grinned at her. "Why don't you just cut your ear off or something?"

"Already been done."

Burt stared down at the desk the way he did when he was trying to solve a problem. "Okay, give me fifteen or twenty minutes." He picked up the gun and the shells and headed for the back room, but turned halfway there. "Oh, I knew there was something I wanted to tell you." Burt walked back to Mary and continued. "I've got something for you to see. I think you artist types call it a 'found object'. Well, it's an object anyways, and I found it behind my shop this morning. Somebody must have dropped it off last night." Burt pointed behind Mary. "Have a look at that."

Mary spun around on her stool and spied an old pine box, soiled and dented by time, grimy rope handles emerging at either end. It was about three feet by one foot, with a corroded lock which hung open on its hinge. Strange foreign writing had been printed along the side, and the only thing she could comprehend was a date: 1943. Mary placed her hands on the box, gently rubbed the rough grain of the wood, and then leaned close to absorb an odor of pine resin and time. She was about to remove the lock when Burt spoke.

"Just a minute. Before you open it I want to tell you something. I thought the writing on the box might be Slavic, so I showed it to Mr. Standinsky, who lives up the road. Turns out its Czechoslovakian. Get this – the box originally held grenades. World War II grenades. That's what the writing is about. Now, I'm gonna sort out your gun. Have a look inside the box and we can talk about it when I'm done."

Mary gave Burt an appreciative grin, conscious yet again of the way they conspired in the name of art and ideas. Burt certainly knew how to create an atmosphere of intrigue. Slowly, she removed the lock and opened the lid, which gave a rusty squeak. She set her eyes upon several baby dolls, piled on top of one another, all wearing colorful dresses. Delicate and feminine things, they stared up at Mary with large glass blue eyes and rosy cheeks.

Burt returned twenty minutes later to find Mary still staring into the box. He placed the gun and shells on the desk.

"This is an incredible find Burt. What about the dolls?"

"I think someone collected them during the 1970s."

Mary gently stroked the cool cheek of one doll, her mind emptying of thoughts momentarily. When she spoke it was with a dreaminess her voice took on at such moments.

"Baby dolls turn up in a World War II Czechoslovakian grenade box behind your store. It's mysterious, but… there *is* meaning in it, isn't there?"

"There's whatever meaning you might attribute to it Mary," said Burt, his expression inquisitive and patient.

"It just seems sad, that's all. Dolls piled into a grenade box."

Mary stared vacantly into the rafters of Burt's shop for a few moments. "It's the contrast which is important," she said at last. "The baby dolls are innocent, uncorrupted, beautiful. A filthy World War II grenade box represents violation, desecration, ruin, defilement."

"Innocence lost?" suggested Burt. His words were careful and he watched Mary's reaction closely.

"Yes…" Mary replied, abstractly, a pained expression coming over her face. And then her tone lifted abruptly. "And still it refuses to explain itself, which is important! It's the mysterious and inexplicable which needs to be evoked."

"Yes, very mysterious. Anyway, your gun," said Burt, patting the shining stock. Mary looked at the shotgun, a surprised expression forming.

"Burt, you've sawed off the barrel. I've got a sawed-off shotgun."

"That's right," replied Burt. "You can now rub shoulders with the most hardened criminals and not feel out of place. Maybe there's a conference you can all meet up at. The shortened barrel will mean a lot less paint gets stuck on the inside of the gun.

"Oh, of course," replied Mary. "Good thinking."

"But that's not even the clever part. The clever part is that I've reduced the amount of powder in a few shells." Burt held up a zip-locked plastic bag with the doctored shells. "Reduced powder means that you won't get quite so high a temperature inside the shell. It'll give your paint a better chance, and you'll still get all the violence you need. Just try not to shoot while sitting on a stool next time."

Mary placed a warm hand against Burt's cheek and offered him a smile of gratitude.

"Be careful, okay?" said Burt.

CHAPTER 3

A man from Albuquerque, New Mexico was given the birth name Snaphappy Fishsuit Mokiligon. Recently Snaphappy won a legal suite to change his name to Variable. A previous ruling indicating that the name Variable would be "contrary to the public good" was overturned by the NM State Appeal Court.

From the journals of Professor Charles Kidding, extract #88.

Michael woke suddenly at 3:54 am and found himself in a state of acute agitation, conscious of a nightmare he'd just had. He'd been driving his car through somewhere downtown at night, though the streets were lighted. He hadn't recognized where in the city he was, but all around him the buildings were dilapidated, the streets filthy with litter. Strangely, the whole area was deserted, and he felt very alone. As he slowed for an approaching red light, a large shadowy man ran up the hood of his car and landed on the roof above him with a loud metallic bang. Michael felt this monstrous form shake his car with inhuman force. He had now come to a stop at the light and wondered if he should run the light in hopes that the man might get off of his car – but he had never run a light, and couldn't conceive of doing something as anti-social as that. In his panicked state he could only grip the wheel hard and gaze up at the roof of the car. Michael's horror increased when he heard a metallic screech, a sure sign that the roof was being ripped off. Within seconds the man had peeled back the roof and was now staring down on him. Petrified, Michael could do no more than stare at this huge figure, a figure screaming 'who the hell are you… who the hell are you'? This enraged man glared at him from a pock-marked face and dark eyes which burned intensely. The weight and strength of his form indicated solidity, corporeality, and yet, he seemed a shadowy force, a man made of a translucent darkness. This man-beast stared fixedly at him. 'Who the hell are you'? the man screamed one final time, and then Michael had slipped from the grip of unconsciousness.

In the drowsy stupor of waking he felt relief that it was only a dream, and then a moment later the events of the night before came over him all at once, and the agitation stirred again. He recalled the vacant space where his car should have been, phoning the police, standing in the parking lot and filling out a police report with Sergeant Can't Remember His Name, calling the bank's out of hours number to cancel his debit card, and then wandering around downtown until he found someone who told him which bus to take back to Pittsford. The image of his wallet and multi-file came to mind and a vague nausea tugged at his stomach. He again recalled the shadowy hulk of the dream-man, sighed, and pushed the image away.

Michael decided there was little point in remaining in bed and made himself his bowl of cereal. Then, breaking with ritual, made coffee as well. He dressed and sat at his table, sipping at the brown liquid, staring at his safe. An impulse to check the safe arose, as if per chance his multi-file had returned in the night, or perhaps had never left the safe in the first place. Conscious of the irrationality of the act, he scurried to the safe, bent on one knee, spun the dial, opened the safe and gazed inside. The empty space where his multi-file should have been produced a physical pain. He gazed at the contents of the safe – a leather zip bag containing cash, gold coins in a plastic bag he'd purchased when the price had been good, a notebook he'd written some poetry in, a small stack of porn magazines. Sighing deeply, he counted the cash, noting absent-mindedly that there was a little over $12,000.

Michael shut the safe and decided he needed to be pragmatic. Things get lost and then you find or replace them. He would be fine. The police will look for his car, and there must be procedures for replacing lost identification.

He found a lined notepad and sat at the table, noting his coffee was almost gone, surprised how quickly he'd drunk it. He made another cup, got dressed, and returned. Today was Saturday and all municipal offices would be closed, so there was little he could do about getting his ID back until Monday morning. Still, he needed to do something. Opening the notepad he wrote: *Lost Items*, and then:

Birth Certificate
Social Security Card
Passport
Driver's license
Visa Debit Card
Health Insurance card
Library card
Car title and car insurance document
Apartment lease
Finances: Tax returns, bank statements, investment contracts

He stared at the list, eyes glazing. He looked around the room – at his desk, the top of his dresser, the bedside table, wondering if he might find anything that even had his name on it... and then like a desperate gunslinger he made a reflexive grab for his back pocket, feeling only the smooth emptiness of the khaki cotton.

He sat there for some time, staring into space, and then suddenly recalled he had a check book in the top drawer of his desk. He jumped up from the table, jogged to the desk, opened the drawer, and there it was. It even had his name and address printed on each check. There was also an extra wallet in the drawer. He picked up the fine leather wallet and opened it out, noting the many empty folds and spaces. He liked the idea of at least having a wallet to carry around, but what to put in it? He tore off three checks and slid them in. The police had given him a crime reference number which he'd written down on a slip of paper, and he put that in as well. Michael got down on a knee in front of the safe and pulled out a small stack of twenties, which he put in the wallet as well.

At 7:30 am Michael made the effort to walk to his local Pittsford Starbucks to drink coffee and study the markets. But he couldn't concentrate, and the print before him kept blurring into obscurity. At 11:00 am he gave up, and walked home. Michael stood in the middle of his living room, like a foreigner in a strange land. The question was: What to do? He was stuck here in his own skin, not wanting to stay in and not wanting to go out, and unable to fix anything. Mrs. Deveroix was at her

Bridge Club, but he could feel the deep throb of Sam's stereo two floors below. Michael felt a strange impulse to visit with Sam. It was not so much that he wanted to spend time with Sam – more that he did not want to remain standing here in the middle of his living room.

At the bottom of the basement stairs, Michael found himself facing a flimsy wall of pine 2 x 4s which had been covered in fake wood paneling. The wall lent at an odd angle, and he recalled Sam dragging these materials through the house when he moved in, and the hammering as he built this wall in order to create a bedroom. There was a sign hung on the door:

The Dark Lord Is In

Michael had never visited Sam's room. He'd never really expressed interest in speaking with Sam – only a polite receptiveness whenever Sam had ventured up to visit with him. What was he doing here? Michael knocked loudly enough to be heard over the music, and Sam opened the door, obviously pleased to see him.

"Hey Mr. W, come on in."

"I hope I'm not intruding Sam – I thought you might like a visit."

The pungent odor of stale pot hit Michael as he entered. The room was dimly lit by a single small window at ground level and Sam's computer screen. As Michael's vision adjusted, he took in the room – death metal posters on the paneled walls, an electric bass guitar in the corner, a filthy goldfish tank containing ragged fish who appeared to be fighting for their lives, an unmade bed with a duvet featuring Spock, Jim, and McCoy. There was also a three-foot-long shelf over the bed displaying a single trophy.

"So what are you up to then?" asked Michael.

"I'm d-jaying my internet radio station," said Sam, motioning with a chubby hand to a computer in the corner of his room. Sam led him to the corner, and Michael was struck by the rumbling dirge of a note forcing itself from two large speakers, apparently connected to the computer.

"An internet radio station? How interesting. And you created the radio station?"

"Yeah, I only went live a couple of weeks ago, but I've been broadcasting 24/7 ever since," Sam said as he sat before the screen.

Michael looked over his shoulder.

"I've heard of internet radio, but I didn't know anyone could just create a station."

"Oh, sure they can," said Sam. 'It took me a while to figure it out though. I'll show you my Home Page."

The Home Page which came to life featured a large photo of Sam, his chubby face soaked in a glossy coat of grease and adorned with long shaggy black hair. The print above the photo read *Dark Star Radio*, and beneath Sam's photo was printed the words *DJ Sam, The Dark Lord.*

"Ya see," said Sam, "if you want to listen you just click launch radio player, and then you can go to another page which shows what's playing currently, what's been played, the most requested songs – stuff like that."

Michael could see what he was talking about – the current band playing was called *Vacant Scream* and previous groups played were displayed, as was the other information Sam had mentioned.

"Wow Sam, I'm impressed. I mean this is all very sophisticated. I didn't realize you had such computer skills. Do you have many listeners?"

Sam shrugged his beefy round shoulders. "Not really. I've got a hit counter here which shows me how many listeners I've got." Sam pointed to a small box which was indeed labeled *Current Listeners*, and there was a zero next to it. "I keep an eye on it while I'm deciding what I want to play next."

"You've had some listeners, then?" Michael said encouragingly.

"Naw, not yet," replied Sam, his tone cavalier. "I haven't got *Dark Star* onto Google yet, so all my listeners can't find me – but they will, and then we will RULE THE WORLD!" Sam gave Michael a large goofy grin, and then returned his attention to the screen.

"Just a second, Mr. Wilson. I've got a break here." The current song ground down into what might have been guitars or animals growling – it was hard to tell – and then Sam began speaking into a small microphone. "Hello again my children, your listening to DJ Sam, the Dark Lord of the darkest radio waves available to man or beast. That was *Vacant Scream* with My Pretty Homicide, which was from their first and self-titled album. It's pretty hard to find *Vacant Scream* on vinyl these days but apparently they're on Napster which seems pretty fucking impossible, but there you go. I've got some *Slayer* coming at you now, so keep that fucking dial right where it is – oh I don't suppose you have a dial – this *is* internet radio isn't it…" Sam laughed too hard at his own joke and when he clicked a tab a rather impressive reverb effect made his laughter sound ominous, and then the sound of grinding guitars wrenched itself from the speakers.

Michael stared at the big zero next to *Current Listeners*, wondering if it might turn into a 1, but it didn't. Sam turned to face Michael, a rather proud expression on his face. Michael tried to think of something positive to say, eventually coming up with, "Well, you certainly have worked hard at it."

"Yea, it takes a lot of time to run a radio station. For one thing, I have to keep up with my tracks. You can't allow for dead air – dead air is the worst sin a DJ can make."

A rather awkward silence followed, and Michael, feeling stuck for something to say, stared around the room. He again noticed the trophy.

"So what's the trophy for then?"

Sam pushed himself up from his chair and plucked the trophy from its shelf, inspecting it. The base was marble, and contained a copper plaque. The trophy itself was of a man in gold, covered in impressive muscles and naked except for a loin cloth, tall wings stretching straight up behind him. Sam read the inscription on the plaque.

"I'm not sure. All it says is *First Place – Monroe County Regionals*."

Michael was thrown into confusion and struggled to find the right words. "But… I mean… did you win the trophy?"

Sam burst into laughter. "Yeah right. As if! Like I would want to win a trophy of gold loin-cloth man." Sam bent over in a state of hilarity, rolls of fat jiggling rhythmically, and he had to sit down on the bed. Finally, he said, "I got it at a garage sale for a dollar."

Sam replaced the trophy carefully, ensuring that it sat right in the middle of the shelf, and they again fell into an awkward silence. Michael thought of telling Sam about the events of last night, but he didn't really want to divulge that sort of experience.

Back in his living room, Michael discovered that he was standing in front of his oak book case, gazing at hundreds of novels he'd collected. The material world could be reassuring because it gave him something to do with time, like researching and collecting novels. He'd consulted several lists of *the greatest novels*, lists developed by various experts, before deciding which books he should own. His eyes passed over the books, alphabetized by author name, and he wondered how many he'd actually read. Probably not many. He was meant to read them all, and he wondered what had happened.

At 2:30 PM Michael decided to visit the Rundel Memorial Library, downtown, something he did most every Saturday. Michael thought about renting a car, but realized almost immediately that this would be impossible without a driver's license and a debit card. So he walked the three blocks to Main Street Pittsford and took the bus the ten miles down Monroe Avenue and into the city centre. Michael got off at Woodbury Avenue, walked one block west, and stood at the foot of Washington Square Park.

This small park often had a rather hypnotic hold on Michael, and he frequently stopped on the way to the library to sit on one of its benches. Michael sat on a bench at the south end of the park, a bench which was 'his bench' in the sense that he always sat here if it was available. The park itself was a perfect rectangle in shape, bordered and formed by the intersecting of South Clinton Avenue, Court Street, St. Mary's Avenue, and Woodbury Avenue. Two hundred yards in length, there was a tall statue of Abraham Lincoln in the centre and two cannons at the far end. Tall oak trees dotted the park amidst symmetric pavements and plush green grass. Many birds made their home amongst the oaks and sprightly chirping could almost always be heard. Impressive buildings and skyscrapers presided across the roads which bordered the park – the Frontier building, The Geva Theatre, the Xerox tower, the Bousch and Lomb building, and the quiet dignified structure of St. Mary's Church. Sunlight dappled the ground. To Michael, the park was a different world in relation to the suburban landscapes he so often inhabited. The park was the heart of the city. The park was a place where it was okay to be alone.

Today, some of the benches were occupied, others empty. Michael noticed a middle-aged woman reading a novel, a man in a suit eating out of a brown bag, an older man walking his dachshund, and a couple eating a late lunch. He also noticed the park bum sitting on 'his bench', a bench nearest the park centre, not far from the Abe Lincoln monument. Today, for reasons he did not understand, Michael found himself inspecting the bum in detail.

He was certainly not the city's only bum, but he was a peculiar bum in some respects. For one thing, he drank red wine out of a wine glass, a half empty wine bottle there on the bench next to him, an empty wine bottle at the foot of the bench; most bums you see drink cheap stuff straight out of the can or glass bottle it comes in. He might be about fifty years old and he was tall with lanky limbs. He had a scruffy graying beard, and wore a non-descript button-up shirt, a dirty baseball cap, and powder-blue nylon slacks. The slacks were too short and they revealed an expanse of white athletic socks and tatty basketball shoes. He wore headphones attached to a CD player.

The bum inclined on the bench, his long legs crossed and stretching out before him, one arm loosely around the back of the bench, the other holding the wine glass which rested casually on a knee – and he stared into space, lost to some inner word of his own making, or maybe just listening to the music. Michael had seen this bum, this drunk, many times in the park, always sitting on the same bench, always in the same state of repose, drinking bottles of wine, staring into spaces incomprehensible to all but the bum himself. Normally, Michael ignored his presence rather easily, but not today. Why does he just sit there getting drunk on wine? Did he have a life before he became a bum? Michael was struck by what a non-person this drunk seemed to be. There's probably a law against public consumption of alcohol, but even the police don't care to bother with him. No one talks to him. He just sits there, inebriated, staring into space. What happened to him? Michael felt a sudden anger at the bum for reasons he did not understand, and then, inexplicably, he wondered what it would be like to bring several bottles of good ale to 'his' bench, perhaps in an iced cooler bag, and get slowly drunk over the course of an afternoon and evening, all the while staring into space, maybe listening to some music too.

CHAPTER 4

A Man has been convicted of stealing six 350 pound electrical transformers from a power plant in Stanberry, Missouri. Twenty-one-year-old Michael Marcum explained that he needed the transformers to build a time machine so that he could transport himself a few days into the future and learn the winning lottery numbers.

From the journals of Professor Charles Kidding, extract #106.

Julie Miller walked her terrier, Bobby, down the street. They were heading for the local park, completing a daily ritual which Bobby seemed to depend on with all the urgency of life itself. It was just after 7:00 pm and the sun was mellowing into shades of warming yellow. Julie found herself recalling the day's events. Managing the Vital Records Department had presented her with the normal run of bureaucratic nonsense, plus two especially weird interviews. Her staff dealt with 99% of people who needed help, but she acted as 'back up' for the really odd and probably illicit cases. There was this Mexican family she'd seen – a man and woman and their two solemn little children. He must have spent time working on our side of the border, because his English wasn't too bad. The amazing thing was that he wanted birth certificates so he and his wife could get social security cards, and some work. The guy had absolutely no idea how the system worked. He had an expired work visa, and the rest of the family had nothing but the tired smiles they plied her with. And they didn't even bother to make up some story about the visa problem – the man just said, "Oh no, we don got no good visas." Julie realized that she was sitting there with four illegal aliens. She wondered what they were doing so far north of the border. Julie didn't have the heart to call the INS, so she just gave them the best advice she could, including the location of the nearest soup kitchen.

Bobby was straining at the leash, giving these little yelps, pleading with her to go faster. She tried to train him not to do that once, but she'd given up years ago. After the Mexicans, she'd seen this Russian fellow with hair that had been slicked with about half a jar of shiny gel. He wanted a death certificate for his father. God knows why. Greasy-man presented her with one of the phoniest coroner's reports she'd ever seen and tried to win her over with smiles, jokes, and silly stories. When it was clear he was getting nowhere, he mentioned how fabulously wealthy his family was back in Russia (oil money, naturally, because we all know that Russians are getting stupidly rich on oil). He actually opened his wallet and fanned through a stack of twenties. As bribes go, it was as comical as it was clumsy. Did Russians like this guy really exist, or were they a product of the Hollywood films they watch about themselves? It was sort of a chicken and egg thing, really. She sent him away with his money but wondered if some day the job would really get to her, and then… just maybe.

They reached the park and Julie took Bobby off his lead. The little guy pranced about in tiny circles like a deranged circus pony. It was time for the big event of the day, time for Julie to toss Bobby his ball so he could retrieve it… again and again and again. She stared at the beloved, half-chewed object for a moment, and then threw it hard. A blur of terrier sped off. Julie's friend Margaret had called earlier that evening. Margaret had cried and raged down the line about her shitty kids and even shittier husband. Julie had held the phone in the crook of her neck while pouring herself a big glass of chardonnay. You really need a glass of wine to lubricate all those *uhg hughs*, and *that's awfuls*, and *Mmmmsss.*

Bobby dropped the ball at her feet and looked up expectantly, tail flashing frenetically. She threw the ball, and he was off. Margaret didn't get out much on account of her kids, so this was the sort of relationship they seemed to have. She'd probably watch a movie again tonight.

Bobby arrived and dutifully dropped the ball, eager for the next throw. Julie picked up the ball but held onto it for some reason. Bobby gave out an exasperated bark and bounced up and down on stubby legs, encouraging her to *GET ON WITH IT!* Julie watched Bobby, wondering why she was being so sadistic to the little guy. He spun around in a circle, stopped, and stared at her in utter disbelief. She and Bobby had spent so many evenings together that she seemed to know just what he was thinking.

Throw the ball, throw the ball, throw the ball. Oh my god, you're just standing there holding onto my ball! Throw the fucking ball!

Julie discovered that she was annoyed with Bobby and his insistence on this simplistic and repetitive routine. It wasn't rational, but there it was – she was irritated with Bobby, her best friend. Come to think of it, he was about the color and size of a football, and a well-aimed place kick would… Now Julie felt bad. How could she think that?

She brought her arm back for a throw and noticed the pond. Were terriers swimmers? she wondered. Terriers weren't built much like seals, but some dogs enjoy swimming, like those hunting dogs that retrieve birds she'd seen while flipping through the TV channels. Julie walked closer to the pond, Bobby barking excitedly at her heels. The little guy was crazy as a box of frogs.

Julie held the ball out and locked eyes with her friend. "Come on Bobby," she said enthusiastically. Julie threw the ball about ten feet into the pond. Bobby raced to the water's edge and skidded on four stubby terrier legs. He barked at the ball and looked back at Julie, his face filled with despondent disbelief.

My ball, oh my god, my ball. It's in the water. Oh Jesus, it's over there and I can't get to it. Oh no…"

"Come on Bobby," she said in that perky tone which she knew Bobby liked. "You can do it. I'll bet terriers are great swimmers."

Bobby gazed at her, eyes large and panic stricken. *It's in the water. I don't go in the water. Oh my god, why are you doing this?*

Bobby barked, a pleading and distressed utterance. Julie sighed, and quite suddenly felt bad and wasn't annoyed with him anymore. She understood at that moment how hard it was for him. She knelt down and ran her hand over his curly, rough fur.

CHAPTER 5

An unknown resident of San Francisco attached a hen to 100 helium balloons. The confused and disoriented bird floated over the city for 2 hours. Police eventually popped the balloons with an air rifle, and the bird floated to the ground. The hen, nick-named Amelia Earhart, is recovering in a shelter.

From the journals of Professor Charles Kidding, extract #214

Michael woke at 4:06 am Sunday morning and tried to rest in bed, but the thought of his absent wallet and multi-file kept forcing itself upon him. It was like a hard fought game of tennis. The image of the missing wallet and multi-file would come to mind, dragging with it a sense of agitation he could feel in his stomach like a vague sickness. Michael then worked hard to reassure himself that everything would be okay – he would get his identification back and his life would resume its normal shape. At 5:15 am, in a fit of frustration, he at last leapt out of bed and had cereal and coffee, studying his list of lost items with a hazy eye.

He determined to keep to his routine, and promised himself that he would take the bus to the Clover Commons Starbucks and study the markets until 2:00 pm, do a bit of shopping at Eastview Mall, and then get a work-out at the YMCA.

The café had just opened and he was the first customer through the door. He stood back from the serving counter for a few moments, pretending to make up his mind about what he wanted, appearing to examine the equipment and signs. He knew he would have the House Blend, but he needed to look over the seating and the staff situation. There were two college kids, a handsome boy who looked the football type and a slim attractive girl with blond hair framing angular features. As he approached, the college girl offered him a small perfunctory smile.

"Morning, what can I get you?"

"House Blend, grande please."

As the girl poured coffee and rang up the sale, her gaze was fixed on her duties, and Michael noticed that for these few moments he could view, inspect even, her person in detail. He noticed very fine and soft hair, almost indiscernible, covering the back of her neck. Michael wondered if all women were covered in this downy hair and if he had managed to overlook it all these years. Her hair was parted in the middle, and on close inspection he saw that she was not the natural blond she appeared to be, as there was a very thin streak of auburn running in the parting. And just as she at last looked up at him to announce the cost of the coffee, Michael noticed a petite speck of whitish material on her upper lip – could it be dried milk or just a dry patch of skin?

Taking a seat by a front window, Michael placed a pile of newspapers and magazines on a chair beside him and opened *The Harvard Business Review*, scanning the table of contents. Sprightly acoustic world music echoed about the place and he was aware that the college girl and boy were chatting.

Michael was conscious of being the only customer. He did not have his back to the staff, but neither did he face them, and as such they could observe him if they wanted to. How easy it had been for him to inspect the college girl in such detail, and what a strange pleasure it had given him to notice those subtle idiosyncrasies. Michael suddenly recalled being made to dissect a worm at the age of twelve in science class, and the clearest image came to him – the two rows of pins holding the ribbed colorless skin back, the entrails revealed in order that they might be examined and prodded. He wished that other customers would arrive, and he drank his coffee too hot and burnt his tongue. He couldn't see the college boy and girl but could sense them just the same.

Other customers eventually arrived, and Michael had managed to read three newspapers, a few magazine articles, and visited some websites. He felt it was a good day's work considering his precarious state, and he left Starbucks at 2:00 pm, dropped his reading materials and laptop at home, and took a bus the eight miles down Jefferson Road to Eastview Mall.

As he entered the wide doors of the main entrance he was struck, as always, by the enormity of the mall – a materialist's Mecca for anyone with money at hand. To Michael, nothing ever seemed quite real in malls. Maybe it was the celestial quality of the 'muzak' floating around the soaring ceilings, ceilings which spread overhead like some hard-edged and creamy cathedral. Maybe it was the trance-inducing sound of the fountains, or the mingling of so many impenetrable conversations. Even the air pressure had about it an indiscernible other-worldliness. Whatever the case, the unreality of Malls was, for Michael, like an ointment applied to the concrete actuality of things, and he felt strangely at home there.

Michael slowly strolled the long stretches of marbled flooring, gazing obliquely into shops, taking in the presence of thousands of items. In a dreamy and abstracted state, he drifted into certain shops, feeling the fabric of a sweater or jacket here, pressing a thumb into the bottom of an expensive sneaker there, moving on, almost losing himself to it all.

And then Michael came upon the first shop which sold wrist watches. The predicament that was Michael Wilson seemed to involve timepieces. Michael was oddly infatuated with watches. He never made a conscious decision to shop specifically for a new watch, but when he was in the Malls he invariably drifted towards each plexiglassed wristwatch display. This *drifting towards plexiglassed displays* occurred for reasons which could only whisper inaudibly to Michael.

He owned nine watches already and always felt slightly ridiculous as he gazed at the shop displays, scrutinizing the details of each watch like a gambler studying his cards. Because the real reasons concerning his affection for watches were mysterious, he could only conjure rationalizations for his habit. Top three rationalizations: 1. People should dress appropriately for different social settings, so you might need a range of watches handy to choose from; 2. This new watch has some unique and useful bit of technology which is of practical use; 3. Everyone has some acceptable oddity about them and his happens to involve watches, and that's okay. But no one really gets away with rationalizations. Rationalizations have subterranean currents which are felt, currents which crackle in the brain cell synapse and fizz just beneath the skin. And so Michael was forever ill-at-ease about his watches.

He once threw out a whole collection of watches in disgust. He lasted less than a week before starting over again. One day, when he was feeling particularly low, he even bought a little pine watch stand with ten pegs for organizing his watches. He felt excitement and shame in equal measure every time he surveyed his collection, displayed as it was on those varnished pine pegs which sat in the middle of his dresser. Desire and shame wrapped itself around this fixation, and he could understand little more beyond these feelings.

He knew he would buy one today, and he knew he would spend most of the afternoon cruising each display in the mall, analyzing every watch, agonizing over which one to purchase. Occasionally he just felt low enough to need that, and today was *definitely* one of those days.

Michael stepped off the bus at the corner of Jefferson Road and Main Street. Carrying his new watch in a plastic bag, he walked down Jefferson Street, heading home. He hated this feeling of apprehension, this vague and objectless sense that something was wrong. He sensed it in the thin electrical buzz which had taken up residence in his stomach. He felt it in the subtle pressure on his chest; it was there in the foggy-mindedness of his thoughts.

Michael was just about to turn down Sutherland Street when he noticed that he wasn't at the corner of Sutherland Street at all. He was standing at the four corners of Pittsford, amidst the traffic and shops. How had that happened? He must be really absent-minded today. So he continued down Monroe Avenue, and decided he would approach home from the other end of Sutherland Street. What the hell was wrong with him? He looked up at the green metallic sign as he approached his street. Michael stopped dead, the electric charge in his stomach leaping in intensity. The sign said Lincoln Avenue. How was that possible? This was supposed to be Sutherland Street, his street. Michael closed his eyes hard and felt his fists clench. Jesus, he can't even get home. Okay, just walk down Lincoln Avenue. Lincoln Avenue crosses over Sutherland Street, only two blocks down. He quickened his pace, scrutinizing each home like a sailor reading landmarks on the shore. It's not much further. But where was Sutherland Street? He should be able to see it from here. He noticed a teenager raking up dead and decaying leaves left over from last fall. Impulsive now in this growing state of panic, he stopped and called to the boy.

"Sutherland Street is just up there, isn't it?"

The boy squinted and leaned on his rake. Michael noticed the sly smile which grew on his face, the sort of self-pleased smile you get from a teenager who has appraised an elder as dim-witted.

"Sutherland Street? This *is* Sutherland Street."

Michael's face screwed up into a knot of confusion, and he whirled around, scanning. There was the school! Farther down, there was his own house! How was this possible?

"Of course, of course, thank you," he called to the boy, barely turning to address him for fear of losing site of his home. He rushed down the street, fixing his home in his sights like some trotting torpedo making for its target.

CHAPTER 6

An organization in England is set to launch a telephone hotline for people who work at telephone hotline centers, so they can express their feelings about work conditions.

From the journals of Professor Charles Kidding, extract #189

Michael checked his watch: 8:59 am. He was sure that municipal offices opened at 9:00 am, and he had already planned his approach. No reading through financial papers and magazines today, no Starbucks either, not unless he managed to get his identification back. Earlier this morning he had looked in the White Pages of the phone book and had found a section covering Government Departments, where he felt he'd found most of the contact information he needed. What bothered him most was not having his birth certificate, social security card, passport, and driver's license. He wanted his ID back and he wanted it back as soon as possible.

Michael dialed the number of the Social Security Administration Office. An automated voice answered and reeled off several choices. Finally, the voice said "If you are applying for a Social Security card, a replacement Social Security card, or need to indicate a change of information to your record, press 3." Michael pressed 3 and the voice continued.

"To apply for a Social Security card, a replacement Social Security card, or to indicate a change of information to your record, you will need to complete form SS-5. Form SS-5 and related instructions for completing the form can be downloaded on our website… "

Michael jotted down the website information, hung up the phone, spilled what was left of his coffee, jogged across his living room, and turned his computer on. Finally, he got form SS-5 up on the screen and read through the instructions. Okay, he could fill out the form and mail it in with the required proof of identification or take the form down to the Social Security office and process it there. But the phrase *proof of identification* leapt out at him. They want proof of his identity before they will give him a new Social Security card? Well, of course they do. They just can't hand them out to anybody. He skipped to a section labelled EVEDENCE DOCUMENTS WE NEED TO SEE. As proof of age, they needed to see a birth certificate, and for proof of identity they needed to see a US driver's license, US state issued non-driver identity card, or a US passport.

Michael read the instruction over again, and then just stared at the screen, a feeling of numbness crawling over his consciousness. He didn't have anything they wanted. How was he supposed to get his SS card back? Michael thought of that book Catch 22, and how he hadn't read it. He looked over at his book case and spotted it on the third shelf. This was depressing. Michael thought about taking a bus down to the Social Security Department. He had an image of himself explaining to some underpaid employee about how he didn't have any of the proof of identification they wanted. He shuddered at the thought.

Alright, he shouldn't get hung up on the social security card for the moment. Michael dialed the number for the Department of Motor Vehicles and was not surprised to get another automated voice and a list of choices. He pressed 5 for *obtaining a replacement driver's license*, and was told he would need to submit form MV-44 at a local DMV office. Michael downloaded the form and there at the end was a section labeled FOR OFFICE USE ONLY, and then **proof submitted**, followed by: birth certificate, learner permit, INS papers, social security card. Michael sighed. How the hell can he get any of his identification back if he doesn't have any to start with!

Michael looked down at the number for the immigration office, and decided to go straight to the web to find out about getting a new passport. He googled *US passport* and soon found the information. The problem was of course the same. To get a replacement passport he needed his old passport or a valid birth certificate. Failing that he needed something called a letter of no record, which documents that a search had been made and no birth certificate is on record for you. That was no good.

Michael stared into space and felt blood rising into his neck and face, felt his fists clenching. "That's it!" Michael spat out in disgust, "I need to get my birth certificate back". With a birth certificate he could get his passport, and with his passport and birth certificate he could get his driver's license and then Social Security card… and library card and what ever the hell else he needed! The phone book had listed a number for birth certificates. Apparently it was the Health Department which dealt with that, and they had an office downtown. He dialed the number. When the phone was picked up, all he could hear was a burst of laughter at the other end, and then several people talking, and then more laughter. Thank god. Finally he was going to speak to a human being.

"Hello, dis is de vital records departmen. Haaa haaaa. Dis is Juanita. How may I hel ju?" The cheery Hispanic accent was strangely comforting to Michael, as was the laughter. He pictured a middle-aged and overweight woman in very good spirits. Surely this woman would help him.

"Yes, hello, my name is Michael Wilson. I've lost my birth certificate."

"Oh dear me. Are ju lost? Where are ju now? Maybe we can hel you fine yo way back. Haaa haaa." More laughter in the back-ground. "I jus kidding wit ju. Don ju worry Mr Wilsin – we gonna hel ju out." It was a terrible joke, a pointless joke, but Michael joined in with her joviality, laughing himself, sensing that this woman was important to him."

"Yes, I mean if you could just tell me how to get a new birth certificate, I'd really appreciate it."

"Das no problem. Ju got to come on down to da office and jus show a photo id. Could be a driver license or passport."

"I… I had my driver's license and passport stolen. Is there any other way?"

"Ju had dem bot stolen? Das bad luck. But don worry. Ju can bring two utility bills in your name and maybe some other form of ID. Dat might work."

Michael thought about that. All the utility bills were in Mrs. Deveroix's name. Shit!

"Juanita… I realize this is going to sound strange, but I haven't got that sort of thing. Is there any other way?"

Juanita let out a laugh. "boy, ju a tough one. Da only udder way would be a Supreme Court Order. Ju would have to get a lawer and petition da Supreme Court. But I work here for two years an I neber seen nobody do dat."

"But that's..." Michael was going to say *that's ridiculous*, but thought better of it. He needed to keep Juanita sweet. "That does sound a bit extreme. It's just that I've had all my identification stolen, so it's really hard to figure out how to get any of it back. This could happen to a lot of people, I would have thought."

"I know, I know. Ju a nice man, Mr. Wilson. Listen, ju want to talk to Julie Miller? She da head of Vital Records. Maybe she cou help you."

"Yes please – that would be really helpful."

"Old on a minute."

Julie was staring absent-mindedly at a photo on her desk of Bobby and herself when the phone range. They were at the park, and Julie was down on one knee, scratching the little guy behind the ears. She'd asked a passerby to shoot the photo of them. She took the call and listened to Juanita explain the case of a Michael Wilson. She sighed deeply. This was one for her, alright – this guy sounded like another square peg. She had a busy morning, so he'd just have to be patient.

Michael could hear the sort of chatter you expect in large municipal offices while he was on hold. He was really relieved to be speaking with human beings rather than recorded messages and websites. He wondered what this Julie would be like, and hoped she'd understand his predicament.

"Mr. Wilson, Julie got a lot of appoinments diis morning but you cou call her back after 3:00 PM tomorrow. I tol Julie about ju an yo problem, okay?"

"Yes, thank you. That's very kind of you."

Michael entered through the back door at 7:30 PM and made his way quietly through the kitchen and into the main hallway. He'd spent the evening at the Pittsford Pub, making conversation with Mitch and Bob. He hadn't been able to get a seat right next to them at the bar, which made talking somewhat awkward. As he reached the foot of the stairs, he heard a sound coming from the direction of the living room, though he was not sure if it was human or some gush of air or water coming from the innards of the house. Stopping in mid-step, he held his breath and listened. There it was again, and this time he knew it was human. A low moan, muffled, as if someone were in pain. It must be Mrs. Deveroix. What should he do? If she is distressed, she may not want to be disturbed. Would his presence be an intrusion into her privacy? But what if she was in trouble? Perhaps a medical problem? She is elderly, after all. And then Michael heard something else.

"The trains… oh my god, what can be done with the trains?"

The trains, thought Michael. What trains?

"There's so much up there." A long anguished sob followed.

Mr. Deveroix had died not so long ago, and Michael realized that this was the sound of grief. Not a medical problem, at any rate. Best to leave her alone. He took another step, but a loud creak sounded beneath his shoe and Mrs Deveroix's sob was cut off sharply. Michael held still, not daring to remove his foot from the creaky board. And then a faint voice.

"Michael, is that you?"

"Yes it is". What else could he say?

There was a pause, and then finally, "I'm sorry if I've upset you with my carrying on. I didn't know you were there".

"That's quite alright," Michael said in a tone which sounded far too cheery.

And there he stood, frozen like a leaning Giacometti figure, one foot pressing upon an insolent floorboard, not knowing what to do. He wanted to carry on up the stairs and escape this messy awkwardness, but he found himself moving softly into the doorway and looking down upon a bent Mrs. Deveroix and the many tissues strewn about the coffee table. She seemed to know he was there.

"It's just the trains Michael. There's so much of it up in that attic of his and I just can't face it. I've tried going up there, but it was always his place and it must be filled with his things."

Everything seemed to register for Michael all at once. The door to the attic was just opposite Michael's bedroom, and prior to his sudden heart attack, the introverted and polite Mr. Deveroix had passed by Michael's room countless times on route to his attic space. Michael never had any idea what he spent so much time doing up there, but clearly trains were involved.

A pause followed, and Michael searched in desperation to find the right thing to say.

"Can I help in some way?"

"I don't want to trouble you Mr. Wilson. But… but maybe you could have a look up there sometime. I never went up there when he was alive. It was his space, you know, and he was so private. Maybe you could have a look up there sometime, just to see what's there."

"Yes, of course Mrs. Deveroix – I'd be happy to," Michael said, but he really wasn't sure if he was happy about it at all. It seemed rather an overly-intimate thing to do.

Michael stared at the door leading to the attic stairs, fingering the key Mrs. Deveroix had given him, his back to his own rooms. It had always seemed somewhat odd that Mr. Deveroix had kept the door locked with just the three of them in the house. Michael recalled the many times Mr. Deveroix had scuttled up to the door and then worked the key with such swiftness it was clear that he wanted to avoid any hallway conversation in order get to the safety of his space. Once on the stairs to the attic, the door would be closed swiftly and softly, and Michael could hear the bolt being thrown from the inside. The task felt heavy just now, and Michael decided it could wait a day or two.

CHAPTER 7

A bus driver transporting twenty mental health patients to a hospital in Zimbabwe stopped on route to get a drink at a bar. On returning to his bus, the driver realized that the patients had all escaped. Unable to round up the patients, the driver offered free rides to 20 sane people, and dropped them off at the mental hospital. It took three days for the 'patients' to convince authorities that they were not mentally ill.

From the journals of Professor Charles Kidding, extract #135

Michael walked up the steps of the Rundel Memorial Library and pushed through the heavy oak doors at 12:30 pm. He walked through the darkened foyer, noticing a heavy-set black lady guard at the desk, and then made his way into the generously proportioned main reading room on the ground floor. Michael was very fond of this room. There was a sense of timelessness in the old bookish smells and the perfect symmetry of the place. The near silence which wrapped itself around marbled floor, oak paneled walls, and the polished pine reading tables created an atmosphere of ease and forgetting.

Michael found a couple of novels which looked interesting and then scanned the main reading room, trying to decide where he should sit. There was an old woman near the centre, a couple of students at another table, and, remarkably, a man who appeared to be asleep at his reading table. Michael looked closer at the figure, and then suddenly realized it was the bum he often saw in Washington Square Park – the one he'd watched getting drunk this past Saturday. Michael positioned himself a couple of tables over, a place where he had a good view of the bum. He opened one of the novels, but felt compelled to study the bum in detail.

He wore the same clothes as the other day – tatty basketball shoes, powder-blue nylon slacks, and a button-up short sleeve shirt. His head lay upon folded arms and Michael noticed that a viscous string of drool ran from the edge of his bearded mouth and stretched to the table.

He heard footsteps move past him and saw a librarian stop about ten feet from the bum. Michael knew the librarian because she had helped him find books. She was a lanky, fretful woman who seemed the type to jump at the slightest note of conflict, and Michael wondered what might happen because he was sure that bums were not allowed to sleep in the library. The librarian placed a slender hand against her mouth and looked around nervously, no doubt wondering what she should do – she made Michael think of a spindle-legged stork. She took a step towards the bum, thought better of it, and made a hasty retreat to the foyer. Michael didn't hear what the librarian said out there, but the library guard's voice bellowed into the main room.

"Oh yea, well you better show me to 'um."

The black lady guard led the librarian into the room. She strutted in her officious uniform of blue, rolls of fat pushing at the fabric. Her body language told Michael most of the story. Probably grew up in the inner city, tough as nails, took no shit from anybody, probably shouted and laughed a lot, had a lot of kids, maybe a husband as big and as tough as her with a job as crummy as hers. She put two chubby thumbs into her belt, tilted her head, and sized up the bum. The storkish librarian towered over her in height, but was slightly bent, and seemed really to be hiding behind her.

"Do you want me to get Leonard, to help?" said the librarian.

"Leonard? You think I need that college drip to manage one bum?"

As if on cue, what could only be Leonard strolled into the room from the book stacks.

"Oh thank god, here's Leonard," said the guard. "I guess we'll be okay now." Leonard ignored her remarks and stood next to them, surveying the bum.

"Leonard," sputtered the librarian, "this… um… gentleman fell asleep and there's that policy about people not sleeping in the library."

"You make it sound like an accident," said the guard, "like he got tired and accidentally fell asleep. He's a drunk and he's about to get his sorry ass throwd out."

"Oh dear," whispered the librarian. The guard took a step forward but was stopped short by the sound of Leonard's voice, who addressed her.

"Tamisha, do you know who that is?"

Tamisha squared on Leonard, drew her short fat frame up to full height, and cocked her head. "Yea, he's a sorry-ass bum who's sleeping in my library, on my shift – dats who he is!"

Leonard looked at Tamisha with a hint of distain at the corner of his mouth, and Michael sensed there was history between these two. "That's Professor Dembrowski," said Leonard. "He was regarded as the leading authority on the Philosophy of Logic in the country – maybe the world. He was the head of the Philosophy Department at City University."

"He don't look like no professor to me. He look like a drunk." Tamisha bent close to the bum and then jerked back dramatically, eyeing Leonard. "Damn Leonard! He's drooling on my table!"

"Ssshhh", said Leonard. "Can you keep your voice down. He might hear you." The librarian nodded in agreement.

Tamisha folded her arms and cocked her head. "HHmmmph. Professor my ass!"

Leonard sighed heavily. "Okay, he's probably not a practicing professor any more. I heard he left the University a few years ago. But I could go back into the philosophy section and show you about four or five books that he wrote. One of them is considered a classic in the field."

"Point is Leonard, he's asleep and drooling on my table and he's got to go." She took a step forward, but Leonard intervened.

"Okay Tamisha, but let me talk to him, alright?"

"Suite yourself collage boy, but I want him out."

Leonard placed a hand on the bum's arm and shook him gently. "Professor… Professor Dembrowski…"

The bum slowly came around, instinctively wiping his mouth and then rubbing his face with his hands as he looked up. He gazed, bleary eyed, at three discordant library staff, his eyes moving slowly from one to the next. Michael wondered if he was drunk or just very groggy.

"Professor, I don't know if you remember me. I'm Leonard McKnight. I took Introduction to Logic and Intermediate Logic from you a few years ago, and then I was one of your graduate assistants for a semester. I'm really sorry to have to wake you…" Tamisha rolled her eyes and the librarian seemed to edge even further behind the guard. The bum sat up straight now, squinting at Leonard through watery vision.

"Leonard… sure, I remember. You liked to sit in the front row. Asked a lot of questions."

Leonard's face brightened and he seemed to forget his immediate circumstances. "I guess I did."

"What was your dissertation on?"

"*Necessity and Contingency and its Place in the Field of Logic,*" he replied. "That was the title." The bum rubbed his forehead hard and squinted now at Leonard.

"Did I give you a good grade?"

"You gave me a C+ sir. I think I got a bit confused in the way I described free logical necessity, abstract logical necessity, and broad logical necessity. But you met up with me and explained it all – you sorted me out."

The bum nodded groggily and then seemed to be taken unawares by a large belch which exploded from deep within.

"Excuse me," said Tamisha, "it really pains me to break up your school reunion, but there's no sleeping in the library. You wanna take a nap, I suggest a Motel 6." Her tone shot up sharply on *Motel 6* and she did that strut with her neck, the one some black woman will do when they mean business. The bum looked at Tamisha square in the eyes, but there was a softness in his gaze, no hint of anger or offence. He nodded his head slowly and with an air of resignation.

"Motels…" he said, gazing off into space, as if speaking his thoughts to himself. "Motels are mysterious places. They are home, but only for a little while. In a motel room couples have arguments, people hatch business plans, lots of people have sex, people harm themselves in one way or another… and it's all okay as long as you leave by 11:00 am and don't unscrew the framed posters. Then the motel staff sanitize the rooms to create the illusion that nothing has happened there. I don't know, there's just something *peculiar* about motels."

The bum stared now at the varnished table, as if he had forgotten the others were there. Tamisha folded her arms in under her bosom, rocked back on her heels, and said, "hhhhmmmph, I don't know motels, but I'm DAMN sure there's something peculiar about you." The bum looked at Tamisha again and seemed to recall the point she had made a moment before. "Was I asleep?" he asked.

"You damn right you asleep. And there's no sleeping in the library allowed. I got every right to kick you out right now. I'm gonna be straight wich you. We got a particular view of transients. Library ain't no place for transients and I don't care what you was."

Michael was transfixed by the scene. The bum stared at the table again, maybe collecting his thoughts, maybe not thinking anything at all. Finally, the bum looked up, groggy, his head rolling a bit, taking the three of them in. He spoke, his voice establishing some evenness. "I don't really feel like a transient. Transient comes from the same root as transition, from the Latin *transpire*, meaning change or development. That's not really right, is it? I mean, does it look like I'm going through some important developmental period of change?" He gazed at Tamisha, groggy-eyed, before continuing. "I'd prefer it if you referred to me as a bum." He wiped more spittle from his salt and pepper beard with the back of his hand. "Actually, I'm not too fussy – bum, tramp, vagabond, hobo – it's all good. Just not transient. It puts too much pressure on me."

"Fine. You a bum. A bum asleep in the library on *my* shift. So you got to go."

"Tamisha, come on," interjected Leonard. Tamisha turned and squared off on Leonard and opened her mouth to speak, but it was the bum who intervened.

"Okay…" he said.

Tamisha cocked her head at him. "Okay? Okay what?"

"Look, you people got a job to do. I understand that. I came in to read. I'm not drunk… yet." He looked at Tamisha squarely, a look which wasn't subservient or pleading, but it was a look without much dignity either. "I know you've got to make this library nice for people," he said. "I'll stay awake when I'm here. If I need to sleep, I'll leave."

Tamisha shifted her gaze from the bum to Leonard to the librarian and back, deciding. Michael saw that things sat on a knife edge. She blew out a deep sigh of exasperation, and pointed a chubby finger at the bum. "You fall asleep again, and you out. And I'll make it difficult for you to return."

"As you say," the bum replied.

When the three library staff drifted off, the bum picked up a pair of metal-framed reading glasses and took a magazine off the top of a nearby pile. Michael noticed that the glasses had only one arm and so they hung cockeyed across his face. He tried to read but he kept wondering about this bum and what had happened to him. He wondered about those books in the philosophy section that the bum had written.

The section was alphabetized and he got down on one knee in order to search the texts for *Dembrowski.* He found four books written by the bum. He had one of his fingers on the spine of the first book when he heard what he thought were the whispered tones of the librarian and Leonard. Michael peered over a row of books and realized that he was looking at the lower portion of their bodies – he recognized the librarian's dress.

"Was he really a professor at the University?" asked the librarian.

"Yea, he was a great teacher. You had to sign-up for his classes the first day of registration because they filled up so fast. He was a big shot on the international scene too. He often had assistant professors standing in for him because he would be away giving some address at an important conference. And he was a visiting professor at a lot of other universities – Harvard, Columbia, Oxford. But that was before he lost it."

"Lost it?"

"Yeah", said Leonard. "He started drinking. He had a nick-name – Professor Lush. Professor Larry Lush."

"Larry? Is Larry his first name then?"

"Yeah. Larry Dembrowski. I guess *Professor Larry Lush* had a ring to it. It caught on as a nickname. I always thought it was mean for people to call him that. I never called him that, but a lot of students did. He didn't do himself many favors though –stumbling around campus or wandering through the university library drunk."

"Gosh, that's so awful…what happened to him?"

The voices faded into obscurity as Leonard and the librarian walked away, and Michael crouched motionless for a moment as he absorbed their words. He picked up the four books and brought them back to a nearby table. The first book was entitled *The Application of Logic to Critical Thinking and Argument.* On the back cover was a black and white photo of Larry. He didn't have a beard and looked about ten years younger, but it was him, no doubt about it. The man in the photo appeared very serious and quite formal. Michael scanned the table of contents and felt immediately overwhelmed: *Tautologies, truth functions, quantifiers, extensionality*... good god, what was all this? He flipped through the pages and stopped somewhere near the start of the book, reading a paragraph his eye fell on:

We must not underestimate the importance of the most basic syllogism:

A is A
A is not B

Here we begin to comprehend logical analysis and, more importantly, the role of logical analysis in relation to truth-values.

Michael squinted and rubbed his forehead. He flipped through the book. There was a lot of text, but there were also many pages filled with diagrams containing letters and strange symbols he had never seen before, all joined up with lines. It had something to do with Truth Functions, whatever that was, but Michael didn't imagine that he would be able to make much sense of it. The image of the bum suddenly came to mind, and he saw that glutinous string of drool hanging from his mouth, forming a tiny puddle on the varnished desk. That image seemed at such odds with the intimidating orderliness and intellectual gravity of the book he held in his hands.

CHAPTER 8

A waxwork of track star Linford Christie in Madame Tussaud's, London, has to be given a new leotard every six weeks because of the number of women who manhandle his crotch.

From the journals of Professor Charles Kidding, extract #53

Julie's phone range.

"Hey Julie. Ju remember da man I tol ju about. Da one dat needs a new birth certificate but he say he had all his ID stolen."

"Yeah, I remember Juanita."

"He on line one for ju. His name es Michael Wilson, okay."

"That's fine – put him through."

Julie wasn't really looking forward to this call. It wasn't uncommon for people to try to get illicit birth certificates – you run into people evading debt collection agencies, illegal immigrants, people running scams.

"Hello, this is Julie Miller– how can I help you?"

"Yes hello Julie, I understand you're the head of the Vital Records Department. I'm very sorry to trouble you this way. My name is Michael Wilson and I seem to be in a pretty difficult spot. I had my car stolen last Friday, and I realize this seems hard to believe, but they made off not only with my birth certificate, but virtually every other form of identity I had. Your colleague, Juanita, was as helpful as possible, but I seem to be in a bit of a quandary. The problem seems to be getting a replacement birth certificate when I haven't got the identification you need."

"I see. Well, that does seem to be a bit of a quandary. We normally need to see a passport or driver's license – they were both stolen?"

"I'm afraid so – they were in my car when it was stolen. I was just on my way back from renewing my driver's license, so I had all my ID with me. I've got a police report documenting the theft of the car and everything that was in it. I've got a check book and hopefully I'll get my visa debit card returned to me before too long, but I realize your department doesn't accept that as proof of identity. I'm having problems getting my driver's license and passport back for the same reasons. It's all really quite disarming."

Julie was staring down at the shape of her thighs as they pressed against the cotton fabric of her dress, wondering about this Michael Wilson, and thinking that her legs were in pretty good shape. There was something about the quality of his voice which was strangely appealing. Yes, he was nervous and quite worried, that was plain. But there was a depth to his voice and a politeness – no, that's not quite right – *a civility* to his voice which she liked. *It's all really quite disarming* – he actually said that. An image of a cultured male character from a period film came to mind.

"There's a legal process you can go through but that would seem really excessive in your case," said Julie. "To be honest, that's the sort of process that non-citizens have to go through occasionally. It sounds like you've just had some really bad luck."

Michael felt a wave of relief wash over him. Here was someone who understood.

"I quite agree. If there's a way we could sort this out, I'd really appreciate it."

Julie tried to imagine what Michael looked like and wondered whether he was married, or how old he was. It wouldn't really be inappropriate to ask about his personal situation – after all, she had to make some determination concerning the legitimacy of his case. On the other hand, she knew this was a load of crap – his personal details were irrelevant. She was meant to simply tell him the policy and procedures for obtaining a replacement birth certificate. That was the remit of her job. So the appropriate course of action would be *not* to bother with personal details.

"Mr. Wilson, can I just take a few personal details?"

"Of course, I'm happy to help in any way I can."

"What's your birth date?"

"July second, 1980."

Julie did some quick math. Thirty-two years old. "Occupation?"

"I'm an independent investor, futures market mostly… I work from home."

"And are you presently married?"

"No, I've never been married."

Could mean he's gay, but there was something in the quality of his voice which suggested otherwise.

"No children then?"

"No."

"I see."

Julie reflected on that last phrase – *I see.* But what did she see? And more to the point, what was she doing? There was what felt like a long pause. Julie pressed a hand between her thighs, squeezed her knees together, and bit her lip.

"Perhaps it might be helpful to meet here at the Department of Health," she said finally.

"Of course, I'd be glad to meet up. You're on State Street, aren't you? Should I bring the police report and my check book?"

"Uhm… sure," Julie replied, a rather abstracted tone in her voice which she did not intend.

CHAPTER 9

A strip club in Boise, Idaho was nearly shut down when it was found to be in breach of local 'indecency laws'. They got around the problem by handing each customer a pencil and piece of paper on entrance, and advertising a new life-drawing class.

From the journals of Professor Charles Kidding, extract #67

Mary came through the door of Burt's shop, offered a smile and walked past him into a kitchen area off the main store. Her voice drifted in.

"You okay Burt? I've got an idea I really need to talk over with you, but it's pretty involved so I need a coffee. I love this idea so I hope you like it too, but be honest with me, okay?"

"Honesty – you got it."

Mary returned a few minutes later, flushed and animated, and sat at a stool on the opposite side of the desk. She placed her coffee on the desk and a cup for him and launched straight in. Burt was used to this. Mary didn't do small talk. Mary wasn't interested in greasing the wheels of human interaction.

"Okay, what I was thinking about is that at any point in time a particular individual could make a decision, in theory, to do any one of a million things. They could get drunk, start a revolution, write their congressman, look at pornography, get one of those spray-on tans, and so on. This individual couldn't choose to flap their arms and fly because that goes against physical laws, but what they could choose is still so wide open, the options are nearly infinite. But people don't really get it – there's something really uncomfortable about seeing how vast the landscape is. And so people rarely see what's available to them."

Burt took a reflective drag on his cigar. "Heidegger used the term *the clearing*, but it's like the sort of thing you're talking about. He meant a *clearing*, as when you walk out of a forest and into an open space. And that experience of coming out of thick trees into a clearing – imagine a large meadow – that's a metaphor for being able to see the vastness of life's possibilities."

"Yes, that's it. I like that metaphor. But most people live in the woods and don't even realize that there might be a clearing. Every day they see the same trees, or maybe new trees, but it's the same dark forest, and the trees pretty much look the same as the trees they saw yesterday."

"Okay," said Burt. "But why? I mean why aren't people aware of the possibilities available to them? I think you're right in what you say. But why do people forget that they have choices and just act out of habit, or impulse?"

"Because they're afraid."

"Afraid of what?"

"Can we just leave it there for a moment. I need to tell you about the idea I have," said Mary.

Burt scratched his head.

"I thought you were telling me about your idea."

"No – I've been telling you about the idea *behind* the idea."

"Oh… of course," said Burt, a note of friendly sarcasm in his voice.

"Before I tell you about the idea," said Mary, "I want to show you something." She pulled out a photo from her purse and placed it on the desk. "This is a photo I created a while ago."

Burt looked closely at the image. In the photo he saw Mary. She was wearing a black shirt, plaid skirt, and was holding a bright orange umbrella. Mary seemed to have black lipstick smeared across her lips. Beside Mary was a box with the words DO NOT OPEN THIS BOX written on the front.

Burt took his time looking at the image, feeling unsure how to respond. He could feel Mary's impatient eyes on him, so eventually he said, "you look a lot younger in this photo – when did you shoot it?"

"Probably about ten years ago," said Mary. "I think I was about sixteen at the time."

Burt gazed at the photo again. Eventually, he said, "it's a beautiful image – really good use of lighting and color, but…".

Mary interrupted him. "Burt don't worry about that. It's the box I really want to talk about."

"Oh," said Burt. "Yes, the box is interesting. Adds an element of mystery."

"Yeah," said Mary. "When I created that photo I had my own reasons for including the box, but when I was looking at the photo the other day, I had another idea for how to use a box like that."

"And this is the idea you've been wanting to tell me about?"

Mary nodded. "Okay," said Burt, "let's hear it."

"Right," said Mary. "Let's say you come across a box. It's about two feet by one foot and maybe six inches deep – and it's hanging on a wall. There's a door on the front of the box which has a handle, so you could open the door and look inside. But…" and here Mary paused and raised an index finger for effect, "across the front of the box are printed the words DO NOT OPEN THIS BOX. What do you do?"

Burt gave the proposition some thought, and Mary smiled expectantly. "I think that depends. It depends on the reasons why I'm not meant to open the box."

"Aha," replied Mary with all the enthusiasm of a detective who has tripped up a criminal. "Of course you want a reason – you want to know to what extent opening the box means that you have been a bad boy. But in this instance, the reason is hidden. There's no context to the box. You simply don't know why you are not supposed to open the box, you don't know who or what authority doesn't want you to open the box, and you don't know what consequences might occur."

"And there's no lock on the box?"

"No, which is interesting because there is a hinge which would easily take a lock, but the lock is absent."

Burt gazed into slowly drifting plums of cigar smoke. "Okay, but where is the box? Is it in a public place or am I alone with the box?"

"Good question. You were in a public place and there were probably people milling about, and you came across a room about the size of a closet, and on the door of this room is printed the words ENTER HERE. When you went into the closet, the door closed behind you because it's on a spring and the room lit up, and the box is hanging on the wall in front of you. The only other thing in this little room is a CCTV camera which is pointed at you."

Burt squinted at Mary, trying to get an image of it all.

"Right, so I'm in some sort of public place and I see this closet-sized room. I'm curious and I go in, and now I'm alone with this box which reads DO NOT OPEN THIS BOX and…" Burt frowned before continuing… "and a camera videoing me?"

"That's it."

Burt thought for a moment more. "I'd really like to think that I would open the box, but I can't be sure. It's like that theoretical scenario about whether you might give up your life to save someone else."

"Good point – the box is like that theoretical scenario – it's *that* important."

Mary felt an impulse to continue, to explain her thoughts about the box, but she wanted Burt to *get it*, so she left him to feel the weight of the silence between them. She knew that explaining why art has value is like explaining why the punch-line of a joke is funny. Burt looked down at his desk, but he was really just looking into nothing as he tried to understand. Finally, he found some words, but the words came slowly, as if he was feeling his way.

"This box thing is difficult. I really don't like being confronted with the box. It's disturbing. I do want to open it, but of course I'm not meant to. It might be a mistake to open the box, but it might be worse to walk away. And if I walk away, it might really bother me that I didn't look. I might feel compelled to go back."

Mary interjected quickly. "Ah, there's something else you need to know. Let's say you stood in that room and thought about opening the box, but decided not to. And let's say that you regretted your decision later and returned to the closet. Guess what would happen when you tried to re-enter?"

Burt took a long drag on his cigar and watched the plume of smoke he'd blown out thoughtfully. "Oh God," said Burt finally. "The door to the closet wouldn't open for me?"

"That's right."

Burt's mouth hung open, and then he laughed and shook his head. "But why? Why won't the door open for me?"

"Because while there may be millions of boxes we come across every day, we usually only get one fucking chance to open them. Later on, it's usually too late." Mary looked triumphant, and Burt gave her a smile of admiration. Finally he said just what Mary had been hoping to hear.

"That would be really awful – screwing up my courage, going back to that closet, turning the handle, and discovering that the door was locked. Especially if I had to watch other people going in."

Mary nodded slowly, encouragingly.

"Okay," continued Burt, "I get it. Human beings have a tremendous range of choices, but they are scared to acknowledge such potential, and so they deal with this fear by pretending that their freedom to choose is much more narrow than it really is. They remain in the forest, rather than looking for the clearing. They deny the possibilities of existence, they deny their own potential. But when a person stands in front of a box which tells them not to open it, they are being confronted by a choice, a choice which is so *in their face* that they cannot pretend it doesn't exist. And they have only one chance to make that choice… They will have to live with the consequences of opening that box and they will have to live with the consequences of not opening that box."

Mary nodded slowly and with much gravity, and simply said, "Yes."

"Your artistic vision has a cruel streak, you know."

"Of course. Isn't art meant to mimic life? There are boxes all around us every day Burt. We're scared of opening them, we're scared of not opening them – so we cope by *not* seeing the boxes. All I want to do is present people with a box they cannot help but see."

Burt grinned in a knowing way.

"And I suppose you would like help building this box?"

"Are we not co-conspirators, you and I?"

"And help building this closet?" asked Burt.

"Yes please."

"And how will the door to the closet lock itself when someone tries to re-enter?"

"You'll find a way Burt. You always do."

"And the closet and box are going to be located in a public place?"

"Yes."

"Don't you think we're screwing with people's heads a bit?"

"Of course, but look at the people who make up our culture. Look at the conventional, wearisome, cautious lives they lead – they prefer reality TV to reality. Porn to sex. Don't you think most people need there heads to be screwed with a bit? Honestly Burt, it's for their own good."

Mary offered an encouraging smile, and continued. "Come on, you know you want to."

Burt's grin acknowledged the truth of her statement. "Well," he said finally, "we are the dreamer of dreams – we call the tune." It was his abstract way of saying yes.

"Who said that?" asked Mary.

"Willy Wonka – but the movie, not the book."

"No shit? Willy Wonka?" replied Mary. "He was a good man."

"The best," replied Burt sadly, and then he and Mary laughed together because they realized it sounded as if they were talking about a close friend who had died.

"I liked what you said earlier," said Mary. "You said that you would like to think that you would open the box, but you couldn't be certain, and that was similar to the way people like to think they would give up their life for another, but they can't be sure unless they were in that situation. I think facing the box is similar, except it's not about whether you are going to save someone else's life…. ."

"Yea," said Burt. "It's about whether you're going to save your own." He eyed Mary closely. "That's good Mary. That's very good."

They sat in silence for a moment, absorbing the exchange. Burt pulled out a note pad and began making a sketch of the box, absently-mindedly stroking his frail and ancient cat with his free hand. He looked up. "You got a CCTV camera?"

"Yeah," said Mary. "Picked one up at the dump. I'll even bet you can get it to work."

Burt smiled and shook his head, and then a thought occurred to him. "So what's in the box then? I mean if someone opens it up?"

"Isn't that obvious?" replied Mary.

CHAPTER 10

Staff at a Turkish prison were very confused when one of their female inmates fell pregnant, until they discovered a hole in the three inch wall of her cell. The woman, a convicted bomber, had been having sex with a convicted murderer in the next cell. They were each fined for damaging prison property.

From the journals of Professor Charles Kidding, extract #113

Juanita had just rung through to let Julie know that Mr. Wilson had arrived. Julie recalled the tone of this man's voice and his strange circumstances, and she pulled a pocket mirror from her purse and inspected her face from a few angles. Satisfied, she buzzed Juanita and asked that Mr. Wilson be shown in.

As Michael came through the door, Julie's reaction was immediate and visceral. People use that expression 'took my breath away', and as tired a cliché as it may be, there must be an underlying truth about it, because Julie felt herself take a sharp and deep breath and then seemed to need to hold it. Her heart banged against her ribs and a constricted feeling took hold in her throat. She absorbed his appearance – green sports jacket made from some fine material, a button-up Oxford in dark blue, and smart khaki trousers. Tall and slim, athletic in build, but it was the eyes which drew her in. They were deep blue and glistened in a way which seemed to make her look straight into them. She saw him hold out his hand and she knew she was responding mechanically, appropriately, responding in a way which the situation called for, but she was acutely aware of the need to contain her physical reaction – she must be blushing in her throat and cheeks.

"Hello, it's Michael, isn't it? Michael Wilson?"

"Yes, thank you, it's really good of you to see me. Can I call you Julie?"

"Of course," Julie replied, constructing a smile which she hoped looked natural.

Julie noticed the softness of his hand in hers as they shook. He was not a manual laborer and never had been. She had shaken thousands of rough, callused hands over the years.

"I really do appreciate your time. This is such a disorientating experience. It's lovely to deal with a human being rather than phone mills or internet sites."

"Yes, it can all get rather bureaucratic I'm afraid, but we try to be helpful and flexible– I mean, we know that sometimes people just find themselves in unfortunate circumstances."

Julie was inwardly appalled by the insincerity of her words. Her department was poorly staffed by underpaid and under- motivated individuals, and the senior management was too preoccupied in meeting targets to be helpful. Flexibility? Flexibility was unofficially banned.

"I'm happy to be as helpful as I can," said Michael. "I've brought along the checkbook and the police report concerning my stolen car and identification. I should receive a replacement debit card from my bank any day."

Michael produced the items from his jacket pocket and handed them across the desk. Their fingers touched briefly in the exchange, and Julie felt the throb in her veins accelerate. She was glad for the distraction provided by the checkbook and police report, and then realized how difficult it had been to look at Michael. When she did look at him she felt she was *gazing* into his eyes in ways he must think odd, even invasive.

She scanned the checkbook and police report. They certainly seemed legitimate, but rather useless against the juggernaut of State and Federal officialdom. The checkbook and replacement debit card are not acceptable forms of identification, and while the police report demonstrates that he claimed his car and identification were stolen, it certainly doesn't prove they were.

She glanced up at Michael, smiling, surveying his expression, trying to read him. Reading people – that was something she knew about. You don't do this job for ten years without getting good at seeing beneath the surface. Michael looked dignified given his precarious position, but there was an edge of need and anxiety around his eyes and in the purse of his lips. Julie realized she had been looking at the items far longer than she needed to, but so much was going through her mind. Should she really just give him chapter and verse of Health Department policy and send him on his way? That's what her management would expect of her. But that wasn't fair, was it? Here is a nice man who's been a victim of a crime. Why shouldn't she find a way to help him? And then Julie smiled inwardly to herself, appreciating the real reason she didn't want to give him the conventional bureaucratic treatment.

If she did, she would never see him again.

She put the items on her desk, looked into his eyes, and realized that she wanted him to feel better.

"Well, I for one believe you're Michael Wilson," she said in as charming and encouraging a way as she dared muster. She was smiling and wondered if she'd actually said it in a way which was too playful. Jesus, was she flirting?

"Ah, well. That's great to hear. You just feel a bit naked walking around without the familiar feel of a wallet and all that's supposed to be in it… So how might we proceed? I mean, is there a way we can sort things out?"

Julie was taken aback by Michael's request to *proceed*. To *sort things out*. Why does he need to go so quickly? Wasn't he supposed to show some interest in her? Is that all he wanted? She noticed her disappointment and how irrational it was. She realized she had fallen silent now, and fought to get a hold of herself before her reaction became transparent. Of course there was really nothing she could do for him at the moment. She needed some time to think.

"Why don't you leave it with me Michael," she said, noticing how strangely intimate it felt to use his name.

CHAPTER 11

A policeman in Orlando Florida gave a lecture to a classroom of primary students on gun safety. He informed them that he was "the only one here professional enough to handle a gun", and then accidentally shot himself in the leg.

From the journals of Professor Charles Kidding, extract #26

Sam slouched deeply in a fabric deck chair he'd positioned at the edge of the lawn, right up next to the sidewalk which passed in front of their house. It was almost 3:30 pm, and he often sat here about this time, especially on sun-drenched afternoons like this. He sucked lazily at a Budweiser and scanned the pages of a large hard-backed library book entitled Atlas of the World's Worst Natural Disasters. He'd placed a large boom-box on the grass next to his chair, speakers facing out into the street. Today he was bringing to the neighborhood the music of a group called The Machinery of Despair, a guitar and synth-laden quartet who played in a genre he referred to, when d-jaying, as Dutch Industrial Metal. He might have even made that term up. He had programmed the next twelve songs into Dark Star Radio before leaving his basement room, so he had about forty-five minutes to hang out on the lawn. Sam was still waiting for his first listener, but what if someone found his station and went on line while he was out on the lawn, and all they heard was dead air? That would be an unforgivable sin for a DJ of his caliber. No way was he gonna do that.

Sam was reading about the Krakatoa volcanic eruption of 1883 when he heard the final school bell ring. Soon, many of the High School students would make there way down the sidewalk across the street. He drained the last of his Bud, dropped the bottle on the grass, and reached down to get his reefer tin. It turned out to be a difficult stretch because rolls of fat had him pretty well jammed into his chair. He thought about getting up, but he was awfully comfortable. He made one last attempt, grunted and stretched, and the chair toppled over. Laying on his side, he realized that his ass was still stuck in the chair. Sam pushed himself free of the canvas and aluminum, collected his reefer tin, righted the chair, and got settled again.

"Fucking Chinese," he said to himself. "Can't make a chair for the full-figured man. Don't they have fat fuckers too?"

Sam casually rolled a joint and lit up. When he saw the first groups of students making there way along the sidewalk he reached down, turned up the volume, and gave the bass a boost. A group of three pretty seniors strolled past, blond hair flashing in the sun, muscular thighs pressed into faded jeans which seemed to fit each girl in an identical fashion. Sam's head rested on his chins, inclining towards his book, but he watched the girls through up-slanted eyes and police style mirrored sun glasses. Extraordinary – despite the booming groans of Machinery of Despair and the close proximity, these girls took not the slightest notice. The next group through consisted of four muscled football players and two more pretty girls. Sam recognized the boys and readied himself for it.

"Yo fat boy," one of them called out, laughter from the others drifting over. Sam remained unmoved, head *down* and staring *up* at the offending footballers. Another shouted, "That music make you go deaf fat boy?"

Sam slowly lifted his right arm, middle finger half-raised, as if these human beings meant so little that half a finger was all the effort they warranted. The pretty girls giggled and the boys hooted in mock fear. When the student's voices had faded, Sam took a slow reflective drag on his joint and spoke in low and serious tones to himself.

"And he gazed upon this parade of the attractive and trendy as you might watch the monkeys at your local zoo."

Sam figured that was like poetry. He'd made part of it up and probably heard part of it in a song somewhere. It helped a bit, but he still felt that age-old pull in his gut like anger and hurt that was so mixed up it was something he really had no name for.

CHAPTER 12

Both the mayor and chief of police in a tiny Mexican village have been arrested for bribery. During a recent election, a mule named Pickles was put up for election against the discredited mayor. Pickles won the election, and is thought to be the world's first mule to win public office.

From the journals of Professor Charles Kidding, extract #92

Julie knew that if she was going to help Michael, she would need to go through Martin Simmons, her manager, and this meant going through Martin's PA. It turned out that Martin didn't have time to meet with her until next week, but she had pressed the PA and got her to acknowledge that, yes, there had been a cancellation for later this afternoon, and yes, she could see him. Martin Simons was senior manager at the Department of Health. He made a big deal at staff meetings about how his "door was always open", but this must have been a metaphorically open door, because his actual office door was always closed. Julie knew how it worked. Unless you truly needed something from Martin, it was best to avoid his open door policy.

Knocking on Martin's door she heard him shout "come on in", but as she entered she noticed he was on the phone, a strained expression on his face, the sort of expression you might associate with a blockage in the lower bowel. She sat in the chair facing his desk.

"Jesus Mark, I can't work miracles. Brendon's working on the policy right now, but I doubt he'll have it ready for tomorrow. I've already taken him off his other duties." Martin offered her a curt smile as he listened to whoever was on the other end of the phone.

This was a bad sign. Martin was already in a foul mood. Foul mood may mean uncharitable and inflexible frame of mind. Julie fought to arrange her thoughts. She knew the case she wanted to make for Michael and she had, at 11 pm last night, found a strategy she wanted Martin to support. But Martin needed to be approached in the right way. She noticed his tea mug on the desk – it was empty, and Martin was famous for the amount of tea he could drink over the course of the day. Catching his eye, she held up his mug and motioned that she'd be right back. Martin nodded endorsement to the idea and she made her way to the staff room. When she returned with two cups of tea she was glad to see that Martin was off the phone.

"Bless you," Martin sang as he accepted the tea, blowing out a breath laden with the stress of his phone call.

"Sounds like you're having one of those days," Julie said sympathetically.

"You could say that. Thanks for the tea. What's up?"

Well, that's Martin. His tone said *get to the point girl, I haven't got all day.*

"You've got a lot on your plate so I won't keep you long. It's just that I've got an unusual case I need to talk over with you. I had an appointment with a man named Michael Wilson who wants to get a replacement birth certificate. The problem is that he had his car and wallet stolen and he lost all his identification in the theft. He really needs a valid birth certificate in order to get other forms of ID, but of course we need to see a driver's license or passport to reissue a birth certificate. The thing is, he's a very genuine case. He brought in a check book from a local bank with his name and address on it, and the police report documenting the stolen car and identification. He's clearly legit."

Martin's eyes were already starting to glaze over.

"Julie, it's not our problem. There's a procedure we have to follow – you know that."

"I know, I know. But if we follow the policy to the letter, do you realize that means this poor guy will have to actually get a lawyer and petition the Supreme Court. I mean, that's just ridiculous. It seems really inflexible for us to force this guy through that sort of machine, especially when he was the victim of a crime. That policy was never intended for US citizens who had virtually all their ID stolen. And it's not necessary."

"Not necessary?" Martin asked, a pained and perplexed expression forming. Julie winced inwardly at her mistake. She knew that for a bureaucrat like Martin, policy and procedure were the very life-blood of any civil office. Questioning the value of policy amounted to something like spitting in the face of one of his family members.

"Up until about eight years ago we had a policy for people like this guy. Do you remember?"

Martin reflected for a moment. "Do you mean that external validation thing?"

"Sure," replied Julie.

This was the idea she had hit upon late last night. In the past, some discretion could be used on the part of the vital records department. Perhaps the individual had some forms of ID, but not the required ones. This would happen once in a while, just as in the case of Michael. External validation had been a supplemental process where the individual could get three credible persons to verify his identity. There was a form they had used.

Martin looked at Julie as if she had lost her mind.

"External validation? Are you kidding? We haven't been allowed to use that for years."

Julie had been prepared for this.

"Actually, when the new policy was written eight years ago it never said we couldn't use external validation to supplement forms of ID the individual might have. It's just that the external validation process wasn't mentioned in the new policy. I don't see why we can't use our discretion in exceptional cases. There's even a line in the current policy about the need for vital records staff to use good judgment in all cases. Couldn't we say that using something like the external validation procedure represents good judgment in this sort of case? Besides, aren't we supposed to be more oriented towards customer care these days?"

Julie knew she was taking a gamble by mentioning customer care. There was a lot of customer care policy around at the moment, and manager's like Martin hated the stuff. It meant that Martin had to create the illusion of giving a shit. She wasn't sure whether mentioning it would nudge Martin in the direction she wanted or just piss him off. Martin stared at her for a moment, a quizzical expression on his face. He opened his mouth to speak when his phone rang abruptly. Martin exhaled heavily, raised his hands in weary surrender, and picked up the receiver.

"Okay… tell him I'll call back in one minute. Yes, literally one minute." He hung up and gazed at Julie, a figure of frustration and fatigue.

"Look, if you want to go into this case and the external validation process, be my guest. You know more about vital records than I do. To be honest, as long as you don't do anything that gets us in trouble, I couldn't care less. Good luck finding the old forms."

Back in her office, Julie was pleased and excited. *If you want to go into this case…* Martin had said. So she could *go into the case*, and if she interpreted the rest of Martin's response in a liberal manner, she could pretty much just use her discretion. By the end of the work day, Martin would forget all about the conversation. She wanted to call Michael straight away, but she needed to collect her thoughts. The external validation form is important. She'd have to make sure they still had one. The secretaries probably chucked them out years ago, but copies of all the old vital records policies and related forms will be in the appendix of policies which are 8 years and older. Julie scurried to an old store room, found the year 2004 policy, and opened it up to the appendix. Yes, there it was. Excellent, thought Julie. An external validation form, a check book, a debit card, and a police report. She could make this fly.

She noticed her hand was trembling slightly when she placed it on the phone receiver. She pulled her hand away, took a large breath of air and held it, then slowly blew it out. Hey, it's just a phone call to tell him about the form, she thought. You won't see him again until he brings the completed form in to you. Just calm down.

He answered the phone on the first ring, and she knew his voice immediately.

"Hello."

"Hello, this is Julie from Vital Records. Is this Michael?" she asked.

"Yes, hello Julie. Thanks for getting back to me so quickly."

"I've got some good news for you Michael."

CHAPTER 13

A 21-year-old student named Brendan San from Norwich, England has made the final round in an art competition. His work consists of two checks, each for £1,000, made out to the judges of the competition.

From the journals of Professor Charles Kidding, extract #64

Michael found a corner seat in Starbucks which allowed him to scan most of the café, if he felt like it. It was just after 10:00 am and he was making pretty good progress. British beef was in trouble again and the odds were good that things would only get worse over the next six months, so that was going to be a fairly sure bet.

He wasn't surprised when Mary's bread truck lumbered up to the store front, grinding and clattering in the way it did. She seemed to like Starbucks too, and every few weeks their paths would cross at one of the stores around town. Michael kept his head down when she entered, pretending to concentrate on his reading. He'd probably done that out of habit – he'd always ignored Mary whenever they came across each other in public. She had made it harder for him in the early days of their relationship. Mary used to plunk herself down at his table, uninvited, and start chatting to him as if they had been close friends for years. Or she'd sit at a table near by, and if he looked up she might wink at him provocatively. If she walked past him she might run her hand through his hair. It had annoyed him. Why couldn't she just stick to their weekly arrangement? It was simple enough. Over time, though, Mary had seemed to get the message, or maybe she just got bored trying to provoke him.

But things felt different this morning, and he looked up from his magazine and found himself watching Mary as she ordered her coffee, even staring at her as she made her way to a table and arranged her newspaper. She had a camcorder on the table as well. What was that for? Mary didn't look over, though she sat facing him about halfway across the room. She must know he was there – it's not such a large room. Maybe she had got used to him ignoring her. Strangely, Michael wanted her to pester him, to tease him. At least to look at him and smile. He couldn't blame her for sticking her nose in her paper these days, could he?

But why couldn't *he* join her? Michael scanned the handful of patrons. What would he say to her? She would be surprised, that's for sure. Michael put his papers and magazines into a canvas bag, picked his coffee up, and made his way over. As he neared, Mary looked up and smiled broadly.

"Hi there, would you mind if I joined you?"

Mary continued to smile at him, looking straight into his eyes, a quizzical expression forming around the edges of her mouth.

"You want to sit with me?"

"Well, if it's okay. If you'd rather I didn't, that's alright," replied Michael.

"Of course you can sit with me."

Michael got himself comfortable in the chair and found a place on the table for his coffee. He struggled for something to say. Normally Mary gabbled on about god only knows what or it was clear that it wasn't the right time to talk. They were on new territory here. Michael hoped Mary might say something, anything, but she just gazed at him, an expression of curiosity on her face. Michael looked down at her newspaper.

"So what are you reading about?"

"I was reading the obituary notices and the personals. It's all about death and love, as it turns out, but I guess that's not surprising."

"No," said Michael, "I guess that's what it would be about."

They fell quiet for a few moments, Mary examining her coffee, Michael taking the opportunity to look closely at her. Strands of dark black hair fell over her pale complexion, and he followed the clear line of her profile, noticing her dry flaking lips. She wore no make-up, never did. Lots of young woman worked really hard at their appearance, and it showed in the shining hair, the glinting gold and silver, the fashionable clothing, the feminine aroma of expensive perfumes. At a distance, they were beautiful and their presentation absorbed your attention. But when you got close enough to *really* look at them, you could see that their beauty was a mirage of sorts, that their bone structure just didn't work, that they were soft or bony in the wrong places, that their skin was blemished beneath the make-up. Things worked in reverse with Mary. At a distance, she looked a mess. Unkempt hair falling over her face, that ashen complexion, those dry and often peeling lips, black skirts and ridiculous t-shirts which looked like they were picked up off the floor this morning, and yesterday morning as well. Then you looked closer, and you saw the striking contour of her face, those luminous eyes, and the subtle girlish shape to her figure as it moved in that strangely self-possessed way.

Mary looked up from her coffee.

"Michael, are you alright?"

He heard the sound of his own name, spoken this morning, here in Starbucks, and he really liked hearing it.

"Yes, I'm fine. I just wanted some company, I suppose. It's okay, isn't it?"

Mary smiled and uttered a brief laugh through her nose, as if what Michael had said was deeply amusing.

"Of course. That's what human beings do when they want company. They go and sit with someone they know in a café and ask them what they're reading about. It probably happens a lot."

Michael felt a warmth slip over him, a warmth tinged with a strange anxiety. She was acting refreshingly normal this morning, which helped.

Michael noticed the camcorder.

"What's the camcorder for?"

"It's for a little project I'm working on. You know how people get fascinated with exotic wildlife and they take a camera to places like Borneo or Zimbabwe, and then do naturalistic observation. It's exactly like that except I'm going to be filming in *Mega Home Supply.*"

Well, so much for Mary's normal behavior. Michael had been in *Mega Home Supply* a few times. It was one of those large chain stores. There was one in Pittsford Plaza.

"Why are you filming there?"

Mary leaned closer and looked around the café as if spies might be listening. She whispered, "because the natives wear special ceremonial attire and perform straaaaange rituals." Mary's eyes widened, as if she was inviting him to join in on the fascination of her discovery.

"Natives?" he said. "What natives?"

Mary looked at him expectantly, as if waiting for him to *get it.*

"Store staff," she said finally. "The people who work there."

"Oh," Michael replied, as if he now understood.

"In fact, it's not really naturalistic observation. It's more like participatory observation, which, come to think of it, means that I need a film crew." Mary's eyes widened. "Hey, you could be the film crew. You'd be great."

"What?" Michael spat out.

"Yea, definitely," said Mary. "You could be my film crew. It's gonna be really interesting."

"Mary," said Michael, "what ever this is, I really don't think it's a good idea for me to get involved."

Mary stood up. "Michael, don't you see? You're already involved – it's already happening."

Michael noticed a group at the next table looking at them. "Mary," he said, lowering his voice to a whisper, "I don't know what you mean, but I really think you should get someone else."

She lent down and took him by the elbow. "Come on, you'll miss out." Michael noticed a cashier gazing at them with voyeuristic intent. He sighed heavily and allowed himself to be pulled out of his seat.

They made their way through the doors and stood in front of Mary's converted bread truck. Mary waved her hand at the truck.

"Welcome to Hacienda Mary – all the comforts of home on four wheels, and it'll take you wherever you want to go except when it's broken down. I'll give you the grand tour."

She walked around the truck and opened two back doors. Michael was surprised at what he saw. The exterior of the truck looked like a shoddy mess, covered as it was in dented and tarnished silver siding. But the interior was rather extraordinary. Mary had obviously taken great care in the little world she had created. She must have had a long window put in along one side, which gave the interior a warm glow. Along the right-hand side was a kitchen, complete with stove, oven, shelving, and sink, inlaid by exquisite hand-built woodwork. Nearest the open door and carrying on from the kitchen was a tiny desk with a laptop, and a small stereo above the desk on a shelf. A thick, soft beige carpet lay on the floor, with a colorful throw rug on top. At the far end of the space was a small couch.

"Wow," Michael breathed. "It's really nice. I mean it's really comfortable. Where do you sleep?"

"The couch opens into a bed. I can lounge on it during the day and sleep on it at night. It's missing a bathroom and shower, but that's what the YMCA is for."

She closed the doors, walked to the driver's side, and climbed into the seat. Michael felt uncomfortable about joining her, but found himself following her lead. Opening the passenger door he climbed into his seat next to her. The ex-bread truck gave away its age when Mary started it up. There was a loud bang from the tail pipe and then the engine rumbled into life, clanking and grinding. As Mary guided the lumbering truck down Monroe Avenue Michael was suddenly aware of the camcorder in his lap. Mary must have handed it to him. He really didn't like being pulled into something he couldn't fully understand, but he didn't want to say 'no' either.

"So I'm the camera crew?"

"Sure," replied Mary.

"Is the camera easy to use?"

"It's simple. Just push the *on* button, look through it, and push record when you're ready. Push the same button again to pause, and again to start recording. There's a button here you can use to widen or narrow the angle of the lens."

"Why are we filming in *Mega Home Supply*?"

"I was in there last week and noticed something very strange happening. I mean it was all very normal, which was what made it seem especially strange."

Michael saw Pittsford Plaza at the bottom of the hill they were on, and he felt a wave of anxiety coarse through him. For goodness sake – what was she talking about?

"But Mary, are you sure it's okay to film inside a store? Don't you think they might have rules against that?"

"I don't know – maybe."

Mary pulled into the large Pittsford Plaza parking lot. Two hundred yards of stores spread out before them, and Mary negotiated her way through hundreds of parked cars and traffic, finally finding a space quite near *Mega Home Supply*. Michael looked at the store front, and it appeared larger than he remembered. He felt a hard pit forming directly beneath his sternum.

"Mary, I don't know about this. What am I supposed to be filming anyway?"

Mary turned off the ignition and looked over at him.

"You can film me and the people I'm speaking with, and maybe bits of the store or other store employees. You're a part of what's happening – you're a part of the process." Mary placed a hand on his arm. "Your *involved*."

"What if we get in trouble?"

"Then getting in trouble is part of the process as well," said Mary. She gave him a broad grin and pointed an index finger at him playfully. "But if we get in trouble, make sure you film that too."

Mary opened the door and got out. Michael got out too, closed his door, and breathed "Oh shit" under his breath. As they walked towards the store front Michael asked, "When do I start filming?"

"Michael, you're the director. You're like Scorsese. You can make the creative decisions about filming."

"Oh God," he said as he stopped and turned the camcorder on. Bringing the camcorder up to eye-level, he saw the slim figure of Mary walking towards the store through the viewfinder. He pushed the record button and was pleased to see a red light illuminate. Michael started walking, following the figure of Mary as she entered the door. He decided it was best to remain about ten feet behind her, filming from this perspective. His heart was thumping as he struggled to hold the camera as still as possible. Through the doors now, he entered the store and followed Mary into a rat's maze of isles.

Navigating was a rather disorienting challenge, because his field of vision was more narrow than normal – Michael had all of Mary in the frame, but felt he might bump into or trip over something closer to him. He felt for the telephoto button and widened the angle of the lens. Now he could see the shelving on either side of him and more of the floor ahead – that was better. Mary led him up an isle containing a lot of plastic ware and a member of staff walked past him, an inquisitive expression on her face. Michael noticed her uniform, a white shirt with the store logo stitched into the pocket, and recalled what Mary had said about the natives wearing special ceremonial dress.

Mary stood in front of a selection of plastic cooking implements and chose a measuring cup. She headed back towards the camera, passed by Michael, and walked for the front of the store. Michael turned and followed her, and as they came out of their isle he scanned the area through the lens, taking in the eight check-out counters. The first five of them were manned by cashiers, and Mary joined the end of the line in number three. Michael didn't get in line, but got a good angle so he could film Mary, the line of people ahead of her, and the cashier. Michael scanned all five lines now and noticed that the twenty-five or thirty customers were silent and stony-faced as they stood there, waiting their turn. But the store was filled with subtle sounds – the electro-mechanical chuntering of the cash registers, the soft shuffling of feet, the conventional exchange of conversation between customer and cashier.

Michael recalled Mary telling him he was like Scorsese, and he slowly scanned the store front and saw the cashiers, now the entrance way, and **now** the camera focused squarely on what must be a store manager. Michael's heart suddenly banged harder against his ribs as he absorbed the image of this fat middle-aged man in a sports coat with store logo and tie, acutely aware of his folded arms and stony facial expression.

And the manager was staring straight at him.

Michael lost his nerve and let the camera drop down to his side, releasing the record button. He found himself looking around *Mega Home Supply*, a bemused expression on his face, as if he had suddenly realized that, inexplicably, he was in *this* store, using a camcorder. He probably looked terribly guilty about something, which was strange because he didn't even know what he was involved with? This was ridiculous. Why doesn't he just whistle absent-mindedly to himself as the manager stares at him?

And then Michael looked at Mary.

He was behind and to the side of her, so she couldn't see that he had stopped filming. She was bound to be disappointed that he didn't get the film she wanted. And then Michael was aware of something else. She might be disappointed in *him*. Was he a coward? Michael took a deep breath, blew it out, brought the camera to eye level, and pushed record.

There were three customers in front of her now, and he focused the camera to take in Mary, the other customers, and the cashier.

Okay, he'll go through with this. But what the hell was she up to? Why was she putting him through this?

The cashier was a tall, lanky redheaded boy who looked about twenty – probably one of the local college students. The next customer placed her items before him.

"Telephone number, please," the cashier asked politely.

The young woman reeled off her telephone number in a mechanical and bored manner, and the cashier tapped at his computerized cash register in response. He scanned her items.

"$22.57, please."

The customary exchange occurred and the next customer approached, a middle-aged man with what looked like a blender.

"Telephone number, please."

The telephone number was offered, the cashier tapped at his computer, and the exchange was made with the standard *thankyous* and *have a nice days*.

Mary moved forward, her plastic measuring cup at her side. Michael imagined he should pan over to the manager again. He didn't want to, but Scorsese would probably do that. Maybe the manager had got bored with him and had gone off to do something else. He panned to the left and gliding into the frame was the manager and, standing next to him, a store security officer. They were leaning close, looking directly at him, and talking things over.

Oh God.

Michael quickly panned back, but the image of that security officer was still in his mind. Another balding fat fellow, and although his uniform had the store logo, it was mostly black. A lot like the police, but no gun. The next customer was a somewhat graying, older woman.

"Telephone number, please?"

The woman offered up her number, the cashier typed at the computer, and the transaction was made. Finally, Mary moved forward.

"Telephone number, please?"

Mary paused for a moment, and then responded in a clear voice.

"Could you tell me what sort of underpants you're wearing, please?"

The cashier was struck dumb. His pimply countenance offered a rather stunned expression, and then his eyebrows narrowed in confusion and alarm.

"What?" he replied, his mouth gaping in astonishment. Michael only had Mary, the cashier, and a few other customers in the viewfinder, but the hairs on his forearms sensed a hum of ferment all around him.

"Well," Mary continued, "I wonder if you wouldn't mind telling me what sort of underpants you're wearing? I mean there's lots of different types – boxer shorts, Y-fronts, g-strings. And do you mind telling me what size they are?" There was something really incongruous about the way Mary spoke – what she was saying might be outrageous, but her manner was very discreet and polite, as if she were discussing the weather.

"But… I don't… uhmmm" the boy sputtered, looking now at his row of customers and then straight into Michael's camera. Finally, he looked over at the manager and Michael widened the lens angle to take them all in. His heart was hammering away and it was hard to breathe, but in this near occasion of panic, even Michael couldn't help wondering what would happen next. And he was getting the hang of this camera business. The manager gave the security officer a hard glance and then the two of them approached Mary's counter. It was the manager who spoke.

"Is there some difficulty, Ma'am?"

"Oh, that's very kind of you to ask, but there's no problem. I was just talking with your cashier." She returned her attention to the college boy. "So then, where did we get to?"

The cashier looked at the manager with pleading eyes, and then addressed Mary.

"Uhm, you were sort of asking me about something, but… ."

"Oh yes, now I remember. You wanted to know what my telephone number was and then I got to wondering what sort of underpants you had on."

Michael heard muted laughter now from the other customers, and noticed the security guard place his hands squarely on his hips.

"Excuse me Ma'am," the guard said calmly. "Our staff have a right to their privacy and they have a right to be treated with dignity. There are health and safety laws which guarantee employee's rights to safety. I don't really think that sort of conversation is appropriate in a store."

"Not appropriate?" Mary asked, affecting a surprised note in her expression and tone. "What's not appropriate? The question about my telephone number or the one about his… ." Mary stopped abruptly and turned to the cashier. "I'm sorry, I don't even know your name. That's really rude of me to keep calling you *he* and *his*, isn't it?"

"It's Brian," the cashier responded hesitantly.

"… or the question about Brian's underpants? Which is the inappropriate one?"

"It's not appropriate for you to ask our staff private questions like that, especially in front of a lot of other people," the guard said.

"Oh," Mary replied, looking genuinely surprised. "Brian, I'm so sorry. Did my question about your underpants upset you?" More restrained giggles from the customers.

"Well…" Brian stammered, and he looked down, as if in deep thought. Staring at his counter, something must have fallen into place in that college-boy brain of his, and when he looked up he leaned closer to Mary and spoke in a low tone.

"Is this because I asked you for a phone number? You know, you don't have to give me the number. We have to ask everyone that. It's the store policy."

"Oh, yes, I was wondering about that. You ask everyone for their phone number and then you tap something into your cash register. That is a curious thing. Why do you do that?"

"Uhmmm… I think it's just for our records," Brian replied.

Mary began to sing quite suddenly, and though Michael was impressed at the quality of her voice, it was quite shocking that anyone should sing in this context.

We'd like to know a little bit about you for our files
We'd like to help you learn to help yourself
Look around you, all you see are sympathetic eyes
Stroll around the grounds until you feel at home

A Simon and Garfunkle song, thought Michael, but he couldn't recall which one.

"Well," said Mary, "if it's just for your records, what could be the harm in that? It's probably important for your records to be complete, and I actually feel safer knowing that a huge and morally reputable international corporation such as yours has my personal information in their records. I'm quite happy to give you my number."

Mary smiled, and Michael was suddenly aware of how quiet the store had grown. No cash registers chuntered, no feet shuffled, and the only conversation which could be heard was drifting up from the back of the store from customers oblivious to what was happening. What was going on? The sincerity and naive pleasantness with which Mary spoke was beguiling. Was she being serious? Was she being ironic in order to amuse herself or make some sort of point, or just cause trouble?

"Well," the manager said. "If you're happy to give our cashier your number, he can complete your purchase."

"Okay," replied Mary. "It's... uhmm. Oh goodness me, now I've gone and forgotten my number." She looked over at Michael.

"Michael, what's my number?" she called out.

Michael was desperately aware of several sets of eyes being trained on him. What's she doing? She knows he probably wouldn't have her number memorized. But he had to respond, if only to get everyone to stop looking at him.

"Uhmm... sorry, I don't think I know it off hand."

"Oh," Mary replied. "I've just remembered my number anyway. It's.... You know though, I am curious about what you do with my phone number. Not that I don't have every confidence in this fine corporation, but it's just that, well, like I said, I'm curious." This time the manager was not going to leave Brian to deal with this strange young woman.

"Ma'am, everything we do with phone numbers is entirely in compliance with Federal regulations concerning data protection."

"Oh, of course it is, but what do you actually do with my phone number? You must keep it for some purpose." The manager seemed caught off guard, looked around at the customers, and leaned closer to Mary.

"Look, I'm not completely sure, but I'm sure it's okay."

Mary swallowed a deep intake of breath while placing a hand against her chest, and looked rather shocked.

"But you're the President of The Corporation. If you don't know what happens to the Information, then we could all be unsafe."

"I'm just the assistant store manager, Ma'am..."

But now the security guard could restrain himself no longer, and moved directly to the side of Mary with a menacing gait. Michael saw the look in his narrowed eyes and knew that something had tipped over inside this man – some stockpile of masculine pride had overwhelmed the last line of professional restraint, and Michael knew instinctively that they were *in for it*.

"Excuse me Ma'am," he said harshly. "We're a busy store and we do not have time for your silly games. You are holding up customers. You need to make your purchase **now** and leave the store. And you," he bellowed, pointing at Michael, "need to turn your camera off and leave as well." He didn't care who heard him. He was going to take control now. Michael felt a reflexive impulse to put the camera down, but was stopped short by the sound of Mary's voice.

"Sir, you're a brave and muscular sort of fellow and that's good because I feel a bit safer with you around, especially since discovering that the President of the Corporation doesn't know what happens to the Information, but I really don't want my camera crew to get upset."

"Okay, I've had enough of this nonsense," the guard replied. "You are causing a disturbance and you need to leave. And you," he said to Michael, "are leaving with her."

The security officer walked straight for him, and Michael felt his muscles constrict as the shaking image of the officer grew larger in his viewfinder. And then he felt the camera being pulled downwards, smelled the sweaty odor of the guard, and sensed heavy pressure on his upper arm as he was being pulled towards the door. And now Mary had swept around to cut them off and she seemed to have transformed entirely. Barring the way, she brandished her plastic measuring cup threateningly at the guard, and shrieked, color flooding into her face.

"TAKE YOUR FUCKING HANDS OFF MY FRIEND."

But the guard knew his business, and in an instant he had Mary by the arm with his other hand and they were both dragged through the electronic doors and tossed out onto the sidewalk and into dazzling sunlight. The pressure on his arm was gone now and though he had his back to the guard, he heard his parting words.

"You're not to return to our store."

Michael reeled around to look back into the store, and noticed for the first time that the entire store front was covered in reflective silvery glass.

He wondered if he should run, but for the moment felt so shaken that he seemed barely able to move. Rubbing his aching arm, he gazed at those silvery plates of glass. How strange – from this perspective, the store looked as normal as ever, as if nothing had taken place. And then he was aware of Mary laughing wildly and he looked at her in disbelief.

"I'm getting out of here," he spat at her.

Michael trotted down the walkway in front of the stores with Mary at his heels. She caught up, faced him, and took Michael by the arms.

"Michael, you were fantastic. The way you hung in there. Hey, is that camera still running?" Mary took the camera and trained it on him.

"This is Michael, camera crew par excellence. Michael, tell us about your experience. How was it?" Michael looked grim and trampled as he spoke, an edge of anger in his tone.

"Awful, Mary. It was really awful, okay." Mary softened, and a look of empathy came over her as she stopped recording and let the camera down by her side. She blew a breath of air out, grinning broadly.

"Michael, what happened was really important, and that film we just made is far beyond anything I'd hoped for. And you were great. You kept filming right through it all. I couldn't have done that without you."

"Done what, exactly? I mean, what was that?" he demanded. Michael could hear the blood pounding in his head and his ears felt astonishingly hot. He seriously wondered if his legs might buckle.

"Mary, I need to sit down." He looked momentarily through the store window they had stopped in front of, and identified the type of shop immediately – a place smelling of synthetic flowery aromas, selling pointless and expensive nick-knacks which well-off people give to their well-off friends. He sat against the red brick of the store front, pulled his knees up, and put his face in his hands. Mary sat close to him, resting a hand on his thigh, and they were silent for a few moments.

"I'm just not used to things like that," Michael finally said, looking very glum. In response, Mary held up a plastic measuring cup so he could get a good look at it.

"Free Tupperware," she suggested, offering him a broad smile. Michael stared at her for a moment and then smiled in spite of himself, shaking his head.

"You were really angry at that guard," he said. "I've never seen you like that."

"I was. I was really pissed at him." She waved the measuring cup. "I tried to stab the fucker right in his big fat gut, but he was too strong."

"I think I missed that."

Mary laughed and they sat in silence again. Michael's mind drifted and he noticed that his physiology was finally slowing down. Disjointed scenes of the past five minutes flew before his eyes.

She had called him *my friend*, he thought.

CHAPTER 14

Although now retired, Dennis Grey, age seventy-two, continues to patrol the streets of Woodbridge, England, where he was traffic warden for twenty-four years. He takes photographs of illegally parked cars which he then hands onto the local police.

From the journals of Professor Charles Kidding, extract #209

Michael held the external validation form out in front of him. He had felt genuine relief when Julie called and told him there was another way to get his birth certificate back. She had been surprisingly helpful. But the more he thought about this form, the more anxious he seemed to be. There were four sections. In section 1, Michael was to offer his name, address, phone number, email, and other information, like where he had been born, addresses he had lived at, etc... No problem with that section. Below that there was one section for each of the three individuals who would verify his identity, and there were general instructions at the top. Michael read the instructions for the third time:

In order to assist in identifying an individual requesting a vital record (e.g. birth certificate), three individuals are required as a means of external validation. These individuals must complete their section of the form below in full, and may in certain cases be contacted by the Department of Health. Individuals providing external validation must:

1. *Have known the individual requesting a record for a minimum of two years.*
2. *Provide a photo copy of their birth certificate (do not enclose originals).*
3. *Be deemed to be persons of "legitimate standing in the community", who have*

been gainfully employed for the past five years, and who have no criminal convictions.

What was worrying Michael was the issue of who could validate him. Mrs. Deveroix hadn't been employed for many years and Sam's radio station hardly represented 'gainful' employment. He'd known Mary for long enough, but didn't really want to ask her. And was she a person of legitimate standing in the community? That seemed doubtful. He could ask his family doctor, but that was only one person. So that left Bob and Mitch and another regular named Pete at the Pittsford Pub. He'd known them for more than two years, he supposed. But the idea of approaching them left him feeling really uncomfortable. Still, it was Thursday, his night for visiting the Pittsford Pub. If he didn't ask them tonight he'd have to wait another week, and Michael wasn't sure he could manage another week of this purgatory.

Michael arrived at the Pittsford Pub a little after 6:00 pm. As he made his way into the bar, the clinking glasses, chattering clientele, and fizzing drinks struck him as noisier than usual. The reason was immediately apparent. The local ham radio group was in tonight, and they were standing around like a restless heard of cattle. They all wore matching jackets, with *The Hamsters* embroidered across the back. Looking over several heads, he made out Mitch and Bob, who were sitting at the bar. Reflexively, Michael slipped his hand into his suit coat jacket and felt the external validation form. He squeezed his way through the aged and graying pack of ham radio amateurs, smiling politely, and then glimpsed Pete. Pete had also managed to get a seat at the bar, but was sitting a couple of stools down from Bob. Michael cursed inwardly. As he worked his way to the bar, he noted that there were no remaining stools. He accepted his fate – he would have to chat with Bob and Mitch, include Pete if he could, all the while jammed into a mob of Hamsters.

Michael carefully squeezed himself between a few Hamsters, acutely aware that Mitch and Bob didn't know he was there as they had their backs to him. Their conversation had stalled apparently, and they were both watching the baseball game. Pete was chatting to a woman Michael hadn't seen before.

"Hiya Mitch, Bob," said Michael.

They both turned in unison.

"Oh hi there," said Bob. Mitch nodded acknowledgement.

Michael was immediately struck by the way that neither had used his name. What's so difficult about saying *Hi Michael*? Of course they know his name. He'd been chatting with them for almost three years. But then Michael had to think. Did they actually address him by name when they greeted and spoke to him? Michael always used their names. That was one of the things Dale Carnegie had written about. *Remember people's names and use people's names when speaking to them. The sound of a person's name is the sweetest sound in the world to each individual.* He was sure that they must use his name from time to time, but he couldn't remember it happening. How could he be uncertain about something so simple?

"Wow, is it ever busy tonight," said Michael.

"Well, it's the Hamsters. What are you gonna do?" said Mitch. "It's Hamster heaven in here tonight."

Michael worried about the Hamsters feeling offended by Mitch's remark, but he noticed that the two guys closest had hearing aids stuffed into thick grey ear hair, so he relaxed a bit. Michael had planned to make some small talk for a while, maybe ask them how their week had gone, and then bring up the car theft and the form later, after everyone had had a couple of drinks. But this situation was intolerable. He wanted to collect the three of them, take them to a nice quite table in the restaurant next door, and explain everything carefully. But he just didn't feel like he could do that.

Bob was saying something about the pitcher. Michael never could follow any conversation about baseball, and cursed himself for not being able to join in. He'd just have to bring it up. He could be standing here all night listening to a conversation about baseball. They should find the story about the car theft interesting, at least.

"You guys wouldn't believe the week I've had."

Mitch and Bob turned to look at Michael.

"I stopped in at this news shop downtown last week. When I came out my car had been stolen."

"Your kidding," replied Bob, laughing somewhat.

"No shit," said Mitch. "Did you get your car back?"

"No, not yet. I gave the police a statement and I guess they're looking for it. But the worst thing is that my wallet was in the car when it was stolen."

"Jesus," said Bob. "That's bad luck."

"Oh, it gets even worse than that. I also had a lot of other ID in the car – social security card, passport. I'd been down at the DMV renewing my license, and everything was stolen," said Michael, trying to make the story sound natural.

Bob and Mitch looked at each other for a moment, and Michael wondered why they did that. Did they wonder if he was making the story up? But why would he? He knew he had to press on, though he felt a flush of heat crawling up his neck. A hamster was trying to squeeze himself between Michael and other customers in order to get to the bar, and Michael could feel the weight of his bony body pressing against him.

"It's just been hell trying to sort everything out. You try to get one piece of identification back, and you need identification to do that. It's been a real mess."

The crack of a bat hitting a ball sounded and then cheering from the TV, and Bob and Mitch reflexively turned to see what had happened. Michael looked at the TV as well, and noticed that what looked like a home run had drifted out of bounds. He swallowed hard, and was glad to see that Bob and Mitch looked back towards him a moment later. The Hamster had managed to get a bartender's attention and shouted that he wanted two gin and tonics.

"So what are you gonna do?" asked Bob.

"Well, you won't believe this. In order to get my birth certificate back…".

"Birth certificate?" asked Mitch.

"Yea, that was stolen too," said Michael. "I've got to have three people who know me fill out this external validation form."

Michael pulled the form from his jacket and held it up for them.

"I guess I've got to put my name and information here at the top, and then I've got to have people who know me fill out one of the sections below. There's not much to it. They just need to give their name, address, contact details and a few other personal details, and then just indicate here that I'm Michael Wilson. The only other thing is that they need to include a copy of their birth certificate.

There was a pause as Michael waited for Mitch or Bob to respond. They were supposed to offer to help him, but the pause seemed to stretch out until Michael finally said, "it's really pretty simple." Still, they didn't answer.

Michael continued, a feeling of desperation and indignity coming over him. "It's just that the people who validate me have had to know me for at least two years and I've been coming to the Pittsford Pub now for longer than that and…" Another crack of bat on ball was heard, the TV crowd roared, and Mitch and Bob looked back at the game in unison. This time it was a shot deep into left field and the batter rounded first and held up safely at second. Mitch and Bob turned back to Michael, but slowly, as if with reluctance.

"It's just that… I could use some help with the form."

The Hamster had finally received his gin and tonics and was trying to maneuver past Michael, elbows tucked in, drinks clutched tightly. But other customers had their backs to the old man and didn't know he needed space, and he couldn't get past. The Hamster looked up at Michael with pleading eyes. Michael sighed, stepped back, and gestured for the old man to move through. He made it past, spilling G and T down his wrists and mumbling thankyous. Mitch was looking back at the game now. All Michael felt he could do was look expectantly at Bob.

"Jesus," said Bob. "That's a heck of a spot. My cousin had his car stolen once. Right in front of him too. He actually saw the guys take it and …"

Michael was not really hearing Bob's story. He was holding his form up, waving it slightly, hoping the image of it might register with Bob, but he could see that Bob and Mitch didn't want to fill out this form – they didn't want to get mixed up in it. Maybe they even thought there was something illicit about what he was asking them to do. Michael thought about being more direct, but they didn't want to help him – he could see that. He felt a strange mix of anger and humiliation stirring in his veins, and he just wanted to leave. When it was clear Bob had finished his story, he said he had to use the bathroom. He said it curtly, and maybe Bob got the point.

Michael was glad he was the only one using the bathroom. He needed a moment to collect himself and decide what to do. He took a piss, washed his hands, and then stared into the mirror. It was his face. The same reflection he had looked at for years. Maybe he looked a bit distressed and tired, but that was definitely him. And then he found himself speaking to his reflection in a way which was surprising.

"Hello, I'm Michael Wilson. It's a pleasure to meet you."

His reflection spoke the same words, which for some inexplicable reason struck him as odd. Michael splashed cold water on his face and then dried himself with toweling. He knew he wanted to leave immediately. As he pushed his way through the front door he glanced back towards the bar and whispered "assholes" under his breath.

Michael walked up Main Street. At the four corners he turned left onto Monroe. Kids flew about the sidewalks on skateboards or skipped along under the falling dusk. He should be at Sutherland Street, but he was still at the centre of the village. The yellow street lights came on suddenly, ushering evening in. Michael looked for Sutherland Street on the left… but it wasn't there! He stopped, the now familiar current of anxiety pulsing and straining at his stomach, the weight pushing on his chest. Was he lost again? He should definitely be at the corner of Main and Sutherland Streets. Oh God, not again. He turned around. Where was he? Where was his home? This was crazy. He saw the Pittsford library. Okay, he wasn't lost, but he wasn't where he was supposed to be either. There was a taxi out front. He jogged up and the driver opened his window.

"Have you got a fare," Michael asked?

Michael entered his rooms and sat on his couch. His hands were shaking – in fact a tremor of agitation vibrated through his body like an electrical circuit which had no switch. Imagine taking a taxi four blocks. The taxi diver must have thought he was nuts, or disabled. Maybe he was… disabled. Who knew? He went to the kitchen and pulled a pint glass from a cupboard and placed it on a counter. Standing at his ale cooler, he looked through the glass door at a variety of fine imported ales and wondered which to choose. It needed to be just the right one at a moment like this. He went for the Fuller's London Pride. The same ale can sometimes taste quite different depending on the mood your taste buds might be in. But the London Pride never failed him. That's what he needed.

Michael sank into his couch and took a large mouthful. He might need a couple more of these. The image of the man from his dream came to him, the vast form of his shadowy figure appearing before his eyes. Michael pushed the image from his mind, but not before he looked into that face of his, not before he glimpsed the pock-marked countenance, the heavy forehead. He took another full mouthful and held it there on his tongue, and the scene from the Pittsford Pub played out before him, the images clear in his mind. It was the blank expressions on Bob and Mitch's faces which really got him. *It's just that I could use some help with this form.* He'd said that, all right. How much clearer could he be? He'd pretty much asked them straight out. And Bob had changed the subject. Even worse, Mitch had just turned away. They knew he needed help. He'd been making conversation with those guys for almost three years, expressing interest in their dreary lives, sitting through dull games of baseball and football and basketball. But what was he going to do about this form?

He found himself thinking about Mr. Deveroix's clandestine attack space, and the image of Mr. Deveroix's death forced itself into his mind. He'd come back from Starbucks one afternoon about six months ago and had been surprised to see an ambulance in the drive. He saw it clearly now – walking into the kitchen, Mr. Deveroix lying on the lynoloium and staring fixedly at the florescent lighting on the ceiling, oxygen mask on, his hands fixed into two claws pulled up near his shoulders, Mrs. Deveroix standing in the corner and staring, hands covering her mouth as if to prevent herself from screaming, two paramedics bent over him, wires everywhere. And Michael remembered his eyes clearly, those wide glassy eyes fixed on the ceiling. Mr. Deveroix might have been aware of these people in the room with him, but he did not look at others, not even his wife. Was he so gripped by the pain and the terror of it all that he could only attend to the inner workings of his failing heart? Michael had felt like a voyeur, the way he'd stared dumbly into this man's helplessness.

Michael decided to visit the attic. Mrs. Deveroix had, after all, asked him to look into it, to see what was up there. Michael noticed his pint was half gone, so he grabbed another London Pride from the cooler, the bottle opener too, and made his way to the attic door. He managed to hold onto everything and unlock the door. He flipped a light on at the bottom of the stairs and made his way up a dozen steps, a note of suspense and intrigue finally catching hold of him. On the landing, he flicked a further three switches. The switches illuminated a series of carefully placed ceiling lights and the scene he gazed upon left him transfixed. Michael stood stock still for several minutes and slowly scanned the whole of the space. Finally, he breathed out an astounded "Wow." Michael's image of an attic was one of dust, rough unfinished wood, and piles of flotsam which no one wanted but which someone couldn't bear to throw away. This was different altogether.

A plush cream carpet covered the floor, which also had a few expensive rugs placed carefully on top. The wooden ceiling and beams had been stained and gave off a tasteful semitransparent sheen. There was a beautiful antique desk with a reading lamp, and against three walls were custom-built book cases which were filled with books and expensive marble bookends. There was a comfortable leather recliner.

But it was what sat in the middle of everything which really caught his attention – a train set. Michael felt a need to move slowly and carefully to the edge of the set, almost as if by walking in this space he might somehow cause everything about him to collapse. This was not some simple store-bought set. Aside from the trains, it looked like everything had been hand-made and painted – the railway station, the railway men and waiting passengers, the farm animals in the countryside which lazily ate from the realistic grass. The whole thing was enormous, taking up most of the room, and there were several trains. It must have taken him years to build all of this. He sat on the stool in front of the control levers, and was suddenly aware of what it must have been like for Mr. Deveroix to sit here hour upon hour watching his trains go round and round, pushing buttons which produced a steam whistle, changed the track signal lights, or put the crossing bar down to keep the cars off the track.

Michael walked around the train set and inspected the tidy corner of the room that Mr. Deveroix must have used for working and relaxing. He took in the leather arm chair, the fine oak desk, the compact stereo, the small refrigerator, the wine rack filled with reds, the book case, and the filing cabinets. He opened the refrigerator and saw a few bottles of white wine. He picked one up and read the label. He wasn't much of a wine drinker, but he knew that anything from the Napa Valley was very expensive stuff.

So Mr. Deveroix was a wine connoisseur then.

He placed the London Pride carefully in the fridge next to the other bottles, and closed the door. There was a photo on the desk, somewhat aged by time. Michael recalled that Mr Deveroix had worked for a bank, and there he was with the other bank staff, smiling in what looked like a staged group shot. There was a plaque over Mr. Deveroix's desk.

To Morrise Deveroix, Assistant Bank Manager, In Appreciation of 32 years service… it began.

Michael eased himself into the arm chair, sinking into the soft leather. He wanted to put his pint down, but noticed there was a lot of condensation on the glass. Looking around, he saw that the blotter on the desk had numerous circular stains, and Michael realized that Mr. Deveroix must have put his wine glasses down there when he sat in this chair. When he placed the pint on the desk he felt a strange need not to put it over one of Mr. Deveroix's rings.

Michael was struck by the silence and stillness of the place. He gazed at the enormous and complex train set, astounded by the amount of work it would have taken to build. He must have spent half his life standing over some miniature boxcar or station guard figurine, carefully gluing, sanding, or painting. What a peculiar fellow. Never more than a few words of polite small talk whenever they happened to pass one another in the hallway. And Mr. Deveroix hardly socialized at all. Michael didn't want to feel critical of Mr. Deveroix, but there was something so empty about this room. Not that the space was empty, what with the trains and everything else. It's just that… and Michael was lost for words. He recalled Mr. Deveroix's wide glassy eyes again, fixed on the ceiling.

You drank wine and played with your trains and went to the bank. Jesus.

He took a large drink, held it in his mouth, and let the aroma drift up into his nose before swallowing. But what did you do at the desk then? Michael sat up in the chair and opened a large desk drawer. He was immediately confronted by a tall stack of fine leather notebooks. He pulled them out one by one until he had eighteen of them on the desk. The notebooks were dated and in order. Note book one covered the period 1962-1966, and the others seemed to carry on right up to the point where he died. He opened the most recent notebook and immediately realized that it was poetry, written carefully in blue ink. Michael quickly scanned through the notebook, and saw page after page of poetry, hundreds of poems, just in this one notebook. He read the first few lines of a poem his vision fell upon.

The Original Ache, a sadness like dry leaves
falling silent in the sudden cool air;
And She was never there.
He looked into the sky and trees
and found himself alone.

The other notepads were the same. Poem after poem, all in neat ink, though the older poems had faded somewhat. There must be thousands of them, thought Michael. Mr. Deveroix, a poet? It must be. Did anyone else know about his poetry? Somehow, he doubted it.

Michael looked over at the two filing cabinets. Well, Mrs. Deveroix had wanted him to find out what was up here. Pulling himself out of the chair he placed his pint on top of the first cabinet, and pulled at the top drawer. Gazing inside, it looked like the entire drawer was filled with magazines. He pulled a few out and smiled at what he saw.

Pornography. They couldn't all be porn, could they?

Michael pulled out other magazines, and yes, every one was a porno mag. He opened the other three drawers and all he found was porn, magazine after magazine. He flipped through one of them, absorbing the images, but then he noticed that the edges of the page were worn with use, and he reflexively put it back in its place.

Sliding back into the arm chair, he placed his still cold pint glass between his legs. Michael's head was swimming. Banking, trains, wine, and a life of virtual social isolation. And then piles of porn and poetry. *Piles of porn and poetry.* That was rather poetic, wasn't it? Michael thought about this life he'd intruded upon.

There was something familiar about it which bothered him.

And then he saw that image of Mr. Deveroix's gaping glassy eyes, and he swigged down the last of his pint, rubbed his eyes hard with both palms, and opened the fridge to get the other ale.

CHAPTER 15

A female psychology student from NY rented out a spare room to a carpenter to study his reaction to incessant nagging. Several weeks into the study, the carpenter snapped and beat her with an axe handle.

From the journals of Professor Charles Kidding, extract #113

Michael woke early, as usual, the red numbering on his digital clock reading 3:59 am. He forced himself to lay inert in bed, trying his best to keep his eyes closed and get some rest, but his mind drifted. He thought about that drunk, or professor, or whatever he was. That sure was weird, seeing him drooling on that desk and then getting hassled by that library guard. That photo of him in the book he'd written had looked impressive. What the hell happened to that guy? He thought about Julie Miller. *I've got some good news for you Michael.* She'd put it that way, hadn't she? She even seemed pleased to be able to help him. Good news? He was starting to despise that form of hers …

The sleepless early morning hours had felt especially obnoxious today, but an idea had at least occurred to him, and as he ate breakfast he turned the idea over in his mind again. He has an internet broker, a broker who has been responsible for the transfer of his money in and out of countless companies for years. He and that broker have been sending each other emails for a long time, and that brokerage service has probably made thousands of dollars in commission off his successful investments. Maybe they would help him. Maybe his broker would even sign that form. His visit to Starbuck's could wait today.

At 9:05 am Michael fired up his computer and went to the Web Ventures Internet Brokerage homepage. He typed in his password and the normal greeting popped up:

Hello user #43666002371-L

Welcome to Web Ventures Brokerage Service, provider of the largest range of financial instruments. Please click below to indicate the financial instrument you wish to use for investing, selling, or altering a financial contract (where possible). You may contact me directly via the email link below to ask any questions you may have, and I will be pleased to offer you my personal attention.

Yours Sincerely,

Broker LH884562

Michael clicked the email icon and Outlook Express popped up with his personal broker's email in the address box. He typed:

Dear Broker LH884562,

I wonder if you would be kind enough to help me with what has become something of a problem. I had my car and wallet stolen recently and

He groaned inwardly at the complexity of this email, realizing how difficult it would be to explain his problem without sounding like a lunatic. Michael considered calling his broker up. Maybe that was best. He could explain everything fairly quickly by phone, and maybe it would sound more believable that way. He went back to the brokerage home page and looked for a contact number, but found none. Typical, he thought. Another internet company trying to reduce costs. But they must have phones, and he'd made a lot of money for them – the least they can do is spend a bit of time on the phone with him. *I will be pleased to offer you my personal attention.* Well, he needed some god-damned personal attention at the moment.

He scoured the home page again, and there, at the very bottom, in tiny print, was the word *contact.* Michael clicked on it and a postal address in New York City and another email address appeared. No phone number.

Now Michael was getting pissed-off. There is a person out there who has been his broker for years, and all he needs is a simple phone call with him, or her. He minimized the homepage, brought Google up, typed in *web ventures brokerage service phone contact*, and clicked the first internet address in the list. He found it immediately in the emerging webpage. Okay, they hadn't made it easy, but he'd found a contact number.

Feeling entitled to some help now, he dialed the number. Michael groaned when he heard the usual automated answering mill. How about push 1, he thought, if you want to speak with a live human being – that would be ideal! He listened to all of the choices and realized there was nothing close to what he needed. But what was he expecting? *Push three if you have lost all your identification and need your personal broker to help identify you as a real person.* He pushed five for *questions about personal accounts.*

"Hello, Web Ventures Brokerage Service. How may I help you?"

"Yes, hello. My name is Michael Wilson. I have an investors account with Web Ventures and I was hoping to speak with my personal broker."

"Oh…" the receptionist responded, a note of surprise in her tone. "Normally our users use email for communication with their brokers, sir."

"Yes, I have emailed my broker several times over the years, but it's the sort of issue which needs more of a discussion, really."

"Right. Can I please have your user number?"

Michael pulled up the welcome page on their site. "It's 43666002371-L," Michael replied, and then he heard the receptionist tapping on a computer.

"And who is your broker, sir?"

"My broker is LH884562."

"Yes, that's what I've got in my records. I just need to check this out quickly with my manager. Can you hold a moment?"

"Certainly."

Michael's confidence in this approach was waning, and he thought over the many emails which he had received from his broker. Was this person a man or a woman? What would they be like to speak to directly? The broker's emails had been strangely inconsistent – sometimes very thoughtful and comprehensive, and other times rather rushed and curt. Was his broker a moody sort of person?

"Hello sir. I'm going to put you through to your broker now."

"Thank you."

"Hello, Web Ventures Brokerage, can I help you." A man's voice. But why was his greeting so formal, so distant? Surely the receptionist must have told him who was calling.

"Hello, this is Michael Wilson. I do hope you don't mind me contacting you in person. There's a particular issue I need to talk over with you, but it's nice to speak with you after all this time. Is it alright that I'm calling?"

"Uhm, yes, that's fine… how can I help? Is there a problem with your account?"

"No, the account is fine. It's just that I've had a rather unfortunate turn of events. Recently I had my wallet and a number of other items of identification stolen, and it's become really difficult to get my identification replaced. It's sort of like a catch 22. You need identification in order to get identification replaced. It's been a bit of a nightmare dealing with different agencies… ."

Michael paused, wondering if his broker might express a bit of understanding or sympathy, but there was only silence on the line. Did his broker even believe him? Did he wonder if this was some sort of scam?

"I'm working with a member of the Health Department in terms of renewing identification, but you wouldn't believe how complicated it all is just proving who you are." Michael paused. More silence. "I know we haven't met, but you've been my broker for several years now and we've had quite a lot of email communication. I mean we've had to work through a lot of decisions together, make a lot of purchases, you know. And I was just wondering if you might be able to help me with this identification problem."

"Oh, I see," the broker replied. "Mr. uhm… (Michael heard the sound of shuffling paper)… Wilson, I'm not sure you quite understand how we work here. There are about 150 brokers and we tend to share the role of helping individual clients. Any one of us might have responded to your queries over the years."

Michael was stunned, and somewhat confused. "But aren't you," he said, looking at his computer screen, "broker number LH884562?"

"LH884562 is a broker number attached to your account. Any one of us who responds to your questions responds as that broker number. But you will have had many different brokers helping you over the years."

"Oh," replied Michael, the facts of his situation sinking in. He felt an impulse to ask this man his name. How was he supposed to get understanding and help from a number. In fact, this man was less than a number – the broker number was a reference to his account, not a particular person. How could he have not known this for so many years? He had to ask:

"So… have you worked on my account before – I mean, have we communicated?"

"Uhm, let me have a look," he said, and then Michael could hear tapping on a key board. "I'm afraid not. This looks like the first time. I suppose you could talk to our records department. They would keep a record of your name, address, and bank details. They might be able to confirm that you have an account with us. I don't really know. We don't normally speak with our clients directly."

Michael considered the offer, but didn't really see the point. He could provide banking information himself. What he needed was personal help from… his broker. But he doesn't have a broker, he has… what does he have? Michael felt as if his head was in a fog.

"No, that's alright. Thanks for speaking with me," he said finally.

When Michael hung up, he gazed at his computer screen, the numbers absorbing his attention for some reason. LH884562. 43666002371-L. The numbers had always seemed rather normal – now they seemed strange and foreign. He walked to the window and gazed, empty-headed, out across the lawn, across Sutherland Street, over to the empty sun-drenched tennis courts.

This identification problem was difficult, but what he really found hard just now was what to do with himself, what to do with time. He wished that he could get out of his own skin, and sometimes he had a fantasy at moments like this. He would close his eyes and imagine that his whole body became absolutely still, even catatonic, and then *he* left his body in the form of a vapor which floated out of his mouth, and then the vapor went somewhere (he didn't know where), and the vapor became content and rested, and when the vapor re-entered his body through his mouth, his body re-animated, but now he felt much better. But that was just a fantasy.

CHAPTER 16

The world's first prison beauty contest has been won by a 24 year-old Lithuanian woman. The Miss Captivity Pageant was held in Lithuania's Panevezys Penal Labor Colony. The winner, a woman named Samantha, fought back tears while being crowned. When asked what she wants to do with her life, she responded, "get out of prison".

From the journals of Professor Charles Kidding, extract #196

Julie stood in the middle of her kitchen. She'd come into the kitchen for something, but what? Her mind groped for the reason blindly. She stared at the fridge. Maybe she'd come into the kitchen to open a bottle of wine? She was pretty sure that wasn't it, but now that she was here, it seemed like a good idea. She pulled an icy bottle of Chardonnay from the fridge, placed it on the counter, and got the wine opener from the drawer. As Julie worked at the cork she thought the evening over. She didn't really like Saturday evenings. It was more acceptable to stay in on a Friday; after all, people could be quite worn out after a week of work and they might just like to relax on a Friday. But Saturday evening was really the sort of evening people go out. It was 8:30 pm. She could call Margaret, but it's too early for that because Margaret won't have the kids down yet. She didn't really feel like talking with Margaret anyway. But why couldn't she just have a nice time staying in? She had an excellent camembert cheese and some crackers. She could curl up on the couch with Bobby and watch some TV.

Julie got herself settled in – Bobby tucked happily against her thigh, wine glass and crackers and cheese handy on the side table. She turned the TV on and surfed through the channels. A couple of feel-good romantic comedies she'd already seen, a religious preacher bellowing, a rather somber news reporter standing somewhere in the Middle East telling us that the Israelis and Palestinians were at it again. The land behind the reporter was a barren, rock strewn desert, and Julie wondered why all those people lived there anyway. Maybe they feel like killing each other all the time because they live in a shit-hole. She continued flipping through channels. A talk show featuring a jeering audience and an unrepentant guest, a weight-loss infomercial, Judge Judy haranguing an irresponsible man covered in tattoos, a documentary about cops who are too eager to use their guns. She gazed numbly for a few minutes at an exercise show featuring an oily muscle-bound man and woman in spandex. They jumped about in unison on an exotic beach and she supposed they were meant to be really motivating.

An old Western came on next, and there was Clint Eastwood riding slowly into an apparently empty town – but there were probably town-folk watching him through shop windows or those little doors that swing open in dusty saloons. Clint was giving the town one of those severe looks, chewing slowly on a small cigar, bobbing along, probably thinking that he wouldn't mind shooting a few people if he had to. He didn't need anybody, apparently. Julie had to admit he looked pretty good in that Mexican-style woolen poncho. She considered watching it, but you had to wait about twenty minutes for Clint to say anything, and meanwhile there's just a lot of long hard stares, cigar-chewing, and spitting.

She pushed a button on the clicker and watched the QVC Shopping Channel – not because she wanted to make a purchase, but because the whole thing seemed so absurd. Two platinum blonds covered in layers of make-up sat on a studio couch and were getting very excited about a necklace, mostly because it was *genuine* zirconium. That's reassuring, thought Julie, because you sure wouldn't want to make the mistake of buying *fake* zirconium. Didn't zirconium get cooked up in a laboratory anyway? Well, there were only 200 of those necklaces left, so you'd better call in now because they're gonna go fast. Despite how enamored these women were with the necklace, they managed to shift their loyalty rather quickly to a Quesinart, some machine which slices things up. As one of them reached for the Quesinart, an awful lot of gold glinted and clinked.

"Oh Cindy, don't tell me that's the Quesinart. I love this item. I've got one at home and there's simply no way I could live without it. Now, tell our viewers what the Quesinart can do?"

Does it make you queasy? wondered Julie.

"Well Heather, what **can't** the Quesinart do? I guarantee you that it will satisfy all of your slicing, dicing, and chopping needs."

Julie wondered whether her slicing, dicing, and chopping needs were satisfied. She was pretty sure they were. She took a mouthful of wine and winced at the dry bite.

"But I'm so clumsy with electronic gadgets. Is it easy to use?"

Of course it was so easy to use that even someone as stupid as Heather could make it work, and Cindy was going to prove it by putting a carrot in the Quesinart and slicing it up. Cindy held up a six inch carrot, a carrot which seemed rather disproportionately fat. She gripped the carrot firmly, the gold rings on her fingers flashing in the harsh studio light. Did she just stroke the tip of the carrot with her thumb? And then in it went, emerging a moment later in slices at the bottom of the machine. The studio audience clapped in appreciation.

Julie was surprised at how angry she was feeling at Heather and Cindy. She hit the mute button and Heather and Cindy galloped on in silence. She suddenly found herself imagining that they were selling a handgun.

Oh Cindy, don't tell me that's the Magnum 35? Julie didn't know if that was a real gun, but it sounded like one. *I've got one of them at home and I just couldn't live with out it. Let's tell our viewers about it.*

Well Heather, the Magnum 35 is ideal for home defense, it fits nicely into any handbag, and it's really good for… uhm… killing stuff.

Wow Cindy, it can do all that? But you know how clumsy I am with handguns. Is it easy to use?

You bet it is Heather. All you do is pop open the chamber, load the bullets, point and shoot. Cindy popped open the chamber easy as pie, slid 6 bullets into the cylinder, aimed the gun towards the camera and fired, a loud blast echoing in Julie's imagination. Heather addressed the audience, mouth gapping in astonishment.

Wow Cindy, that ***is*** *easy! But is the Magnum 35 as deadly as they say?*

Even more deadly Heather. Watch this. Cindy slid the barrel into her mouth, offered her audience a wide-eyed smile, and blew her bloody brains all over the studio wall behind her.

My goodness, that is deadly! said Heather, but Cindy probably couldn't hear her because she lay back on the couch, glassy dead eyes fixed on the ceiling. The audience applauded in appreciation.

Julie had a moment of amusement at this scene she had created, but felt deflated almost immediately. Heather and Cindy were fake and annoying, but she had killed Cindy. That wasn't nice at all, and what did it say about her anyway? She took another large drink of wine and noticed that Bobby was watching her, a look of concern around his eyes. She switched off the TV and held the wine glass against her lips, feeling the cold wetness of it, her gaze unfocused. She noticed the orange-yellow sunlight on the carpet. The day was slipping into evening, the sun sinking over the edge of the world. Some Pink Floyd lyrics came to mind, something from *The Wall* album. She gazed into the middle-distance, vision unfocused, and sang to herself, lips pressing softly against the wet coldness of her wine glass.

I've got elastic bands keeping my shoes on
Got those swollen hand blues
Got thirteen channels of shit on the TV to choose from

She paused, smiling sadly. She's got way more than 13 channels of shit to choose from. How did that song go?

… I've got wild staring eyes
I've got a strong urge to fly
But I've got nowhere to fly to

She sang the *fly to* part a few times, like the way it reverberates in the song. She remembered more…

And that is how I know
When I try to get through
On the telephone to you
There'll be nobody home.

Perhaps the whole evening had somehow been secretly designed to ensure that she would end up thinking about Michael Wilson, remembering their meeting, recalling the two phone conversations, wondering what might happen. The image of Michael was squarely fixed in her mind now, almost as if he were coming onto a stage, right on cue. He was supposed to call her when the external validation forms were completed, but she hadn't heard from him. Maybe the friends he had given the forms to were taking their time filling them in.

She recalled that she had written Michael's address and phone number down on a yellow sticky note, and that the note was in her wallet. Why had she done that? She hadn't thought much about what she was doing when she copied it from his file – all she knew was that she liked the idea of having it.

Julie pulled the yellow sticky from her purse, returned to the couch, and turned the side-light on. She stared at his address, forty-two Sutherland Street, and a strange and compelling impulse took hold of her. She felt a little ashamed at what she wanted to do, but that wasn't going to stop her.

Julie turned off Monroe Avenue and onto Sutherland Street, making her way slowly, looking out for number forty-two. Night had fallen, but a large moon had recently risen and the street lights cast a yellow glow. She pulled up at a stop sign, then eased the car forward, noticing that almost all the houses were on the left because of the school grounds across the way. The broad street was quiet, peaceful. She'd been down Sutherland Street before, but she hadn't appreciated how beautiful and refined the houses were. And then she saw it, number forty-two. She glided past, not wanting to stop right out front. About one-hundred yards further on she pulled over in front of Sutherland High School and killed the engine. Julie looked over her shoulder at the school grounds and noticed an elevated grassy area across from Michael's place.

She pulled a wicker picnic basket she had prepared from the passenger seat and headed across the school grounds, walking out of the street lighting and into relative darkness. Fifty yards into the school grounds, she put her basket down on the fresh-cut grass. She could see the shadowy shapes of the tennis courts on one side, the school on the other, and decided this was as good a place as any. She pulled a blanket from the basket, spread it out, sat down, legs folded beneath. The June air was warm against her skin, but she had goose pimples on her arms somehow. She looked at his house and saw one light illuminated in a room on the second floor. It was a lovely place. Julie got the bottle of chardonnay and a wine glass out, and poured a drink. She thought about her apartment. It was empty now except for Bobby, but it would be emptier if she were in it. Funny how that works. She wondered if people could see her from the street, and if she was doing something illegal? She imagined a police man walking up to her. He'd probably be polite, but it would be the sort of politeness that had a purpose.

Good evening ma'am. Is everything okay here?

Yes officer, everything's fine. I'm just having a little picnic. I was supposed to be going out on the town with about fifty of my closest friends but they all had to cancel at the last moment.

I see. Kind of a strange place for a picnic, isn't it? It's pretty dark back here.

Oh, that's because there's this man I've fallen in love with. He lives across the street and I'm stalking him.

Julie smiled when she heard the words *stalking him* in her mind, but then she worried about that. Jesus, is that what she's doing? Isn't sitting in dark places and looking at someone's house just the sort of thing that stalkers do? She thought about that and had a couple of mouthfuls of wine, but then decided she didn't really mind if she was a stalker. She probably wasn't one of the dangerous ones, anyway. It wasn't like she was going to jump out from behind a bush at him. Or maybe that's the way all stalkers start out – they couldn't possibly imagine going mad, but then one night they just find themselves hiding behind a bush and jumping on someone. Anyway, maybe Michael would fall in love with her. People don't fall in love with stalkers, they just press charges and get restraining orders. If Michael fell in love with her, she definitely wasn't a stalker. That was logical. But what was she doing here?

She felt something moving across her ankle, and she peered through the dimness, straining to see what was there. Ants. A busy column of tiny ants making their way industriously from somewhere to somewhere else, marching along, each of them assured of their role, each of them working in perfect unison with the rest of the group, no-one stopping to stare into space and wonder what it's all about. She decided to just let them use her ankle as a thoroughfare – it would be easier for everyone that way.

Julie listened to the muted echoes of cars moving down Jefferson Street, suddenly aware of the distant sound of music, a deep throbbing bass. She gazed across the darkness of the school grounds, beyond the glow of the street lights, and onto his home. She was aware again of the warm summer air against her skin, like a velvet wrap, but she somehow sensed the night air all the way between them, all the way to that lighted window. She wondered how Michael had decorated his house, how the rooms were laid out. The one on the second floor with the light on – that was probably a bedroom.

She let her mind drift and an image of Michael and herself seeped into consciousness. They stood close to one another, in some bedroom. No, not just any bedroom. It was *that* bedroom over there, but the lighting was much lower. Michael didn't have his suit coat on, just the oxford button-up and trousers he wore in her office – and what was she wearing? That blue summer dress she never takes out of the closet. The bedroom was lavish and warm and they were perfectly content to just be there. Michael looked straight into her eyes and she returned his look. Now she could sense his sure hands on her waist, and he pulled her close. Her pubic bone pressed against him through the thin fabric of her dress, and he felt hard down there already. She placed her hands on his upper arms and slowly moved them down, sensing the solid form of his biceps. Michael came closer and now Julie could feel the warm and soft sensation of their lips meeting. His kiss was slow and gentle and warm, and she wanted to explore him. Julie pulled back and unbuttoned his shirt, moving her hand against his chest, feeling the strength of him. Michael was breathing harder now, and she was aware of how much he wanted her – it was something in his eyes. She found his hand and pressed it against her breast.

CHAPTER 17

In response to a prediction made by Nostradamus, many Japanese people are worried that something calamitous is going to happen to them. In response, a Japanese lingerie firm has produced a bra with a sensor which alerts the wearer to incoming missiles. The "Armageddon Bra" contains a sensor in the strap which can detect falling objects.

From the journals of Professor Charles Kidding, extract #210

Michael walked into the entranceway of his medical centre and was struck by some pictures children had drawn. There were about a dozen of them, all pinned up in the corridor. Michael noticed that the corridor was shared with a speech department for deaf and hard of hearing children. Across the cork board an adult had written *How I Feel About Having a Hearing Problem* in large letters. Children had drawn happy pictures of themselves and written something about their difficulties. Most of the responses were the sort of thing adults would approve of with smiling nods:

I have to work harder to learn

I have learned how to read lips so I can understand

I can be just as good as hearing children

But Michael was drawn to one of the images, a drawing which had been hung at the bottom edge of the display. He looked at it for five minutes and read the caption several times. A boy had drawn a scowling impression of himself, the paper ridged with the heavy force of his pencil. In the speech bubble the boy had written: BEING DEAF MAKES YOUR LIFE SUCK! Michael smiled at the drawing and shook his head, feeling a sense of sadness and admiration for the kid. He liked the boy, whoever he was. This kid told it like it was. Being deaf sucks. Of course it sucks. No amount of adult encouragement and glass-half-full admonitions can change that.

Michael checked in at reception and then waited for his doctor in one of the consulting rooms. He could hear his doctor talking to a colleague out in the corridor, and couldn't help but listen in. He'd seen his doctor last week and had told him about not being able to remember how to get home. His doc had done the normal stuff – tapped his knee, listened to his heart, had him touch his nose and walk on an imaginary line. A nurse had taken some blood and given him an ECG. Michael had an MRI scan a few days later. He supposed it was possible that his doctor was talking about him.

"The results came back this morning," the doctor said. "He had an abnormal lover function test."

Abnormal lover function test? Michael wondered, perplexed.

"The enzyme levels were way off," his doctor continued.

"Well," the colleague said, "he has a history of drinking, doesn't he?"

Michael smiled. Abnormal liver function test. That must be what they'd said. He didn't drink that much and he didn't suppose they tested his liver anyway. They must be talking about another patient.

The consulting room door opened and his doctor greeted him warmly, and then got straight down to business.

"Well Mr. Wilson. I've got good news for you. The MRI scan, the blood tests, the ECG all came back completely normal."

Michael felt relief, but it was a relief colored by confusion. "That's great… but I don't understand why I'm getting lost, I mean why I don't know where my house is?"

"To be honest, you seem to be describing episodes of cognitive impairment. But there's nothing I can see that would cause that. You haven't had a history of this sort of problem, you haven't had a knock on the head, the MRI suggests that there's nothing structurally wrong with your brain. Memory loss is something we see commonly with many of the dementias, like Alzheimer's Disease, but you're quite young for that and that sort of memory loss develops gradually – you don't have bouts of it. I've talked this over with our neurologist, and as far as we can see there's just no… medical explanation for what's happening."

Michael's doctor paused and they stared at each other for a moment. "Sometimes," his doctor continued, "these sorts of problems are just idiosyncratic. Maybe you're just working a bit too hard at the moment. This memory problem may just sort itself out."

"Sure," said Michael. "I'm sure you're right." But he didn't feel sure of much.

Out in the parking lot, Michael stopped and stared into space, his mind numb and drifting. What the hell did idiosyncratic mean?

CHAPTER 18

A Mexican widow put $32,000 in the Banco del Atlantico in 1988, and has subsequently become the world's richest women. Interest rates rose by 150% during the financial crisis of 1994, with the result that Celia Reyes is now worth 60 billion. The bank was unsuccessful in making a legal appeal, and has been ordered to pay the entire amount.

From the journals of Professor Charles Kidding, extract #264

At 5:00 pm Michael walked to his local YMCA . It was rather up-market as YMCAs go, and Michael appreciated the chrome, colorful synthetic materials, and good smells – all quite different from the battered heavy wood and sweat of the downtown Ys. Having changed into shorts and a t-shirt, he made his way to the work-out room. This afternoon there were only two solitary college kids, a housewife, and himself. He stepped into the circuit of lifting, rowing, and bicycling in a rather mechanical way.

Between exercises, Michael stole glimpses of his form in the huge mirror which ran the length of one wall. He was aware that he had developed a peculiar relationship to the large mirror, though he did not like to think about it. Michael was conscious of not wanting to be caught staring at his reflection, but he did seem to need to look at his body and face, especially from particular angles. The image which looked back at him did so in ways which elicited the same recurring set of thoughts, thoughts he also encountered when looking into his bathroom mirror. He was tall, slim, and muscular. He compared well to male models or celebrities, so he should be considered handsome and desirable. And yet, the moment he began to feel a sense of pleasure or reassurance through the comparison, he quite definitely had a sense of *not* believing it. What ever the objective nature of the positive comparison, it just felt wrong. A sinking feeling in his chest took hold, and he returned his attention to his circuit.

Michael arrived home and spent a few minutes staring out his window, wondering what to do. He became aware of Sam's music vibrating softly through the floor boards. He could check in on Sam and see how that internet station was going.

Michael paused at Sam's bedroom door, his knuckled hand raised, ready to knock. He didn't have much in common with Sam, but Sam was always keen to see him. He knocked, and when Sam opened the door, Michael noticed that he didn't look too good – bleary eyes, hair in a mess, still in his Star Trek pajamas.

"Hey Mr. W. – come on in." Sam slumped down on the bed and waved a chubby hand in the direction of the desk chair.

"I hope you don't mind me stopping in. I thought I'd see how that internet radio station of yours was going?" Sam rubbed his face hard with this hands and Michael had a quick scan around the room. There were several empty Budweiser bottles on a side table and on the floor, an empty bag of potato chips on the bed, and a large purple bong lying on its side on the brown shag carpet.

"Dark Star Radio lives," said Sam, but his tone was quite depressive.

"So you've got some listeners then?" asked Michael. Sam yawned deeply and then buried his face in his thick hands. Michael glanced at the computer screen next to him and scanned the home page, noting a prominent zero next to *current listeners.* Sam spoke into his hands, his voice muffled.

"The mother ship calls to her children, but the children cannot hear. No, I haven't got any listeners. Fucking paid Google twenty-five bucks, but do you think you can find Dark Star Radio on Google? You try and find it and you get a bunch of shit about Darth Vader. It took me an hour to find it, and it's my own station."

"Well, maybe it just needs some time. When did you get onto Google?"

"Week ago."

Michael tried to think of something positive to say, but came up with a blank. He listened to the song playing. The singer was droning on about a beast, blood, and something about a festival.

"Sam, these lyrics are a bit on the dark side, aren't they? I suppose that's just the sort of music it is?"

"Oh, it's not all like that. Some lyrics you hear are quite beautiful and sensitive. You take AC/DC for example. There's a love song they do which goes like this." Sam cocked his head and held a hand out, palm upturned, and sang with a soft and sensitive voice.

Let me put my love into you babe
Let me put my love on the line,
Let me put my love into you babe
Let me cut your cake with my knife

Sam smiled at Michael, inviting his response.

"Yeah, I guess that's nice," Michael said tentatively.

Sam laughed loudly, rolls of fat jiggling rhythmically. "Are you shitting me? That's pure misogyny. Absolute pure misogyny. Nothing nice about it at all." Sam playfully punched Michael in the arm and waved a hand in the direction of the computer. Fact is, it's not nice. But that's Dark Star Radio. The Dark Lord feels your pain and plays the music. I can't seem to help myself."

Silence fell between them, and Michael wondered what to say. Sam just didn't make a lot of sense. Perhaps he should just go back to his rooms? But he thought about how he had become lost, and didn't feel like being alone. That was strange. He'd always been pretty okay with being alone. Not great. But okay with it. Something was changing, and he didn't like it.

"I had a pretty extraordinary run of bad luck recently," said Michael.

"No way, what happened?" Sam asked.

"Well, my car was stolen from the down-town area."

"No shit. Those fuckers. Did you call the cops?" asked Sam.

"Yea. The police filled out a stolen vehicle report and I suppose they'll try to find it."

"So how are you going to get around without a car?"

"I'm taking the bus at the moment. Hopefully the police will come up with something." Sam's face lit up and he snapped his fingers and pointed at Michael. "I got just the thing for you Mr. W. – come with me."

Sam led Michael out to the garage and wheeled a black moped onto the driveway. The sun was blazing and the glare off the bike was considerable. "Here you go Mr. W. – the Honda 50. That's 50 cubic centimeters of pure pavement punishing power. You're looking at 30 miles an hour if you get a tail wind. I souped it a bit at one point, and I guarantee that she'll kick the ass of any 50cc moped out there. She's black, she's evil, she's willing, and she's yours."

Michael was rather speechless as he stared down at this tatty moped. Numerous stickers had been applied across the body and seat, and Michael read one which caught his eye: *It's because of people like you that I'm on medication.*

"Sam, this is a lovely thought, but I wouldn't want to take your moped away from you."

"It's no problem at all – I'm riding a motorcycle now. I don't use it." Michael recalled seeing Sam on what looked like a blue dirt bike lately, roaring up and down Sutherland Street. Michael felt acutely uncomfortable.

"Honestly Sam, it's very thoughtful, but…"

Before he could protest further, Sam pulled up the seat and produced a black helmet which he held out for Michael. A sticker reading *Never Mind the Bullocks* was plastered across it, and Michael wondered what that meant. He knew Sam expected him to take it and put it on, but there was something really distasteful about this whole business.

"I… I… are you sure this is okay Sam…I've never been on one of these. Don't you need some sort of special license?"

"Who knows – who cares? How are we gonna smash the State if we follow every rule they make?" Sam said. The big boy pressed the helmet down onto his head and did up the strap. Michael found that he had been ushered onto the moped, and Sam was showing him how to start it up, explaining the brake, the throttle.

"Oh wait," said Sam. "You'll need a riding jacket – I got an extra one."

He disappeared into the garage and returned with a ragged black leather jacket. Numerous leather tassels hung off the shoulders and back, silver rhinestones and several buttons adorned the front, and there was an anarchy symbol hand-painted in white on the back. Michael was appalled at the sight of it and opened his mouth to object, but Sam guided one of his arms into the jacket, and before he knew what was happening, the jacket had been zipped up and Sam was instructing again.

"Worn leather is the trademark of any true moped man, and it will protect you when you go overboard. Now get yourself comfortable in the seat. It's just like riding a bike except you pull back on the throttle rather than peddling". Sam pulled a plexiglas visor down over Michael's face. "Keep this down when you ride. Otherwise all kinds of shit can fly up and smack you in the face. Okay now – just pull back on the throttle and lift your feet and pretend you're riding a bike."

Michael opened the throttle slowly, lifted his feet onto the foot stands, and the world was quite suddenly moving past. He motored down the driveway and steered onto Sutherland Street, picking up some speed, everything feeling unsteady. At the end of the street he steered around, almost fell, and headed back. On the return trip he felt like he found his balance. He gave the moped more throttle, the engine whining like an angry bee. As he approached he saw Sam out on the road applauding his performance, hands above his head.

"Yeeeesssss! You ARE moped man!" shouted Sam.

Michael had felt absurd and quite self-conscious under the gaze of a few pedestrians he'd past, but there *was* something exhilarating about it. He pulled into the driveway and puttered to the garage. Looking over his shoulder, he could see Sam jogging up to him. Sam placed his beefy hands squarely on Michael's shoulders, and strained heavily to catch his breath. At last Sam was able to speak – "You... you were born to ride Mr. W.," he wheezed. "I got something else for you – hang on."

Sam emerged a couple of minutes later from the garage holding a battered pair of leather trousers. "I remembered I got an old pair of riding leathers. They're pretty mashed, but when you've come off your bike as many times as I have, your leathers take a beating."

"You've had crashes?" Michael asked.

"Oh yeah. The good news is that really fat people are great bike crash survivors. We hit pavement, bounce a couple of times, and roll around for a while. Skinny-ass hits pavement and slides for about a mile – that's a lot of abrasion." Michael suddenly wasn't so sure about this moped idea.

"Where do I fit in?" he asked.

"You're somewhere in the middle. You might get one good bounce, roll for a bit, and then slide for a while. But these leathers have got padding in the ass and thighs. It'll help a lot when you get launched."

"Sam, is it really that dangerous?"

"Oh it's dangerous, but Moped Man doesn't know the meaning of fear. Moped Man laughs in the face of those things which make the common lot tremble. Moped Man…" Michael tuned Sam out. He appreciated what Sam was doing for him, but he didn't know how much of what he said was meant to be helpful, and what was nonsense. Maybe Sam didn't know either.

Back in his room, Michael felt an impulse to put the riding leathers on and stand before the full-length mirror. The trousers were somewhat short and very baggy, but they had a belt built into them which he pulled tight. He was still wearing the jacket, and he pulled the helmet over his head, visor up, which completed the outfit. Staring into the mirror, a battered blackness looked back at him, a rough man, maybe a man who had done dangerous things. He pulled the tinted visor down, and he was surprised and fascinated by the reflection. What was it? The image just wasn't him at all, and yet of course it was *him.* That seemed to explain part of the surprise he experienced, but there was something else. His mind emptied for a moment, and then he had it. In this strange attire he had become something other than himself, but he had also become completely *anonymous.* On the exterior he was still every bit the deranged misfit represented by this anarchist's outfit, but he, Michael Wilson, was hidden. This *thing* reflected in the mirror could go out into the world, and yet *he* could not be identified. Michael felt a sudden impulse to try it out, and wondered where he should moped to. It would be the city, certainly. Moped man does not ride in the suburbs, he thought. Moped Man. How ridiculous. But he smiled just the same.

CHAPTER 19

At a pet show in Shendai, Japan, a dog won first prize for "keen intelligence and unquestioned obedience". It was later discovered that the dog was in fact stuffed. When asked to return the $2,000 prize, the owner refused, indicating that "nobody said the pets had to be alive".

From the journals of Professor Charles Kidding, extract #11

Michael puttered down Monroe Avenue, all the way into the city. A big bright afternoon, the sun glinted off the shop windows and cars around him. He told himself to pay close attention to his driving so he wouldn't crash, but it was easy to lose himself in the whining engine, and the easiness with which he could turn in and out of lanes. He was getting the hang of it. As he waited at a light he saw his reflection in a car window, and then noticed the dim image of young children in the back seat, staring at him, mouths gaping. He nodded his helmet at them and they gazed back in that solemn, big-eyed, and unselfconscious way that kids do, and he wondered what significance this exchange had.

Michael crossed over the Genesee River and saw Washington Square Park ahead on the left, which made him think about that bum he'd seen in the library – Professor Larry Lush. It did have a ring to it, like that librarian had said. He wondered if Larry would be on his bench at the park. Michael pulled his moped over to the curb at the near end of the park, killed the engine, and swung his leg over the seat. He stood there for a moment, scanning the oak trees, the statue of Lincoln at the centre, the cannons, the dappled sunlight strewn about the bright grass.

Larry was on his bench, his back to him, and Michael wondered what to do with this anarchist's uniform. His impulse was to take it off with subtle quickness, stash it in the storage area beneath the seat. But this was the city, and it was early evening. By day wealthy white folks drive in and take elevators which move with soundless precision up towering glass buildings. By 6:00 pm the city returns to the people who inhabit the place - Blacks, Hispanics, Asians, poor White folks. Their world is different and when they look at you it is with eyes which do not care to judge because you can be no more strange to them than they are to you. Michael decided to leave his leathers on. He hung the helmet over a handle bar, pretty sure that no sane person would steal it, and walked towards the park.

But Michael had only gone a few steps when something made him stop. He looked carefully at the bum, noticing his arms stretched out along the back of the bench, the empty wine bottle on the ground, another half-empty bottle nestled strangely between the bum's shoddy high-top basketball shoes. An idea was forming in his mind. He recalled a liquor store a couple of blocks over.

Michael noticed a tired, older black man leaning on the counter by the register, smoking a cigar and staring at him, eyes tracing his slow and hesitant path through the crowded and dusty isles of booze. He found the reds and scanned the labels. What sort of wine does a disgraced philosopher drink? Does he drink what all winos drink, or is it a better vintage? Michael decided to get him something good to be on the safe side. Trouble was, he didn't really know wine. He might know more about quality ale than anyone in the city, but to him, wine was just grape juice that had gone bad. Michael thought about getting some advice from the man at the till. He looked over to the counter just as the old man hawked something up and spat into a garbage pale. Maybe not. He picked the most expensive red they had, $7.99, and moved along to the beer isle. Everything was refrigerated, a bad sign if ever there was one. He settled for a six pack of Saranac Pale Ale. He wondered if he was actually going to drink in the park too, and whether there was a law against that.

How are we gonna smash the State if we follow every rule they make?

Michael shook his head and made his way to the cash register, picking a cork screw off a rack on route.

Michael felt warm as he approached the South end of the park, carrying his beer and wine. He sat at 'his' bench, put the beer and wine down, and unzipped the leather jacket. He looked over at Larry, who reclined in a relaxed posture, staring into space. A CD player and headphones were on the bench beside him. Michael imagined him for a moment as a finely detailed and painted statue. Larry took a sip from his glass and the image was broken, but a moment later the statue took shape again. Michael felt a wave of anxiety move through him and then settle around his sternum. He took a large breath, blew it out, and approached. He stood near Larry for a moment, hoping the bum would look at him, but he just continued staring into space.

"Excuse me. I hope I'm not disturbing you... ." Larry slowly looked up and Michael felt his glassy blue eyes rest upon him, eyes which wondered what this could be about. Michael noticed a cut over his right eye, and the dark red of congealed blood. "I know this might sound strange, but I was wondering if I could join you?" Michael held out the bottle of wine. "I've brought along some wine."

Larry just continued to stare, a quizzical expression forming around the edges of his eyes. Finally, he offered Michael a wave of his hand and a subtle shrug. He moved over and Michael sat down.

"I'm not sure how good this wine is," Michael said as he pulled the cork and filled Larry's glass. Larry nodded and smiled at Michael, and then took a large mouthful. The wine glass went back on his knee and Larry continued staring into space.

Michael pointed to the CD player. "So what are you listening to?"

"A Mozart piano concerto. Number 22, I think."

Michael nodded enthusiastically. Mozart and his piano concertos had been part of his listening routine when he had been collecting classical music. "I really like Mozart's piano concertos... they're just so... ." Michael couldn't find the right word.

"Perfect," said Larry.

"Yes, that's it. Perfect. Everything exactly right. Beautiful, everything in place."

"Yes, flawless music. If god could sing... but is it *too* perfect sometimes? I can only listen to perfection for so long..."

"Hmm," said Michael. "Maybe." They sat in silence for a minute, the leafy oaks waving slowly in the late Spring breeze.

"I know you're a philosopher," Michael said, and the words

immediately felt like some sort of accusation. "I've seen your books in the library. I haven't read much of them, but they seem quite impressive."

"I'm not a philosopher," Larry said dreamily, continuing to stare into space. "I'm a bum – I thought that much was pretty obvious".

"But you wrote those books. You were famous, in a way."

"I was a bum then too," Larry continued. "A bum trapped inside the body of a philosopher. I just found my true self and came out of the closet." They sat in silence, Michael struggling for something to say.

"Look, I don't mean to be intrusive, but I see you sitting here and you always look like you're thinking things over. You were a professional philosopher. A really respected one, I hear. You must have developed a way of seeing the world, a way of understanding things about…" Michael lost his way for a moment. Larry just smiled slightly, looking into space. He would have to continue.

"I mean, philosophers have a perspective, they take positions. Do you have a perspective you've developed?"

Larry looked over at him. "What's today?" he asked.

"Tuesday," Michael answered.

"Okay, I'm a Nihilist."

"A Nihilist?" Michael said, trying to recall what that meant. "Isn't that when a person doesn't believe in anything?"

"Sure," responded Larry, who took another mouthful of wine.

"Why are you a Nihilist?"

"Tuesday is a good day for Nihilism."

Michael was confused. "You mean you could be something else on another day?"

"Sure," Larry said.

"Like what?"

"Oh, I don't know. Maybe an agnostic. That's a good one. I could be a really devout agnostic. A fundamentalist agnostic. Really evangelistic about my unbelief." Larry chuckled to himself and drank more wine.

"So you could be a nihilist or an agnostic?"

"Okay," said Larry, which seemed a strange response.

Michael thought about the Saranac, and pulled a cold wet bottle from the box at his feet. A mother and her son, a boy of maybe six, walked past them holding hands, and the boy stared at him. Michael felt self-conscious about his leather outfit and the beer in his hand, but he popped the cap off the ale with the opener on the cork screw and took a sip from the bottle. It felt wrong not to drink from a glass, but he somehow liked the coldness and this ale was better than he remembered. They sat in silence again, and Michael wished that Larry would say something, anything.

"So Nihilism or Agnosticism then," Michael said hopefully.

"Sure," said Larry. "A little Nihilism or Agnosticism never hurt anyone. Or maybe it did. I don't know."

Michael wasn't sure how to read Larry. There was something quite disorientating about this conversation, and he was wondering if he'd made a mistake in approaching him. Maybe Larry had lost his mind. Still, there was something compelling about this battered man. And who else could Michael talk to?

"A bit of phenomenology is nice too," said Larry, "especially when your brain starts to hurt from trying to decide what you are. We could be phenomenologists, you and I."

"Phenomenology? What's that?"

"Look at the park, listen to the birds, taste the beer. Just do it with no thought present, no cognitive interpretation of anything, and… that's it. You might just discover the true nature of parkness, birdness, and beerness. The phenomonologists thought that maybe they could do it."

"Did it work?" asked Michael.

"No, it was a complete failure. But the practice of phenomenology is charming, isn't it? A real balm to the soul if you can pull it off."

"So you're a phenomenologist then?" asked Michael.

Larry laughed, clapping Michael on the shoulder. "Only on Thursdays and religious holidays, okay?"

Michael felt a mixture of confusion and frustration, and Larry saw it in his eyes and the set of his lips. Larry's voice softened. "Come on, I told you – I'm a bum."

"But you traveled around visiting important universities. You were sort of a star in your field, weren't you?"

"You think it's difficult to be a hot-shot academic?" Larry said, staring up into the trees. "I'll tell ya, it's simple. In my case it was especially simple because in the field of Logic most of your would-be competitors are borderline autistics. My colleagues were lucky if they could string two sentences together in a public venue without falling over and succumbing to a panic attack."

Larry eyed Michael closely now and placed a weather-beaten hand on his shoulder. Michael felt anxious over the intimacy of the physical contact, but worked hard not to let it show. The bum continued. "You want to be a speaker who is admired and envied? By purchasing this exciting new video for only $29.99 and following three simple steps, you will learn everything you need to know." Larry wiped wine from his lips and salt and pepper beard with the back of his hand before continuing. "First, litter your presentation with bits of knowledge which fly off your tongue so easily that your listeners barely have enough time to digest one nugget of wisdom before you lay into them with the next. You're inspired, you see. Never read from a prepared text. They won't believe you're a natural genius. No, always memorize and thoroughly rehearse your presentation, then deliver it in a way which looks inspired and seamless. It's *you* the audience needs to resist and adore – your words are only a vehicle. It's your *presence* which counts. Second, just appear to care about someone or something. Care about truth, the purity of Arian blood, starving babies, men's souls, the revolution – it doesn't matter. Apparently wearing an eccentric mustache can help. Third, be passionate. Don't ever say 'I feel passionate about…' – that's a dead giveaway. Just *be* passionate. You see, you are so filled with knowledge and concern that you cannot help but be passionate. The blood moves to the extremities and your face pinks up nicely as you gesture and dance about the podium. A certain rhythm is developed. Never mind their skepticism at the outset, they cannot help but love you in the end because you *believe* in what you say." Larry chuckled to himself, but then look a large gulp of wine and stared expressionless at the ground.

Michael was befuddled by Larry's words and his mind searched for some sort of useful meaning in them. Why was he telling him all this? He said the only thing he could think of. "So you made a video then?"

Larry stared at him, then broke out in laughter. "Sure, available at all fine retail stores near you." Larry leaned back and the wine glass went on his knee, the stem fingered lightly between index finger and thumb, and he resumed staring into space. Michael unconsciously did the same, beer bottle held in an opposing hand on an opposing knee. Given that they were sitting at opposite ends of the bench, they resembled a set of peculiar bookends.

"Look... I get confused," said Michael softly, as if he did not want to be overheard. "I get confused, I guess, about who I am or what I should do. It's been more of a problem recently, I guess. It... can make it hard to know where I am... I can get lost with it all. I just thought philosophers were good at understanding what's true."

Larry didn't respond for a while, didn't move, and Michael was anxious that he wouldn't. "Understanding what's true?" Larry eventually said. "There's a terrible law which concerns philosophic and scientific investigation. It's unnamable in polite academic circles, and it's the sort of thing which simply doesn't occur to the person in the street. I call it Larry's Dreadfully Upsetting Law of Philosophic and Scientific Enquiry."

"That's quite a title," said Michael.

"I just made it up," said Larry.

Michael frowned. "What does the law say?"

"It says that the more certain you can be that something is True, the less important that Truth is likely to be. Am I wearing shoes today? Yes I am, and ain't that the truth. Of course, who gives a shit if I'm wearing shoes today. If you want the Truth about anything really important, you're pretty-much screwed. And it's all proportionate – the more important the question, the more screwed you are."

Michael didn't like this law – in fact he was irritated at the very idea. "But maybe it just seems that way because we don't know enough yet. Maybe when we learn more we might discover the Truth about really important things."

"Nope. Larry's Dreadfully Upsetting Law of Philosophic and Scientific Enquiry is not dependant on how much we know – the law works the way it does because human existence is rigged. You might cheat the odds for a while, but you will never beat the House in the end."

Larry looked up into the sky and put a hand on his heart. He continued, a reverential tone slipping into his voice. "The late Professor Charles Kidding put it this way. 'I'd rather have a poetry of paradox than a symmetry of logic'." Larry caught Michael's eye. "Now that's beautiful, isn't it?"

"I guess," said Michael. "Who was Charles Kidding?"

"He was a colleague of mine for a time. One day he gave up his career, left academia completely, and made a private study of paradox, irony, and illogicality. For the rest of his comparatively short life he kept journals. He had given up on the search for truth and all the conceptual claptrap attached to it. Instead, he collected *stories*. Every time he came across a story which he felt illustrated the absurd nature of human experience, he added it to his journal. He filled four journals, if you can believe it."

"But he's dead now?" said Michael.

Larry gave him a questioning look. "Did I say he was dead?"

"You said he was the *late* Charles Kidding."

"Oh yes, that's right," said Larry.

"How did he die?" asked Michael.

"Let me think," said Larry. He drank more wine, his head bobbling on his neck. "I think he gassed himself. No, wait a minute, that's not it. He … shot himself." Larry seemed to need to think that over as well. "Nope, that's not right either." Larry stared into the trees for a while, and when he replied, Michael thought there was an edge of sadness in his voice. "I remember now – someone backed over him with their car."

"Really?" said Michael. "That's just so senseless."

"Yes," said Larry. "He would have liked to hear you say that. A senseless death for a senseless man."

"But why did he give up his career?" asked Michael. What was wrong with him?"

"He certainly didn't suffer from any recognizable mental disorder such as neurosis or psychosis. I think Charles succumbed to a philosophical disorder, a disorder you might call 'intractable absurdity'. He was unable to hold any stable metaphysical or moral perspective."

"Was that… serious?" asked Michael.

"Quite serious. The main behavioral manifestations of the disorder are flippancy, laughing out of context, and a tendency towards innuendo, all of which made Charles unsuited to human relationships – a sad but inescapable feature of the condition."

Michael was having a hard time following the conversation. "A tendency towards innuendo?" he asked. "What are you talking about?"

"Innuendo refers to an oblique hint. No more truth for Charles Kidding. No, an oblique hint at something possibly true was as much as life could offer Charles. So yes, a tendency towards innuendo. And he would find these hints in strange human circumstances, brief stories he would record for his own private reasons. He was more of an archeologist towards the end – an archeologist of the absurd."

They stared into the park and trees for a while, drinking, Michael noticing that the shadows were lengthening. He was thinking about what Larry had said concerning truth, about how it was hard to know the truth about important matters. He found himself recalling the way he had got lost in his own neighborhood. He didn't want to tell Larry in detail about that, not yet anyway.

"People can feel that things are out of control," said Michael. "You said Charles Kidding gave up on truth, but maybe people want to understand what's true because they want to feel in control."

Larry took another drink and seemed to be remembering something. "You wanna feel in control, huh? I knew of this guy whose wife was often angry with him. The angrier she got, the more impotent he became. Finally, his dick just wouldn't function at all. He tried Viagra, read some self-help books, saw a therapist – but nothing worked. He was at the end of his rope when his doctor said that there was a device which could be inserted into his dick which would give him something like a proper erection. It even came with this remote control for inflating and deflating. He tried it and wouldn't you know, it worked, and he bonked the angry wife – once. The next day he was sitting on his own couch, minding his own business, and he got an erection just as his next door neighbor drove into the garage. Turns out that the remote control for his neighbor's garage door opener operated his dick too." Larry inclined his wizened face towards Michael and raised his eyebrows before concluding, "so what do you think about THAT?" Small flecks of red wine flew out of Larry's mouth and landed on Michael's face, though Michael tried not to notice.

"I don't know…" said Michael. "Is that really a true story?"

"There you go about truth again," Larry spat out, laughing in a way which struck Michael as rather maniacal.

Larry leaned back once again on the bench and continued staring into the park while Michael searched his mind for something to say. He stared at Larry out of the corner of his eyes, wondering what happened to this guy and whether he had lost his mind. Maybe he doesn't know how to have a conversation or how to be with people anymore. They sat in silence, and after a while, Michael looked over.

"I'm Michael Wilson," he said.

Larry smiled and slowly nodded. "Larry Dembrowski."

Michael took another sip and realized that his ale was empty. Maybe he should leave. Or maybe he'd just sit here and stare into the park for a while. He popped the top off another bottle and noticed Larry reaching slowly into a small tatty duffle bag under the bench. Larry pulled out a second wine glass and offered it to him.

"You've got two glasses?" inquired Michael.

"You'd be amazed at how many glasses I've dropped on the pavement."

CHAPTER 20

A group of Antarctic helicopter pilots have invented 'penguin bowling', a game in which a pilot flies close to the ground and knocks over as many penguins as possible by creating wind turbulence. The current record was set by Klaus Doer, a German pilot who knocked over 27 birds in a single flight. Animal rights activists have condemned the sport, though Doer has said, "they just fall over and get back up again – what's the problem"?

From the journals of Professor Charles Kidding, extract #61.

Mary had completed the massage. She stood before Michael, who sat on the edge of the bed and watched her, his gaze abstracted. It was late evening, but moonlight seeped through the thin material of the curtains. Mary slowly pulled her black skirt up to reveal white silk panties which framed the inch wide space between her slim, muscular legs. There was something exquisitely contradictory about Mary's white silk panties. Her clothing – grubby black cotton skirts, crumpled t-shirts, sweaters which looked as though they'd been run over by a lawn mower – stood in stark contrast to those immaculate, white, silken panties.

The exterior of an alley tramp, and yet hidden beneath, something… beatific?

As Michael gazed at Mary's slim arc of waist and subtle hip bones, he wondered if there was enough light to allow him to see the scars on her inner thighs. It was a momentary but recurrent dilemma – he wanted to look at the slim curved musculature of her thighs, but he did not want to see the scars. He did not want to think of Mary that way. Michael had initially *felt* the presence of those scars before he had seen them. In the early days of their relationship, he had moved his hand lightly over an inner thigh and discovered several parallel ridges, definitely cuts which had healed. He assumed that Mary had been injured, though he couldn't fathom what sort of accident would result in cuts like those. But then one evening there had been more light in the room, and he noticed that there were fresh cuts, cuts only partially healed. He had read about people who did that to themselves, had seen something on TV about it too. He tried not to think about it after that.

Mary lifted her shirt and Michael placed his lips on Mary's warm belly now and cupped her round soft bottom in his hands. He remembered the paintings of biblical angels he'd seen in an old church when he was young – they seemed to float about in all their glossy goodness, bathed in celestial light. If Mary was an angel, she was a bruised and disheveled angel.

Michael was annoyed at himself for letting these thoughts distract him, and he cleared his mind, allowing the ritual to unfold. This wasn't the only ritual which helped ease him through his days, but it was the one he needed most.

Mary slipped off her skirt and t-shirt, and stood motionless before him. He focused again on the subtle curvature of her small belly, the trajectory of a hip, and then he followed the curve of an inner thigh to a bony knee, relieved that the cuts could not be seen. Kneeling down, he pressed his lips to her warm belly again and brought a hand up which he moved lightly over her thigh and hip. He turned his face and rested his cheek against her belly, inhaled the soft feminine scent of skin, and became aware of how the moon had painted the room, and Mary, a translucent pale blue. Some paperwork on his desk was caught in the moonlight, and he realized it was the external validation form. He shut his eyes tight, pressed his lips into Mary's belly again and gripped with both hands at the soft roundness of her silken bottom, grimacing and trying to forget.

Sex occurred as it always did, but something was wrong. Michael hadn't felt that hard, and he had even needed to use his hand to push himself into her. He had hoped that once he had entered Mary he'd become harder, but that hadn't happened, and his orgasm was hasty and weak. He had watched Mary's face beneath him, wondering how aware she was, but she had disappeared again and he could see nothing in her eyes.

Michael lay on his back now, staring at the nondescript space of the ceiling for several minutes. He felt Mary's gaze on him, and he realized that she was back from wherever she had disappeared to. She lay on her side, her head held on a slim hand, her other hand warm against his chest. He did not know *what* she was thinking, but he was aware that she *was* thinking – as sure of her thinking as he was of her soft, rhythmic breathing.

"Are you okay?" she whispered.

"Yeah, I'm fine," Michael replied, trying to sound natural and convincing. But it wasn't fine – nothing was fine.

"Mary, I know it's none of my business, and you don't need to tell me if you don't want to, but are there many other men you… spend time with?"

"You mean other men I have sex with?" asked Mary.

"You don't have to tell me if you don't want to."

Mary rubbed her hand over his chest lightly in a gesture which was soothing, nurturing, a gesture silently acknowledging that this thing Michael was asking was not easy for him. "It's not something I do a lot of," she said with a smile. "At the moment, there's just one other man."

Michael reflexively wondered about this other man. Did sex happen in a similar way? Did Mary enjoy it? He determined not to ask her these questions. They lay in silence for a moment and then the long sad call of a neighborhood cat floated up from the street. Mary continued to look at him, and eventually he couldn't bear the laden silence anymore.

"Mary, this other guy you see. Is he like me or is he quite different?"

"Well," said Mary, "he's a nice guy, and he's successful and good looking, so I suppose he's like you in that way. But it's quite different, I mean in the way things happen, in what he needs."

"Different?" asked Michael.

Mary stared thoughtfully into space. "Sometimes I think about sexuality. Do you want to hear my theory?"

"Okay," said Michael.

"Sexuality comes in three flavors – the needy, the confused, and the sadistic."

"Sadistic," queried Michael. "How would you know if they were sadistic?"

"There was this guy I knew briefly who wanted to have anal sex with me. In fact, he had no interest in massage, just anal sex."

"What did you say to him?"

"I said you can have anal sex as long as I get to shove a tennis racket handle up your butt." Michael couldn't believe he was hearing this.

"What did he say to that?"

"Not a lot. As it turns out, most people don't really want to have someone shove a tennis racket up their butt."

Michael turned this conversation over in his mind. He was wishing he hadn't said anything, but now he was worrying about what Mary was saying about sexuality. He was quite sure he wasn't the sadistic, and hoped he wasn't the confused. In fact, he didn't want to be any of these flavors. But he had to ask.

"Which one am I?"

"I guess you're the needy," Mary said. She must have noticed the subtle mark of hurt in the way his eyes went to the bedcovers, because she added, "there's nothing wrong in being needy. You need me to come here and spend time with you, that's all."

Michael didn't look up. "This other fellow you see, the one besides me, which type is he?"

"He's the confused."

"What's the confused?" asked Michael.

"Sometimes desire gets all tangled up," said Mary.

"And this other guy, he's the confused?"

"Yeah, he's a really nice guy. He just needs to do something, and he needs me to help him, and I don't mind."

"What happens?" Michael asked. He wondered if he was going too far, but Mary didn't seem to mind.

"His sexuality involves white high-heeled shoes which have some mud on them. I arrive at his house and he gives me a gift. The gift is always the same, a pair of clean white high-heeled shoes. I put them on and we go for a walk, but always through a grassy area which is damp enough to ensure that the white shoes get a bit muddy. When the weather is hot and dry, he needs to create a muddy area ahead of time. I think he takes a watering can to this park down the road. After the walk, we come back to his place and both undress. I have to be sure to put the dirty shoes at the foot of the bed, right next to each other. We get onto the bed and have the normal sort of foreplay, then he has sex with me, and at one point he goes to the foot of the bed, gets down on his knees, and comes onto the shoes."

Michael tried to hide the alarm and distaste he was feeling. "And you don't mind helping him in that way?"

"I don't mind. The fact is, he's a good guy. I imagine women liked him quite a lot. Before he met me he used to give his dates a pair of shoes, buy them a nice dinner, take them for a rather sodden walk, and then bring them home for a sexual encounter. The problem was that most women didn't like it. I guess it would be pretty upsetting if you're having sex with this guy you like and he suddenly goes to the foot of the bed and does his business all over your new pair of high-heels. He used to feel really bad about it. He didn't want to upset anyone."

"But isn't there some sort of treatment for his problem? A psychologist or someone?" Michael asked.

"He's seen therapists and he understands his problem, but understanding a problem doesn't always make it go away. I think I'm sort of his therapy now. Spending time with me must be better than sitting in front of the computer and whacking off like so many men do. I've even got an installation I'm working on which is all about that."

Michael noticed that he was clenching his jaw. An installation about men looking at internet porn – what sort of art is that? He was really annoyed with himself for starting this conversation. He didn't like being *the needy*, he didn't really want to hear about Mary's latest art project, and mostly he didn't like being connected to this confused guy through his relationship to Mary.

"Mary, this whole conversation just makes me feel abnormal."

"Michael, you're very normal. I wouldn't worry."

Michael didn't like the way she said *normal*. Coming from Mary, it sounded derogatory. Michael laughed, a nervous laugh meant to hide his irritation. "I'm not sure I want to be normal, not the way you say it."

Mary smiled broadly. "Okay, let me see if I understand this. You don't want to be abnormal, and you don't like the sound of being normal. Is there another option? Would you like to be semi-normal? How about quasi-abnormal? Subnormal? Trans-normal? Any of those appeal to you? I'm sure something could be arranged. Do you think there's a *Department for the Advancement of Normality* we could contact?" Mary released a rather spastic explosion of laughter, obviously very pleased with her joke.

Michael stared at the bedcovers, irritated, half-disbelieving they were having this conversation, wanting to cut the conversation short, and wanting to continue. Michael had been the one who had cultivated and maintained the boundaries in this relationship. He had been the one who had politely side-stepped her pushy questions and eccentric observations. What was he doing? Michael sighed deeply, his irritated gaze glued to the bedcovers.

"Come on, don't sulk please," Mary said. "There's something really unattractive about a sulking man. History is shot through with impressive male figures, some because they were wonderful, some because they were awful, and the only thing they all shared in common was that they didn't sulk."

Michael looked up. "Okay, I'm not sulking. It's just that I really didn't like the way you said *you're very normal.*"

"Alright, then tell me something abnormal about you," Mary replied.

"Abnormal?"

Mary nodded, and Michael had to reflect. "Okay, I have a problem with ticking clocks. I can't stand the sound of them. If I buy a wrist watch it needs to be quiet enough so I can't hear any ticking. See my wall clock?" Michael pointed to a clock above his desk.

"Yea, I see it," Mary replied.

"It's electric – plugged into the wall socket. Completely silent."

"I zee. Und Mr. Vilson, can ju tell me veen ju firs started to ave dis problem vith time," Mary asked.

"I don't have a problem with time. I just don't like ticking clocks."

"Of course… of course Mr. Vilson. So dis problem vith time. It is very upzetting, no?"

"Are you meant to be a German Psychoanalyst?" asked Michael.

"Austrian, actually."

They lay in silence for a few moments before Mary continued. "Well, good for you. See, you're not so normal, are you? Seriously, did you always hate ticking clocks?"

"I guess."

"Do you know why?"

"No idea," said Michael.

They lay there in silence for a few moments, and then Mary knelt up in the soft glow of pale blue moonlight and looked down on him, suddenly animated. "Alright, this is fun. Now ask me about me."

"What?" replied Michael.

"Ask me about me. Come on, ME ME I MINE ME. It's my turn now. Ask about ME!" Mary's black chaotic hair fell over most of her face, and as he looked up at her, Michael was aware of her pouting lips and small pointy breasts, which made her parody of a girlish outburst unnervingly realistic.

"Okay, okay… so… I don't know anything about your past," he said.

Mary flopped down on her side again, head propped on a crooked hand. "I grew up in a large house on East Avenue, the sort of place people might call a mansion. It had so many rooms that a lot of them didn't even seem to have a purpose. My dad was a big shot lawyer, still is. His law firm has offices in the Baush and Lomb building, but he traveled a lot, all over the North East and sometimes overseas."

Michael pictured the Baush and Lomb complex. Built from attractive red brick and piles of glass windows and atriums, it was one of the most prestigious buildings in the city.

Mary continued. "My mom was lonely most of the time and she got drunk almost every day. When I was really young I didn't know what alcohol did to you, but I knew that my mom was sad most of the time, that she cried a lot, and went to sleep in the afternoons. Everyday she made these exotic drinks. I didn't know what they were at the time, but they were probably daiquiris, margaritas, pina coladas – everything tropical you could imagine. It was like a science to her. If dad was home at all, he would leave for work before we were up. Mom and I would have breakfast cereal, and then she'd start mixing all this fruit and cream and booze and ice in the blender. Sometimes she would try to play with me in the mornings before she got too drunk, but by lunchtime she was really tearful and tired. When I was old enough to go to school, it was the same when I got off the bus. At some point in the afternoon, mom would tell me it was nap time and take me to bed with her. I had to lie there with her clinging onto me, and she had the most amazing smells on her breath – strawberries and pineapple and rum and vodka. I didn't want to lie there with her because I was a kid and I wanted to play. But I somehow knew that she needed me to be there so she could sleep. When her breathing would find a regular rhythm, I would try to slip away, but that was strangely difficult. I'd slide a little bit out, and even in sleep her limp arms would jerk to life and stiffen and cling to me. Sometimes I could get away, and other days I would just have to lie there."

"But what about your father?"

"When he wasn't traveling, sometimes he came into my room late at night and put his hand on my head, thinking that I was asleep. He smelled like cigars. I would try hard to stay awake for him, just in case he would come into my room, but I would get tired and fall asleep, so most of the time I never knew if he put his hand on my head. Sometimes I would wake up very late at night because my mother was screaming at him, and some mornings there was broken dishes all over the kitchen floor."

Mary looked into space, as if remembering.

"He went to Japan once and some Japanese businessmen gave him a portable CD player, and he gave that to me. That was nice, I guess. My dad was the grey-suit man.

"What do you mean?" asked Michael.

He always wore a grey suit, even at home. He might loosen his tie, but I can't really remember him when he wasn't in the grey suit. My mother hated him so much and when she was drunk she would tell me how awful he was to her. But I didn't believe her. There was a large room on the top floor which he used as a den. I wasn't allowed to disturb him there, but sometimes he would read the newspaper in the living room. I remember once, when I was about six, I stood next to him as he sat in that chair reading his newspaper, and after a while he said, 'What do you want?'

Mary gazed at Michael, a questioning expression on her face. "Do you know what I wanted?"

Michael thought about it. "Did you want him to play with you?"

"Well yes, but it was something else. I wanted him to touch me. There was nothing sexual in it – I was six years old. I just really wanted him to put his arms around me. And then do you know what happened?"

"No," replied Michael.

"I developed a little trick I played on him. It all happened by chance. One day I got something in my eye and it was really irritating, and there was my father in his reading chair, and I told him. To my surprise, he took me up to the bathroom where the light was better, and he held my face in his hands, and he looked into my eye for a long time. And then he ran a bit of toilet paper under warm water and he carefully swabbed something out of my eye. His hands were big and warm, and as he leaned close to me my heart beat so fast I thought it would burst. After that day, I developed all sorts of problems whenever my father was back in town. I stuck a bead into my ear, I gave myself splinters under the skin, I forced my hand over rough street pavement until it bled. And my father would grumble each time I showed him my latest ailment, but he would get out of the chair and take me to the bathroom and he would come close to me and he would touch me and he would attend to me, and my heart would pound. I got bored with my self-inflicted injuries and developed a reckless style of play. I took chances with scooters and bicycles which no other six-year-old would dream of. And then one day I presented my father with a skinned knee. I can still remember his words. 'For God sake, can you be more careful. You know how to do it. Just clean it with soap and water and put one of the large bandages on it. You know where they are.' And then he looked away from me and he flapped his newspaper in this forceful way and there was nothing for me to do except go to the bathroom. I sat down on a chair by the tub, and stared at my bleeding knee. I can still see it now. A tiny, nobly, bleeding, grubby knee."

Mary threw back the bed sheet and pulled her knee up to show Michael. "If the light was better I could show you a very faint scare – I think you can still see the scar."

Michael nodded and Mary continued. "The blood was starting to dry, but I pushed at the edges of the cuts and forced a flow of blood to ooze up through the dirt, like a tiny volcano. Eventually, I let the blood congeal, and it darkened into a blackish-red. I started to cry but I stuck my wrist into my mouth to hide the sound. And that was it. I was all out of ideas."

Michael felt an impulse to touch Mary, but something did not allow it. She had explained it all in a matter-of-fact way, the old emotion being well-contained.

"What happened then?" asked Michael.

"When I was seven, my mother took a large overdose. It wasn't the first time she'd overdone it on her medication and booze, but this time was different. She nearly died, damaged her liver, and spent a long time on a psychiatric ward. I visited her a few times, but she would either sit there and stare at me or she would start sobbing and shaking. One day a doctor told me that I shouldn't visit with my mom for a while because it was making her more upset. *A while* turned into a year. Dad was of course too busy to deal with any of this – he just wasn't around."

"But who looked after you?"

Mary looked away and Michael noticed a sudden hardness about the set of her jaw. "My uncle Ken moved in with us," she said. "My mom's brother. Dad arranged it."

Mary turned on her side, facing him, and curled her knees into her body. Her eyes slowly closed and then opened. "Michael," she said, "can I rest here for a while before I go?"

"Sure," he said. Mary's eyes closed again and he pulled the sheet up over her shoulders.

CHAPTER 21

A linguist from New York City conducted an exhaustive research project in order to determine the most phonetically melodious word in the English language. He eventually had to conclude that the word was diarrhea.

From the journals of Professor Charles Kidding, extract #112

Michael spent the morning at Starbucks, drinking too much strong coffee in an unproductive attempt to jump-start his brain and get focused on market trends. He did manage to stumble across a company called *Marshal's Specialist Cleaning Products*, and spent far too much time analyzing it. Odd company. They make products to clean things you never imagined required a specialist product. Soap and water will do, you might think. Oh no, says *Marshals*. They've got a scrubbing agent specially formulated to clean, for example, burial headstones. There's a picture of a widow on her knees lovingly cleaning what you imagine is her husband's headstone. We're all supposed to feel bad these days if our loved one's headstone gets mossy or tarnished. But in the future's game, the relevance of the product or service is not the point. The point, Michael well knew, was being smart enough to predict the future. And he was good at it. A small master of the material world. An analyst of consumer inclinations and the vicissitudes of growth and decline.

But by 10:00 am he was fed-up and pulled a book he'd purchased yesterday out of his work bag. He gazed hopefully at the title. *Super Memory: Can't-miss strategies for developing a powerful memory*. Idiosyncratic, my ass, thought Michael. He'd sort this memory problem out for himself. On the back of the book it said *this fail-safe system will help you discover how easy it is to remember phone numbers, figures and appointments, right in your own head!*

Where else would you remember something, thought Michael. It didn't say anything about remembering where you live, but there must be something in there which can help. Michael read chapter one which had some ideas about developing vivid and unusual visual cues and something about a memory technique called *chunking*. He'd never heard of chunking.

At 3:30 pm he arrived home and sat in front of his computer. He placed a futures bet on Marshal's Specialist Cleaning Products, predicting that they will do well over the next quarter, which was a stupid thing to do, but it amused Michael for some reason. *Marshal's* was a ridiculous company and the bet was more hunch than science, which wasn't like Michael at all. Of course people buy ridiculous shit all the time, but that was no reason to back this company. He was keeping to his work routine, on the whole, but he seemed to care an awful lot less about investing.

He turned his computer off, rounded the back of the house, and walked down the driveway to check the mail. But what he saw at the edge of the front lawn brought him to an involuntary stop. There was Sam, wedged into a folding lawn chair, awash in June sunlight, a rumbling dirge of a song forcing itself from the portable stereo at his side. This scene was not unusual. What had brought Michael to a standstill was what was on the end of the leash which Sam held in his right hand. A large Doberman, sitting on its haunches, alert and staring up the street. Michael approached carefully, not wanting to startle the animal.

"Hi Sam. That's quite a dog you've got there."

"Oh, hi Mr. W.. Yeah, he's something, isn't he?"

The Doberman ignored his presence and continued looking up the street. Michael was struck by the powerful lean muscles beneath the shining coat of black and tan. The dog wore a thick black collar featuring sharp silver spikes. Michael looked back at Sam and was about to speak when he noticed that Sam was wearing an identical collar around his rotund neck.

"Sam…," he began cautiously. Sam looked up, squinting, a greasy sheen of sweat glinting in the mid-day glare.

"You've got… matching collars."

"Yeah," said Sam. "I bought Brutis the collar the other day and thought I'd get one myself. I think it's helping us bond."

"Is he dangerous?"

"He's a born killer, Mr. W.." Sam held up the lead and gave it a shake.

"If Brutis managed to break free, I'd hate to think what he might do if Johnny High School happened to be walking past. It's the sort of mess you'd need a mop to clean up." Sam rested a hand on the dog's shoulders. "We're not so different, Brutis and I."

Michael heard the sound of young children approaching from up the street. There were three coming into view now, a boy and two girls. Brutis emitted a sharp whine and watched the children intently.

"Is he your dog, Sam?"

"Naw. He belongs to this old lady who plays cards with my grandma – she lives two blocks over. She's in the hospital, so I'm taking Brutis for walks every day."

As the children approached, Michael noticed the dog lifting his hind quarters ever so slightly off the ground. A moment later, a blur of black and tan bolted for the children, the leash ripping out of Sam's hand with an audible *snap*. Everything happened so quickly that Michael's disbelief and horror could be no more than visceral. And then, just as Brutis reached the children, the dog dropped to the grass and rolled over on his back. The children gleefully shouted "Roger" in unison, and one of the girls got down on her knees and wrapped her arms around the dog, burying her face in the dog's neck. "Roger," she squealed. The boy was on his knees now, vigorously rubbing the dog's exposed tummy. "Rooogger – you're such a good boy, aren't you!" The dog's long tongue hung out, and his stubby tail jerked back and forth appreciatively. So great was his pleasure at the attention received, that he lost control and urinated on himself.

Michael looked at Sam, seeking understanding, his heart still pounding. Sam sighed loudly, and then spoke quietly as if to himself, his tone a mixture of weariness and sarcasm – "kill, Brutis, kill." Michael was at a loss for words, but thought it best to remain quiet anyway. Eventually Sam broke the silence.

"All right, his name's Roger – not Brutis. And there's something completely defective about that Doberman." The other boy was on the ground now as well, scratching behind Roger's ears.

"He looked pretty dangerous though, didn't he?" asked Sam. "I mean, before the children came along."

"Sure Sam," replied Michael. They watched the children fawn over Roger for a while, the birds twittering in the trees overhead.

"How's the radio station going?" Michael asked, imagining a change of subject might help. "Have you got some listeners yet?" Michael hoped he had.

"Naw, not yet. I got a new idea though about how I can make the website even more interesting. People like to participate in polls, don't they. You know, top 100 greatest albums, top 100 most important inventions, top 50 most successful athletes. Stuff like that. The thing about all these polls is that they're just so nauseatingly positive. Ooohhh, let's celebrate yet another human accomplishment. These polls are about as useful as electing a prom queen, and I hate prom queens. Now what we need is a poll which appreciates what a bunch of fuck-ups humans can be. Sooooo…. ." Sam craned his gelatinous neck to catch Michael's eye…. "Humanity's Top-ten Fuck-ups." Sam raised his eyebrows, encouraging Michael to appreciate his idea.

"Sounds interesting Sam, but how's that gonna help your radio station?"

"Dark Star Radio is posted on Google. So in the description of the station, I can now add Dark Star's famous pole of Humanity's Top-ten Fuck-ups. I think people – Dark Star's kind of people – will love it. When they log onto Dark Star they can suggest their ideas for the worst fuck-ups. Come on, what would you choose?"

Michael wasn't sure if he quite knew what Sam meant. "What about when they sent that space shuttle up, the one which exploded."

"Oh, come on," replied Sam. "Don't under-rate us. The space shuttle was nothing – not even in the top 100. How about Mao Tse Tung's five-year plan which shot holes in China's economy and starved 30 million to death? Hitler invades Russia? Now those are fuck-ups. You could vote for the invention of gun powder if you like. Good idea at the time, but not so good with hindsight, huh? What about when pre-human life forms crawled out of the sea? Maybe that was the original fuck-up. Course we weren't quite human then, so you probably can't count that one." Sam was grinning broadly, obviously pleased with his idea.

"Yeah, I guess it does make you think."

They watched the children. The girl was showing the others the spot where Roger *liked to be scratched best*. Sam groaned and positioned his hands on the arms of the chair, readying to heft himself up. "I'm goanna get him inside before he humiliates himself any further," he said.

The phone was already ringing when Michael entered his rooms, two pieces of junk mail clutched in his hand. Telesales, he thought, irritated at the intrusion.

"Hello."

"Hello," the female voice replied. "Is this Michael? Michael Wilson."

"Yes."

"This is Julie… Julie Miller."

"Yes, hello Julie, it's very good of you to call."

"It's no trouble," he heard her say. "I just wanted to check in on you – see how you were getting on?" The voice was soft, feminine.

"Oh yes, the external validation forms." Michael felt an electrical current of anxiety pull at his chest, a school boy unable to produce his homework. "I'm sorry not to have got the forms back just yet. It's taking me a bit longer than I'd hoped. Some people feel a bit strange about filling them in. It's a funny world we live in." Julie laughed at his remark, which relieved his tension somewhat.

"Yeah, it's a strange world," Julie said, "and this whole process must seem awfully overblown. The external validation forms are there to support identification we normally can't consider, like a bank book. My last appointment on Friday is in Pittsford. We could meet up at your bank if you like, and verify the account. I seem to remember that you live in Pittsford – Sutherland Street, isn't it?"

"Yes, that's right," replied Michael.

"Did you create the account with the Chase Bank in Pittsford?"

"I did, yes," said Michael. "And you'd like to meet at the bank?" There was a pause on the line as Michael waited for Julie's reply.

"We could, I mean if you wanted to," Julie said. "We could talk to the bank manager together about your account, if that was okay with you?" Michael was struck by a shift in Julie's tone. She seemed suddenly unsure of herself. Her voice had even broken when she had said the word *together*. He didn't mind her offer to meet at all. He was delighted at the interest she was taking in his case.

"Yes, of course," replied Michael. "This has all been quite disorienting. I appreciate any help you can give."

"Shall we meet at Chase Bank at 4:30 pm?"

When Michael hung up, he found himself staring into space, trying to absorb the import of this unexpected phone call. He recalled his meeting with Julie, and tried to visualize her. He had a vague sense of her office – tidy and officious. But he struggled to get an image of Julie herself. She had auburn hair, didn't she? About his age. But beyond this, her form remained blurry, non-distinct. He'd been so anxious about his lost identification that he hadn't noticed much at that meeting. And now he was going to meet her at Chase Bank. What a strange idea, but he supposed that the Department of Health had a particular way of working, and this was probably one of the things they did in cases like his.

He decided he'd read a bit more of that memory book and opened his work bag. It wasn't in there. Michael glanced around his living room, but he was sure he hadn't taken it out of his bag since returning home. Where the hell was it? And then he had an image of it – he'd left it on the table at Starbucks. How stupid.

As Michael entered Starbucks he looked over at the table he'd been sitting at. Some customers there, but no book. He approached the service counter and noticed two staff members chatting to one another – a skinny youth with pimples and thick glasses and a pretty girl. He had to wait for them to finish an annoying conversation about a party last Saturday night. The skinny boy looked at him.

"What can I get you?"

"I don't need anything to drink," said Michael. "I was reading a book over at that table this morning and I think I may have left it behind."

"I'll have a look in *lost and found*," the boy said. He reached under the counter and pulled out Michael's book, eyeing the cover closely. The boy glanced over at the girl, raised his eyebrows, and grinned.

"We got a few books here," said the boy. "What was the title of the book you forgot at the table?"

Michael felt the back of his neck growing red and hot. "The Memory Book," he said, realizing that he was mumbling his words and staring at the counter.

The boy glanced at the girl again and Michael saw her smile out of the corner of his eye. "Sorry Sir, I didn't catch that," said the boy. "What was the title of the book you forgot?"

Michael felt anger mixing with humiliation. He forced himself to look straight at the boy. "Super Memory," he said clearly. "Can't-miss strategies for developing a powerful memory."

The boy smiled. "Here you go," he said, handing Michael the book. "How's that book working out for you so far?"

"Just fine," snapped Michael. The girl giggled.

Michael exited the café and chucked the book into a trash can next to Sam's moped.

CHAPTER 22

A toy designed to stimulate children's imaginations has been created by an American company. 'Invisible Jim' is simply an empty box costing $4.00.

From the journals of Professor Charles Kidding, extract #6

Mary trundled down Clinton Avenue, her van creaking and grinding in the orange-yellow glow of late afternoon sunshine. It was just before 5 pm, and the city walkways were busy with employees leaving work. She parked near the Baush and Lomb building, killed the engine, and stared up at that towering mass of modern redbrick and glass. Mary looked over at the passenger seat and checked the items she'd brought along. One shotgun, one grey suit on a hanger, one hammer, two concrete nails, one video camera affixed to a tripod.

It was only yesterday that her shotgun project had found the next step forward. She had been in the Salvation Army on East Main Street, staring for some reason at a long line of men's suits. She had run a hand down the row of them, feeling the worn and sometimes stained fabric – the wool, the cotton, the nylon. Her hand came to rest on a grey suit. Mary had taken the suit off the rack and hung it up on the wall behind her to get a good look. It was the full works. Suit coat, trousers, vest – even a rather characterless handkerchief protruding from the breast pocket. Unlike most of the suits, this one was in great shape. Hardly worn and barely a crease. At one point her gaze had softened and she relaxed inwardly, and then the idea was simply there, right in front of her. She wasn't supposed to shotgun a canvas in the privacy of her studio. She was supposed to shotgun a grey suit hung on the ruddy red brick of the

Baush and Lomb building.

Mary climbed out of her van, and collected her items. She carried the camera and tripod in one hand, the suit and hammer in the other, but left the shotgun in the van for the moment. She made her way to the cobbled turning circle outside the entrance of the Baush and Lomb building and inspected the site. The central doors led into a massive glassed atrium, and she saw a steady stream of businessmen and woman coming and going. Next to the entrance doors was a large mass of red-bricked wall, warm in the early evening sunshine. A good back-drop, Mary thought. She set up the tripod and looked through the viewfinder, zooming back to get the right section of wall. Mary pushed *record*, saw the red light illuminate, and felt the subtle whirring vibration of the camera's innards. It was then she thought about security. The mirrored glass prevented any sight into the entrance hall, so if there was a guard in there she couldn't see him. All part of the process, she thought.

She wanted to work quickly now. One of Burt's special bullets had been preloaded. She had decided that blood-red wasn't right anymore. She just wanted a vibrant color. Something signifying life or growth. She decided on a lime green. Lime green on lawyer grey – that was the color relationship. She hoped the shade of the color would hold up to the temperature of the blast. Mary knew it was unlikely that her father would emerge from the building at this particular moment, but the thought that he might crossed her mind, and a wave of anxiety passed through her. She pushed the thought from her mind and focused on the work. Mary returned to the van, picked up the now stubby shotgun off the seat, and walked quickly to her camera.

Everything moved fast, images rushing up to meet her, and she glimpsed gaping mouths, widened eyes, people moving away from her. She put the gun on the ground next the camera, picked up the hammer, and got a nail out of her pocket. She placed the nail in a horizontal slice of concrete between two bricks, and hit it fairly hard. A small hole, but not enough to hold the suit. Three more blows of the hammer and the nail was in far enough. She picked the suit off the ground by the hanger and hung it on the nail. It hung perfectly straight and needed no adjustment. Her heart was banging against her ribs as she picked the gun off the ground and put the stock into her shoulder, raising the gun to look down the sight. She was surprised to find that she had actually gripped the end of the barrel, forgetting how short the gun was now. She moved her hand down the barrel and sited the suit. The electronic doors whooshed open suddenly and a man emerged, briefcase in hand. Mary heard him utter a cry of "Oh shit", and he seemed to jump off to her left. She remembered how hard the gun had bit into her armpit the first time she fired it, and she tensed the muscles throughout her upper body. She squeezed the trigger and was struck by the loud blast, the smoke, the jolt to her body, and then… the image of splattered green on lawyer grey. The main blast was just off-centre, creating the impression that she had shot this imaginary man in the heart.

Mary's limbs felt weak and she wondered if she had pushed things too far this time. She grabbed the tripod and jogged for the van, taking in the image of a frightened business woman speaking frantically into her cell phone. There was a shout behind her and she quickened her pace. Mary threw the gun and tripod onto the passenger seat, hopped in, fired the still warm engine up, pulled a U-turn across Clinton Avenue, and headed for 490 Eastbound. It was when she turned onto 490 that she heard the siren, but the siren was fading as she drove. The cops were driving to the Baush and Lomb building, she was heading away.

Mary realized she was gripping the steering wheel hard and forced her hands to relax. She took a large breath and blew it out slowly. There was no label for what she was feeling. This wasn't even feeling yet, just the raw physical material which a feeling gets made from.

CHAPTER 23

A Chinese man residing in Jaixing put his soul up for sale on a popular internet sales site.

From the Journals of Professor Charles Kidding, extract #76

Michael spotted Larry's filthy baseball cap and the crop of longish graying hair as he walked across Roosevelt Park. Larry looked at him, removed his headphones, and turned his CD player off.

"Hello, I hope I'm not disturbing you," Michael said cautiously, raising a wine bottle slightly as he spoke. "I'm told this is very good."

"I'm willing to take the risk," said Larry.

Larry moved over on the bench, and Michael sat down. Larry accepted the bottle and inspected the label, smiling. He put the bottle next to a half empty one beneath the bench. Larry's head bobbled a bit when he spoke, and his speech was slowed. He was certainly tipsy, but didn't seem very drunk.

Michael pulled a bottle of ale out of a small cooler he'd brought, and noticed that the bottle was soaked in droplets of condensation. Larry produced the extra glass from his duffle bag again.

"Thanks," said Michael. He poured his ale slowly and they stared into the park. Larry didn't seem to mind if they spoke or not, and that made it easier. Still, there were things Michael wanted to discuss. They sat in silence for a bit, eyes moving lazily over the dappled sunlight on the grass, cannons, and statue of Lincoln.

"Larry," said Michael, his tone careful. "Can I ask you a personal question?"

"Is there anything impersonal?"

"I guess not," said Michael. "Do you mind if I ask… how… I mean, you're not working anymore and you… ." Michael lost his way.

"You want to know why I just sit here most days getting drunk?" said Larry.

"I guess," said Michael.

"You wonder how come I don't do more with my life?" said Larry.

"I know it's none of my business."

Larry stared into the trees for a moment. "You know what lichen is?"

"Isn't that a type of mould?" suggested Michael.

"It's a fungus – actually it's a synthesis of fungus and algae, but that's not important. The way I look at it, you've got to admire lichen. It's been around on planet earth for millions of years. It's seen out the dinosaurs and countless other species. And what's the secret of lichen?" Larry eyed Michael closely before continuing. "Lichen keeps things simple. Lichen has almost no aspirations of any sort. It grows at a modest rate of about one centimeter per year, and is happy *not* to evolve into anything else. This self-effacing and unpretentious organism is quite content to just attach itself to a rock and hang out. Most species like to make things complicated. Mammals are the worst perpetrators – never content to leave well enough alone. Homo hebelious, homo erectus, Neanderthal man, homo sapiens – each one with more grandiose notions of development, each model flashier than its predecessor. And where will it get us? Long after we're gone…" Larry paused and raised his glass to the trees and sky overhead… "the humble lichen will stare out at the empty plain and crumbling cityscapes and giggle, knowing all along that it got things right."

"And so that's why you're…" Michael struggled to find the right words… "opting out?"

"I've gone the way of lichen," said Larry, a sloppy smile crawling across his face.

"Okay," said Michael. "So why do humans make things complicated then?"

"Drama," said Larry immediately, as if anticipating the question. "We can't seem to live without it. I think we're quite unfair when we say that Margaret or Lucy or Penny is a drama queen. For one thing, it's always a woman we blame, which is awfully chauvinistic. But also, why should singular persons hold all the blame for humanity's love of drama? We should say, 'Oh human beings, such a bunch of drama queens'." Larry laughed and took a swig of wine.

"So why do we love drama then?" Michael asked.

Larry leaned close, putting a finger to his lips, and Michael could smell the thick odor of wine coming in waves as he breathed. "We love drama," he whispered, "because we can't bear boredom, and we can't bear boredom because it is the state of consciousness which most reminds us of death." Larry's voice rose, gaining a triumphal tone, and he held up and waved his wine glass as he spoke. "So we love drama in any form – tragedy, personal catastrophe, natural disasters. Ideally, we'd all stand on the sidelines and watch, but you can only watch for so long before you have to take your turn." Larry laughed, obviously quite pleased with his assessment. Eyeing Michael closely he concluded, "Humanity – what are you gonna do with 'em?" Michael thought he was serious, but then noticed the wry grin on Larry's face, and couldn't be sure. That was the thing with Larry. It was so hard to know how to take him. And they always seemed to end up talking about something miles from where they started.

"But… you stopped teaching."

Larry eyed him, his expression satirical. "Did I *stop* teaching? Did I ever *start* teaching? Movement is a curious thing. Ever hear of Zeno's arrow?"

"I think I've heard of Zeno," said Michael. "Wasn't he an ancient Greek philosopher?"

"He certainly was. Zeno argued that if an arrow is moving, it can't move in the place it presently is, since it is only there for an instant, and an instant has no duration of time. Doesn't this mean that an arrow is at rest at every instant along a supposed line of flight, and so never moves. And if this is true," said Larry, an authoritative index finger wavering, "then everything is always at rest. So Zeno proves that movement isn't possible, and I think that's quite a supportive position for bums who never get much done."

Michael's mouth hung open, limp and dumb, his mind glazed. Finally, his brows narrowed boldly. "Larry… that's… ridiculous." Larry chuckled gleefully and spilled some wine on his trousers, and Michael noticed a number of brownish stains there.

"Well, you're probably right," Larry said. "I guess all Zeno proved is that you can advance a valid and internally consistent argument which is a load of horse manure in the real world. I don't know… sometimes I think the only good philosophizing is the sort which ends with a good punch line. Like that story about the guy who was dating a beautiful student of metaphysics. She wanted to break up with him but didn't want to hurt his feelings, so she just proved that he didn't exist instead." Larry chuckled, shaking his head.

"Did that really happen?" asked Michael.

Larry put down his glass and rubbed his temples. "It might have happened, or I might have made it up, or it might be something Woody Allen said. My life's a lot like that lately." Larry sipped more wine and Michael wondered if he was drunker than he thought. He felt irritated, thinking about his own problems.

"But that argument that Zeno made about the arrow," Michael said, "I mean, how is that sort of thing supposed to help anyone?"

"I have no idea, but I wouldn't be too hard on Zeno. His teacher made him wander around Athens carrying a pot of lentils and then snuck up on him and smashed his pot with a staff. That's pretty rough. It might have messed him up." Larry belched and wiped his mouth with the back of his hand. Michael was feeling frustrated. Maybe he needed to focus the conversation somehow.

"Your specialism was Logic, wasn't it? Why did you choose Logic?"

"Oh the usual motivational factors," said Larry. "Status, power, a feeling of self-importance, adoring and naive co-eds."

"That sounds pretty cynical. People must study… what ever they study… for other reasons as well."

Larry continued to stare into the trees, but Michael noticed a smile growing across his face. When the face could no longer contain the smile, Larry broke out into laughter. He was shaking his head now and wiping tears from his eyes with his shirtsleeve, still cackling. Michael wondered how drunk he was.

"What's so funny?" asked Michael.

"I was just remembering something. You want to know what motivates academics to study a particular subject? Here's a good story. There were these three social philosophers I knew, all bachelors, all of them awkward as hell around women – the bad complexions, the premature balding, the awful dress-sense. They were the full package. Now the three of them embarked on a joint research project. Their research question was this: Is there an ideal female form? And if so, what is it? They ended up authoring a single article which was published in an anthropological journal, of all places. And how long did they spend studying the female form?" Larry looked at Michael expectantly, eyebrows raised.

"I don't know."

"Seven years! For seven years these three bachelors studied the female figure throughout history and across cultures. And these guys were willing to get their hands dirty. They took actual measurements on countless attractive women. One of the guys worked in my department. A lot of the time you'd pass by him and he'd have this measuring tape slung around his neck, like a doctor wearing a stethoscope. You had the impression that he might need to suddenly drop to one knee at any moment and measure up some pretty woman." Larry chuckled again. "Human motivation – what a thing."

"Did they discover the ideal form then?" asked Michael.

"Ya know, as strange as it seems, they did. We all just thought that the research was an excuse to get their measuring tapes around the particulars of a lot of attractive women. Turns out that the buggers stumbled onto a genuine finding. I read the article – I guess we all did. Apparently the ideal female form appears to vary quite a lot throughout history and across cultures, but there's one factor which always stays the same – the relationship between a woman's waist and hips. The ideal female form is a waist-to-hip ratio of 7 to 10."

This was all quite interesting, but Michael couldn't remember why they were talking about woman's bodies. They sat in silence for a few minutes. Michael found himself staring at Larry's filthy basketball shoes and tatty baseball cap. His powder-blue nylon slacks were six inches too short and those white athletic socks covering his skinny shins were ridiculous. Larry poured another glass of wine and reached into the duffle bag at his feet. He pulled out a box of crackers and a block of cheese, and then cut slices of cheese and placed them on four crackers. He handed Michael two of the crackers.

"Dinner time," he said.

"Thanks," Michael replied. The cheese and crackers were of good quality and tasted great with the cold ale. Michael brushed crumbs off the sleeve of Sam's riding jacket. They sat in silence for a while, just watching the people passing and listening to the birds. Larry finished his glass and put it on the bench while he reached for the bottle of wine Michael had brought. He knocked his glass when he pulled the bottle from beneath the bench and it smashed on the pavement at their feet. "Oh shit," Larry groaned.

Michael finished the last sip in his glass and rubbed the rim with his shirt. "Here," Michael said, holding out the glass. "You can use mine."

"I've got another glass," Larry said as he reached down into his duffle bag.

"You brought three glasses?" asked Michael.

"Like I said," replied Larry. "I seem to break glasses." They were silent for a moment before Larry continued. "And I thought you might be along."

CHAPTER 24

A group of Russian train conductors became bored whilst on a 3,000 mile journey from Novosibirst to Vladovostok. They agreed to a competition in order to see who had the strongest head, which involved banging their heads against a train window. As the contest progressed, it became necessary to stop the train in order to seek medical help.

From the journals of Professor Charles Kidding, extract #39

Michael checked his watch as he walked down Monroe Avenue towards the Chase Bank: 4:25 pm. He should arrive at 4:30 pm, as planned. A lovely summer evening, his shoes moved rhythmically over light and shade which dappled the sidewalk, and there were plenty of birds singing in the broad-leaved trees overhead. He recalled his conversation with Julie Miller, and noted that they had only agreed to meet at the bank, but didn't say where exactly. If she arrived before him, would she be waiting inside? Or would she be at the entrance? He said her name to himself a couple of times, just to get used to it.

As Michael neared the four corners of Pittsford, he noticed that someone had erected what looked like a bed sheet across two wooden poles by the edge of the road. They had painted *Joe loves Melanie* across it in large red lettering. He imagined two lovesick high school students caught up in a fawning and ingratiating love affair. Michael was surprised at the strength of feeling this juvenile banner elicited in him. He felt revulsion, even anger. What right did Joe and Melanie have to advertise their foolish infatuation, to promote it like some new product everyone should own?

As Michael approached the bank entrance, he noticed a woman outside the main door in a blue summer dress, a smallish handbag on her arm. He supposed she was waiting for someone to pick her up. Maybe she was a bank employee. But as he came closer, the woman smiled and called out to him.

"Hello Michael."

Michael's brow furrowed and a few seconds elapsed before he realized that this was Julie Miller. Hadn't she worn some sort of Department of Health uniform when he'd met her – blue dress slacks and a white button-up, or something like that? He was sure she'd had a name tag on.

"Hello," he said cheerfully, trying to sound unphased. She was smiling at him.

"Beautiful evening, isn't it?" said Julie.

"Yeah, it's really nice."

Julie motioned to the door. "Shall we?"

"Of course," replied Michael.

Inside the bank, Julie made her way to a teller, Michael in tow.

"Excuse me," she said to the teller. "I'm Julie Miller with the Vital Records section of the Department of Health. Mr. Wilson and I have an appointment with Mr. Barns for 4:30 pm."

"I'll let him know you're here. Do you want to take a seat over there?" the teller said, pointing to a couple of chairs on the other side of the room. "There's coffee if you want some."

There were only two rather small chairs in the waiting area, and they were placed directly next to one another. Michael motioned for Julie to take a seat, but felt uncomfortable about sitting so close to her.

"Can I get you some coffee?" he asked.

"That would be nice," Julie said. Michael poured the steaming black liquid into two styrofoam cups.

"Do you want milk or sugar?"

"Just milk please," Julie said. Michael poured milk into the two cups, handed one to Julie, and thought about the seats. Why have they only got two seats and why did they have to arrange them right next to one another? He couldn't stand around with Julie sitting there.

Julie looked at Michael over the edge of her cup while taking what seemed like a large sip. "Ow," she blurted out, and Michael saw some coffee spittle fly out of her mouth. Julie involuntarily leant forward, her hand going up to her mouth.

"I'm sorry," said Michael. "I didn't know how hot it was." Julie held her hand up and smiled through the pain. "No, no, it's alright. I'm fine, really." But Michael could see that she was in pain. Julie had coffee on her chin which she wiped with her hand, an apologetic expression forming.

"I'm going to get you some water," Michael blurted out. He looked around and was relieved to spot a customer toilet.

"No, please," said Julie. "God, what an idiot I am. Really, I'm fine."

Michael picked up an extra cup, went to the toilet, ran water over his hand until it was cold, and then filled the cup. Returning, he handed the cup to Julie, who gave him a grateful smile. Julie drank.

"You are a gentleman, Mr. Wilson. Thank you. That was very stupid of me."

"Better now?" he asked.

"Yes, thank you."

They sat in silence and Michael checked his watch. 4:37 pm.

"So... uhm..." Julie began. Michael leaned forward, waiting. "Well, here we are then... at the bank," she said.

"Yeah, funny isn't it," Michael said, smiling.

"Yeah," said Julie. Michael noticed that Julie had a habit of looking at the carpet after she had spoken to him. She seemed quite different from when they had met in her office. She had appeared very self-assured, pleasant but officious. He hadn't really seen her as a woman then, just more as a functionary who might be able to help him. The sheer material of her blue dress hugged her form closely in the right places. They needed something to talk about.

"Do you remember when that businessman put his briefcase on the roof of his car and drove off," Michael said. "And those two high school boys found the briefcase and there was 300,000 dollars in it."

"Oh yeah, I remember," said Julie. "It happened here, just outside this bank."

"I didn't know that. And the kids kept the money but they bragged about it at school and that's how the police tracked them down."

"Extraordinary," said Julie. "Can you imagine what that guy must have thought when he got home and his briefcase wasn't in the car. Must be worse than having your car and ID stolen, huh?"

"Yeah," Michael said, laughing. But he wasn't sure, really.

Just then, a small slim man in a blue pinstriped suit approached them.

"Hello," he said, extending a bony hand. "I'm Alan Barnes." They all shook hands and were led to his office. Michael had seen him once or twice before, but he had never needed to speak with the branch manager. In fact, he rarely ever needed to come into the bank. Cash machines and automatic money transfers were handy enough. Julie and Michael sat down in front of his desk.

"Well Mr. Wilson, I'm sorry to hear about your stolen vehicle. Mrs. Miller here…" Julie interrupted politely. "It's Ms. Miller," she said.

"Oh, I do apologize. Ms. Miller contacted me on your behalf and told me her office is helping you renew your identification."

"Yes, that's right," said Michael. "She's been very helpful."

"Yes, it certainly seems that way," said Mr. Barns, a note of mild cynicism in his tone. "At any rate, I've pulled Mr. Wilson's file and I've made a copy of the account application form which was filled out when he joined our bank." Mr. Barns slid the form forward on his desk.

Michael scanned the form and watched Julie's expression.

"Well, that helps," said Julie. She pointed to a section labeled *Personal Identification Shown*. Boxes next to *driver's license* and *passport* were ticked.

"Did you make copies of his driver's license and passport when Michael provided those documents to you?" Julie asked.

"I'm afraid we don't do that. We're not required to keep copies, and having copies lying around just creates liability."

"Oh," said Julie. "That's a shame. Still, having a copy of the application form will help, I'm sure."

Mr. Barns looked suddenly uncomfortable. "Ms. Miller. Have you got some form of work ID – sorry to ask."

"Oh, of course," said Julie. "Sorry, I should have shown you that straight away." Julie pulled a Department of Health ID card from her small handbag and handed it to Mr. Barnes. He looked it over and handed it back.

"If I can be of further help, please let me know."

They shook hands and Michael opened the door of Mr. Barns' office for Julie. He scooted ahead in order to open the main entrance door for her as well. As Julie walked through the door, her form was lit through the sheer material of her summer dress by the evening sun. Michael felt compelled to gaze at her waist, bottom, and thighs. Her dress was reasonably snug against her figure, and Michael made out subtle panty lines beneath the thin blue material – a single horizontal line hugging her waist and then two separate lines materializing from below and circling beneath her bottom and up around her hips. He quite suddenly recalled Larry telling him about those social philosophers who discovered that the ideal female form was a 7-to-10 ratio between waist and hips. Michael watched Julie as she walked ahead of him into the sunshine, hips canting. That, he thought, has to be what a 7-to-10 looks like. But Michael noticed that she seemed unsteady on her high heels, as if she wasn't used to wearing such shoes. He made an effort to catch up to her, guilty about his behavior. He couldn't have been the first 'gentleman' to open a door for a lady and then stare at her ass in this way, but it still wasn't right.

They stood in the late afternoon summer heat, facing one another in the nearly empty parking lot. Michael expected Julie to speak first. She was the professional, he the client, so he waited. But she just ran a hand through her auburn hair and looked past him. He was suddenly very aware of the sounds around them. There was a buzz in the air, the sort of buzz you get at the end of a work week. A quitting-time Friday evening buzz. Over Julie's shoulder he saw people hanging around the entranceway to Thirsty's Bar, beers in their hands. Younger people in fashionable cars were driving faster than normal down Monroe Avenue, roofs down on some of the cars. Laughter came from somewhere.

"Well," said Julie finally, "I suppose we could talk it over. I mean the bank form and everything else. I'll tell you though, it's been a hell of a week – I'm glad it's over. I could kill a cold glass of Chardonnay just now. Maybe some of those nachos too – you know the ones with cheese and peppers?"

"Yeah," said Michael. "Oh," he added. "If you're tired, we can talk about it another time. I really appreciate the fact that you met up with me at all."

Julie's eyes narrowed into a subtle expression of consternation. "It's not that," she said. "I'd like to talk it over. It's just that it would be nice to get a glass of wine… you know, after a long week of work."

"Oh," said Michael. "You mean… getting a drink... you and I… together…?"

Julie smiled. "That's a really nice idea. Do you know a good place to get a drink and a meal?"

"The Pittsford Pub is good. It's just down State Street. It's only about a five minute walk from here."

"I know it. It's a nice walk. Over the river, isn't it?"

"Yeah, that's it," Michael said.

"Well then, shall we?"

They walked together to the four corners of Pittsford Village, crossed the intersection, and carried on down Main Street. Michael thought about his attire. He'd worn a pair of brown corduroy trousers, dress shoes, a blue oxford button-up, and a tweed sports coat. That would be fine for the Pittsford Pub. They passed by older colonial-style homes and expensive shops, the air warm on their skin. To other pedestrians, they probably appeared like just another couple out for a walk. To Michael, it was all very strange, even surreal. They approached the village bridge, a bridge crossing the Genesee River.

"I love this section of the river," said Julie. "Can we stop on the bridge and just watch for a bit?"

"Of course," replied Michael.

At the centre of the bridge, they stood and stared down the river, watching the slow-moving green water, the ducks, the shops along Shoen Place. "When I was young," Julie said, "my parents used to take us to Shoen Place to feed the ducks. It seemed like such a big deal then – I mean, just tossing some bread to a duck." She looked over to see the expression on Michael's face before continuing. "I suppose that's a silly thing to say. Not very interesting conversation, really."

"No, it is interesting," said Michael. "It's funny how things make such a strong impression when you're young."

"Have you got family locally?" Julie asked.

Michael smiled faintly and looked into the green water. "It's a long story," he said. The words sounded wrong the moment he said them. It wasn't quite clear what they were doing at the moment, but Julie was the head of Vital Records. He didn't really want to talk about what had happened, but it sounded like he was trying to hide something. "I'm sorry," said Michael, "I don't mean to sound evasive, it's just that it was a long time ago." He took a deep breath. "I was an only child. When I was six years old there was a fire in our house. They said it was some sort of electrical fault. It happened at night. I don't remember anything about the fire. The fire department was able to get me out... but not my parents."

"Michael, I'm so sorry. That must have been awful."

"It was a long time ago. It's fine."

"But what happened then?" Julie asked. "I mean after your parents...went."

"I was in different foster homes and then one day I was grown up. Well, one day I turned eighteen, and that's when social services say you're grown up. Turns out I had a knack for finance and investment, and so I was able to make it fine on my own." Michael didn't want to make a big deal of it.

They stared for a while in silence, gazing into the lazy green water. It seemed to have a hypnotic effect on Michael, and he wondered if Julie felt it too.

Michael was a jumble of thoughts as they entered the Pittsford Pub. What about paying for the bill? His impulse was to offer to pay, but would Julie think he was trying to bribe her in some way? Would Mitch, Bob, or Pete be at the bar? He hadn't seen them for a couple of weeks now, and didn't really want to come across them tonight. They found a table and settled into the booths across from one another. Julie was very animated, smiling, getting very enthusiastic about the menu. She seemed to really be enjoying herself. They'd probably order and then talk about his ID problem.

"Do you drink wine Michael?" Julie said.

"No, I'm afraid not. I'll get an ale."

"That's a shame – now I'll have to work on a bottle all by myself," Julie said. The waiter arrived and asked for their orders.

"Do you like Nachos?" Julie asked. "We could share a platter if you like. Or we could get something else, if you want."

"Nachos sound good," said Michael.

"One order of Nachos, large platter," Julie said, "and a bottle of your Chardonnay please." Michael smiled in surprise. He thought she was joking when she talked about drinking a bottle on her own.

"Do you have Saranac Ale?" he asked.

"Yes sir."

"I'll have one of those please."

When the waiter left, Michael decided he should let Julie choose the conversation. She'd probably want to talk about the visit to the bank now. Their eyes met squarely for a few moments, and that seemed too much for Julie. She smiled broadly, seemingly embarrassed, and looked down at the table. And then it struck Michael. She was nervous. But why? They needed some conversation.

Julie looked up. "You said you make financial investments. Is that interesting?"

"I suppose it can be. I have to read a lot about the markets and world news. Sometimes my head gets so full of the stuff I get sick of it. But I seem to have a knack for it, so I keep doing it. How did you get into working for the Department of Health?"

"My dad worked for the Department of Health in the accounting department. He was the consummate civil servant, a born bureaucrat. He didn't figure I'd do much with my B.A. in literature, so he helped me get a job with the Department." Julie stared into space for a moment. "My dad did accountancy with the Department for decades and died in the saddle, three months shy of retirement."

"That's awful," said Michael.

"I worked in another building, so I didn't see it happen, but one of his colleagues told me about it." Julie stared reflectively into space before continuing. "Death is cruel by nature," she said, "but ironic in only some cases. Dad's death went the ironic route. He pushed paper for forty-two years without complaining, but his death was so cruel that he couldn't contain the suffering. The poor guy. He fell from his cubical, shouting and clutching at his chest. It must have been awful. I had to talk to the coroner later that week and he was really apologetic because he couldn't be sure of the cause of death. He assured me that 'foul play' was not likely." Julie smiled sadly before continuing. "If you knew my dad you would know that the idea of foul play was absurd. It was more likely that he was killed by boredom. I could have asked the coroner that. I could have said, can forty-two years of civil service accountancy induce a sudden death?"

Michael found himself smiling. She had quite a poetic way of talking. Their drinks and food arrived, and it was while Michael was pouring his ale that he noticed Mitch heading in their direction. He looked away, hoping that Mitch might not see them. No such luck.

"Heeelllooo Michael. Haven't seen you in a couple of weeks."

"Hi Mitch," said Michael. He'd have to introduce Julie. "Mitch, this is

Julie Miller. Julie, this is Mitch…" Michael remembered that he didn't know Mitch's last name, so he'd have to leave it at that.

"Nice to meet you Julie," said Mitch, shaking Julie's hand.

"So Bob and I been sitting at the bar wondering where you found such an attractive lady-friend," Mitch said, giving Michael a solicitous eye. Michael groaned inwardly at Mitch's misreading of the situation, worrying that Julie would be embarrassed.

"Well," said Julie, looking at Michael. "You do have charming friends."

"Mitch," said Michael. "It's not quite like that. Julie is… I mean we're…". How was he supposed to describe this? *Julie's with the Vital Records Department and she's helping me renew my identification, and we're out for a drink together.* Michael felt the weight of Mitch and Julie's expectant gaze. "Julie is helping me… with something," he offered.

There was an awkward silence before Mitch spoke. "Well, you're lucky to have a helper who's that easy on the eyes." Michael willed Mitch to go away, and felt relief when he finally excused himself following a few pointless exchanges about the civil service and the weather.

Michael pissed his second ale into the urinal, washed his hands, and stared at himself in the toilet mirror. This evening was getting rather disorientating. Julie had nearly polished off a bottle of wine and had picked up the menu when he got up to go to the bathroom. He checked his watch. It was nearly 7:00 pm. Julie had told him funny stories about the things which can happen at the Department of Health. She'd touched his hand a few times, but she was probably that type, the physically affectionate type. A lot of women are. She was intelligent and funny, but what were they doing? She hadn't mentioned his problem with ID once, and their conversation had galloped on in such a way that he supposed she didn't really want to. Maybe it was because her work week was over, and she didn't want to talk shop anymore. She was getting quite tipsy now, anyway. But they were supposed to talk about it, weren't they?

Julie was smiling broadly when he sat down, her blue eyes glistening. They were very blue, those eyes. How had he not noticed that? She seemed to be laughing inwardly at something she found funny, but he couldn't imagine what.

"Julie," he said. "About my identification problem. Do you think the trip to the bank will help?"

Julie turned her wine glass up and finished it. Empty glass, empty bottle. She raised a playful finger at Michael. "Definitely. Very corroborating evidential evidence," she said through a broad smile, her speech slurred. She's drunk, thought Michael.

"I mean, that's just the sort of thing that we need to support those validation forms you gave me, right?"

"You know Michael," said Julie. "Now would be the perfect time for us to go on a crime spree. You got no ID. They capture us and they got no way to identify you. You're off the grip… I mean, off the grid, my friend." She touched his hand and laughed, encouraging him to see the humor in it. It was funny somehow, even if it didn't make any sense.

"Hey," continued Julie. Did you know that the best time to go on a crime spree would be before the age of three months. Know why?" Michael shook his head. "Because," Julie continued, "babies are born without fingerprints. Babies don't get fingerprints until they're three months old. If we were about two months old, we could go on a great crime spree together." Julie laughed and took hold of his hand. "Shall we get terribly drunk together Michael?" she said, a mischievous grin on her face.

"I don't think that's too good an idea," said Michael. "You're not going to be able to drive as it is." Michael saw Julie's smile transform into a subtle mix of confusion and disappointment. "I really appreciate everything you've done for me," he added, "and I don't want to take too much of your time." Julie nodded, and Michael felt quite unsure of himself.

As they crossed over the river, Michael felt Julie against his side and realized that she had placed her arm into his elbow. The sun was low on the horizon now, casting a yellow-orange glow over the western sky. The air had cooled and Michael felt Julie shiver against him.

"You're cold," Michael said. He took off his suit coat and put it over her shoulders.

"Oh I'm fine," said Julie. "But thank you – you're a gentleman."

When they approached Chase Bank, Michael noticed the taxi waiting in the parking lot. "There's the taxi," he said.

Julie looked confused. "The taxi?" she asked.

"Yes, I called one for you before we left – when you were in the bathroom." They stopped and stood facing one another in the lot, several feet from the taxi.

Julie stared down at the pavement, and moved closer to him.

"I'm sorry Michael," she said. "I'm so sorry. I got drunk and I talked about such a lot of nonsense." Her voice was breaking, and Michael noticed that her eyes had suddenly become moist. He was afraid she might cry.

"Oh, not at all. Don't mention it, really." He felt an impulse to put his hands on her upper arms, but he didn't.

Julie shook her head. "Very very bad Vital Records management. Getting drunk with a nice guy who needs my help." She looked up at Michael. "Very bad, very bad," she said, smiling sadly.

"Well…" Michael said. "Thank you – thank you for your help."

Julie looked into his eyes, her head wobbling slightly. She put her hand on his arm. "Michael, what do you want?" Her voice had taken on a strangely serious tone. It was such a vague question. What did she mean?

"I'd like to get my life back in order. I'd like things to go back to the way they were." He thought about telling her that he'd been having problems finding his way home, but he was aware of the cab waiting.

"Michael, you know what you told me about your mom and dad. I'm really sorry that happened."

Michael smiled. "It's ancient history… really, it is."

Julie nodded slowly and wrapped her arms around him, pulling herself into him. Michael felt the large fullness of her breasts against his chest, and was surprised at the soft authority of her femininity. Now he was aware of a floral scent and the subtle press of her pubic bone against him through the sheer material of her dress. Julie turned and walked away, weaving a slow course towards the cab. A high-heel suddenly turned over on itself and Julie lurched to the right. Michael instinctively took a step towards her, sure that she would fall, but Julie staggered a few steps, arms flailing, and righted herself. As she was getting into the cab, Michael was aware that she still had his sports coat over her shoulders. He thought about asking her for it, but didn't want to get tangled up in that. Julie didn't look up at him as she was driven off. In fact, she made an unsuccessful attempt to hide her face, but Michael noticed that her cheeks glistened in the street lights.

CHAPTER 25

Martin Narlow of South Carolina has been ordered by a US Supreme Court judge to stop selling his urine for $50 over the internet to people wanting to pass a work-place drug test.

From the journals of Professor Charles Kidding, extract #53

Michael sat in Starbucks, scanning the screen of his laptop computer. He'd made a futures bet on the airline industry and was checking stock values using the internet. He was getting careless. He had learned over many years that the futures game required dedicated study and then patience. It was a hard slog and there was no alternative. Impulsivity and intuitive hunches will kill you. And here he was making futures bets on the airline industry, one of the most volatile areas in the market. What was he doing? And this identification problem was bugging him. The forms had sat on his desk untouched for days now. You can only detest something to the extent you need it. Apathy and hatred are mutually exclusive, and he was coming to hate those forms. He remembered Julie's breasts… . That had been some evening. Her getting drunk and hugging him like that. The softness and fullness of her against him. In a way, it made it harder to ask her for help now. Maybe she'd had a bad week. Maybe she had some personal problems he didn't know about. *Was there something wrong with her?* He should probably get his sports coat back. Maybe she'd been embarrassed about that evening, maybe she felt like she'd been unprofessional. She might want to forget about the whole thing. He needed to sort those forms out though. Maybe there were other people who had problems with those forms. There probably wasn't. He was pretty screwed up about all of that. *Was something wrong with him?* And why did Zeno's teacher make him walk around Athens carrying a bowl of lentils'? He should have asked Larry about that. Sam's anarchist jacket was on the back of his chair. He'd thought about folding it up and putting it on the other chair when he sat down, but he'd thought 'screw it'. He recalled the anger on Mary's face when she went for that security guard. It was more than that – rage maybe. He'd seen something in that moment he didn't quite know existed in Mary. He checked his watch – it was the new one he'd bought last week, a shiny digital watch with a data bank you can store lots of information on. Maybe he should put some data in there. He sort of wished that Mary hadn't told him about that guy who had a problem with white high-heeled shoes. He didn't like thinking about that guy and what he did, but it was hard not to. It was just so weird, maybe even sick. He didn't like thinking about it, but sometimes an image of this guy and Mary would just pop into his head.

Michael looked up and noticed a man who had just taken a seat on the far side of the room. The man was looking down, but there was something familiar about him. Strange, but familiar. A huge guy. He wore a loose fitting t-shirt, but Michael sensed the unearthly reserves of strength coiled in chest and arms. The man looked at a book, his dark hair obscuring his face. There was no need to stare, and yet Michael did. And then the man raised his large head, and Michael saw the pock-marked face and dark eyes … Jesus! That was it – this guy looked so much like that figure from his dream. The resemblance was uncanny, but it wasn't just that the two figures looked alike – Michael hadn't even had a good look at the man in his dream – there was a similarity between the two men that was more than just physical. There was something about the *presence* of this man sitting here in Starbucks which recalled the memory of the dream quite vividly. The man looked down and dark hair fell over his face again. Michael's heart hammered against his ribcage, his face unable to conceal the bewildered disbelief which held him.

He stared for 2,3,5 minutes, and still the man did not look up. He told himself he was being silly – men who tear roofs off cars and scream at you in dreams exist *only* in dreams, and they exist in dreams for perfectly sensible psychological reasons. They do not visit you in cafes. Michael felt that a decision needed to be made. He could ignore this man, be sensible, and just get on with his work. He could leave the café, or maybe he should get a closer look. He knew it was ridiculous to think this way, but the idea of a malicious dream figure wandering around Pittsford just made him feel uneasy.

Michael eased his chair out cautiously and stepped warily towards the man, his legs feeling jellified. He worked his way around the line at the counter and then positioned himself behind a display of coffee bags, making a pretense of examining one. Now he could see the face. Yes, dark-skinned, pock-marked, dark eyes, and really powerful. The man might have sensed the intensity of his observation, because he looked up from his book and gazed straight at Michael. A quizzical expression formed on the man's face.

"You okay buddy?" the man asked. Michael was surprised by how deep and gentle the man's words were. An impulsive burst of laughter escaped from Michael, a constriction of anxiety suddenly released.

"Yeah… I'm fine, thanks."

Michael turned and walked quickly to his table, accidentally joggling a customer on route. He collected his work materials and jacket hurriedly, and made his way out the door. Phantoms from a dream drinking coffee in your local café? He must really be cracking up.

CHAPTER 26

Twenty-four year old Abrie Kruger of South Africa won the World's Biggest Liar competition, but has been accused of cheating. Other participants indicate that Kruger read from a script and used props.

From the Journals of Professor Charles Kidding, extract #182

Michael was staring out his bedroom window when his phone rang.

"Hello."

"Hi Michael, its Mary."

"Oh hi Mary, how are you?"

"Fine, yeah, just great. What are you up to?"

"I've been checking on some of my investments. Nothing too interesting."

"Everything okay in the world of money?" Mary asked. "Is it a bull market or is it … what's the other one?"

"There's a bull and a bear market."

Michael heard rather strange noises in the background, other people talking on telephones and a door opening and closing. Where was Mary calling from?

"The bull one is when people are buying stuff isn't it?" Mary said. "Is the bear one when people aren't buying?"

"Sort of – it's when people are selling."

"Why is that? When they say that the market is bullish, don't they mean that people are being aggressive? But I would have thought that a bear was as aggressive as a bull. They should call it a bear market and a mouse market, don't you think? They probably wouldn't want to do that though because everything you tycoons do is meant to be virile. A mouse just doesn't fit the picture, does it?"

"No, I guess it doesn't." Why was Mary calling him, and where was she?

"So have you had lunch yet?" Mary asked.

"No, I was just going to get some."

"Eating in or out?"

"I've got some chicken in the refrigerator," Michael said.

"So are you going to have a leg or a breast," Mary said, her voice adopting a seductive tone.

Michael smiled. "Um, I haven't looked yet."

"Okay, but which would you *prefer*? Leg or breast?"

Michael heard a deep male voice in the background, louder than the others. "You got two more minutes missy, and that's your only call."

"Oh yeah," Mary said. "I'm at the police station downtown."

"Why? What's happened?" said Michael, concerned.

"Do you remember I told you that I was doing an installation about the male use of internet pornography? Well, I used a vagina as part of the installation."

"You used a what?" asked Michael.

"A vagina, as part of the installation. I hired out this disused shop on State Street, by the Inner Loop – that's where I have the installation. Someone must have called the coppers and made a complaint. Can you believe that? Anyways, the coppers think that maybe I've stolen it, or dug someone up, or maybe even killed someone. I don't really know what they think, but I got to be interrogated, and it was just like on TV. I'm not kidding – I was in this room with a one-way mirror and the harsh light. I swear they even did the good-cop bad-cop thing. They didn't try to get me talking by offering me a cigarette, but that's probably because you can't smoke in municipal buildings anymore. It was so funny."

"My god Mary, this doesn't sound funny at all."

Michael heard the male voice again. "One more minute!"

"Do you want to keep your panties on Sarge," Michael heard Mary shout.

"Sarge here was the bad cop by the way," Mary said. "Weren't you Sarge?"

"Mary, listen," said Michael. "Have they charged you with anything?"

"Uh, hang on a minute." Michael heard Mary addressing the man. "You guys charged me with anything?"

"Not at the moment. You're in for questioning," the male voice said.

"Sarge says I'm in for questioning."

"Mary… what do you want me to do?"

"Uhm, I don't know. It would be nice to see you."

"Times up, little lady," Michael heard the male voice say.

"I gotta go Michael – bad cops' in a snit." The line went dead.

Michael drove his moped with a sense of anxious urgency down Monroe Avenue. He might have thought that if there was an emergency, and if you pulled back on the throttle handle extra hard, and if you really wanted to go faster, that your 50cc moped would somehow find extra speed. But every time he glanced at the speedometer, the little red needle waved spastically somewhere around the familiar twenty-eight miles per hour. Cars thundered past, weighty and patronizing, and the whole situation seemed brutally unacceptable. What did Mary mean when she said she had used a vagina in one of her installations? How is that even possible? Had she broken the law and how much trouble was she in? He didn't want to be associated with any of this. Still, he hated the idea of her being locked away. What if she went to prison for a long time? Michael had to break hard to avoid slamming into the back of a BMW that had stopped at a light. He had to concentrate. Should he contact a lawyer for her?

As Michael drove into the downtown area he saw Roosevelt Park on the left and calculated that the police station was seven blocks up. A foreboding sense of apprehension gripped him hard as he *imagined* entering the station, introducing himself at reception, explaining who he was and why he was there. He slowed and peered into the park, looking for Larry. He was there, on his bench. Michael felt like he should get to the police station straight away, but he really didn't want to deal with all that. Maybe he'd just have a quick chat with Larry. Maybe he'd run this dilemma by him. Larry was pretty weird – maybe he'd have some useful thoughts about how to handle a weird situation. Michael doubted that was true, but stopping off to see Larry meant he didn't have to face Mary and the police straight away.

Michael could tell that Larry was drunk – drunker than he'd seen him yet. As he sat down he noticed the bleary eyes, the slowness with which Larry's smile came to light across his flaccid face, the fact that the wine glass had come off his knee and was now held more securely between his open legs. Maybe this was a mistake.

"Hi Larry, you okay?"

Larry's head bobbled. "Just ducky," he said, words slow and slurred. Michael dropped down onto the bench.

"You're not going to believe this," said Michael. "A friend of mine, Mary, she's at the police station for questioning. All she could tell me was that someone complained about an art installation she's got on display, and the police have taken her in."

Larry leaned forward, blood shot eyes squinting, as if to see Michael more clearly. He grunted, "Hmmph," and then nodded.

"The fact is," Michael continued, "I really don't even know if I want to get mixed up in it. I mean, I don't even know what Mary's done. I've known her for a while, but maybe the police are gonna want to question me. To be honest…Mary… she's a bit *out there*."

"She's your fend?" Larry asked, wiping spittle from his lips.

"Well," replied Michael, blowing out a breath of exasperation. "Yes… I suppose she is a friend."

Larry nodded, as if to himself, and then reached up and removed his baseball cap. He grunted himself up from the bench using both hands and stood rocking in front of Michael for a moment before the cap came swinging around, slapping Michael squarely across the face. The blow knocked Larry off balance and he lurched forward, catching himself against the bench.

"Hey – what the hell did you do that for?" sputtered Michael.

"She's your fend."

"Well, yes, but it's complicated, isn't it?"

Larry shook his head, a new vigor suddenly making itself known. "Come on then," he said, clutching the lapels of Michael's leather jacket with two wizened fists. Anticipating that Larry was about to drag him off his seat, Michael spat out "fine" and was relieved when he was released. He made his way to the moped, Larry in tow, half-expecting Larry to kick him in the ass, a state of disbelief and humiliation coursing through his being. When they reached the moped, Michael picked the helmet off a handle bar, and was surprised to see Larry climbing onto the back portion of the seat.

"You're coming?"

Larry pointed a wavering and accusational finger at Michael. "Hhummphh..." he said.

"But you haven't got a helmet." Larry's head just bobbled. Michael had a quick look around and noticed a couple on a park bench watching them. He crouched down and spoke into Larry's ear.

"Larry, this is really not a good idea. Please get of my moped." Larry waved a finger at him and smiled. "You gotta help yo frien."

"Yes, I know Larry, but…" A group of adolescent boys carrying basketballs slowed their pace to a near stand-still, clearly taking an interest. Michael didn't like the idea of Larry on the back of his moped, but he liked the idea of a public scene even less. He shook his head and climbed on, started up, and rocked the moped to get a feel for Larry's weight. Michael sighed heavily and pulled slowly out into traffic. The moped seemed remarkably sluggish and unsteady. They stopped at a light and Michael felt uncomfortable with Larry's arms wrapped around his midriff. And was that Larry's chin resting on his shoulder? They were going to have to turn left.

"Larry, you have to lean with the bike. Lean into the turn," Michael shouted. Larry didn't reply.

The light changed and Michael accelerated into the turn. Larry's weight just went with the centrifugal force and Michael had to throw his weight extra hard into the turn to keep them upright. The next intersection approached and Michael noticed that the light was green – they needed to turn right.

"Larry," Michael shouted. "We're going right – LEAN INTO THE TURN." As he went into the turn Michael realized that Larry was following his instructions, so well in fact that he was practically falling off the bike. Michael gritted his teeth and pushed the handle bars hard into the turn to try and compensate, the pavement rising upwards, an angle of descent impinging, and it wasn't going to be enough. The curb approached rapidly and Michael knew that they we're going to either slap down on the pavement, or, if they stayed upright long enough, hit a US postal box. Michael squeezed the brake hard and it was the postal box, the front wheel hitting hard, and then for a dreamlike moment, they were airborne.

The sudden impact of leather and bone with concrete was as unreal as it was shocking. When it was over, Michael discovered that he was gazing through the helmet visor at the sun, a dazzling mesh of confusion. Lying on his back, he sensed the hardness of concrete beneath him and something quite heavy pressing down on top. It was either the mailbox, the moped, or Larry, and because it was laughing, he decided it was Larry. He felt at the mass above him with his hands.

"Larry, get off, you're crushing me."

Larry was in hysterics. "We crashed," he shouted, "my god did we crash." Larry must have rolled off because the weight was suddenly gone. Michael wondering if he had injured himself. He felt sore, especially his right shoulder, but nothing seemed serious, so he pulled himself slowly into a sitting position. There was Larry, sitting up as well, facing him, grinning and chuckling, a small river of blood making its way leisurely down his forehead.

"You okay Larry?"

"Yeah, yeah."

"You're bleeding," said Michael, pointing to Larry's forehead. Larry made a groggy and clumsy swipe at his forehead, and smiled. "Jes a scrash – no problem."

Michael imagined he should get up but he just sat there, his mind numb and wandering. *You might get one good bounce, roll for a bit, and then slide for a while… But these leathers have got padding in the ass and thighs. It'll help a lot when you go overboard.* He and Larry had come out of it okay. Michael could sense pedestrians closing in around them, gawking, probably wondering if they should offer help.

"You okay buddy?" Michael looked up to see an older black gentleman hanging over him, a warm smile of concern.

"Yeah, were fine," he said. The black man seemed somehow to float backwards into the small crowd of spectators. Michael looked into the street, trying to orientate himself. Jesus, this was embarrassing. He wanted to get out of here. They were about four blocks from the police station. They needed to cross over State Street at the next intersection and… . Michael recalled that Mary's exhibition was on State Street – in fact, it wasn't far from here. A few minutes walk.

"Hey Larry. That's State Street," said Michael. "That's where Mary's exhibition is."

Larry craned around to look. "Les go."

Michael pushed himself up from the pavement and thought about that. "Maybe we should. If we're going to the station to see Mary, maybe we should see what all the fuss is about. Of course maybe they shut the exhibition down, but it's probably worth taking a look." Michael pulled the moped upright. The headlight was bent and there was a dent in the gas tank, but it looked okay otherwise. "Let's park the bike and walk. You're a menace Larry – I'm not putting you on the back of this thing again."

Larry waved a hand – an expression of apologetic resignation.

They walked down State Street and Michael was surprised at the state of urban decay. The street was filthy with litter and graffiti covered most of the store fronts. He saw a pawn shop, a cheap liquor store, and a bail bonds business. Many of the shops had long ago been abandoned, and the ones still open for business had barred windows. Why would Mary put on an exhibition here? He saw the inner loop overpass just ahead and noticed a store which, at first, he thought was abandoned. But taking a second look, he saw a security guard sitting behind a desk through a cracked window. Next to the door, a hand painted sign:

Exhibition
Mary Magellan

Liberte la entrada
Befreien sie eingang
Liberare l'entrata
Befri inngang

"What's the sign say?" asked Michael.

"It says free entrance in Spanish, German, Italian and…". Larry leaned in closer and squinted through streaming eyes, and then fell forward, just managing to catch himself with an unsteady hand against the wall. Michael pulled him upright. "Nnnoorweigian. Gotta be Norwegian," he concluded.

"Well I'm sure that'll be very helpful for the local residents," said Michael.

They made their way into the well-lit room, and Michael had a close look at the security guard. He was an older man dressed in the sort of standard security guard uniform you see everywhere. There was a monitor in front of him, but the guard was positioned so that Michael couldn't see the screen. He imagined there were probably CCTV cameras in the place, and that's what the monitor was for. The old man was reading a battered, coffee stained paperback – a book which looked like philosophy. He stroked a cat while he read, an old cat which looked like it had been through a combine harvester. The old man put the book down when they approached the desk.

"Good afternoon gentlemen," said the guard. Michael glanced at Larry, worrying about the state of him. The blood had caked up and mixed with pavement dirt and small pebbles. Well, this was probably about the only gallery in town that wouldn't be fussy about a disheveled bum who's just been in a moped accident.

"Hello," said Michael. We'd just like to have a look around, if that's okay."

"Of course," said the guard, who returned his attention to his book. He looked too old to be a guard, and Michael wondered how he was connected to Mary.

Michael scanned the room. There were a few installations, but his attention was seized by the display which had been cordoned off with yellow tape bearing the words 'crime scene - do not cross this line'.

It was as if the guard had read his thoughts. "Don't worry about the tape," said the old man. "The police are coming back later to pick up the installation. Apparently they need some sort of special vehicle to transport it. But you can see it fine."

"Thanks," said Michael.

Michael and Larry stood at the boundary of the tape. What Michael saw was, in one sense, a very ordinary scene. There was a chair and desk. Sitting on the desk was a computer, monitor, mouse, and a half empty bottle of beer. But inside the computer monitor was… Jesus, was that a vagina? Michael squinted. It was dreadful to look at. The folds of tissue were a grayish pink, and the thing floated slowly within the monitor. The monitor must have been filled with some sort of fluid. The only visual image he had of a vagina was of the bit you might see in the ruder men's magazines, meaning the outer bit. But this was apparently the whole thing. It was quite unpleasant, something no man, well, no remotely normal man, could find exciting. There was a label next to the installation which simply read *Internet Pornography*.

Larry smiled drunkenly at him. "That is brivlent," he slurred. "Jes brilliant."

Larry walked off, heading for what looked like a closet which had been placed in the centre of the gallery. Michael noticed a sign on the closet door which read *Enter Installation Here*, and when Larry disappeared into the closet, a door swung shut behind him.

Michael viewed an old pine box which was filled with baby dolls. The exhibit was labeled *WWII Czechoslovakian Grenade Box*. He couldn't quite see the point of that, but at least it wasn't as unsettling as the computer he'd been looking at. Larry emerged from the closet a moment later, shaking his head and laughing quietly to himself.

As Michael entered the closet he was aware that the space had no lighting, but when the spring-loaded door closed behind him, a light came on. He found himself staring at a medium-sized wooden box which was hung on the wall in front of him. The words DO NOT OPEN THIS BOX were printed across the box door. There was a hinge on the box, a hinge which could have easily taken a padlock – but there was *no* padlock. The only other object in the room was a CCTV camera up in one corner, a camera which displayed a blinking red light and emitted a subtle mechanical purr, a camera pointed straight at Michael. Michael thought of the security guard at the desk and of his monitor. He felt an impulse to reach out for the pine knob on the face of the box, and then made a pretense of looking around the rest of the closet, as if there might be something else to see. What sort of art was this? In fact, is it art? He suddenly wondered if he had stumbled into some back room of the gallery by mistake. This was of course ridiculous. He'd gone through a door which had a sign on it – *Enter Installation Here*. A moment later the bold words on the front of the box and the flashing red light on the camera got the better of him, and he left, feeling annoyed and a little confused.

There was only one further object in the room, and Larry was looking at it. Michael joined him, and they looked down on a digital watch which lay on top of a simple pine plinth.

"What do you make of that," asked Larry.

Michael shrugged. "It's just a watch, isn't it?"

"Well," said Larry, words still coming thick and slow, "If I were in a shop, I'd figur it waz jes a watch. But this friend of yours haz a deblish… a devilish mind."

Michael continued to stare down at what looked like an ordinary digital watch, a fairly simple one, actually. "Look," said Larry, pointing to the label on the wall.

The label read *A Watch for Michael.* "Doz tha mean you?" asked Larry.

"I don't know."

They stared at the watch for a moment longer, and then Larry picked it up and examined it closer. "Larry, are you supposed to do that?"

Larry ignored Michael and held the watch close to his ear. A slow sloppy smile spread across his face, and then he began to chuckle.

"I think you'd bever listen to thiz," said Larry, handing Michael the watch.

Michael looked over at the old guard who was watching them with interest, a pleasant expression on his face. He held the watch to his ear and at first thought he heard a faint ticking, but a moment later he realized that each apparent tick was actually a word coming from somewhere inside the watch. What he heard was *death, death, death, death…*

Michael placed the watch back on the plinth abruptly. He knew immediately that the label did refer to him, and he tried to remember the conversation he'd had with Mary about his problem. He knew what she was driving at. He wasn't an art expert, but he wasn't stupid either. Still, he hadn't made the connection. That bothered him a little. He avoided Larry's eyes. He didn't want a drunken conversation about the watch. He'd have to think about it more later.

They had seen everything now and so they drifted together towards the door. Michael looked at the closet on route, and he felt angry, not quite knowing at whom or what. That sign, *Enter Exhibit Here*, struck him as obnoxious and claustrophobic.

"Just one minute," he said to Larry, an edginess in his tone.

Michael walked to the closet, placed his hand on the door handle, and turned. He was stunned when the door refused to open. He tried again. Same result. Was someone inside? No, that wasn't possible. They were the only ones in the room. Michael approached the guard.

"Excuse me, the door seems locked," he said, pointing to the closet.

"Yeah," said the guard. "It does that sometimes."

"But," stammered Michael. "Why would it be locked?"

"I don't know," said the old man, "I'm just the security guard." Michael thought it strange that a security guard wouldn't know why doors locked and unlocked, and he wondered why the old man was smiling at him like that.

"Oh," said Michael. He thought about trying the door again, but decided against it.

After they were searched and put through a metal detector, Michael and Larry were allowed to see Mary. She sat at a table in a plain room, bare except for an imposing one-way mirror and wall-mounted camera. Mary smiled broadly.

"Did you bring me the cake?"

"What cake?" asked Michael.

"You know – the one with the file in it."

Michael glanced up at the camera on the wall. "No Mary, there's no cake," he whispered.

"Well, that's just great. Now I'll have to tunnel out. You know what that's likely to do to my fingernails?" Mary said, holding up both hands for inspection. Michael had noticed her nails before, many times actually. They were routinely chewed to a painful nub.

"So who's your friend?" Mary continued.

"This is Larry Dembrowski," he replied, embarrassed at Larry's appalling appearance. He looked like an island castaway. Like an island castaway who'd just been chucked off a moped.

"Pleasure to meet you Larry. I'm Mary."

Larry nodded groggily, a sloppy grin forming. Mary looked at Michael, her eyebrows converging into an unspoken question. Michael was actually more than embarrassed by Larry. He was mad at him as well – crashing the moped, looking like this. "Disgraced philosophers," said Michael, "shouldn't ride on mopeds when drunk." It seemed a rather cruel thing to say, but he needn't have worried because Larry burst into laughter, Mary joining him. Larry grabbed hold of Michael's arm, pleading for attention.

"Michael… Michael… they should have a health warning on da moped… print it on the seat… vehicle not suitable for disgraced philosophers, especially when drunk." Larry practically fell out of his seat with laughter.

"Are you really a disgraced philosopher?" asked Mary enthusiastically.

"I certainly am," said Larry, raising an index finger to emphasize the point.

Mary smiled. "You never know when you'll need a disgraced philosopher." She looked at Michael. "Haven't I always said that?"

"No, you haven't," said Michael.

"An by the way," interrupted Larry, "we saw your exposition."

"Mary," said Michael, ignoring Larry. "Are you in real trouble? What do they think you've done?"

Mary sighed. "They wanted to know where I got a vagina from and I wouldn't tell them, so they locked me up."

"But Mary," said Michael, an expression of revulsion forming, "that thing… floating in the computer monitor… is that really… a vagina?"

Mary leaned close to Michael and Larry, whispering, "the walls have ears. No, Michael, it's not a real vagina. I mean, where am I going to get a real vagina? I've only got access to one, and I need that occasionally."

"But what is it then?" asked Michael, adopting Mary's hushed tone.

"I went to a butcher's shop. I made my vagina out of a cow's intestine."

"A cow's intestine?" whispered Michael. Larry was laughing.

"Yeah. And you know what's interesting? I wasn't even sure exactly what it was supposed to look like. I had to look in a medical encyclopedia at the library."

"I thought it was a wery insightpul piece," said Larry. His voice was even but drained, his eyes half closed, head nodding slowly to some wine-addled rhythm. Michael could see now that the crash and all that walking had finally exhausted him. "It will give men cause to think about ow they look at a woman," Larry continued, "but more important, and more to the point, what happens to everyone when we experience each other as *objects*. A very humanistic piece."

Larry had made a great effort to say these words and Michael could tell that he had been moved by the installation, probably moved by the whole exhibition. He felt a moment of jealousy, wishing that *he* had been able to say these words. Mary smiled warmly at Larry, obviously pleased. She reached across and took Larry's hands into hers and Michael noticed for the first time that there was quite a lot of dried blood on Larry's palms.

"Mary," said Michael. "Just tell them it's only a cow's intestine. There's no reason for you to be locked up here."

"Fuck them Michael – it's all part of the process," she said.

In leaving the police station they faced several steps they would need to walk down. Larry asked if they could rest, and so they sat on the top step, staring out into the city streets and the soft orange haze of summer evening. Michael felt disoriented, and he worried about the need to find his way back to his home, and there was a question pressing upon him.

"Larry, you know that installation with the box – the one which you weren't supposed to open."

"Sure."

"Did you open the box?"

"Uh huh."

"What was inside?" asked Michael

Larry smiled groggily and looked at Michael. "I really shouldn't tell you."

Michael looked at the ground, his teeth clenching, a smoldering sense of shame warming his neck.

"But I will tell you," said Larry. "There was nothing in the box. It was empty."

Michael felt annoyed. "But what's the point of that? Mary went to all the trouble… or someone went to all the trouble to build that whole thing and then there's nothing in the box."

Larry looked at Michael, a drowsy softness in his gaze. He spoke slowly, carefully. "I don't think that whatever might be in the box was the point."

CHAPTER 27

A 26-year-old widow from Sydney, Australia, has had the ashes of her husband placed in her breast implants, so that she will always "have him close to her heart".

From the journals of Professor Charles Kidding, extract #125

Julie's hand lay atop her office phone, heavy and inert. As she stared at her hand, an absent-minded languor seemed to take hold, and she found herself wondering about the innards of her body. She was aware that this was an odd thing to be thinking about at 3:30 pm on a Tuesday.

In a way, the whole body was constructed out of tubes which were different shapes and sizes – arteries, intestines, nerve fibers, and so on – all tubes. And all sorts of things rush about the body through the tubes – blood, lymph, electrical impulses, hormones, oxygen, urine. She could sort of sense the whole internal works now just by thinking about it. She had never taken hallucinogenic drugs, but people who did probably thought about this sort of thing. Why was she thinking about her innards, anyway?

That was obvious, wasn't it?

She'd said goodbye to Michael on Friday evening, and then the taxi had ground its way through Pittsford and she had been halfway home before she noticed she was still wearing his sports coat. She woke the following morning to find that something felt quite different about her innards. This something felt particularly strange because it *wasn't* tube-like, and it didn't transport. It did throb though, and it was painful. She had sat up in bed Saturday morning and had felt, had actually *felt*, something very hard lying just beneath her breastbone – something like a stone or… or an avocado pit. Yes, that was it – this inexplicable sensation was just the shape and size and color and hardness of an avocado pit, and there it was, in the centre of her chest, right between her boobs. As she put on her bra, she had even tapped her breastbone with her knuckle, wondering if this thing had a particular sound – it didn't, especially. And just when the sensation seemed to be like a solid avocado pit, she could just as easily experience it as an emptiness, as if a space inside had been scooped out. A moment passed, and now it felt solid again. It was like when someone asks you to close your eyes and hold your hand out face down, and then slowly raises a piece of ice to your palm – it could feel like something very cold or very hot, depending on what you expected. This thing beneath her breastbone – well, it could feel like solidness and pain, or emptiness and pain.

Take your pick.

She gazed curiously at her hand atop the phone receiver, and tried to recall what she had decided to say to Michael. She had developed a few different scenarios, each containing subtle and most certainly pointless variations. Feeling something like a bleak and anxious resignation, she lifted her shaking hand, dialed, and put the receiver to her ear.

"Hello."

Julie opened her mouth to speak, but she could find no words. Or perhaps she could not find the courage to say the words – it was hard to tell.

"Hello…is there anybody there?" Michael asked.

Julie replaced the receiver carefully, and found that she was suddenly gulping for air. How long had she been holding her breath? She placed a deductive palm lightly against her chest, as if the action itself might bring understanding. She knew the sensation well by now, but not what it was made of. If she had been able to describe a sensation like that – a sensation that's avocado hard *and* scooped-out empty – she might describe it as *absence* and *longing*, and she'd know how spiteful these bastard twins could be.

CHAPTER 28

A hunter from Tallahassee, Florida shot a duck. Believing the animal to be dead, he put the duck in his refrigerator. However, he had only grazed the duck's scalp, knocking the duck temporarily unconscious. The man's wife opened the refrigerator to find a recovered duck looking at her imploringly.

From the journals of Professor Charles Kidding, extract #51

Michael saw it out of the corner of his eye as he puttered down Sutherland Street. He saw it, and yet what was seen was so implausible, so inscrutable to common sense, that the mind at first refused to register. A rather short and obese man spread-eagled and bound by wrists and ankles to the High School tennis court fencing. Sensation ground its way unhappily towards perception, perception resisted cognition, and Michael could only gawp stupidly as he slowed the moped to the side of the road. It was Sam, stripped naked excepting a pair of hoary and sagging y-front underpants. Michael squinted through the haze and blaze of mid-day summer glare. Jesus. Someone had painted FAT BOY in red lettering across the gaping hills and gullies of Sam's flesh.

Michael killed the engine and quick-stepped his way towards Sam. He was in Sam's direct line of sight. Sam should acknowledge him, show some enthusiasm for help-at-hand. But Sam gazed numbly into the middle-distance, apparently unaware of Michael's presence.

"Sam," he hissed as he confronted the bound and naked bulk. No response. Michael glanced around, wondering where the rubber-neckers might be. The voyeurs, the bystanders. He saw them, two groups in fact, across the road. A pair of wretched housewives standing together, probably lured away from their soaps by the spectacle. Farther up the street he saw a pair of young marrieds standing shoulder to shoulder. They feigned a negligible interest, as if *this show* was no more compelling than the weekly arrival of the garbage men. And now he was on the same stage, he and Sam together, a pitiable double-act. The drunken image of Larry pushed its way into his consciousness for some reason, and Michael once again felt the sting of that grubby baseball cap on his cheek and nose.

"Sam, let's get you out of here."

They had used duct tape, thick grey wads of the stuff, wound several times around wrist, ankle, and metallic fencing. He needed sharp scissors, really, but he wasn't about to walk through that gallery of gawkers to get some from the house. Michael found the edge of the tape on a wrist and began unwinding it, a painfully slow job as each revolution had to be worked back through the fencing. Great tears of sweat ran down Sam's body, and Michael's fingers slipped on the grimy stuff. He freed a wrist and the arm fell with a sickening metallic clang of blubber against fencing. He worked on the other wrist.

"We'll have you out of here in no time."

Sam still displayed no acknowledgement, his eyes far away. Sam stank of… what? Perspiration? Fear? Damage? The ankles were tougher. The routine of unbinding the tape was the same, but it was cramped down there, and Michael began to feel exhausted by the panic and physical effort. Jesus it was hot. Ten minutes more of yanking, tape breaking, starting again, clawing with fingernails, and he had Sam free. He took him by an elbow.

"Come on, let's go." Sam now expressed a vague understanding and he took two jerking steps forwards. But his trembling legs, reduced to jelly, wouldn't support him. Perhaps it was a knee which buckled. Michael watched helplessly as Sam's great bulk dropped heavily to the ground, and quite suddenly Sam was on all fours in the fresh-cut high school grass. Michael noticed that the young marrieds had had the decency to go inside, though he could sense their hidden gaze from behind the curtain. He glared at the gawping housewives, a direct glare which was quite out of character, the experience unnerving and yet strangely pleasant.

He got Sam by the arm again. "Come on Sam, it's not far. Let's get you home."

With Michael's help, Sam grunted himself to his feet and they managed a surreal and inelegant march across the road, up the street, and into the back door of the house. Sam stood there, lifeless and staring numbly at the kitchen floor.

"Jesus Sam, this is awful. Are you all right?"

Sam slowly turned to look at Michael. He then faced the refrigerator, opened the door, and began to look for something. "Shit," said Sam, "shit… shit… ."

"What's wrong?" asked Michael.

"We're out of Budweiser."

An idea occurred to Michael, and he knew with an unfamiliar confidence what he wanted to do. "Sam," he said, taking him by the arm. "This is an awful thing that's happened. Look, I want you to go and take a shower. You'll feel somewhat better for that. And then I want to show you something. But the shower comes first. Come on, let's go." He applied pressure to the slippery margarine bulkiness of the arm, and Sam grunted in appeasement, trudging slowly to the stairs.

Twenty minutes later Sam appeared at the door to his rooms. Michael was relieved to see him normally dressed – well, normal for Sam. But the vacant look was still there in the eyes. Sam said nothing.

"Ah Sam," he said, joining him at the door. "Do you want to see something?" Sam nodded, and he picked up the plastic bag he'd prepared and led him to Mr. Deveroix's attic door. "Ever been up to your grandfather's office?"

"No," said Sam mechanically. "No one was allowed up there. It was always locked."

"Well, he's gone now, isn't he?" said Michael, holding up the set of keys Mrs. Deveroix had given him. Sam shrugged.

They made their way up the stairs and stood together staring at the vast and complex arrangement of tracks, trains, miniature towns, and stations. Sam slowly circled the set, gazing over everything. He stopped at the tall stool in front of the controls and fingered the blue and white conductor's cap. Sam placed the cap on his head and Michael saw a faint grin breach the sorrow momentarily.

"Always wondered what the old dude got up to. Playing with his trains," he said, shaking his head.

"He must have been fairly obsessed with it all," said Michael. "Have a seat over here." He led Sam to the far end of the room. Michael sat at the desk chair and invited Sam to take the plush leather easy chair nearby. Michael placed the plastic shopping bag on the floor. They sat in silence for a few moments.

Sam pointed to the train set. "So what happens to all this stuff?"

"I've called three train shops locally. No one wants it. Apparently if it's not plastic, mass produced, and made in China, no one is interested. You don't want to use it, do you?" That got a slight grin out of Sam.

"Are you kidding?"

Michael sighed. "In that case, it's all going to the Salvation Army. They're sending a truck to pick it up next week."

Sam nodded lethargically, rested a podgy elbow on the desk, and rubbed his plump cheeks and eyes with his hands. Michael noticed angry red marks circumnavigating both wrists. He waited.

"I'm just so tired of this shit. I fucking put up with it all through school. The wedgies, the toilet swirlies, the noogies. And the names – chunky butt, fat ass, lard ass, fat boy… I put up with it, and when I graduated I thought maybe I escaped." Michael wondered what a toilet swirlie was.

"I'm really sorry about what happened Sam. That was a really terrible thing they did. But you're different now. You've got your radio station."

"My radio station?" he said, a look of angry disgust forming. "Three weeks and not one single listener. This is the fucking world wide web. The entire planet has access to Dark Star Radio, and not one human being has gone to my site. Hit counter – 0. Sam – 0. End of story." Sam eyed Michael before continuing. "Know what? I'm off-line." He looked at his watch. "Dark Star went dead about 30 minutes ago, and you know what – it doesn't matter."

"Sam, it does matter. You said that dead air was the greatest sin a DJ could commit, remember?"

"What's the fucking point?"

Michael recalled the first time Sam showed him the radio station, the way Sam had moved tracks over to a pending play list. It wasn't that complicated. "The point is that there are people out there who need you and your station, and you just need to find each other." Sam shrugged.

"Well, you can't give up now. Wait here."

Michael returned five minutes later. "Dark Star Radio lives," he said, mimicking Sam's tone. "I'm playing some group called *My Vulgar Puppy*."

Sam offered him a small smile. "Yeah, they're pretty good."

They fell back into silence, Sam's eyes on the carpet. Michael reached down and lifted the plastic bag onto the desk.

"Sam, I really want to tell you about ale, if that's okay. It's a hobby of mine, and to be fair, I've kept my mouth shut for quite a while about these cheap fizzy largers you're so partial to. That stuff is just padding for potato chips." Michael pulled four bottles out of the bag and lined them up. "What I've got here are examples of four different types of English ale. Lots of countries make ale, but on the whole, no one can touch the Brits. They've been making real ale since the sixteen hundreds and some of those original breweries are still going."

Michael pulled two half pint glasses out of the bag and put them on the table. "Now, we're going to have us a little ale tasting session. We'll start with the lighter ales and work our way up. By the time we finish we'll be a little bit drunk, and you'll know more about great ale than 95% of Americans. First, I'm gonna give you a quick overview of the ales, then we're gonna try each one together, okay?"

Sam nodded heavily, and Michael tapped the first bottle with an index finger. "This is a golden ale. The brewery's called Shepherd Neame and they've been brewing since 1698. An independent family brewery, and man do they know how to do it." Michael tapped the next bottle. This is a straight forward ale. It's by a brewer called Black Sheep. It's an interesting story. The Theakston family made great ale for six generations in a town called Masham in the Yorkshire Dales. Now in the 1980s the family was offered a lot of money to sell out to a big brewery, but Paul Theakston, one of the sons, objected. A big family argument ensued, but Paul was outvoted and the brewery sold. So Paul got mad enough to start his own brewery using all the know-how the Theakston's had built up over the years. And he called his new company Black Sheep Brewery – get it?"

"Yeah," said Sam, "because he'd become the black sheep of the family." Sam smiled begrudgingly, and Michael could tell he liked the story, that he was coming around a bit. He tapped the bottle labeled Black Sheep Ale again. "This is one of the best straight ales in the world, trust me. The secret weapon is Maris Otter malted barley and a very old system of fermentation."

"Okay," said Sam, and Michael spotted a hint of growing interest.

"Next up – a pale ale, sometimes called Indian pale ale. Fuller's Brewery, out of London. Another independent family brewery and they've been brewing since 1845. And finally," Michael said, tapping a bottle with a strange picture of a goblin on the label, "this one is by a brewery called Wynchwood. The ale is called Hobgoblin and it has to be saved for last because of the strength. The strength isn't so much in the alcohol – it's 5.2 percent – but in the flavor. One sip of this and you wouldn't even be able to taste your Budweiser anymore. Plus, I chose the Hobgoblin because I thought the picture on the label would appeal to you."

Michael pointed to the label which displayed a deranged woodland goblin, a jagged axe in his hand, an evil glint in his eye. "Reminds me of your t-shirts," said Michael.

"Yeah," said Sam. "I guess he's pretty messed-up."

Michael waved a hand over the four bottles. Just remember one thing – great ale is all about flavor – that's why you drink it."

"Okay," said Sam.

Michael poured the first beer, the golden ale, equally into their glasses, explaining how to pour at the correct rate so you get the right amount of head. He taught Sam how to look at the color and carbonation, how to get his nose into the glass and how to inhale through his nose as he was taking the ale into his mouth, how to hold the beer on his tongue, and how to work the ale to the back of the mouth.

The sun had been harsh as it came through the skylight window, but it mellowed and melted into an orange glow as it dropped lower, and they just talked and drank ale. Michael told stories about the breweries, explaining the brewing process, telling him about other great ales, and eventually Sam asked questions, coming out of his malignant inner workings. And the images of duct tape and sweat and struggle receded quietly as the flow of ale steadily warmed Sam's insides. Eventually, they came to the final bottle, the Hobgoblin, which Michael shared out into the glasses.

"It's black," said Sam. "Is it like… what's the name of that beer… Guinness?"

"No, Guinness is a stout, and that really is black in color. This is nothing like a stout. Look carefully and you'll see that the Hobgoblin is quite dark, but it's not black. There is a deep reddish hue there."

Sam held the pint glass up to the sky light the way Michael had shown him. "Oh yeah, sort of a reddish-orange color. What type of ale is it then?"

"Technically, it's closest to a brown or ruby ale, but to be honest, this one is hard to categorize. Pay attention closely because the flavors are very complex. You'll need to rely on your nose a lot."

Sam took a sip, and Michael was pleased to see that he was getting it right. He was paying attention to everything. He wouldn't look out of place at any beer festival. He even looked… sophisticated. But then the big lad threw in the Sam element.

"Fuuuuuck," Sam sighed. "Fuck, that is amazing. What is that? What am I tasting?"

"Come on," said Michael. "What is it then?"

"It's a bit chocolaty… and slightly… spicy… no, not spicy, I mean spiced."

"Yes, very good. But what else?"

Sam sniffed deeply at the bubbling dark liquid and took another sip, exhaling heavily.

"It makes me think of flowers… oh wait, fruit, yeah, it's fruity."

"Yes, exactly! You've got it. Sam, you've really got a knack for ale. Chocolaty, spiced, fruity… yes, those are all there. A hint of caramel as well."

"How do they do it – how do they get all that into a beer."

"The flavors' are partly due to the brewing process, but they mainly come from the hops and malts. This ale uses fuggles and styrians hops and a combination of pale, crystal and chocolate malts. A complex mix of the best ingredients. You could compare brewing ale to baking bread. It's all about what goes into the process. Your fizzy pilsners are like Wonder Bread – very little in the way of interesting ingredients, so very little flavor – it fills you up and gets you drunk. That's it."

"You can get drunk on Wonder Bread?" Sam's timing and the look of feigned incredulity on his face was perfect, and they both laughed. Sam said, "So is there more… more to know, then?"

"It's endless Sam. Wheat ales, porters, double bocks, trappist ales, black beers, Scottish ales… there's no end to it. You'll love certain ales, dislike some, and just appreciate others."

They sat in silence and sipped ale for a couple of minutes. Michael eventually pointed at the four empty bottles. "So which one was your favorite?"

Sam gazed at the bottles and then at the carpet for what seemed like a long time. Michael noticed that Sam's eyes were fixed and defocused, and the big boy seemed to be remembering, rather than reflecting. Sam's eyes filled suddenly with silent tears, and he took a large breath of air which he released painfully.

"The Black Sheep," he said.

CHAPTER 29

A group of thieves planed a robbery of a van on its way to Heathrow airport. They were successful in stealing the van, which they believed to be transporting a large amount of money. They were disappointed to discover that the van contained 75 million dollars in monopoly money, which was on its way to the Czech Republic to be used as part of a TV advertisement.

From the journals of Professor Charles Kidding, extract #126

Three pm. Michael and Larry sat on their bench staring into the sun-drenched oak trees. Michael had got himself more organized this time. He had discovered that the moped could take a small cooler on the back, and he'd put a couple of ales and a bottle of red for Larry in there. Larry had finished his own bottle and had just started on Michael's. They'd talked over Mary's art exhibit. Michael could see that Larry admired her. They were as nuts as one another, so that wasn't really surprising.

Michael had been working up to something, waiting perhaps for Larry to get just a bit drunker, but not *too* drunk. He was catching onto Larry's pattern. He seemed to start drinking in the early afternoon, and by 5 or 6 pm Larry could be pretty out of it. Now was probably as good a time as any.

"Larry, something strange has been happening to me. It's something which has never happened before, so it's pretty upsetting." Michael watched Larry closely, noting how Larry just stared into the park, static as a distant island. Michael used to wonder if Larry was listening. He never did the things people do to *convey* that they were listening – making eye contact, nodding their heads and going hmm, hmm, smiling in acknowledgement at the right moments – and Michael used to wonder if

Larry heard anything. But he knew better now. Larry was listening alright, closely. He continued. "There have been a couple of occasions when I've been walking – I mean I was right in my own neighborhood or close to it – and... well... I seemed to get lost. I mean I couldn't figure out where my house was. I felt all turned-around. Like I said, it's never happened before."

Michael waited for a response, but Larry just took another sip and continued staring into the trees and blue sky. "I actually had to get help finding my way back, and when I did eventually see where my house was, it was like the whole neighborhood had been rearranged momentarily." Michael paused for a minute.

"So then... what's up?" asked Larry.

"What do you mean?" said Michael.

"I mean, what's the crisis?"

"There's no crisis, really." Michael stared into the trees for a moment and took a large breath and blew it out slowly before continuing. "This may sound ridiculous, but a few weeks ago my car and wallet were stolen and I lost all my identification, and I'm having a hard time getting it replaced. It's unbelievably frustrating." Michael glanced at Larry again, wondering if he believed him. There was no way to tell from Larry's expression. "I've been to the doctors, had a bunch of tests, but apparently there's *nothing* wrong with me.

"Does it feel like there's nothing wrong?" asked Larry.

"No! There's definitely something wrong. My doctor said my problem was idiosyncratic – I'm not even sure I understand what that means – is that like when something happens for no reason at all?"

"Idiosyncratic," said Larry, "is when something occurs for no *apparent* reason."

Michael and Larry took a long swig of drink at the same time and stared out into the park. "Anyways," said Michael, "it's just really unsettling not being able to find your own house."

Larry grinned. "More like you can't find your own *home*."

"What's the difference?" asked Michael.

"Sounds to me like you're *not at home*," said Larry, "that you're suffering an acute case of not-at-homeness."

Michael's brows pulled together in an involuntary act of bewilderment. "What do you mean?"

"You're uprooted, estranged – a foreigner in your own country. It's probably for the best."

"Larry, what are you talking about? This is *not* for the best. I feel like I'm losing my mind."

Larry looked over at him now, and Michael saw genuine sympathy in those bleary, bloodshot blue eyes. "That's scary," said Larry. "Feeling like you're losing your mind. Like you'll come apart. I'm sorry about that Michael, I really am. But maybe something can come of it."

Larry poured another glass for himself and motioned to Michael's glass. "Have another drink – I'll get you some crackers." Larry pulled crackers, cheese, and a knife out of his bag and went to work, cutting strips of cheddar against the bench seat. Michael sighed heavily and poured a second ale. His annoyance with the conversation seemed to affect his pouring, and the ale built up too much of a head. He accepted a couple a crackers from Larry and they sat quietly for a few moments. Maybe he needed to explain things better.

"Larry, I just feel like before all this started happening I knew what was going on. Okay, maybe my life wasn't very exciting, but I was in control. I got up and I decided what I was going to do. I thought things through and I made choices, and then I did what I wanted."

"You were in charge were you? Choosing your life. Imposing all that free will onto things."

"Well… mostly, yes. Okay, I don't sleep so well. But I was getting by. And yeah, I could mostly decide what to do with my life."

Larry blew out a big breath, a strange grunting noise coming out with it. "Freedom, huh? Our inalienable right, yeah? Like the constitution says."

"Well… yes, I make choices about my life. That's how people feel in control, isn't it?"

"I don't get too excited about free will," said Larry. "I can will myself to pay my taxes or regrout my shower, but I can't will my heart to beat. I can no sooner will myself to fall asleep than I can will myself to fall in love. Look at what happened to most of the *philosophers of the will.* Freidrich Nietzsche beat the will power drum throughout his career and spent the last years of his life on a psychiatric ward. Ayn Rand did the same thing and she just annoyed a lot of people and ended up bitter, jealous, and alone. You ever pull yourself up by your own bootstraps?"

"What? What do you mean?" Michael noticed a tone of exasperation in his own voice.

"Think about that for a moment. Imagine pulling yourself up by your own bootstraps. Go on, *will* yourself up by your own bootstraps." Michael tried imagining that. He saw himself down on the ground and wearing a pair of black boots with straps, and then pulling at those straps – he had to admit that no one could actually pull themselves up by their own bootstraps. That saying was sort of irrational. But this really wasn't helping.

"Larry, surely people can think things through. They can evaluate options and make choices. They can bring order to their lives. I did it for years and I was fine most of the time."

Larry sipped his wine and reflected. "Okay, people make choices, sure. But then what happens? Huh? Have you ever heard the story of Elizabeth Bunting?"

"No," replied Michael. Larry smiled broadly and started chuckling to himself. He wasn't slurring his words much, but he was somewhat giddy.

"The celebrated Professor Charles Kidding told me this story. Nearing forty, a woman from Roanoke Virginia named Elizabeth Bunting became ever more aware of her husband's roving eye. Feeling insecure, she underwent breast enlargement surgery, increasing her bust from a respectable 34C to a staggering 37 DD. Two weeks following surgery, her husband runs off with his secretary. Feeling at a loose end, Elizabeth did the only thing she could think of – she drove to the local grocery store to get more dog food for Benjamin the dachshund. But Elizabeth drove to the grocery store in a despondent and enraged manner, which is to say that she drove *badly*. On route she managed a head-on collision with a tree at 40 miles an hour – I believe it was an oak. The airbag failed to deploy, and in her poorly state she had neglected to fasten her seatbelt. The result was that her upper body slammed into the steering wheel. Elizabeth Bunting was very badly bruised, but…" Larry raised an eyebrow and lifted a single index finger… "her substantial silicone implants provided the necessary padding to protect her internal organs from any life-threatening damage." He stared at Michael, that sloppy grin on his face. "Now…" announced Larry, "what can we learn from that story?"

Michael squinted in the heat, his head feeling foggy. He really didn't know what Larry was driving at. "Is it something about her self-esteem," he suggested. "I mean if she'd had more self-esteem then she wouldn't need to get her breasts enlarged."

"Very likely, but that's not what I was thinking of," said Larry. "The moral of that story is that a boob job may not save your marriage, but it just might save your life." Larry grinned, a crooked and triumphant grin, but then suddenly looked as confused as Michael felt. Larry stared into space, straining to recall something. "No, wait a minute," he continued, "that wasn't the moral. What I meant was that you can't really know what the right decision is. You make decisions and it's impossible to predict what will happen. It could all seem to go wrong but then end up alright. Or it could all go great, and then go wrong, and then who knows what's next. You decide to turn left and you end up down the wrong street. So in a way, yeah, boob jobs might not save your marriage, but they might save your life. Is this making any sense?"

Michael gazed at Larry, feeling a mixture of disbelief, annoyance, and confusion. "No Larry, not much. You know, I make my living by predicting the future, and I'm pretty damn good at it."

Larry slapped him on the shoulder. "Good for you. Let's have some more crackers." Larry cut more slices of cheese and handed Michael two more crackers. They sat quietly for a while, sipping cold beer and wine in the sunshine, gazing at the dappled sunlight on the grass and pavement.

"Did I ever tell you how Charles Kidding died?" asked Larry.

Michael opened his mouth to tell Larry that he had – something about Charles being backed over by a car – but Larry began speaking before he could answer. "They said Charles died from a congenital weakness of the spleen, but what really killed him was the accidental discovery of the ultimate logical fallacy, an extraordinary example of what's called *affirming the consequent*."

Michael sighed heavily. "What's affirming the consequent?"

"It's when you make an argument where the conclusion is not supported by the premise, like if I say, *when people have the flu they cough – I am coughing, therefore I have the flu.* The conclusion can't really follow from the premise. Charles reasoned that arguments are constructed by humans, and human existence is itself preposterous and illogical. And since the preposterous human being making the argument needs to be considered part of the argument, a part of the premise, then *every* conclusion is preposterous and invalid. When Charles realized this he thought that he had destroyed philosophy and he started laughing, and he laughed so hard and for so long that his spleen burst and he drowned in his own spleen bile, which is more poisonous than rattlesnake venom."

Larry shook with laughter and wine slopped out of his glass and onto his trousers.

Michael squinted in the mid-day sun. "Larry, that's ridiculous."

"Charles would have liked to hear you say that – a ridiculous death for a ridiculous man. But I'll tell you what's really ridiculous. There was nothing in Charles Kidding's last will and testament except a request that people not bring flowers to his funeral because he's allergic to them. Now *that's* ridiculous."

Michael considered pointing out that previously Larry had said that Charles Kidding had died in a car accident, not from drowning in spleen bile, but he didn't seem to have it in him.

Larry laughed again, but he must have noticed the slim line of despondency on Michael's face, because he lost the joviality suddenly. He elbowed Michael gently.

"Hey, I'm sorry. Sometimes I don't take things as seriously as I should." Michael didn't reply. Larry put his hand on Michael's arm and squeezed it. "I don't want you to crack up. That's bad – I mean cracking up."

Michael smiled faintly. "I don't want to crack up either."

CHAPTER 30

Ernest Digweed of Palm Springs, Florida left his entire estate to "Jesus Christ, Our Savior", guaranteeing Jesus an annual income of $615,820 over the next thirty years. Digweed's will is currently being contested by family members.

From the journals of Professor Charles Kidding, extract #129.

Late evening. It was warm, but there was a light breeze blowing through the curtains in Michael's bedroom. He and Mary lay next to one another, under a thin sheet, the moonlight casting its pale blue glow about the room. He'd done something he had never done before – he'd asked Mary to come earlier in the week. Their visits had been as regular as the tides, but he had needed to be in her company, needed to sink into her feminine softness and aromas, needed help in forgetting himself for a while. She hadn't seemed surprised, somehow. She looked at him now, head propped on a crooked wrist, listening, as if expecting him to speak his thoughts.

"That watch at your gallery," he said, "the one labeled Michael's Watch. Were you thinking of me?" Mary nodded. "Michael's Watch…" he continued. "It wasn't really my watch, but it was my problem, wasn't it? Why did you do that?"

Mary emitted a long exhalation through a smile, a drawn-out *mmmmm* sound escaping her nose. She rested a thin hand on his bare shoulder. "Are you angry with me?"

"No," he replied, and it was true. In fact, the gesture had made him feel somewhat important, or… at least necessary.

"After we spoke about your problem," said Mary, "I imagined your wristwatch for a while. At first it was just a chunk of plastic and glass, but

I waited and watched. Then I saw two wrist watches, but without their straps. They were wind-up wrist watches – really good tickers. And I imagined sewing them into the sides of a winter woolen hat, and I saw you wearing that hat, the watches right over your ears, ticking away. I was going to do it – I was going to get some good tickers and sew them into the hat and give it to you as a gift. But then the idea of the death watch came to mind and Burt helped me put that together instead. I've got to introduce you to Burt sometime. He's an older fellow, a friend of mine. He's very good with philosophy and the mechanics of art."

Michael smiled, intrigued and amused, pleased to have played such a role in Mary's life outside his bedroom. "I'm glad you didn't give me the ticking hat… but that was nice… I mean it was nice you thought of me."

"Don't call me nice, Michael. If you call me nice then I will have to be very mean to you." Michael thought she was kidding, but wasn't entirely sure.

"How did Burt make the watch say *death*?" He asked.

"I'm not sure exactly. I think it was a talking watch to begin with – the sort of thing blind people wear. I think Burt got some help reprogramming it or something. I leave all that to him."

Michael stared at the bed sheets and wondered if he felt okay about Mary using his problem with time in this way. "Hey," said Mary, placing her hand under his chin and bringing his eyes to hers. "The death watch was for you and it was about you. I want you to have that watch when the exhibit is over. Didn't you know that? I did it for you."

Michael grinned in acknowledgement, embarrassed that she had read his thoughts so easily. "Thank you. You know, I understand the death watch. I know what you were trying to say to me. It was interesting but… ." Michael looked away and went into himself for a moment before continuing. "It didn't help with my problem – I mean, I still hate the sound of ticking clocks."

"Well, so much for psychoanalysis," said Mary. "So much for the idea that insight sets you free. Hey – what's your favorite organ?"

"What?"

"Your favorite organ. What is it? The liver? Pancreas? Kidneys?"

"Well… I sort of like them all," replied Michael.

"You wanna know what my favorite organ is? My favorite organ is the appendix. Know why?"

"Not really."

"Most people think the appendix is useless, some hangover from humanity's biological evolution. But the appendix is incredibly important. Throughout the whole of our lives we have this little sack of poison inside us, *ticking* away, and it could blow-up at any time and kill us. That's the function of the appendix – to continually remind us of our mortality. We should all meditate on our appendix a couple of times a day. No one seems to *get* the appendix, despite the clues around us.

"Clues?"

"Well," continued Mary, "the appendix in a book comes *at the end* and contains a reference to everything important in the whole book. How did we miss that clue?"

"I don't know."

They were quiet for a while, each listening to their own thoughts and the industrious crickets out on the lawn. Michael considered pursuing Mary's thoughts about the appendix, but he wasn't sure what else to say, and the far away look in her eyes suggested she was thinking about something else.

"You know what happened at *Mega Home Supply*?" Michael asked.

"Hmm," she said sleepily.

"The way you were… I mean how angry you got, it surprised me." Mary just nodded, acknowledging what he'd said. "I didn't really like seeing you so angry."

Mary looked down into the sheets, as if remembering, and then her eyes found his again. "Just think about what that cashier is told to do – to ask everyone for their phone number, and then those robots just hand their number over. No one thinks to ask why it's happening? The cashier doesn't ask why he's doing it, the customer's don't think to ask why a corporation wants their number, the assistant manager doesn't even know what's going on. Everyone becomes an *object* for someone else, and the worst bit is that they don't even know that they're being turned into objects. And all I did was I said 'You know what, I think I'd rather not be an object today'. And what happened then Michael? Holy hell broke out. For a brief moment, something started to break down in the system, and then – bang! The system had to hit back. Now isn't that interesting?"

"But does it really matter if people mention their number? Asking for numbers is just part of a routine – it's a commonplace."

Mary shrugged. "Well, I have a low tolerance for the commonplace. You can make *good trouble*, you know. And by the way, you were disruptive too. A camera man with attitude. You're part of the team now."

"What team?"

"You, me, and Burt. I've got to introduce you to Burt sometime."

They lay in silence for a while and Michael thought about this Burt fellow and wondered when Mary would leave. She always stayed for a while after sex, but she never stayed over night. Michael didn't want her to stay over exactly, but he liked her being here right now. He suddenly worried that he'd forgotten to put two hundred dollars in the cup by the door, but then recalled that he had.

Telling Larry about the loss of his identification had been alright. Mary would probably find it interesting – she'd probably manage to read something into in. So he told her what happened, giving her all the details, even telling her about the external validation forms.

"You want me to sign a form for you?" she asked.

Michael smiled. "Have you paid taxes in the last few years?" he asked.

"Not exactly," said Mary, a wry smile on her face.

Michael smiled appreciatively, but he didn't imagine Mary would count as a 'person of legitimate standing in the community'.

Mary was silent, alone in her own thoughts, and Michael wondered if she was thinking about his identification problem, or something else.

CHAPTER 31

A preacher at an Alabama funeral made derogatory remarks about the deceased, and was attacked by some of those present. Reverend Orlando Bethal described the late Lish Taylor as "a drunkard and a fornicator" who was "burning in hell". When family members turned his microphone off, the preacher continued by using a megaphone. Eventually, mourners rushed the podium and dragged Bethal down the isle.

From the journals of Professor Charles Kidding, extract #198

Michael maneuvered the moped between lanes, working his way over to the park. Even before he reached the curb, he could tell something was up. There were far more people in the park than normal, and they seemed to be grouped around something at the park's centre. A noisy and edgy buzz came from the crowd, and he wondered if there was a fight going on, or maybe one about to start. He climbed off the moped and headed for the crowd. It was 9:15 pm, a Saturday night, and an eerie twilight glow hung in the trees and seeped over the grass and benches, a surreal mixture of fading day and the pale yellow light thrown from the park lamps.

Michael walked past Larry's empty bench, noticing that the philosopher's CD player and headphones were on the ground, the player fatally cracked. As Michael approached, he could see that there were about seventy people in the crowd. This was a discordant gathering – youths that looked like gang members, a couple of small groups of well-dressed people who had most likely been out to dinner, handfuls of college kids who had probably come from the local bars and dance clubs. Some of the people drank from cans of beer, others were smoking. He worked himself to the edge of the circled crowd and his heart sank. Leaning against the marble base of the central park statue was Larry, disheveled and bleeding from his forehead, a wine bottle clutched in his hand. The crowd was in a raucous mood, and seemed to be egging him on.

"Come on… more, more."

"Encore… encore … ."

Whistling, clapping, hooting. Larry's frame swung in a slow and drunken rhythm, his eyes to the pavement, his body slumped. What sort of performance was he giving? And then quite suddenly Larry held his arms aloft, wine spilling from his bottle, and looked up. The crowd cheered.

"Cas ino the infin… ." Larry shook his head like a boxer trying to regain his senses, and started again. "Cast ino the infinite immensity of spaces of which I am ignorant, and which know me not, I am frightened." Larry shook his head, this time in sadness. More cheers and whistles. "*Which know me not.* Oh Pascal, where are you – poor humanity needs ya an your compassion." Larry's form slumped and he looked down again. Hooting and shouts of encouragement, but Michael could see there was an enormous gulf between the sad form of Larry and the Saturday night revelers who had found an impromptu form of cheap amusement.

Larry's arms shot heavenward again and he looked over his audience. "More than the overawing infinity of cosmic spaces and times, more than the quantitative disproportion, more than the insignificance of man as a magnitude in this vastness, it is the silence, the indifference of the universe to human aspirations…" Larry looked to the heavens, raising his arms and bottle further… "which constitutes the utter loneliness of man in the sum of things." The crowd shouted and applauded in mock appreciation. And yet, Michael was amazed at how Larry had been able to speak these words – how he had been able to talk with such an articulate and striking tone, given his drunken state. He had the impression that Larry knew these words so well that the booze did not unseat him. The crowd continued to cheer and clap but Larry's shoulders had slumped again and his head hung down wearily – his speech apparently at an end.

And then the first beer can sailed over the heads of the onlookers, smacking into President Lincoln's stone shoe, ten inches from Larry's head. The response was mixed, some in the crowd calling for more, others unsure they wanted it to go this way. The next can spewed beer as it spun and hit Larry in the knee. Larry looked up, stunned, confused.

"A stoning eh? Is zat it? A good ole fashion stoning," shouted Larry. Many in the crowd cheered, clearly thinking that a beer can stoning was a good idea. Larry raised a hand. "We are all guilty…" he said. A youth near Michael turned to his friend and spoke. "Yeah, you guilty Leroy." The youth replied, "Fuck you Marcus – you guilty." They both laughed. Larry continued. "We are all marooned. We are forever and always falling. There is no final absolution. Humanity… dear humanity… creatures stricken by the need to understand… you, me… each moment in time is never consumed entirely, each moment leaves a little trail of smoke and dirty ash in its wake, and we are the greedy beggars with a neo-cortex large enough to notice." Larry passed his hand over the crowd, as if to indicate all before him. "You were there, standing on the cliff edge and shouting into that dark wind and starless night. You were there calling out again and again until there is no more voice left…" (shouts and cheers) "… but the universe was deaf, preoccupied with itself. Dearest humanity... ." Michael noticed a teenage boy near the front of the crowd. The kid was edging closer to Larry, a beer can tucked in at his side, egged on by other youths behind him. "…Dearest humanity, the field mouse scurries in the crop rows in sunlight and the shadow of the hawk passes over..." Only six feet from Larry, the teen hurled the half-empty can, hitting Larry square on the forehead with a metallic thud. Larry stopped speaking and stared at the shouting and applauding group of youths, then at the rest of the crowd. Suddenly, Larry's face screwed up into a knot of anger and he shouted indiscernibly and stumbled forward in blind rage, the wine bottle bumping softly on the grass. The teenager turned to run but tripped and fell. Michael sensed the whole crowd constrict on itself, moving together as if it were one organism. He lost sight of Larry and found himself pressing in on the other bodies, desperate to see what was happening. Michael got close enough to make out Larry and the youth, both on the ground. The teen was on his back, Larry straddling his stomach. Peering through the bodies, Michael could see that Larry gripped hard at the lapels of the boy's jean jacket, up near his neck. The youth punched out, but Larry's long sinewy arms kept him just out of range.

"Get the fuck off, get the fuck off you freak," the youth screamed – anger, fear, and humiliation written on his face. But Larry's knotted fists had the boy bolted to the ground. The youths circled and screamed encouragement. "Fuck him up Johnnie, mash the old fucker." The crowd hooted and shouted. Michael wondered if he should do something, but maybe Larry had things under control in his own way. A titanic struggle was taking place between these odd opponents, the teen turning red in the face, trying to punch and twist his way out from under Larry, and Larry sitting there, steady as a Buddha, pushing the boy into the earth with all his drunken strength.

"Get the fuck ooffff meee!" the boy screamed.

"You wan me to stop?" shouted Larry, "then you answer a question, and you answer it correctly. If you don get it right, I will hol you down for all eternidy. Like Atlas bearing the weight of the heavens on his back, I will push you down until the end of time you little shit!"

"Fuck you, you fucking nut case," the boy screamed. Someone in the crowd shouted, "Answer the question," and then several others joined in until it became a chant – *Answer-the-question, Answer-the-question, Answer-the-question.* The chant gave way to clapping and whistling and the crowd waited, a sense of anticipation now in the air.

Finally, Larry spoke, his words coming slowly and with a great effort at enunciation: "Two truck drivers neglect to have their brakes serviced at the appropriate time. A month later the brakes on one of the twucks fail and the dwiver kills a child as a result. The brakes on the other truck do not fail and no harm is done. Which driver is more morally culpable?"

An eerie quiet came over the crowd, and Michael could hear hushed voices as people talked to one another and the grunts of the youth as he continued to strain against the force of Larry's clenched fists.

"What… the…fuck are you talking about?" the youth yelled. Some chuckles from the crowd. "Answer the question…" Larry shouted. "Which driver is more so in the wrong. Answer correctly or you will never leave this place."

"Yeah, answer the question," someone shouts. The crowd became quiet, and a serious edge crept into the local atmosphere.

The teen continued to struggle, but Michael noticed that his eyes moved upward and to the left, as if thinking "They're both the same," the boy spit out. "It was an accident. They should have fixed the brakes, but it was just an accident."

Larry's grip tightened and Michael could see the strain in his face and neck muscles multiply. "Wrong," he shouted at the youth. "Wrong answer. The driver who killed the child is *more* at fault. Now you'll have to pay for your miztake." The teen's eyes enlarged and he redoubled his effort to escape, punching and flailing, but Larry's grip was overwhelming. The crowd shouted and closed in tighter as people strained to get a closer look. A man close to the struggle shouted, "No, the kid was right," and a few others support his conclusion, but Larry is not listening. A shrill whistle sounded and Michael noticed the crowd parting opposite him. Four large city police officers appear from the opposite side of the park, and begin to push themselves roughly through the crowd. Seconds later, they have ripped Larry off the boy. More hooting and clapping. "CLEAR OUT PLEASE, THIS IS A POLICE MATTER, GIVE US SPACE TO WORK," an officer shouts. Michael lost sight of Larry and the boy as a sea of bodies swarmed about him. When he spotted Larry again, he and the boy were ringed in by the four officers. Another police van appeared behind Michael and several officers piled out. The crowd was breaking up now, spilling towards the edges of the park, no doubt heading for the next source of entertainment. The officers dispersed the remnants of the crowd. Michael tried to make his way back to Larry, but an officer grabbed him hard by an arm and told him to leave the park. Michael made his way to his moped, somber and perplexed.

Michael entered through the back door and moved quietly through the kitchen. He checked his watch, 10:10 pm, and wondered if Mrs. Deveroix was still up. At the foot of the stairs, he heard her voice coming from the living room.

"Michael, is that you?"

He entered the living room to find Mrs. Deveroix on the couch. "Good evening," he said.

"Your friend came by earlier," said the old woman.

"My friend?" queried Michael, but he knew it had to be Mary.

"Your lady friend, the one who visits you."

"Oh, yes?" he said.

"She said she wanted to drop something off for you. She went up to your rooms. I hope that's okay?"

"Yes, of course, that's fine," said Michael, his curiosity greater than any irritation he might have felt.

Michael turned on the lights in his living room, bedroom, and kitchen and searched the place thoroughly, finding nothing. Feeling irritated and weary, he decided he'd have a bowl of cereal before bed, and opened the refrigerator door. He pulled the milk carton out and was struck immediately by the image affixed to its side. Mystified and intrigued, he placed the carton on the kitchen table, sat down, and inspected it carefully. What he saw there was a black and white photo of himself. The photo had been glued to a piece of white paper, neatly trimmed and attached to the side of the carton. There were words printed beneath the photo.

MISSING
Michael Wilson
If you see Michael or have any helpful information,
please call 555-0172

Michael smiled and shook his head. The telephone number was his own.

CHAPTER 32

Bruno Isliker, of Oberseen Switzerland, has astounded equestrian fans by training a cow to show-jump. Bruno has ridden Sybille the cow through several clear rounds. He hopes to take Sybille to her first proper competition next month in Zurich.

From the journals of Professor Charles Kidding, extract #34.

Michael woke even earlier than normal, 3:10 am. His head throbbed with the lack of sleep and he felt angry without seeming to have an object for his anger. He went to the bathroom and returned to bed with some Vaseline, grabbing a t-shirt from the laundry on route. Maybe having a wank might relax him. He imagined Mary and saw her standing before him, her form bathed in the soft street lighting which had seeped through his bedroom curtains on so many evenings. And then he found himself recalling the softness of Julie's breasts and the hardness of Julie pressing against his groin. The erotic production beneath his sheets was going quite well until he realized he was thinking about the other man Mary helps, the one with the fixation on white high-healed shoes, and that *nearly* ruined it.

It wasn't as if he was jealous of that guy. It wasn't as if he wanted Mary for himself. It was just that he didn't want to think of Mary in that way. She was supposed to represent something else. He wondered if he was as screwed up as that guy. Probably not as *sexually* screwed up, but he was getting lost in his own neighborhood and sleeping worse than normal, and now he was getting so preoccupied with sexual deviants that he could barely pull off a decent hand-job. He chucked the damp t-shirt into the nearby laundry basket and checked his alarm clock: 3:32 AM.

By mid-afternoon, Michael stood in the middle of his living room, wondering what to do next. An agitated lethargy crawled over his skin as he gazed into space, vague images dropping into his mind. He had discovered a couple of promising financial trends in the news this morning at Starbucks, but he couldn't be bothered to place a futures bid. What did he need with more money? It was as if his continued interest in the markets was driven by a reflex – more habit than choice. He had finished the carton of milk which Mary had altered, with his breakfast cereal and he'd washed the carton and put it on a shelf. That milk carton was humorous, but there was a dark edge to it as well. Mary's work was sort of like that, come to think of it. Funny and serious. He wondered how Larry was.

Michael shook his head, trying to break this malevolent reverie. He had to *move*. Keeping still was like fuel for these thoughts. He wandered aimlessly, finding himself standing in front of his CD collection, idly inspected the tidy edges of the plastic cases. He ran a finger along the CDs, just to make sure they were properly aligned. They'd been arranged alphabetically, starting with Bach and ending with Wagner. He decided to reorder them by period – baroque, classical, romantic, modern. It was necessary to look up a few composers to make sure he got them all in the right period, but an hour later the job was finished, and the 200 or so CDs were rearranged. He typed up and printed out little labels for each period and blue-tacked them to the appropriate places on the shelving. Then he wondered if he should have the labels laminated, and this thought depressed him because he realized just then that he didn't want labels, and that he preferred the CDs in their original alphabetical order. He hadn't listened to any of these CDs for weeks anyway, and even when he did it was only Mozart and Beethoven he liked. Why did he have all these CDs? Sam's music was about as enjoyable as hitting yourself repeatedly in the head with a ballpean hammer, but at least he seemed to enjoy it.

The phone rang, and Michael felt relief in the realization that this event took away the need to make the next decision.

"Hello."

"Michael, what are you doing?" he heard Mary say. "Can you get down to *Tasco's Odds and Ends*. I want you to meet Burt. Plus, Burt's got a great scam in mind." Michael heard a voice in the background, presumably Burt's. "It's not a scam, it's a mysterious happening."

"Right, Burt's discovered a mysterious happening, and we'll need your intrepid cameraman skills." This was vintage Mary – an incapacity for small talk of almost disabling proportions, a heedless need for going straight to the point, or, more likely, beyond the point.

Michael followed Mary's directions and twenty minutes later found himself parked in front of a shabby junk shop. Michael entered *Tasco's,* spotting Mary and Burt at a desk in the back of the empty shop. They were chuckling over something as he approached.

"Michael," said Mary, "meet Burt Tasco – Burt, this is my friend Michael." They shook hands in the conventional way. "Ah," said Mary. "Burt's given you the secret handshake. You're one of us now."

Michael's eyebrows converged in puzzlement. "But it was just a normal handshake."

"Well," replied Mary, "it is and it isn't. We don't want others to learn the nature of the secret handshake, so we disguise it as a normal handshake."

"But how do you know when someone is giving you a secret handshake or just a normal one?" asked Michael. Mary and Burt locked eyes for a few moments, perhaps searching one another for some answer. Finally, Burt shrugged and answered. "I think ya just know." Mary nodded in agreement.

"But…" Michael started, and then felt at a loss for words.

"Maybe he's right," Mary said to Burt. "How about this – we'll keep the secret handshake as is, but if we meet an outsider we don't know, we'll shake hands with them like this." She and Burt enacted a complicated handshake of evolving grips and positions which culminated in a strange whistling noise they made as they locked thumbs and their hands fluttered up and down like a headless bird. They laughed and Michael joined in self-consciously.

"Go get yourself a cup of coffee or tea," said Burt, indicating a door behind him. Michael made himself a cup of tea in the back room, feeling like he'd been let into something, but not grasping what. He put his mug down on Burt's desk and sat down with them.

"Go on Burt, tell Michael about the manhole people," said Mary.

Burt smiled. "I was just telling Mary about something I saw earlier. I drove by the Firebrand plant this morning about 7:30 am, and I got stuck in a traffic jam just in front of the employee parking lot. The lot was fairly empty, and I noticed that there were about eight employees standing in the lot. But the weird thing was that they were all standing alone, maybe about fifty feet from one another, and they were spread out in a way which looked oddly symmetrical. It looked weird, unnatural."

"Tell him about the mist," said Mary.

"Well, it was early morning, and there was fog around the place. Seeing all these people in that fog was really eerie."

"Like Jane Goodall watching the chimps in the mist," said Mary.

"That was Diane Fossey," said Burt, "and she watched gorillas – the film was called *Gorillas in the Mist.*

"Burt – you're so literal," said Mary.

"Factual, my dear," replied Burt. Mary rolled her eyes.

"Anyway," continued Burt, "there were two security guards standing close to the road and I was stuck in traffic, so I asked them – I said 'how come those people are standing in the parking lot like that?' And one of the guards says, 'the company banned smoking anywhere on *company property*, and some wise-ass figured out that the manhole covers in the parking lot were City property'. I looked again and saw that all these people were smoking, each one standing on their own manhole cover."

"*Smokers in the Mist*, as documented by Mary, Burt, and Michael," said Mary.

"She wants to film it," said Burt.

Burt's Ford Pinto, circa 1976, farted out a rich cloud of black smoke when the old man started it up. Mary had insisted that Michael sit up front, explaining that if people sat behind her and stared at the back of her head, she felt compelled to kill them. Michael felt a spark of anxiety at the remark, but Burt and Mary laughed so hard that he relaxed. Even Michael felt disappointed when they reached the Firebrand Plant. They could make out the symmetrically spaced man hole covers in the nearly empty employee parking lot, but there were no smokers standing on their circular islands in this ocean of black top. It was Mary who had approached the guard house to ask what was up. She returned a moment later and told them that there are set break periods, and the manhole people weren't due to come down to the parking lot for another hour and a half.

"It's not right anyway," said Mary. "It's all sunny now – we need that mist you saw Burt."

Mary got in the backseat and leaned forward between them. "So what shall we do?" asked Burt.

"Hey Michael," said Mary, you know your friend? The disgraced philosopher. Let's go see him."

Michael recalled the beer can stoning from last night. He had been thinking he'd like to see Larry, make sure he was okay. But maybe he was in jail. Even if he wasn't, he felt uncomfortable seeing him with Mary and Burt. He was likely to be in rough shape.

"I don't know," said Michael. "I'm not sure that's a good idea today."

"Oh, come on," said Mary. "Burt would love to meet him."

Michael looked over at Burt. "Larry's a bit peculiar."

"Are you kidding?" said Mary. "We specialize in peculiar."

Burt nodded in agreement. "That's true," the old man said.

Michael agreed and gave directions while Burt drove. They were quiet for most of the ride and Michael felt on edge. A few weeks ago, his life had ticked along nicely – well, maybe not nicely, maybe adequately – and now he was being driven by some old fellow with Mary onboard, and they were off to see some drunkard. Michael half-hoped Larry wouldn't be there, but he spotted the dirty baseball cap as they pulled up to the park. What were they going to talk about? Michael was pretty good at starting conversations. He had some skills in that area, but those skills seemed to apply better to conventional situations. What were these three odd balls going to say? Maybe it was four oddballs, anyway – what made him so damn sane at the moment?

They walked to the park, rounded Larry's bench and stood there, the three of them, looking down on the bum. Larry lay back on the bench, eyes closed, hands folded in his lap. He looked like shit, like a man who'd been run over several times by a lawn mower. There were cuts and caked blood on his forehead and arms, masses of dirt beneath his fingernails, and his powder blue nylon slacks were filthy. Jesus, he was even missing one of his basketball shoes. As Michael stared at the grubby sock, images of last night flashed before his eyes – that beer can hitting Larry in the head, the rage he'd seen as Larry had tried to hold that kid down for ever, that strange question he'd put to the kid.

"He doesn't look so hot," whispered Burt. Michael felt embarrassed.

"Don't let the packaging fool you Burt," said Mary. "The *man* is quality."

"Where does he live?" asked Burt.

"I'm not sure," said Michal. "I never asked him. I think maybe he just lives here, in the park."

A shrill ringing suddenly shattered the peacefulness of the park, and Michael jumped, startled. Larry stirred to life slowly and reached with a practiced hand into his duffle bag. He pulled out a digital alarm clock and turned it off. Larry rubbed his eyes, still unaware of them. Finally, he opened his eyes and gazed dumbly into space.

Larry spoke, though it was difficult to tell if he was addressing them, or the world itself. "Each morning," he said groggily, "I wake and brush my teeth, have breakfast, and go out into the world… and I always have the same thought: This isn't possible."

Mary and Burt looked at each other, smiled broadly, and tried to suppress a giggle.

"Hi Larry," said Michael. Larry peered back, woozy, bleary-eyed.

"Michael?" said Larry, his voice hoarse. "How did you get here?" It seemed an odd question, even irrelevant.

"We saw a star in the sky," said Mary. "A star far brighter than the others, a new star, and we followed it here to you." Larry grinned, a grin which grew slowly from the corners of his mouth and spilled into laughter.

"What's the alarm for?" asked Michael.

"Meal time. I was gonna go get something to eat." They considered Larry's comment for a moment, and it was Mary who spoke.

"I know, let's all get some take-out and then walk over to High Falls. It's beautiful out. I haven't been to High Falls in ages." Mary was right – it was beautiful. The sun had lost its harsh glare as evening approached, and a light breeze blew warmly on their skins. It was just the sort of evening to sit and watch the falls. Larry reached back into his duffle bag and opened a bottle of wine, placing the cork part way back into the bottle. "Suits me," he said.

With the help of the others, Larry managed to find his shoe under a World War I cannon on the opposite side of the small park. The bedraggled philosopher then led them to a street vendor at the near edge of the park where they bought pitas filled with lamb, tomato, lettuce, and some sauce which was white. Larry informed them that the sauce tasted like mint and was good. Mary insisted that the steaming sandwiches were wrapped in foil and then put into a bag so they could eat them at the falls. Michael had been surprised when Larry paid for the pitas with a fifty dollar bill and waved away their offers of money.

They walked through the park, and as they approached the statue of Abraham Lincoln Michael noticed that the refuse hadn't been cleaned up from the night before. Larry stopped and looked around at the beer cans strewn about the pavement beneath the statue. Larry ran a hand through his hair and groaned.

"You okay?" asked Burt.

"Yea," said Larry. "I think things got a little biblical last night."

Mary nodded. "Excellent," she said.

"Yea, not as excellent as you might think," said Larry. "Come on, let's get out of here."

They walked along the Genesee River, watching the slow green water glide by. The white collar workers had gone back to the suburbs for the day and the city was quiet around them. Michael spotted a stick and some foamy bubbles in the water and noticed that the flotsam kept exact pace with them, or maybe they had unconsciously synchronized their pace to the wide river. Eventually, they came to a pedestrian bridge over the river.

Michael had heard of High Falls, but remarkably, he had never come here. The bridge was high and wide and had benches along it, and Michael noticed the old factories and buildings, quiet and still, straddling the river on either side of the bridge. They walked to the halfway point of the bridge and sat together on a bench. Mary unwrapped each pita and handed them out. Michael looked across and down into a wide gorge, the falls being about a quarter mile distant. The evening light cut the scene in two. Sunlight illuminated the distant city buildings and the slow green water which moved serenely to the fall's edge, accelerated suddenly, and then fell into shadow and the gorge below. The water, now a darker green in the shadow of the gorge, collected itself, and recommenced the slow march down the river and under the bridge beneath them.

"Wow," said Michael. "Those falls are really big. How tall are they?"

"About a hundred feet," said Burt. They sat in silence, soaking up the local atmosphere, listening to the distant low rumble of falling water.

"Looking at those falls makes me think of Annie Taylor," said Larry.

"Who is Annie Taylor?" asked Mary.

"Well, I guess she's a hero of mine."

"You have a hero?" asked Michael. Larry nodded, taking a sip of wine from the bottle. Michael wondered why Larry was drinking from the bottle rather than a glass. Was it a sign of increasing despair? Larry offered the others a sip, but it came as little surprise that no one accepted, considering the state of the philosopher's hygiene.

"Annie Taylor," Larry continued, "was the first person *ever* to go over Niagara Falls in a barrel."

"Oh yeah," said Burt. "That's right."

Larry pulled out his leather wallet, a decrepit thing which looked more like a well-loved dog toy. Slowly, he produced two copies of photographs, unfolded them with great care, and handed them to Michael. Michael saw a black and white image of an older woman in Victorian dress sitting behind a hastily- built pine table. Her barrel stood beside her and a sign was on the ground against the table legs: *Annie Edson Taylor, Heroine of Horseshoe Falls.* In the second photo, Annie stood next to her barrel, which was almost as tall as she was. Mary was looking intently at the photos.

"She was really the first to go over?" Mary asked, her tone conveying wonder and awe.

"Annie had been a school teacher by trade," said Larry, "but she was out of work a lot, sometimes trying her hand at dance instruction. Then one day she decided she was going over the falls, and she got hold of a pickle barrel somewhere. At the time she said she was forty-five, but most reports said she was actually in her sixties. She was pretty imaginative about the truth. It took her a while to actually do it because no one would help her put the barrel in the water – no one wanted to be part of a suicide. But in 1901, she used a bicycle pump to force air into the barrel, climbed in, had her barrel towed to the middle of the river above the falls, and over she went. The few spectators who were there were amazed that she survived the plunge with only a cut on her head."

Michael noticed that Mary had taken the photos out of his hand and was examining them closely. "What happened then?" asked Mary.

"She tried to get rich off the stunt, but people weren't as interested in her feat as she'd hoped. One day her manager absconded with the barrel, which was never seen again. Without the barrel, she wasn't much of a spectacle. She had some financial disasters and at times she tried being a clairvoyant, writing a novel, giving people magnetic treatments. She died alone, penniless."

Mary looked up from the photo. "She *was* a hero, wasn't she? What an incredible woman. Why did she go over the falls?"

"I don't know," said Larry.

"Look at her clothes," said Mary, holding one of the photos out. Michael noticed the Victorian dress of dark cotton which went all the way to the ground, and the elaborate hat with a feather. Mary smiled enthusiastically. "She's really strong, isn't she? Can you imagine the courage to go over Niagara Falls? She was the first."

"Courage?" asked Burt. "Or was she insane? Or maybe she didn't have anything to lose." They were silent for a moment, the sound of birds and the low rumble of distant falling water filling the space between them as they considered Burt's remark.

"I don't know," said Larry. "I just like her."

"She's strong," said Mary. "She didn't give a shit. She did it first and all the others had to follow behind her." She turned to Larry. "Could I make a copy of these photos?"

"Sure," said Larry.

They sat in silence for a few moments, and a thought came to Michael, a thought which seemed morbid, but he seemed to feel less worried about the appropriateness of his thoughts in the company of these irregulars.

"Has anybody ever gone over High Falls?" he asked, pointing his pita at the distant crashing water."

"Guy named Sam Patch did," said Burt. "That was back in the nineteen thirties, I think. He didn't use a barrel though. Just jumped from that ledge next to the falls."

"What happened?" asked Michael.

"Drowned," said Burt.

They went on to discuss which sort of barrel was best and about other people who had tried crazy things, and Mary wanted everyone to look at the old fashioned style of shoes Annie Taylor was wearing in the photo. Burt said that those shoes were called *granny boots* these days and were in fashion again, and he explained that sometimes young women came into his shop and asked if he had any, and then for some inexplicable reason he was talking about some German feminist Michael had never heard of. Larry then said something in German which no one understood but it was funny the way he said it, and then Larry offered his wine to everyone again, apparently forgetting that no one wanted to drink from his bottle.

The slow green water continued its inexorable path below them and the diagonal shadow which cut the scene in two crawled down the churning wall of falling water and into the gorge with silent patience. Burt pointed to Larry's cuts and asked if he'd had an accident and Larry suggested that Freud said *there are no accidents*, and Burt agreed with this position but still wondered if he should see a doctor and then Larry said something in German which made Mary laugh hysterically, and Mary asked Larry what the German meant, and Larry said that it meant that his doctor would just tell him again that he should go to Salzburg *to take the air*, which made everyone laugh. The conversation moved with disjointed enthusiasm from topic to topic and everyone seemed to be enjoying themselves, and Michael was quite suddenly aware that whatever he said was okay and that it would be fine if he was quiet and said nothing at all, and he noticed a giddy lightness within himself that was strange but not unpleasant.

Just following sunset the air cooled and they decided to head off. They walked together and said goodbye to Larry at the park. Mary said she wanted to stop in at her exhibition space and that she'd find her way back to her van. Burt offered to drive Michael back to his moped, which was parked outside his shop.

As they drove, Michael noticed a hardback book on the dashboard, and was surprised at the title, *Through Hell for Hitler*. "Is the book any good?" asked Michael.

Burt's eyes lit up. "I've just finished reading it. It's an extraordinary story. I've read world war two history before, but this was a biography written by a German soldier named Henry Metelmann, a tank driver, who was on the Eastern front. He was only 18 and he spent three years going Eastwards for thousands of miles and then all the way back to Germany again until the war ended. He was such a nice kid, just put in awful circumstances. And you can't believe what he went through. He saw so many friends die, he fell in love with a Russian girl. Once his tank broke down and he got left behind and just moved in with a Russian family for a couple of months. He worked in the fields with this family, went drinking with them, made friends with them, until he got picked up by another regiment. The whole thing was crazy."

Burt's enthusiasm was such that he wasn't spending much time watching the road, but Michael didn't want to interrupt him. "When the Americans finally capture him near the end of the war," Burt continued, "the most amazing thing happens. The Americans take all his clothes and possessions away from him, except his watch. They tell him to take a shower, so he places his watch under a towel in this shower room. It was the first hot shower he'd had in ages and it was like all the horror of the war was washing off him. But when the kid comes out of the shower he discovers that someone has stolen his watch."

Burt looked over and raised his eyebrows. "Then what happened?" asked Michael.

"Well, at that moment the kid realized that the watch was the last thing he had in the world. His friends were dead, the American's had taken everything he owned, and now his last possession, his watch, was gone. And he felt real sad, but it was also like a completely new start on life. He was naked, literally naked, just like when he came into the world."

Michael turned the guy's situation over in his mind, imagining him standing there in the shower with nothing. "Didn't he have family though?" Michael asked.

"His parents had died while he was away at war," said Burt.

"Wow," said Michael. "He really had nothing. What happened to him?"

"Well," said Burt, "I suppose the Americans gave him some clothing to wear, and he had to start over again."

CHAPTER 33

A German reality TV show has been launched which will find the man with the fastest sperm. A chemical identical to that emitted by a female egg will be used as the finish line, and viewers can watch this microscopic race in detail.

From the journals of Professor Charles Kidding, extract #78

Michael could physically sense the house shaking, and noticed that the surface of his coffee trembled in a rhythmic manner. Ruling out earthquake, Michael surmised that for some unknown reason, Sam was *running* up the stairs. There was a pounding on his door.

Sam opened the door. "Mr. W, hey Mr. W, you gotta see this."

Sam was clutching the door jamb and heaving heavily, apparently paying the price for his sprint. "Come," he spat out between labored breaths. Sam led Michael to his bedroom lair, and they kicked their way through the usual detritus strewn on the distressed shag carpet, arriving finally at Sam's computer.

"Well, have a look at that," said Sam.

Michael saw the home page of Sam's internet radio site and listened to the usual dirge of crashing guitars and miserable vocals, but he wasn't sure what he was supposed to see.

"Look," repeated Sam, pointing a chubby index finger at a particular section of the screen. Michael read the words *Current Listeners*, next to which was indicated the number *1*.

"Hey, you got a listener."

"Yup," said Sam. "She started listening about eleven-fifteen last night and didn't log off until 3:30 in the morning." I wanted to tell you last night but I thought maybe you'd gone to sleep. Plus, I didn't really feel that I could leave my post, you know, because what with having a listener and all."

"And now your listener is back?"

"Yeah," said Sam. "She just logged in."

"How do you know it's a woman?" asked Michael.

Sam stared at Michael for a moment, a perplexed expression on his face, as if Michael had asked a rather stupid or irrelevant question. "Oh, she's a chick, I'm sure," said Sam. Michael was doubtful, imagining that Sam's taste in music was more likely to attract other socially awkward and pimply young men who lived out their lives in darkened and cluttered basements. But it seemed cruel to say so.

Michael hung around for a little while, but Sam was pretty focused on the song breaks, discussing the music, doing lead-ins on the songs, and generally clowning around and showing off for his listener. Sam did mention that he thought *she* might email him in order to post her vote for his *Humanity's Top-ten Fuck-ups,* and he was already thinking of ways to make his site more attractive.

CHAPTER 34

Three Malaysian executioners have died between 1988 and 2001 while messing around on the gallows. The most recent death occurred when an executioner posed for a photo with his head through the noose, and the trap doors gave way.

From the journals of Professor Charles Kidding, extract #170.

Michael heard a knock on his door and he looked up from the couch. "Come in," he called. Mrs. Deveroix's head appeared in the door. "Your lady-friend is here," said Mrs. Deveroix, a knowing and mischievous grin on her face. "She wanted me to show her up because she says she has a surprise for you." Normally, Michael greeted Mary at the back door of the house, and he wondered why Mrs. Deveroix was bringing Mary up in such a stealthy fashion. Mrs. Deveroix's head disappeared and the door swung open. Michael's eyes opened wide and his mouth gaped at the image of Mary in the doorway. He jumped up to greet her, but Mary said, "No, sit down on the couch." Michael obeyed and Mary sauntered in. Mrs. Deveroix excused herself and closed the door. Mary took two paces towards Michael, smiled broadly, and opened out her arms.

"What do you think?" she asked.

Michael's eyes widened in astonishment. "You're that lady – the one who went over Niagara Falls in a barrel."

"Annie Edson Taylor," said Mary, twirling around once to give Michael a fuller view.

Michael had only had a brief look at the photos, but Mary's reproduction of Annie Taylor was truly remarkable. The elaborate hat with the feather, the detailed dark cotton Victorian dress, the granny boots Burt had made reference to – it was flawless. Mary had even had her hair made up in the correct style.

"It's amazing," said Michael. "How in the world did you find the clothing?"

"Burt made some phone calls. He's pretty connected in the world of second hand cast-offs."

"And your hair – it's just like the photos."

"Burt's niece is a hair dresser. We showed her the photos and she did me up, right in Tasco's."

"It's remarkable Mary. You've got everything but the barrel."

"Aaahhh," said Mary, reaching into a pocket in her dress. She handed Michael a black and white photograph of herself dressed as she presently was. She posed next to a large oak barrel in just the same fashion as Annie Taylor had done in one of the photos Michael had seen. He scrutinized the photo closely. Mary's oak barrel was very similar to Annie's, though perhaps a tad squatter. Mary was of course much younger, thinner, and prettier than Annie, but the spirit of the original photograph had been captured with remarkable authenticity.

"I stand corrected," said Michael. "You *have* got a barrel."

"Well how am I supposed to go over High Falls without a barrel," Mary said matter-of-factly.

It took Michael a moment to absorb what she had said, but when he did he was pretty sure she was serious. He saw Mary for a moment, washed up on the rocks at the bottom of High Falls, soaking wet, her body broken and lifeless. And then, for the briefest of moments, he imagined the world without Mary in it.

"What?" he sputtered. "That's crazy. You can't go over High Falls in a barrel. You could get killed."

"Well, it's funny you should mention that. You see, it's possible I might not have to go over."

"Why not?" asked Michael.

"Because I might get rescued."

"What do you mean rescued?"

"Michael, I need your help making a flyer," she said, ignoring his question. "A flyer which advertises my stunt. Can you help me?"

Michael made a token effort to get Mary to explain why she was doing it and what she meant about being *rescued*, but Mary was quite unhelpful. In the end, Michael found himself sitting before his computer with Mary leaning over his shoulder, giving directions. An hour later, the promotional flyer was complete, and Michael had printed off a single copy. He and Mary sat next to one another on the couch looking it over. At the top it read:

On August 10th, at 7:00 PM, Mary Magellan will
go over High Falls in a barrel.
Never before has this death-defying stunt been attempted.

Just beneath these words was the photo of Mary and her barrel, which Michael had scanned and inserted into the flyer. Below the photo was a final message, which Mary said was important:

Ms Magellan will be entering the Genesee River, above the falls, near the St Andrews Street bridge.

Michael shook his head. "How many copies do you want?"

"Copies?" asked Mary. "No, I just need the one we've got."

Michael thought he should point out that using one flyer doesn't really amount to much of a promotional campaign, but he saw that Mary was working towards something in her own way, and she knew what she wanted. He decided he would just see where it led.

"Come on," said Mary, "Let's go hang our flyer. You can drive me on that motorcycle of yours."

"It's just a moped, and a rather sad and underpowered moped at that."

Mary put a finger to her lips. "Shhhhh, you'll upset the motorcycle."

"But how can you ride, dressed like that?"

Mary disappeared into his walk-in closet. Ten minutes later she emerged dressed in a pair of his jeans cinched-up with a belt, one of his t-shirts, and a pair of his tennis shoes. Everything hung on her, and the tennis shoes gave her a clownish appearance.

After the shambles which had ensued from sitting Larry on the back of the moped, Michael was worried about having anyone else riding behind him – but Mary made it easy, leaning with him at every turn. She told him to go to the Baushe and Lombe building down town, and in twenty minutes they had parked out front. Michael had never entered this impressive red-bricked building with its glassed atrium. As they entered the atrium, Michael suddenly recalled the scene at Bed, Baths, and Beyond, and a shudder of anxiety ran through him. He took Mary by the arm and stopped her.

"Mary, is this alright? I mean, is anything… crazy… going to happen?"

Mary smiled. "I doubt it. We just need to hang one flyer, and leave. Don't worry."

She seemed genuine enough, and Michael relaxed a bit. They took the elevator to the 14th floor, Michael absorbing the fine wood paneling, brass, and glass all about him. When the elevator doors opened, he found they faced enormous glass doors, upon which was written:

Magellan, Smith, & Cline
Attorneys at Law

"Mary, it says Magellan," Michael whispered. "Is that your dad?"

Mary didn't respond, and Michael noticed an intent and focused expression on her face. She even looked… scared, and Michael had never seen that in her. She touched his elbow. "Come on Michael," she said. They headed towards the glass doors but just as Mary's hand touched the handle, she tugged at Michael's arm and led him away from the doors and down a corridor.

When they were out of sight, Mary stopped and put her head into her hands. "Oh Christ," she moaned. Michael put a hand on her shoulder. "Mary, what is it? What's wrong?"

She looked up at him, pleading – "Michael, I can't do it. I've lost my nerve. You've got to help me. Can you give the flyer to the receptionist? Just tell her it's for Mr. Magellan. Please Michael?" Michael was shocked at the state of Mary – it was a side he'd never seen. He sensed that something was going on which was way beyond his comprehension, but he hated to see Mary like this.

"Of course." He took the flyer from Mary and moved quickly through the glass doors. The pretty young receptionist greeted him politely and with the exuberance which was no doubt expected of her.

"Hello," said Michael. "I have a promotional flyer for Mr. Magellan."

"Oh," the fresh-faced receptionist sang out. She took the flyer from him and looked at it. Even her customer care training could not prevent the subtle lines of surprise and confusion which formed around her mouth and eyes. But the receptionist collected herself, smiled too broadly, and offered the most positive remark she was capable of.

"Well, that's very interesting. I'll make sure Mr. Magellan gets it."

Michael looked for Mary on the other side of the glass doors, but discovered that the corridor was empty. He found her sitting on the edge of a fountain outside the main doors to the building. She was kicking her feet to and fro, and in his oversized cloths she looked like a ten year old girl who was sitting on her own for some reason. Michael sat beside her, thoughtful, quiet. Mary spoke at last, her voice strangely small. "Thank you."

"Of course Mary. I'm glad to help."

They sat there for several minutes enveloped in birdsong, the rhythmic rush of passing traffic, and the warble of fountain water. Sunshine was everywhere. Michael didn't really understand what was going on, but he was getting a strange sense for it.

"So, do you think you'll get rescued then?" Michael asked.

Mary smiled sadly at the ground, still lost in her own thoughts, and put a hand on his thigh. They sat like this for a while until Mary pointed at the brick entranceway to the building. "Ya see that brick wall? Wanna hear a story about something that happened there?"

CHAPTER 35

Roger Douglas, a man highly attuned to the need for law and order, sat alone for two hours at a rural traffic light which was stuck on red. He was eventually waved on by an Arizona police officer in the early hours of the morning.

From the journal of Professor Charles Kidding, extract #213

Michael stared into his wardrobe, wondering if he and Larry were the same size. Larry was thinner, but he thought they were a close enough match. He chose a brown tweed suit coat, one he thought might be suited to the academic type, and folded it neatly into a plastic bag.

Michael was roasting in his anarchist's leather as he rode down town. He thought about that young German soldier Burt had told him about as he maneuvered the moped through traffic. Michael had this weirdly clear image of that kid in his head – he could see him standing in the shower room just after he realized that his watch had been stolen. That young man really had nothing now, and he probably didn't even know what was going to happen to him next. He should probably get that book and read it himself.

Approaching Larry as he walked across the park, he stripped the jacket off and put it at the foot of the bench. In his left hand Michael held the bottle of wine, in his right, the jacket in the bag. Michael handed him the wine, which Larry accepted with a smile.

"I thought you might like this," Michael said, offering Larry the bag.

Larry opened the bag and pulled the jacket out, holding it up for inspection. "I thought it might suit you." Larry smiled and stood up. He slipped his long arms into the suit coat and stood before Michael. For a moment, Michael worried that Larry would feel patronized, or that the expensive suit coat might not fit his lifestyle. But Larry looked himself over and seemed genuinely pleased. "Thanks," he said, sitting down again.

Michael checked his watch – 1:35 pm. A couple of months ago it would have been unthinkable to crack a beer at this time of day, but he got a cold one out of his cooler and popped the lid. Larry handed him the extra glass in silence and they stared into the trees, idly noting the passing pedestrians.

"Mary's planning to go over High Falls in a barrel," said Michael. "Seven pm on August the 10th."

Larry raised his eyebrows slowly and grinned, then took a sip of wine. "Is it artistic expression, or maybe something personal?"

"I don't know, but she thinks she might get rescued – I mean so she won't have to go over."

Larry smiled. He was somewhere inward, alone with his thoughts. "Well," he said eventually, "I suppose we all need rescuing." Michael was annoyed with Larry's impassive response.

"We need to stop her Larry. I appreciate all this artistic stuff she does, but this is ridiculous. I just… I don't want something bad to happen to her."

Larry looked at him closely. "She's important to you, isn't she?"

"Yes."

Larry gazed into the trees. "The Genesee River certainly has a current," Larry said, "especially above the falls. Charles Kidding once said that *time is a river with no source and no ocean, but it does have a current.* Mary is already caught in a current, one that we don't understand, one that she may only partially understand."

"Larry, those are nice words, and I'm not saying you're wrong, but don't we need to help her?"

"I don't know." A long pause followed before Larry added, "I just don't know Michael."

They sat quietly for a while, each attending to their own thoughts. Michael wanted to pursue this conversation concerning Mary further, but he didn't see how. Eventually, his thoughts came around to his own problems.

"You know how I lost my ID?"

Larry nodded.

"Well, I've had this dream a couple of times. There's this man who rips the roof off my car and screams at me. He shouts, 'who the hell are you'? And then I wake up. Well, the dream is unsettling enough, but then last week I'm in a Starbucks and I see this guy from across the room, and he looks just like the guy in my dream. I walk over to get a closer view and he just looks at me and asks me if I'm okay. I must have been staring at him, I don't know."

"Why don't you have a word with him?"

"What?" said Michael. "A word with who?"

"The guy, the guy you saw in Starbucks. The next time you see the guy, why don't you tell him about your dream."

"Larry, are you nuts?"

"Yes," said Larry.

"No – what I meant," said Michael, "is that it would be crazy to walk up to a complete stranger and tell him that he's been showing up in your dreams."

Larry shrugged. "It's just a thought. I might talk to him."

"Well, I'm not going to just go up and talk with him," said Michael. This was just more of Larry's cryptic nonsense.

They sat in silence for a while, each absorbing the import of the exchange. Michael's own thoughts collided off one another, noisy and chaotic, like a malevolent game of pinball.

"Larry, I just *hate* not having my identification. I really hate it," he said, surprised at his anger. "I've got a wallet. Do you know what's in it?" Michael pulled his wallet from his back pocket and plucked out his debit card. "Look, I've got a debit card." He opened out the wallet for Larry to see better. "I've got some cash I carry with me." As Michael looked at the cash, he noticed the business card he'd put in there as well. He pulled the card out. "And I've got the name and number of this woman down at the Department of Health who's helping me get my ID back. That's it Larry, that's *everything* I've got left."

Larry reached down and retrieved the bottle Michael had brought him. "Yeah," Larry said. "Things get lost, I guess." Michael wondered if he was going to say more on the subject, but Larry just took a big sip of wine and stared, glazed-eyed, into the trees. Michael looked at Larry, and it occurred to him that the philosopher-bum didn't seem especially well today. No quirky stories or disjointed pieces of off-the-hanger wisdom.

Of course, why should Larry be well? What did he expect?

CHAPTER 36

A convicted murderer in Romania named Pavel M attempted to sue God for failing to protect him from evil. Pavel claimed that his baptism was a contract between himself and the Almighty, which had been broken.

From the Journals of Professor Charles Kidding, extract #114

At 6:00 am Michael pulled himself from bed, had breakfast, and paced his rooms. He realized he had finally come to the point were he could no longer find the energy to pursue the financial markets. There was simply no interest left. This left a hole in the fabric of his day, and it took quite a bit of pacing before Michael decided to visit the library. Maybe he'd chat with Larry on the way.

Larry was asleep on the park bench, a grubby blanket wrapped around him, his filthy baseball cap covering his face. Michael recalled how Larry had produced that fifty dollar bill to pay for the sandwiches, and wondered why he slept here. There was evidence that the previous night had been a rough one. A broken wine bottle lay on concrete nearby, and there was an unpleasant pale yellow substance caked on the side of Larry's face. Michael wondered if Larry had been sick, and then he felt angry at him. Maybe he felt let down as well. But this was not rational. Larry didn't owe him anything, and Michael wondered why he cared about the bum and why he was important to him. It wasn't the first time he'd felt this way. But when he let his thoughts and feelings settle down, he realized he just felt disappointed that he wouldn't be able to talk with Larry.

Michael walked the two blocks to the city library and made his way through the heavy wooden doors. He stood in the main reading room and gazed around him, aware of the warm yellow sunlight, the fine oak paneled walls, and the mostly empty tables. He found himself recalling the time when Larry was almost kicked out. The table Larry had sat at was empty, and as he stared at it he remembered that stand-off between Larry and that fat guard – he even remembered her name – Tamisha. Tamisha had been sitting at her desk when he came in just now, so she was easy to recall. The memory played itself out, and he saw that college kid arguing with Tamisha, the frightened bird-like librarian, the way Larry had drooled on the desk.

Michael needed to use the toilet, and as he sat down on the commode he noticed several messages written with black marker, or pen, or even scraped into the stall wall. They seemed like the usual collection of regressive, angry, and solicitous material you find in most public toilets.

Sheila Adams likes it in the ass

For a good blow job, meet me here on Friday at 7:00 PM

There was even a running debate about the value of hand-jobs, produced by four different authors. How's that for high-brow philosophy? Michael had just about lost interest when he spotted something written in thick black marker – *Normality is today's most widespread psychological disorder.* Michael was struck by that line and how incongruous it was to the other messages; he was still thinking it over when he walked into the main reading room.

Michael spotted that college kid who worked here. What was his name? Michael couldn't remember, but as the kid passed by he got a good look at his nametag – Leonard, that was it. And then an idea suddenly came to him, an idea laden with opportunity and anxiety.

He strolled to a nearby library stack and pretended to take an interest in the books there, keeping an eye on Leonard's movements. He idly picked up a book off the shelf and gave it a quick glance. It turned out to be a remarkably thick romance novel depicting a handsome bare-chested man. He realized that this wasn't a very believable cover, so he replaced the book and strolled to another stack. Leonard pushed a trolley laden with books, and stopped at a stack about twenty feet away. The place offered relative privacy, and Michael reckoned this was probably going to be the best opportunity he'd get. He was grateful that Leonard looked up as he approached.

"Excuse me," he said. "I understand you were a student of Professor

Larry Dembrowski." Leonard placed a book on the shelf and stared at Michael, his eyes narrowing. "I'm sorry if this seems intrusive. It's just that I overheard you talking with Larry last month and it's obvious you knew him pretty well. I've sort of become friends with Larry, I mean we spend time talking to each other. I guess I can't help wondering what happened to him."

"You mean why he became a bum?"

"I guess, I mean… yes." Leonard appeared to soften somewhat.

"It's not a secret," said Leonard. "It was front page news a few years ago."

"Really? I don't normally read the local paper."

"Well, you can read about it now, if you want. We keep back copies on disc these days. I think I can remember the date. I'll show you." Leonard led Michael to a computer and invited him to sit down. "I'll be back in a minute," he said. Leonard returned and handed Michael a disc. "This is the disc you want. Just put this in and type October 4th where it asks for a date. The article's there."

Michael popped the CD in the computer and followed Leonard's instructions. A moment later, the front page of the paper appeared. The first thing which caught his eye was the black and white photo of Larry – it was the same photo he'd seen on one of the philosophy books he'd written. There was another photo near by of a pretty young girl smiling brightly. Then he read:

Tragic Accident Claims the Life of Four- year-old Melissa Dembrowski

Renowned local Philosopher Professor Larry Dembrowski was leaving his home for the airport yesterday, en route to an international conference on Logic, where he was scheduled to deliver the Key Note Address. Unaware that his four year old daughter was riding her tricycle in the driveway, Professor Dembrowski backed over Melissa. Melissa was taken by ambulance to Strong Memorial Hospital, and was pronounced dead three hours following arrival. The coroner has yet to examine Melissa, but doctors indicate that she died of severe and multiple internal injuries.

Melissa Dembrowski attended Little Acorn Preschool and was much loved by her teachers and classmates…

Michael read on, numb with the realization of the tragedy. There was information about this 'lovely' and 'beautiful' child, and a summary of Professor Dembrowski's academic accomplishments. The article continued on another page, and there Michael found a truly awful photograph. The back end of Larry's car was depicted, a stylish sedan, as well as the twisted remains of Melissa's tricycle. He didn't want to think about it, but for a moment he saw a younger and healthier Larry running to his car with a briefcase, maybe late for his plane. He heard the hideous crunch of metal on pavement, the scream of a little girl, sensed the shock and horror Larry must have felt when he understood what he'd done. Michael could read no more. There was no need to anyway. He quickly removed the CD from the computer and looked away, scanning the library, as if that might erase the images he'd just seen.

Michael looked for Leonard because he wanted to return the disc, but the librarian had disappeared. He returned the disc to another librarian at the book check-out desk. Michael felt like he was struggling to breathe. He needed fresh air, so he walked briskly for the front doors. He thought he could taste blood in his mouth, though he knew this was ridiculous.

Pushing his way through the main doors, he saw Leonard sitting on the front steps, idly smoking a cigarette. Michael sat down next to him and they were silent together for a couple of minutes.

"I'm not supposed to smoke outside the Library," Leonard said finally. "It's bad publicity." He took a long drag, held it, and blew it out forcefully before continuing. "I hadn't thought about what happened for a little while, but when you asked about it, I couldn't help remembering."

"It's awful," said Michael dumbly.

"Yeah, it is."

Michael gazed in the direction of Larry, though the park was obscured behind an old brick building. "What happened to his wife?" he asked.

"I heard she left him not long after the accident."

"I guess it's hard for couples to overcome something like that," Michael said. He imagined Larry asleep on the bench, under that grubby blanket. "Was that why the university let him go? Because he drank too much?"

"Sort of. In part they sacked him because he failed to show up to classes sometimes, woke up one too many times under a bush on the campus grounds, gave one too many drunken speeches on the quad. But in those last chaotic days, he committed the *real* sin against academia, the one they really hated him for."

"What sin?" asked Michael.

"Flippancy," said Leonard, "a wanton disregard for the seriousness of philosophy. Philosophy is a humorless business, and it's meant to be that way. He's been gone for three years now, and he's still the most talked about professor at the university. Before he drank, he was a brilliant teacher. After he started drinking, he was brilliant but in a pretty out of control way. I think I loved that guy – lots of us did. At one point, the Dean wrote him a letter about how he was bringing the university into disrepute and how he needed to moderate his behavior, etc… and in response Professor Dembrowski wrote a paper entitled *A philosophical analysis of disgrace and public ruin.* It was actually published in a leading journal. They had to fire him in the end, but they wanted to fire him as well. They really hated him."

Michael thought about Larry, imagining his ragged form lying on the park bench. "I still don't see why he has to live that way, like a bum in a park. It seems to me he has some money."

"He must have a pension," said Leonard, "and maybe the university paid something to get rid of him. I've wondered myself about why he lives that way in the park. I've got a theory, if you want to hear it." Michael nodded and Leonard continued. "You know how a couple of hundred years ago we used to put people in the stocks as punishment for certain crimes? It probably wasn't nice being in the stocks, but the real punishment was the social humiliation of being put on public view. Maybe that's what Professor Dembrowski is doing. It's like a self-imposed version of the stocks."

Michael heard the main doors swing open behind them, and then a voice: "Hey, college boy, supervisor wants to know if you gonna put some books away or if you gonna sit round all day smoking?" Michael craned his neck and saw Tamisha's fat, squat frame in the doorway. Leonard sighed and stubbed his cigarette out on the granite. "I better go," he said, a note of sour resignation in his voice.

Michael remained on the steps, watching his own thoughts. He wondered about all those stories Larry had told him and about the odd points of view he had expressed. Maybe Larry had been trying to say something honest, but it was hard to get a clear picture of it.

Michael pushed himself off the marble steps and made his way back towards his moped, unsure of what he wanted to do. He entered the north end of the park and discovered that he was standing very near the place where Larry had held that kid down on the ground. The memory of that chaotic and frenzied evening came back to him, and he could hear again the shouts of the crowd, could see the beer can hitting Larry in the head, could see the look of anger on Larry's face. And then Michael needed to remember what the question was that Larry had forced upon that kid. Something about two truck drivers who had neglected to have their brakes checked, and one of them accidentally killing a child when the brakes failed. Michael felt a tightness grip at his chest as he stared hard at the ground, seeing the boy struggle physically with Larry and then mentally with the moral dilemma.

Which truck driver was more guilty?

The boy had said neither was more guilty, because the accident could have happened to either of them, but Larry had disagreed and he was going to hold that boy down forever because he had failed to understand this. And then Michael recalled the photograph of the crushed tricycle, and he squeezed his eyes tight and shook his head, trying to push it away.

Michael crossed the park and stood before Larry, who was still asleep. The blanket had slipped off his shoulder, and he noticed that the philosopher was wearing the sports coat he'd given him. Michael felt an impulse to put his hand on Larry's shoulder, but he put his helmet on instead and walked for the moped.

CHAPTER 37

A Detroit judge became frustrated when he got no response from a 76 year-old woman who repeatedly failed to answer his questions. The woman was eventually found to be dead.

From the journals of Professor Charles Kidding, extract #151.

Shhhhiitt, thought Michael. It was happening again. All he had wanted to do was get a few groceries from the convenience store. It was a simple trip, no more than a half-mile. He had even decided to walk in order to challenge this silly notion that he couldn't find his house, or home, as Larry insisted on calling it. He stared at the circular suburban turn-around he faced. That wasn't supposed to be there. He was supposed to be on Washington Street – in fact, he should be home by now putting groceries into his fridge.

Michael stared at the houses which lined the turn-around. No cars in the driveways, no activity in the yards or behind the windows, nobody home. He shuffled to the nearest lawn, dropped to the ground, sat there and rubbed at his face with his hands. What was wrong with him? He remembered having to ask that cocky teenager where he was last time he got lost. He'd hated that. Maybe he'd just sit here for a while. He closed his eyes, not really wanting to think about his predicament.

An image came to him, a familiar and ancient image. He was with his mother at an old church downtown. It was the last time he remembered being with his mom before the fire. His mother always took him on a bus to that old church once a year around Easter. There were hundreds of those prayer offering candles, the ones in red glass, and many of them were burning. The place smelled of molten wax and the pine resin they must have used on all those pews. The sun hardly got through those stained glass windows, and his mother was walking him through the stations of the cross, stopping at each station and telling him what was happening. He remembered the old paintings well. They were standing at the one which shows Simon helping Jesus carry his cross, and he could see the figures clearly. There was good old Simon, carrying the cross, and Jesus just behind him, a Roman solder walking along with them too. Jesus looked beat, but Simon was smaller than Jesus and he seemed pretty tired too. That couldn't have been easy on Simon, having to help a convicted man, right in front of that crowd. The soldiers had asked Simon to carry the cross because Jesus just couldn't do it any more – he'd fallen three times already. It struck Michael that this was the third time he'd got lost trying to find his home. What if Simon were to walk out from behind one of those houses just now? He'd have that beard on and he'd be wearing those leather knee trousers and rough brown cotton shirt, and maybe he'd take Michael home. Despite his miserable state of mind, Michael had to smile at the thought. He wasn't religious, and he knew how ridiculous this fantasy was – but the thought amused him anyway.

He was really small standing there next to his mom, listening to her talking about Simon in that soft whisper. There was an old couple kneeling next to one another in a pew not far away, praying, so you had to be quiet. He could feel the cotton of his mother's dress on his cheek and he could smell… what was it? It was perfume, and it smelled like roses, and he could see how she put one hand over her heart when she told him the stories in that hushed and reverential tone. The religious part hadn't meant much to him, but he liked the story, and he liked being there with her. They'd always get chocolate afterwards at the same department store around the corner, which he looked forward to.

Michael felt a pain in his chest as if something hard was there and he realized that he was struggling to breathe. He didn't want to feel this way anymore, so he yanked himself to his feet and started walking back the way he came, angry now and not knowing why or at whom. He saw a street sign, Stone Gate Lane. What the fuck was he doing on Stone Gate Lane? He quickened his pace, legs fueled by the strangest mixture of wrath and desperation. At an intersection he came to Washington Street. He breathed a sigh of relief, turned left, and headed for home. Maybe he'd be okay. Maybe he wasn't going mad. Maybe he'd just been distracted by this lost ID business and took a few wrong turns without knowing it. As he approached the next intersection he made out the street sign – Locus Avenue. Locus Avenue? How the hell… ?

Michael wandered to the edge of the road and dropped down on the grass – someone's front lawn. He hadn't even bothered to see if anyone was at home. He no longer cared. His cell phone was in his pocket and was jabbing painfully into his hip. He pulled it out and stared at it for a moment, eyes glazed. Slowly, as if in a dream, he took his wallet from his back pocket and removed that business card, vaguely aware of birds singing close by. Unfolding it, he read the name to himself – Julie Miller. He looked at his phone and back to the card. The anger was ebbing now, replaced by an unintelligible numbness. He dialed.

"Hello, this is Julie Miller."

Michael opened his mouth to speak, but he could not find the words. He did not know how to ask.

"Hello, is there anyone there?" he heard Julie say, her tone strangely familiar and feminine.

Michael closed his phone, aware only of the overhanging trees and the sound of birds calling to one another.

CHAPTER 38

In 2001, an under-funded Moscow TV station aired a show called Who Wants to be Fabulously Wealthy? The top prize was equivalent to $61.50.

From the journals of Professor Charles Kidding, extract #115

Michael woke at 4:06 am, turned on the bedside lamp, and gazed at the bedroom wall with sleep-stained eyes. The events of yesterday afternoon came back to him. In the end, finding his way back home had been a simple matter of dumb luck. He'd sat on that stranger's front lawn listening to the birds and watching his thoughts float past – worrying about Mary and her impending stunt, wondering why he had called Julie, seeing that image again of the crushed tricycle, thinking about the way Mary looked and felt in the blue moonlight, recalling that German soldier and his stolen watch, feeling depressed about being lost again, wondering if he should call home and see if Sam was in.

And then he had noticed his postman coming up the road. His shoulder bag was pretty full and Michael decided that postie hadn't been to his street yet. He got to his feet and tried to look like he had some purpose, standing there in that yard; that was a pointless exercise really – he probably just looked like a man trying to look like he had a purpose. He couldn't really blame the postman for peering at him suspiciously as he went past, and Michael didn't much care at that point. In fact, he was losing the capacity to give a shit these days about a lot of things, wasn't he? He tailed postie for about twenty minutes before he found himself back on Sycamore Street. He actually hid behind trees and bushes on route. He hoped postie wasn't the paranoid type. They were licensed to mace dogs, weren't they? Why not people who hid behind trees and followed you? If Michael had felt better about things, he might have even found the situation funny.

At 10:00 am Michael sat at the Deveroix's kitchen table. He could hear Sam's abhorrent music throbbing down in the basement, but he didn't mind it somehow. Maybe it was even growing on him. Michael sipped at his tea and heard Sam coming up from his basement lair. The door opened and there he was, the human beach ball, smiling uncontrollably.

"Hey, Mr. W.," he said. "I was coming to find you. You know my listener?"

"Sure, the one who listens till about three in the morning." Michael was smiling to himself. Most DJs probably talk about their *audience*. For Sam, it's *his listener*.

"She emailed me," said Sam. "At first she emailed in about my contest, you know, *Humanity's Top-ten Fuck-ups*. We started emailing each other, mostly about what sort of music she wanted me to play. And then I emailed her yesterday to tell her she had won the *Humanity's Top-ten Fuck-ups* contest. Her list was pretty awesome and she was sort of the only one who entered the contest."

Michael was stunned. Sam had said he was sure his listener was *a chick*, and he'd been right. "Did she say where she lives?" asked Michael.

"Some little shit-kicker town in Iowa," said Sam. "Anyways, get this, she emailed me a photo of her self. Do you wanna see it?"

Sam led Michael to his computer, pressed a few keys, and a screen-sized image of the mystery listener appeared. "Meet Rose," he said, gesturing to the screen. Michael gazed at the image. She was truly one of the least attractive young women he had ever seen. A big girl, she wore black from head to foot. Her rotund face seemed to be covered somehow in silver studs, and she had tattoos down both arms. Large breasts threatened to pop out of a very tight nylon shirt which, unfortunately, was three inches short of covering her protruding stomach and a belly button containing yet more studs. A leather miniskirt and fishnet stockings completed the ensemble. Michael noticed that she puckered her chubby lips in a sad attempt at erotic appeal.

"She's pretty hot, huh?" said Sam, grinning in genuine pride.

Michael was really lost for words. There was something remarkably incongruous about her name. "Did you say her name was Rose?" Michael asked.

"Yeah. I only learned her name after we started emailing each other. She's got a different *log on* name she uses for my internet site."

"What's that?" Michael asked.

"Rock Bitch," Sam said impassively.

Now that makes more sense, thought Michael. The big girl also held a trophy in her hands, posing with it in the manner a model might display the latest household product. The trophy looked familiar, and Michael glanced over at Sam's trophy shelf. It was empty.

"Sam, she's got your trophy."

"Yeah, I mailed her gold loin cloth man – for coming first place in the contest."

They stared together at Rose for a moment, and Michael thought he noticed Sam's face fall, as if he was attending to something difficult.

"I've sort of got a problem Mr. W. Rose wants me to send her a photo."

"Oh," said Michael.

"I was wondering if you could help me. You got any photo techniques that can transform a fat fuck into something… ." Sam was momentarily lost for words. "Something better?"

They talked it over and in the end opted for a biker shot. All the evidence seemed to suggest that Rose was the rebel type, and a biker shot seemed the right approach. Sam posed on his motorcycle in full leathers out in the driveway. Michael repositioned Sam and his biker's jacket several times, looking for an angle which would somehow flatter his physique. Michael took several shots, and they spent a while looking them over closely on Sam's computer. Eventually Sam chose one which he seemed really pleased with.

CHAPTER 39

A sparrow has been killed in the Netherlands after it knocked over 23,000 dominos, nearly ruining a world-record attempt. The bird flew through an open window and into an exhibition centre in Leenwarden, where domino enthusiasts had spent weeks setting up dominos. The sparrow was shot dead by angry participants while cowering in a corner.

From the Journals of Professor Charles Kidding, extract #164

Michael stared at today's date on his wall calendar, August 10th. He had drawn a barrel in that square with a black ball point pen, next to which he had written, *Mary – 7:00 pm.* His original impulse had been to write *Mary goes over High Falls – 7:00 pm*, but he couldn't bring himself to illustrate such craziness in writing, so he opted instead for a symbol of craziness. He checked his watch: 8:15 AM. He had tried calling Mary's cell phone a few times over the last two days, but he'd only been able to leave messages, messages asking that she call him, messages which had gone unreturned.

He wanted to call Burt, but wondered if it was too early. He figured Burt was up though. He'd read about sleeping problems on account of his own obnoxious difficulties in that department. The older you get, the earlier you wake. A healthy growing teen can sleep till noon if they want to. But older people get less sleep, depressed people wake early, and people with what ever the fuck was wrong with him wake really early. He dialed the number for *Tasco's* he found in the telephone book, hoping he'd get an answer, and somehow expecting he might.

"Hello."

"Hi Burt, it's Michael, Mary's friend."

"Michael, I'm glad you called. I was sort of hoping you would."

"Yeah," said Michael. "I was just wondering if you'd heard from Mary."

"I haven't seen her for about three days, and she hasn't returned my calls."

"Same here," said Michael. "I'm worried about her. This just seems like a really stupid stunt she's got in mind."

"Look Michael," said Burt. "I've helped Mary with a lot of her work. When she asked me to build a barrel for her like the one in that photo your philosopher friend gave her, I said no. And I think that's the first time I ever told her I wouldn't help her. That wasn't easy, I can tell you. But when Mary gets hold of an idea, there's no talking her out of it."

Michael sighed, conscious of the fact that he had helped Mary create and deliver her single promotional flyer. "I'm sorry Burt. I didn't mean to sound like I was accusing you of anything."

"That's alright. I'm kind of jumpy about it myself."

"I saw a photo of the barrel," said Michael. "If you didn't build it, where'd did she get it from?"

"You know that nightclub on Jefferson Avenue called Hooters?" Michael knew it. He'd never been in there, but apparently the big attraction is that your waitress has large breasts and wears a tight t-shirt which reads *Hooters* across the front. "They've got big barrels there," continued Burt, "which support tables in the bar. I think it's supposed to be a Country and Western theme, or something like that. Somehow Mary got them to loan her a barrel." There was a pause on the line before Burt spoke again. "Why don't you come on over about 6:00 pm. I can drive us down there."

On route, Burt asked Michael if he wanted to pick up Larry. Michael was unsure. It would be early evening, and Larry might be in pretty bad shape. On the other hand, Mary sure seemed to like Larry, and it was Larry who inadvertently put this ridiculous idea into Mary's head. Who knows – maybe Larry could be of use. In the end, he decided to get Larry. It was a decision which probably made about as much sense as the rest of his life.

By 6:40 pm, Michael, Burt, and Larry stood together at the halfway point on the St. Andrew's Street Bridge, each of them leaning against the railing. The sun was behind them, still high enough in the sky to cast the scene before them in a glowing yellow light. All around them stood city buildings and skyline, and beneath their feet the green river flowed strongly. Two hundred yards in the distance the river passed under a rusted-out and disused railway bridge, and then dropped suddenly from sight. You could see the edge of the green river, a small horizon, straight and clean. The unseen falling water sounded like perpetual distant thunder, its power palpable in the thin summer air.

Mary was nowhere to be seen.

"Where do you think she'll go in?" asked Michael.

Burt pointed along the left side of the river, to an empty and abandoned lot covered in cracked slabs of grey concrete, weeds, and broken glass. The lot came right to the edge of the river, though there was a row of metal railings which had been erected. "She'll have to go in from there," the old man said.

"Can she get through the railings?" Michael wondered aloud.

"They don't look permanently fixed," said Burt.

Michael was struck by the ordinariness of this city scene. He looked about him and saw people walking over the bridge, caught up in their own thoughts or conversations. The buildings gazed back at him dumbly, golden windows blinking at the slowly sinking sun. The city sounds – the whoosh of cars, a jackhammer in the distance, the shouts of children – it all seemed so… mundane. How preposterous that the world should go on acting as it always does at such a time as this. But perhaps this was a good sign. Perhaps it meant that nothing *out of the ordinary* would occur. And just as he began to feel reassured by these thoughts, he saw Mary's van pull into the lot. She parked about thirty feet from the edge, killed the engine, and stepped out onto the decrepit concrete. She was just as Michael had remembered her from their last visit – the Victorian dress, the granny boots, her hair done up under that ostentatious hat with the feather.

Michael heard Burt blow out a long breath, a breath laced with despondency. "Well, here we go boys," the old man said.

"What shall we do?" asked Michael.

"We go down there, don't we?" said Larry. He seemed drunk, but not nearly as bad as Michael had seen him.

"Yeah, we go down there," said Burt.

As they walked the length of the bridge they watched Mary pull the barrel out of the back of her van, and begin to roll it towards the river's edge. Michael checked his watch: 6:52 pm. The lot was huge and they had to virtually circumnavigate it before they found the entrance through which Mary had driven. As they approached, Michael could see that Mary had pulled back two sections of the railing. She stood next to her upright barrel at the very edge of the lot, one arm resting on the top of the barrel, her back to them. The image was really quite arresting, though Michael had little inclination to appreciate the aesthetic side. When they reached Mary, they stood around her quietly for a moment. It was difficult to know what to say.

"Hi boys," Mary said, a matter-of-fact tone in her voice.

"Hi Mary," they said, almost in unison, their voices sounding flat and dumb.

Michael noticed that Mary's gaze was fixed on the St. Andrew's Avenue Bridge, and the handful of spectators who had obviously noticed Mary and her barrel. There were perhaps twenty of them, and Michael scanned their faces, wondering what a successful lawyer might look like in that crowd.

"Mary," he said. "You can't seriously be considering this."

"What time have you got?" she said. "I haven't worn my watch. It's not waterproof."

Michael checked his watch. "7:05," he said.

"Well," Mary replied. "Maybe he had a late meeting or something. He could be on his way."

They stood there in silence for several minutes, watching the crowd of gawpers swell, listening as the conversations grew louder with speculation and anticipation. Someone shouted "go for it," and a few people clapped. Michael watched the expression on Mary's face – it was worryingly fixed, as if she were preparing herself inwardly.

"Mary," Burt said. "I understand…." Mary shot him a sharp look.

"OK," he continued, "I don't really understand. But I understand a little, and I just don't think this is a good idea."

Mary looked at Larry, who had been unusually quiet. "Larry," she said. "How do you think Annie Taylor felt just before she got into her barrel?"

Larry rubbed his beard thoughtfully. "Scared, I suppose."

"Come on Professor Larry," she continued. "You're smarter than that? What else?"

Larry looked at the ground and spoke softly. "Angry."

"That's right," Mary spat out. "She was angry. I don't know at what exactly, but I'll bet she had plenty of reasons to be good and pissed off." She shot a look at Michael. "What time is it?"

"7:15," he said.

Mary scanned the crowd again, her jaw set in stern determination. She looked behind her into the lot, and Michael followed her gaze. It was empty.

"That's it," she announced. Mary yanked the lid off the barrel, held the lid under one arm, and stood on a foot stool she had placed next to the barrel. Michael noticed that a handle had been screwed onto the inside of the lid, presumably so Mary could pull the lid down from the inside. She made an awkward and unsuccessful attempt to climb in, the barrel teetered and almost falling over. "Burt, hold this," she said, handing him the barrel lid. Mary gripped both sides of the barrel, pulled her legs up under her and above the barrel, and then dropped down into it in one smooth and athletic motion. Michael felt a desperate impulse to do something, but at that moment he was quite mesmerized by Mary's supple gymnastics. Her dress had caught the edge of the barrel and worked itself up over her waist, revealing white panties, but she pulled it loose and tucked it down into the barrel. The barrel came up to Mary's midriff and looked larger now that she was standing in it. Michael noticed that the barrel was right on the edge, and he grimaced as he looked at the fast flowing water six feet below.

"Okay Burt," she said. "I'll need that lid now."

Michael heard a disjointed array of shouting and cat calls coming from the bridge. Burt clutched the barrel lid to his chest like a child holding some prized stuffed animal, looking stunned and rather ill-at-ease. "No Mary," he said.

"Burt, just give me the lid," she snapped.

"No," Michael said. "Don't give it to her." He turned to Mary. "Mary, please – be sensible."

Mary glared at Burt, her expression a mix of anger, fear, and determination.

"Mary," said Burt. "I *don't* think this is art. I really don't."

"Come on Burt," she said. "What *isn't* art?"

The four of them stood there for a moment longer, a surreal and frozen standoff, and then Mary made a sudden furious lunge for the lid. Burt backed away and the barrel toppled over, Mary's forehead bumping the concrete as it went down. The bridge went silent as the stunned spectators watched in anticipation.

"The lid," Mary demanded, as she began forcing herself out of the barrel. Mary made her way onto shaky legs and Michael saw blood begin to stream from the cut on her forehead. Burt looked ghastly – part desperation, part confusion. He backed away, but Mary grabbed hold of the lid with both hands and the two of them performed a pitiable and graceless dance as they tugged at the lid. Just as Michael and Larry moved forward to help, Mary lost her balance following a hefty tug and fell hard on her side. She lay there as Michael, Burt, and Larry crowded around. Mary's elaborate hat had come off when the barrel had fallen, and her long black hair had come undone. Beneath the mess of hair, Michael saw that she was sobbing angrily, her hands pulled up to her face. Michael put a hand on her shoulder.

"Mary, please don't cry. It's alright," he said, glancing up at Larry and Burt as if for confirmation that he had said the right thing. Mary's chest heaved with each sob until finally a sound came out of her which was almost like something an animal might make, a strange growl of a noise torn from somewhere deep inside her. And then suddenly Mary was pushing herself to her feet and Michael caught the briefest glimpse of her expression beneath the tear-stained and matted hair – a dark mix of despondency and rage. As Mary got to her feet, he tried to hold her, but she pushed him away forcefully and trotted towards her van. A heel turned over and she fell. They moved towards her in unison, but as she got up she glared at them.

"Leave me alone," she shouted. They stopped in unison and stared dumbly. Her chest heaving, she gazed at the three of them. "Please," Mary sobbed, a small note of understanding now in her tone. "Leave me alone."

She turned and walked on, her gait somewhat slower and more careful. Mary climbed into her van and cranked the rattling engine to life. Michael, Burt, and Larry stared in silence until her van disappeared beyond the metal fencing and into the fading light now washing over the city.

Mary drove down Andrew's Street, taking in the road ahead and other cars, but not aware of much beyond the growing numbness and formless anger inside her. The road t-junctioned at State Street. She stared at the red light, vision glazed. A left turn would lead to the business section with its expensive buildings and ostentatious City Hall. A right turn would take her into the shitty part of the city – the locale of drifters, drug addicts, prostitutes, and dodgy profiteers. That's where she wanted to be. But she thought of Annie Taylor and wanted to get closer to the river in some way, to complete something, though she didn't know quite what. She would need to turn left and drive upstream to be alone near the river. She made her way up State Street and parked, then walked down a footpath which took her to a grassy bank and the river's edge.

Mary was alone. She took off her granny boots, flung them into the river, and watched as the current swept them quickly downstream. She hesitated for only a moment, and then walked slowly into the green water. She could feel a cool current sucking at her legs and then her body as she waded in to her waist. Her dress – Annie's dress – floated up to the surface, and the flowing water was cold enough to sting her skin and take her breath away. The river bottom was still sloping, and she realized that if she pushed her way out a foot or two more, the current would lift her up and take her down to High Falls and a very long plunge. The crowd will have left by now. Burt, Michael, Larry, will probably have left by now – but did that matter? She thought about her father and wondered where he was, and then she took a half step forward and felt herself become unstable in the push of the water. She wavered in that floating purgatory, was nearly wrenched from the rock, felt one foot pull free, then settle back to the zero point of balance again. She smacked the surface of the water hard with her hand, the fierce sound echoing off the buildings around her. She would do it, she was brave enough, and angry enough.

She gazed at the surface of the dense green water, and wondered what was going on down there. Mary took a small step backwards, crouched down, and submerged herself entirely. The chilly water stung her face, especially the cut on her forehead. She could actually *hear* the current down there, a sound like blood rushing through her own veins, or like an injured animal howling far off in the distance. She had never listened to a current, and she could not resist the force of her own curiosity, even now.

This is how it usually began. Different realities finding each other by chance – an experience of the physical world, a metaphor, an image, a memory. Then the realities collapsed in on one another, blending together, and always posing a question: What does it mean? What is it that wants to be expressed? The cold current pushed heavily at Mary, and her lungs began to burn. The current definitely had a voice, a deep and primordial voice, and the images of lonely wolves and blood coursing selflessly were very real. And more images were coming too. Mary stood up, gulping air, the atmosphere suddenly cool on her skin. The sense of *this current* and the abstract and poetic feeling for *Currents* was something she felt strongly. She had a vague notion that perhaps she could create something out of this, and in that moment she forgot that she had wanted to die.

Mary climbed up into her van, vaguely aware that her sodden dress was soaking the seat. She turned around on State Street and headed back into the bowels of the city, passing a charred shop burnt by fire, a shitty funeral parlor, the building she'd rented for her art show, and a breezeblock bar with neon signs and barred windows. Mary saw a budget convenient store and parked the van out front, making her way inside.

She chose a pint of generic vodka and a carton of grape juice, and approached the Hispanic boy who stood behind the counter. She could feel the water still running down her hair and face, dripping onto the floor off the ends of Annie's dress. The tiled floor was cool and hard beneath her feet. The boy stared, mouth gaping.

"What the fuck are you looking at?" she said.

"Nothing," the boy replied.

She opened the driver's door to her van, intending to get in. But why should she drive somewhere else? Maybe she'd just go for a walk. She could find a suitable place and have a vodka picnic. She'd need a glass, so she opened up the back of her van and climbed in. That was when her eyes fell on the shotgun. She'd take that with her too, though she wasn't sure why.

Mary walked down the litter-strewn street, plastic grocery bag in one hand, the sawn-off 12-gauge in the other, the hem of her wet Victorian dress absorbing a ring of muddy filth from the street. She sat down on the pavement against a boarded-up shop and propped her gun against the wall. Mary poured herself a drink, half-vodka, half-juice, and drank quickly, grimacing her way through the sting of the cheap alcohol. She was surprised that the handful of blacks, Asians, and Hispanics who passed by weren't more alarmed. Who knows – maybe cranks with shotguns were pretty common around here. The vodka was warming her up after that walk in the river, warming body and brain. Her feelings were about as dark as they had ever been, but she couldn't help finding her situation kind of amusing. She finished her drink and walked on down the street, her legs feeling a little rubbery.

One block down, Mary saw a dilapidated porno shop. The place looked closed, but porn shops are deceptive like that. They all look closed, but in fact many are open twenty-four hours a day. *Adult Video*, the sign read. Could the name be any more nondescript? She stood in front of the mirrored door, noticing how the reflective glass was designed to hide the clientele inside. She was startled by the clarity of her reflection, and she studied the image, taking in the old dress, the shotgun under her right arm with its barrel pointed downward, the plastic grocery bag in her left hand. She liked it, but there was room for improvement. Mary put the bag on the ground and took out the pint bottle of vodka. She gripped the shotgun in her left hand, barrel pointing down, and held the vodka bottle with dispassionate coolness in her right. Mary surveyed the sodden image. It was part Annie Taylor, part Annie Oakley, part fish.

The door swung open and Mary saw her image fly off into space. Standing before her was a balding man dressed in a business suit. He clutched a small black plastic bag against his chest and gazed open-mouthed, eyes gaping, hand stuck fast to the door handle. Mary gave the man a hard stare, the sort of stare she imagined you see in old Western films. She wished the cap was off the bottle so she could take a swig of the vodka. The man collected himself and scuttled off down the road. Her image reappeared as the door swung back on its hinges, but she was losing interest in it now.

Mary put the vodka back in the bag and realized she wanted another drink. She also wanted to be alone. There was an ally that ran next to *Adult Video*, and she walked down it, stepping over garbage, feeling the rough grit on the bare soles of her feet. Behind the store she discovered a decrepit and disused parking lot with weeds growing up through the asphalt. She looked in both directions and realized two things: she was on the very edge of the city, and she was alone. No more streets here – just garbage, broken glass, wrecked asphalt, and beyond that, a field of sunburnt grass and weeds. Over that field she gazed at a sky lit by oranges, reds, and the beginnings of purple. This shit-hole of a place stood in stark opposition to that sunset, and if she were in a better frame of mind she'd probably appreciate the juxtaposition.

Mary sat down, her back against the grimy brick of the porn shop. She pulled the glass, vodka, and juice from her bag, poured herself another drink, and stirred the booze and juice with a finger. She drank the second glass quickly, and felt the warmth of it, the light-headedness coming in waves. She thought she might be OK, that if she just got a bit drunk and *checked out* for a while, the images might leave her alone. But they happened anyway – intrusive, insistent, coming like they always did. She could get up and walk away from this place, but the chain of memories wouldn't stop, not now.

She was 7 years old and sitting on the couch at home. She could feel the soft warmth of her flannel pajamas, and she had an arm wrapped around a love-worn teddy bear. Mom was in hospital and dad was away, and uncle Ken was sitting next to her, because he was taking care of her now. Uncle Ken had taken her to the video shop and she had been able to pick any film she wanted. They were watching *Cinderella*, even though she had seen it before. Uncle Ken had his arm over her shoulder and sat really close to her, and that was nice. Uncle Ken had been so nice to her. And then uncle Ken put his hand down between her legs, on her thigh, but he smiled at her when he did it, so that was nice too. Her dad never touched her, but uncle Ken liked to be close to her and he was always making her something nice to eat and he always let her decide which movie they would watch. She missed her mom and she was sad that she couldn't see her, but the doctor said it upset mom when she had gone to visit her, and she didn't want to upset her mom.

Mary turned the glass up and the burning liquid made its way into an empty stomach. She should try to think of something else, but she knew that things had gone too far. She didn't want to remember, but when it starts, it has a power all its own, a power which is bigger than her. The memories could be worse if you try to fight them. Maybe she shouldn't have drunk the vodka, or did it matter?

She was in the bath now. Mary had bathed herself for as long as she could remember, but Uncle Ken said that her mom and dad should really have helped because she was only seven, but her dad had been so busy and her mom was unwell. But he was going to do it right and help her. He cleaned like it was really natural and he told her stories as he moved the soapy washcloth all over her, and the stories were so funny that she hardly paid much attention to where he was cleaning and after a while it was just normal that Uncle Ken helped her to have a bath and he was very nice to her when he helped. He was taking care of her. She really liked Uncle Ken and sometimes she felt bad that she liked him so much because he wasn't really her father. But it was like he was her father because she hardly saw her father because he had to go away on the planes all the time because he was important.

Mary poured another drink and worked steadily on it, her eyes stinging and tearing with the strength of the vodka. She wondered if she was a masochist. Why did she have thoughts she didn't want? Why did she relive this shit? Why didn't she tell him to stop? Maybe she really wanted these thoughts. Did she want Uncle Ken to do that?

Uncle Ken had been so kind when he tucked her in at night. He tickled her and bounced her up and down on the mattress and then gave her a big hug and a kiss, and told her how talented she was at drawing, and what a special girl she was. And when she had that bad dream, uncle Ken got in bed with her and she liked that at first because she felt safer and she had always slept with her mom after she drank the strawberry drinks, so it didn't seem so unusual.

Mary felt the tears coming now, tears made of anger and hurt, and the memories didn't come one at a time anymore. They came all at once – disjointed, random, shifting. The thing that happened when Uncle Ken came into her bed happened so many times that what she saw wasn't one memory, but a disordered collage of all the memories: Waking and feeling confused because there was something sticky on her pajamas or her bottom, the feel of uncle Ken pressing himself against her bottom as he lay behind her, the strange sound of his heavy breathing and groaning, the way he touched her down there and the sweaty warm feel of the places he told her to put her hands and mouth. He said it was okay, and she didn't want to but she was afraid that he might be mad at her. He *had* been really nice to her, and what if he left? Would her dad think she had been bad and that she had made Uncle Ken go away? Would her father be mad at her? And who would look after her?

She could see Uncle Ken on top of her now and he was hurting her so much down there and she sobbed because of the pain and confusion and she told Uncle Ken that it hurt but he didn't seem to hear her and at last she looked away and closed her eyes tight but it didn't stop and then she opened her eyes, as if to look through the wall into her parents room, and she thought *Daddy, Daddy, Daddy…* as if her thoughts could penetrate that wall and find her father somehow, but he was away on a plane and Mary knew that he was not coming.

Mary's body rocked in convulsions as the sobs and tears still came and she pulled her knees up, the tears spilling down onto her feet. These feelings were so old, and yet her body remembered them perfectly. The body had no sense of time when it came to these sensations. She was seven and twenty-six years old all at once. She tried to drink more vodka, but her hand shook and the edge of the glass clinked painfully against her teeth. She felt scared but also a smoldering hate – a hate directed at Uncle Ken and then at her father and finally at herself, and then she didn't know where Uncle Ken and her father ended and where she began, or where the hate belonged. More than hate, she felt spilt open and exposed, raw and broken…

Mary had noticed the shattered glass on the asphalt when she sat down. She ran her hand over the smashed translucent pile and selected one with a reliable point. A siren approached, and she wondered vaguely if someone had reported the deranged woman with the shotgun. She didn't give a fuck about the police, but she didn't want to be disturbed. Mary pulled her dress up, exposing her inner thigh. She wondered abstractly if Annie Taylor had ever done this. Mary made four slow cuts, watching the blood ooze up, remembering when she had made the blood run as a child so that her dad could minister to her. She felt a numbness wash over her, felt the emotional pain transforming into physical pain, the anger ebb, saw the memories fade as they lost their power… for now. She didn't like that she did this, but at such times nothing but physical pain could soothe her. It didn't make sense, but it was true.

She replaced her dress around her bare ankles and put her chin on her knees. Mary gazed at the fading sun as it dipped and melted into the horizon, the deep red and purple spilling across the sky, the air suddenly cooling against her skin. Her body rocked slightly, and though she was no longer sobbing, silent tears continued to fall from her cheeks and land on her feet, feet filthy with the dirt of the streets. Her long black hair, still damp, had come undone and fell near her feet. She looked around her, wondering if anyone had come by, but she was still alone. She felt a sudden impulse to be clean. Mary Magellan took hold of her hair with both hands and washed her filthy feet with her damp hair and the tears which had fallen.

Michael recognized Mary's converted bread truck parked by the side of the road as he puttered down State Street. He brought the moped to a stop, climbed off, and looked around. Night had fallen now, and the streets lights were on, casting their glow over the garbage-strewn streets and dilapidated buildings. An hour earlier, Larry, Burt and himself had stood staring dumbly at one another after Mary had bolted from the scene of her near plunge over the falls. They had questioned each other in predictable and futile ways, making rather pointless conjectures. *What in the world was she doing? Should we follow her? Do you think she'll be okay? She seems to want to be left alone. She probably just needs some time to think things over.* And then there wasn't much else to say, so they drifted off, carrying with them a shared sense of disorientation and ineffectual malaise. Michael hadn't felt good about just leaving Mary. But how do you find a person who lives in a home which is on four wheels? So when Burt had dropped him off back at *Tasco's*, he puttered home, telling himself he would call Mary's cell phone in a while. But the space he occupied in his own living room felt pointless and oppressive, so he puttered back downtown. It was arriving at the corner of State Street that he recalled that Mary's art exhibit was down there somewhere. He'd have a look around.

Michael peered into the windows of Mary's van – empty. He called out, "Mary," but had no reply. Michael looked around, noting that the streets were fairly deserted and most of the shops were shut, except a convenience store and a porno shop up the road. He wandered the isles of the convenience store and then left, peering up the road at the blinking *Adult Video* sign. Michael walked in that direction, scanning the street, shops, and alleyways as he went. He passed a couple of black youths wearing NBA basketball shirts, athletic dark arms swinging, and then stopped in front of the video shop.

Michael called out, "Mary", the sound of his voice echoing in the street. There was a group of guys standing on a street corner across the road, and they looked over. He felt a little embarrassed, but he needed to see Mary, needed to know she was alright. "Mary," he called, louder. The sound of his call fell back into silence and a moment later he heard her voice, faint, drifting up an alleyway beside the porn shop. "Michael, you can stop shouting. I'm down here."

Michael made his way down the alley, tripping on something he couldn't see, and then emerged behind the store. A large moon was up over a disused field, and he could see Mary well enough, seated on the ground against the building in the pale bluish glow. She gazed up at him, a weary smile on her face. He saw the nearly empty vodka bottle and realized she was drunk.

"Jesus Michael, wha a racket you're making out there."

"I'm sorry," he said reflexively, relieved to see her. Michael looked at her more closely. Her hair and dress were quite disheveled, and her feet were bare. And… she looked damp, as if she'd been in water. He felt an impulse to hold her, to pull her close to him, but he really didn't know if she wanted that. Mary patted the tarmac beside her, inviting him to sit, and that was when he noticed the dull metallic reflection of the shotgun propped against the brick. This was too much – what was she doing with that? He sat down next to her, glad to be near her and yet annoyed that Mary's antics had taken yet another turn.

"Mary, you've got a shot gun."

"Oh yeah," Mary said, as if she'd forgotten it was there.

"Why have you got a gun?"

She gazed at him, eyelids half closed, grinning sloppily. "Is funny you should mention that because I was jus thinkin about it. Is a little project I been working on and it's sort of been developing." Mary leaned close and whispered in his ear. "Is not real bullets. It's paint I put in the what-cha-ma-call-its. I shot a canvas an then I shot my father's suit and jes now I figured out that I'm gonna hunt down my father and shoot him… shoot him jes like Francis Macomber shot that buffalo in Africa, cept I'm gonna hide behind buildings and post boxes and maybe that fountain where he works. You know, you're not supposed to shoot from the Land Rover, you gotta get um from the ground. I could be as brave as Francis Macomber. I got sort of a bright pink I put in my last bullet and that'll liven up dad a bit."

Michael was having a hard time following this, but he knew that Francis Macomber was a character in a Hemmingway story, and he got the clear impression that Mary was planning to track her dad around town with a shotgun. "Mary," he said, trying to affect a tone which was firm *and* sympathetic, "that's really not a good idea."

Mary snapped her fingers listlessly and pointed at him. "Hey, you could be my gun bearer. Maybe you could help flush him out of where ever he's hiding. An urban safari, maybe it'll catch on."

Michael stared, lost for words, trying to read her. She was the same but different. Mary usually discussed her ideas with unchecked enthusiasm – tonight she seemed drugged, depressed, drained. She put the empty pint bottle to her lips and tried to get a few more drops out of it. They sat together in silence and Mary felt very far away from him, and Michael was aware of the extent he didn't understand her.

Mary pushed herself to her feet, unsteady, swaying, and Michael jumped up, taking her elbow. She dropped the pint bottle on the pavement and patted his arm, motioning with her head that they should leave. Mary picked up her shotgun and held it under an arm, taking Michael's arm for support. They turned right at the end of the alley, Mary leaning against him as they gently weaved a path towards the van. Michael was acutely aware of the gun tucked in her arm, the barrel almost level with the street. He scanned the street ahead, but it was empty except for a distracted man and woman about two blocks up. He realized he should have tried to convince Mary to conceal the gun somehow, but they were only twenty yards from the van so he decided to push on.

Mary suddenly leaned close and spoke, her voice a mere whisper. "You are good to me Michael." As he nodded in response, he heard a voice from behind them, a male voice carrying an authoritative tone.

"This is the police. Stay right where you are. Now listen carefully, I want you to put the gun… ." Michael saw an expression of utter weariness crawl across Mary's face, and felt her release his arm and turn around, the gun barrel following her turn. "Oh come on fellas…" she replied, and Michael saw that she was smiling – a sad smile of recognition and absolute resignation. Two shots came in quick succession, like the sound of a cracking whip, and Michael saw the terrified and bewildered expression of the young officer who held the handgun. The shotgun clattered stupidly on the ground and Mary's body dropped away and hit the pavement with a dull thud, the back of her head making a cracking sound. Bizarrely, Michael was horrified to think that Mary had hit her head like that, and it was only a moment later that his faculties of perception could acknowledge the two holes in her chest, and the blood soaking into her dress in slow expanding circles. Michael peered into Mary's eyes, searching for recognition, for connection. But her eyes were glassy, fixed on nothing earthly, as if she were no longer there.

PART 3

CHAPTER 1

Somewhere in the flicker of a poorly tuned television set is the background radiation of the Big Bang.

From the journals of Professor Charles Kidding, extract #164.

Michael sat on the edge of his bed, staring into space. He had either slept very badly or not at all, it was hard to tell. Sharp-edged memories of last night darted in and out of his mind. He knew everything had actually occurred, yet somehow the memories had the quality of a dream. He recalled the sickened expression of disbelief on the face of the young officer, the ambulance and the paramedics, the small crowd that had gathered at the periphery. Just before they had closed the ambulance doors, he heard one of the paramedics say 'I've got no heart beat'.

I've got no heart beat.

Those words had been shocking. They were shocking now. Mary's heart had stopped. That's what the paramedic had said. How could that happen?

He vaguely recalled the trip in the police car, being led by the arm up the steps and into the same city police station he had visited only two weeks previously. They kept him until after 1:00 am in the morning, and he had been interviewed by two sets of officers – or was it three? *Why did she have a gun? Where did she get the gun from? What was she planning to do with the gun? What was the basis of his relationship to Mary?* He remembered explaining that Mary didn't have real bullets in the gun and didn't bother to tell them much more. How do you explain to a bunch of cops that Mary had decided to hunt down her father and shoot him with artist's paint? Michael didn't really care to face an interview with a police psychiatrist.

They were quite decent to him, and he saw the faint expression of worry on their faces. There would be an enquiry, it might be suggested that someone screwed-up; they were going to have to explain things. Michael didn't really care about their problems though. He asked about Mary several times, but they just kept telling him they didn't know anything definite yet. Around midnight, he watched the sergeant take a soundless phone call through a thick glass window. The Sergeant hung up and Michael saw him mouth the word *shit.* That's when he knew.

Michael got up and stood before his book case. He gazed at his collection of books, then over at his collection of CDs, and then his collection of watches. They seemed strangely unfamiliar to him. He placed a finger on top of one of the books, as if to confirm its actual existence. To his surprise he felt mild disgust for the thing.

Why was this book here?

Why were those CDs and wrist watches over there?

He jerked his finger back from the book like a man receiving a shock, and then his mind fell into emptiness. Michael walked to the window and looked out at the fine August morning, but felt nothing for it. He watched a large Salvation Army truck pull into the driveway, its heavy engine cranking noisily, though the scene before him was about as real as an oil painting. He seemed to be gazing at a notional truck, a theoretical truck, a speculative truck. The idea that the truck was *there* seemed no more sensible than the idea that he was *here.*

A young man slammed the truck door, creating a localized compression in air density, a sound wave, which radiated towards Michael at 767.3 miles per hour. The sound wave reached Michael's inner ear, jiggled three tiny delicate bones encased in pinkish tissue, and got passed onto his perceptual faculties via nerve sensations. Michael was not consciously aware of these mechanics, but there was probably a lot of shit he was ignorant of as he moved through his local environment.

The delicate jiggling ear bones and resultant perception of the slamming door did, however, jar Michael into some sort of wakefulness, because he recalled the reason for the Salvation Army truck – Mr. Deveroix's train set was due to be picked up this morning. Not wanting to see anyone, he groaned inwardly.

He led the two uniformed young men to the attic and showed them the tracks and trains. Michael felt obligated to ask if they wanted help, but they assured him that they were happy to load it themselves, and besides, health and safety policy prevented Michael from assisting. It was going to take about thirty minutes, and he signed a release form. One of them asked him if *he was okay,* and he realized that his troubled state must be quite obvious to others. He didn't really care.

Michael imagined that he should do something, and having no obvious sense of volition, he simply fell back on routine and decided to take a shower. He entered the bathroom, took his clothes off, and removed his wrist watch. He placed the watch on top of a white towel which hung on a rack, and stood under a strong flow of water and rising steam. He ran the water unusually hot, and though it practically burned him, he didn't feel the need to adjust the temperature. He washed himself thoroughly, using a lot of soap, and eventually stepped out of the shower. Michael seemed to be moving slowly, like a man walking underwater. He dried himself and then picked his wrist watch up off the towel. Michael had performed this action thousands of time. You dry yourself off and strap your watch on – it was a simple habit, one of many which formed the course of his day. And yet, Michael just stood there, naked, staring at the watch, seemingly unable or unwilling to move. He tried to put the watch on, but he couldn't do it. It wasn't that he couldn't physically perform the action; it was just that he couldn't *bring* himself to do it – he didn't want it on his wrist, he didn't want the watch at all. An image of that German soldier Burt told him about came to his mind. He saw the soldier standing naked in a shower room, contemplating his stolen watch, contemplating his nakedness. At just that moment, Michael heard the roar of the Salvation Army truck engine as it started up. An idea came to him all at once, a senseless idea which had to be pursued. A peculiar and anxious energy flooded his body and Michael threw on Mrs. Deveriox's pink bathrobe and ran down the stairs and out the front door.

The truck was edging down the driveway when Michael shouted, "Hey, wait." They heard him and stopped, allowing him to reach the cab window. "Excuse me boys," he spat out through heaving lungs. "Can I have a moment of your time?" The young men gazed at him with confused expressions, and Michael became aware that the bathrobe had fallen open.

Michael led them to his rooms, and the three of them stood together surveying the material world of Michael's possessions. "I want you to take everything," said Michael. "Everything you see or can find here. There's a bedroom and closet too. Take everything from there as well."

The young men were silent for a moment, glancing over at one another. "Sir, are you sure you really want to do that?" said one boy. "I mean, it's a lot of stuff."

Michael was suddenly worried they wouldn't take his things. Maybe they thought he was mentally ill and wasn't fit to make these sorts of decisions. They might want to call a manager or something.

"Yes, definitely. I don't need this stuff anymore." He walked to his dresser and took a watch off the pine watch rack. He presented watches to the boys, one he had carried from the bathroom and the other he had just removed from his dresser. "This is a lot of extra work for you two. I'll bet you've got a busy schedule, so I want you to have these watches. They're worth quite a lot, so if you don't want them yourself you can sell them."

The boys looked at each other, unsure, small grins growing at the edges of their mouths. Michael took the boys hands in turn and placed a watch in each palm. "Please, he said, take this as a gift. You've worked really hard this morning." He realized there was a beseeching tone in his voice, and he imagined he was starting to sound quite insane. The boys were unsure of themselves, and threw glances at one another. Michael retreated to his closet, opened his safe, and took all of the cash. He pressed it into the hands of the boys. "I want you to have this. It's a lot of extra work. Please." He was pleading now, and he didn't care.

At 11:15 am Michael stood in the exact center of his living room. He made a little whistling noise which echoed around the bare walls and varnished pine flooring. Even the rug was gone. Funny how the sound of emptiness is actually louder. They'd taken everything except Sam's riding leathers and helmet, which, after all, didn't really belong to Michael. Oddly, these items were the only things he might have actually missed. He didn't feel much except a mild sense of detached amusement at the vacant space around him. That, and a dark numbness. He needed a coffee and wondered abstractly about money. After the boys had driven away in their truck, Michael had changed back into the Khaki trousers and blue Oxford he'd hung up in the bathroom earlier. He felt his back pocket and realized that his wallet was there.

As Michael drove his moped to the end of his driveway he noticed a man standing across the road, apparently watching him. The man was about his own age, and Michael wondered what he was doing there. You get used to the rhythms of passing pedestrians and people who hang out on the school grounds. The guy looked ill-at-ease, as if he had no natural business being there. Michael was about to pull out onto the street when the man took a couple of steps forward, as if he might speak to him. The man stopped, hesitated, and then continued across the street to meet him.

"Excuse me," the man said, looking nervous, agitated. "I'm sorry to disturb you. My name is Kevin Greensmith. Are you Michael Wilson?"

"Yes."

"I saw your picture in the paper this morning. You were with Mary when… it happened."

Michael hadn't realized that Mary's death had made the papers. It was something he hadn't even thought about. He didn't recall reporters being on the scene, but someone must have taken a photo of him and Mary. It made sense, really. It was bound to be big news, at least for a few days. "I'm sorry to intrude," the man continued. "It's just that, I was…." The man seemed unsure of his words. "I was… *a friend* of Mary's."

Michael looked at the man more closely. He was handsome, well-dressed, well-mannered. He looked successful. Michael smiled spontaneously as he realized exactly who this man was. He had always thought of him as *the white high-heels man*. Now he had a name – Kevin.

"I was *a friend* of Mary's too," Michael said, taking his riding glove off and offering his hand, which Kevin shook. "How did you find me?"

"Your name was in the paper," said Kevin. "Mary mentioned the town you lived in once, and I just looked you up in the phonebook." Kevin looked around before continuing. "Can we talk for a moment?"

Michael nodded, parked up the bike, and suggested a bench across the street. They remained silent for a moment after sitting down, as if speaking right away was some sort of sacrilege.

"I just can't believe she's gone," said Kevin. "I read the story in the paper, but it didn't really explain much, just that she was shot by an officer and it was all being investigated. Then there was that photo of Mary on the ground, and you were holding her head." Michael remembered. He could feel the sticky sensation of Mary's blood on his hands again, could see her pale face beneath him, those empty eyes. A wave of nausea passed through him. Kevin shook his head and pushed a hand roughly through his hair, his mouth tightening as if to constrain himself. The man was near tears, and Michael recognized his own sense of brokenness in the guy. He told Kevin everything, explaining about Mary's infatuation with Annie Taylor, the promotional flyer he'd made, the scene at the falls, the shot gun, and the encounter with the police in front of the porn shop. There seemed little reason to conceal what had happened. Kevin stared at him, astounded, dismayed, and Michael wondered if he felt a bit hurt at the extent of the relationship he'd had with Mary. They sat in silence for a while, each attending to their own thoughts.

"Did Mary tell you about me, I mean my problem?" Kevin asked.

"Yeah," said Michael, a bit embarrassed for him.

Kevin shook his head, smiling. "She was never very good with boundaries, was she?"

"No she wasn't," Michael agreed. "Did she tell you about me?"

Kevin nodded. "She didn't tell me your name, but yeah.

"You must think I'm pretty strange," said Kevin.

Michael recalled his conversation with Mary about Kevin and certain images came back to him.

"You know," said Michael, "a few months ago, I might have thought it was strange. But so much has happened since then, not much seems strange anymore."

A momentary expression of pained uncertainty came over Kevin's face. "There are probably reasons why I need to do what I do. I'm not a pervert, really. Mary was the first person I could talk to about it. I'd upset a lot of women along the way and I wasn't happy about that. She helped me, and she accepted me for who I was. I'd never known anyone like that."

An unspoken and shared melancholy grew up between them, and they realized that they couldn't talk about Mary any more. They discussed their work as a means of distraction, and traded a few stock tips absent-mindedly. Michael liked this man, but he was relieved when Kevin excused himself for an appointment. Maybe he'd see Kevin again, maybe they'd even be friends some day. But not now.

CHAPTER 2

Brand new cars, including Land Rovers and Mitsubishi Shoguns, were parked in a field in Wales, Britain, as the car dealer didn't have space in his sales lot. A Ram occupying the field saw his reflection in the car panels and thought he was facing off against a rival. He repeatedly charged the cars, eventually causing $20,000 in damages.

From the journals of Professor Charles Kidding, extract #94.

Larry had eaten lunch, a pita sandwich from a street vendor, and was sitting on his bench, working on his second bottle of wine. The weather was fine, and for the most part it was just another Tuesday. A young couple with a baby in a pram sat at the next bench over, and the man was reading to his wife from a newspaper. Apparently, a woman had been shot yesterday evening by the police. The woman pointed to a photo in the paper.

"Look at the clothing she's wearing. That's so old fashioned. That photo could have been taken a hundred years ago."

"Excuse me," said Larry. "Can I see that photo?"

Larry had actually managed to finish four bottles of wine and open a fifth before he decided that he would walk to the High Falls pedestrian bridge. He staggered along the sidewalk, a backpack with his few belongings over his shoulder. Larry fell down twice, and on the second fall he managed to smash his wine bottle and scrape the palms of his hands on the broken glass and rough pavement. He pushed himself up from the shards of glass and puddle of wine, and staggered his way to the nearest liquor store. Outside the store he uncapped the new bottle of red and took a sip, trying to remember where he was going. He recalled that Mary was dead, mumbled "Oh yeah," and shuffled off.

Larry eventually stumbled to the middle of the pedestrian bridge, the visual world jerking wildly about him, and fell heavily onto a bench. The sun was lower in the sky and cast a yellow-orange glow on the falling water which crashed ceaselessly into the gorge. He drank steadily from the bottle. He hadn't known Mary well. He'd only met her a couple of times, but she had affected him. His memories were of her smile, her art, and the infectious enthusiasm she felt for whatever was at hand. He wondered how Michael was, and where he was. He wished he hadn't told Mary about Annie Taylor. Maybe he shouldn't have become involved with human beings again. He noticed blood on the palms of both hands, still tacky the way blood is before it dries completely. He gazed at the blood for a while, wondering how it got there, trying to remember if he'd fallen down.

Larry opened his eyes and noticed that the sun was lower in the sky, and he wondered if he had nodded off. He continued to drink from the bottle, belching now and again, his head lolling from side to side. His thoughts of Mary and Michael were interspersed now with a vague and dark introspection, and he considered the choices he'd made. An image of his daughter came to him and he pushed the memory away. For some strange reason he found himself thinking about Christian notions of heaven, purgatory, and hell. The *literal* meaning ascribed to these places was of course nonsense. Still, biblical stories had this accidental knack for getting at something which was *metaphorically* compelling. Quite suddenly he felt the whole of his life pass over him, sudden and shocking, like a cold shadow which soars over the face of the earth. In this moment he sensed something inexpressible and crushing, something which he felt in his body. In its wake there trailed a thought, and he wondered if he should write it down. He didn't know if he had the will or mental faculties to get it down on paper, but the thought had a poetic quality and seemed important. Maybe it would still be important later. He managed to pull his wallet from his back pocket and find a slip of paper in there – it could be a receipt. He discovered a pen in his pocket and smoothed the bit of paper on the bench.

Dear Larry, he began. His watery vision jumped about, and his brain struggled to coordinate his hand in forming these simple letters. He continued. *You are a coward. Purgatory means not having enough courage to live or to die, and there are only cowards in purgatory. So…* . A wave of exhaustion came over him. He'd have a swig of wine and rest for a moment, and then he'd finish his thought. He knew what he wanted to say, he just needed a minute to rest. His bleary vision swept the landscape and the sound and image of the falls felt very far away. Everything felt very far away, and strangely dark.

CHAPTER 3

In order to make a pound of honey, bees have to visit two million flowers and fly the equivalent of twice around the world.

From the journals of Professor Charles Kidding, extract #56.

Michael sat in his local Starbucks, a cup of Grande House Blend steaming in front of him. The espresso machine made its recurrent whooshing noise, the clientele chatted easily, the aromas were just as you'd expect, the staff acted in a fashion consistent with their corporate compliance training. Everything was the same, which struck Michael as quite impossible.

Michael was meant to study the newspapers, finance magazines, and online investor sites. A conjurer of finance, he had developed an intellect for predicting the future. Where others failed (and most did), he succeeded. But what possible relevance did predicting the future hold? What was the point in making more money? And something else was strange. Normally, Michael felt mildly anxious at his inability to understand the perceptions of the café clientele. Today, he experienced the people around him with the same interest he felt when gazing into his coffee. The clientele and staff were mere surfaces now, empty of any capacity to harm him. You have to feel the need to survive in order to fear harm. If the customers at the next table spat in his face, he might not bother to wipe the spittle away. He felt himself to barely exist, a ghost surrounded by animate surfaces. Detached, cut adrift, the world had become *impersonal.*

Across the room, seated alone, he noticed a large man – muscular, dark-skinned, pock-marked face. Michael recognized him immediately – a dream made flesh. Michael was vaguely aware of the shock he'd felt the first time he'd seen this man a few weeks ago, but it now seemed entirely normal that a man from his dreams should be sitting across the room. What had Larry said?

Why don't you talk to him?

Why not? He stood up and walked across the room, feeling a bit floaty, as if his feet weren't quite making contact in the normal way. He stood near the man's table, and noticed that the man had a small stack of books with him. The man continued to read, and Michael examined closely the cover of one of the books. The book was entitled *The Essentials of Plumbing*. Beneath the title was depicted an intricate drawing of a house. The drawing had been made in 'cut-away' fashion and showed a complex array of piping which went through the walls, beneath the floors, and even under the house itself. The large man looked up and gazed at Michael, a surprised and questioning expression forming on his face.

"Are you OK buddy," he asked eventually, his voice deep and even.

"Do you mind if I join you for a minute," said Michael.

The large man paused for a moment and then glanced past Michael, probably noticing that there were empty tables. He shrugged and motioned to the chair opposite. "Sure, have a seat if you want," he said. The resonant depth of tone in the man's voice seemed to set off little local vibrations. Michael sat down, and they stared at each other for a moment.

"This might sound kind of strange," said Michael, "but I've had this dream a few times. There's this guy in my dream and... as odd as this seems, he looks just like you. I mean maybe not exactly the same, but the guy… well, he looks a lot like you." Michael watched the big man's expression, wondering how he was taking this. The man just looked curious.

"What happens in the dream?" the man asked.

"Well, I'm driving, it's late at night, and I'm somewhere downtown – but the streets are empty. I stop at a light and then you… I mean this guy in my dream… jumps on top of my car and rips the roof off. And then this guy is looking down on me through the roof and he's screaming, 'who the hell are you'?"

The large man put a marker in his book and closed it. He looked at

Michael closely, a pensive expression on his face.

"What happens then?" the big man asked.

"That's it. That's when I wake up."

The man smiled broadly. "Well, how 'bout that? And I look just like the guy in the dream?"

"Yeah," said Michael. "Except… except the man in the dream is quite awful. I mean, he's pretty terrifying."

"Hmm," said the man. "Well, I'm sorry about that."

Michael smiled. "That's alright. It's not as if it's your fault. I don't even know why I'm telling you this."

The man laughed, and they looked at each other for a moment, Michael not quite knowing what to say, or if there was more that could be said. He noticed the drawing on the cover of the book he'd seen earlier.

"So are you a plumber then?"

"Yeah, I sure am," the large man said. Michael pointed to the cover of the book.

"Is there really all that piping running through the walls and under the floors in a house?" asked Michael. He was interested, for some reason.

"There sure is. Plumbing is actually very complicated. Most people think of plumbing as just the stuff you can see – you know – the sinks, the tub, the washing machine. But most of the plumbing is stuff that you don't even know is there."

"I've never really thought about it that way," said Michael. "So you have to keep learning about it?"

"Oh yeah. Being a plumber is difficult work. You have to know what's behind the walls and under the floors, and you have to be able to get at the problem and fix it without making a mess of the place in the process. People want you to fix their sinks and showers, but they don't want you punching nasty holes in the walls or ripping apart their floors. The trick is to repair what needs repairing, but without doing any damage, and in order to do that you need to understand how everything works."

"Hmmm," said Michael, and they stared at each other for a moment.

They were quiet for a bit, and Michael realized how tired he felt. He tapped the large man's book with a finger. "Anyways," Michael said, "good luck with the plumbing."

"Well, good luck with… you know, everything."

CHAPTER 4

An innocent Indian gentleman served eight years in prison when staff forgot to tell him he was free to go. Pratap Nayak was found innocent by the Orissa High Court in 1994 and officials forgot to tell him until 2002.

From the journals of Professor Charles Kidding, extract #216

Michael stood at the far end of the High Falls pedestrian bridge. He could make out Larry's disheveled form lying curled up on the pavement near the centre of the bridge, next to one of the benches. He made his way over the bridge, put his flask of coffee down on the ground, and sat on the bench. Larry resembled a corpse. He was wearing the sports coat Michael had given him, which was filthy and badly wrinkled. There was dried blood on Larry's hands and forehead, and his skin had a deathly pallor about it. Michael suddenly worried if Larry *was* actually dead, and he grabbed his shoulder and shook it. Larry groaned and opened his eyes, squinting painfully in the morning sunlight. Larry pushed himself with difficulty to his knees, and then slowly pulled himself up onto the bench. Michael noticed a scrap of paper, maybe a receipt, stuck to the shoulder of his sports coat. He must have slept in some gooey substance because the note was stuck fast to the jacket.

"Larry, you look like you've been involved in an industrial farming accident."

"Good one," said Larry, his voice a rasping croak. They sat in silence for a while, staring in unison at the veil of falling green water and the gorge below. Larry sighed deeply and held his head in his hands.

"I'm sorry Michael – about Mary."

"So am I. I still can't believe it's happened."

"I liked her a lot too," said Larry, putting a trembling hand on Michael's shoulder.

They sat in silence. Michael didn't have the words necessary to express his experience of Mary's absence. Larry could have said a few things, but his head hurt a lot and the crashing waterfall was painful in his ears. Eventually, Michael felt the simple need for conversation, if only as a means of distraction; so he told Larry about meeting the man from his dream, giving him the detail of their conversation.

Larry smiled and then grimaced, as if smiling made his head hurt more. "He was a plumber then?" said Larry.

"Yeah, a plumber."

"Well," said Larry, smiling faintly, "I suppose plumbers know what's beneath your floorboards, which reminds me of something Charles Kidding once told me...."

Michael felt a surprising surge of anger well up and he shot a look at Larry. "Can you do me a favor and stop this Charles Kidding nonsense. Not now, okay?"

Larry put his hands up. "Hey, I'm sorry, I just thought...." The expression on Michael's face had hardened, an expression which held Larry's tongue.

"Now's not really a good time for screwing about, is it?" said Michael. "There is no Charles Kidding, is there?"

Larry shrugged. "Well, isn't there a little Charles Kidding in all of us?"

"I don't know about that. But I think you just made this Charles Kidding person up. The name's even farcical, isn't it? *Kidding*, as in joking. The irony wasn't lost on me – I'm not stupid. It's like you can't bear to say anything important or meaningful, but sometimes you need to just the same, and that's when you wheel out this Charles Kidding figure. You hide behind the guy. I just don't want to hear about Mr. Kidding right now, okay?"

"Okay," said Larry, his tone conciliatory. "I didn't mean to be disrespectful."

Michael softened, his shoulders slumping. "It's alright." Michael and Larry continued to stare into the falls. "Come to think of it," said Michael. "You know these journals that Charles Kidding was supposed to have kept? Do they actually exist?"

Larry looked around for his backpack, and they eventually found it under the bench. He pulled four leather-bound journals out, a thick rubber band wrapped around them. Larry handed the journals to Michael and then raised his hands in an expression of guilty admission. Michael stared at the journals and then snapped the rubber band, as if he needed further physical evidence to substantiate their existence. There was a title written across the top journal: *Clitoral Ambivalence and other Symptoms of Economic Unrest.*

"Larry, what sort of title is that?"

"When I first started the journals I used a different title. I think it was *Examples of Human Absurdity in Everyday Life*. But that title seemed a little too straightforward, so I changed it.

"But you changed the title," said Michael, "to something which doesn't make sense."

"Absurd, isn't it?" said Larry, a tired grin at the edge of his mouth.

"Oh," replied Michael.

He gazed at Larry's battered form, and tapped the journals. "I'll bet this would make a good book. It would be funny and it represents some sort of philosophy, doesn't it? You should get this published."

Larry smiled sadly. "You know Michael, the first time we met you asked me what my perspective on life was? It was practically the first thing you said to me. Do you remember?" Michael nodded. "I talked a lot of nonsense about nihilism and phenomenology. I was just being my usual flippant pain-in-the-ass self. But your question got to me, actually. I've thought a lot about it. You want to know my perspective?"

Michael nodded.

"There's a very old term connected to an odd branch of Christianity. Terminalism, I believe it's called. I'm not a Christian, mind you, but the term is useful to me. It means that people have a certain period of grace, and during that time there is the possibility of absolution, of release. But after that period lapses, they're beyond hope. I'm past my sell-by date."

"Larry, don't you want to even try anymore?"

"Michael, apathy is the last great line of defense – it's where I've marshaled my remaining forces and it's where the final battles will be fought and lost. I've got my strategy worked out, OK? You gotta think of yourself. You've got plenty of chances left."

Michael sighed deeply, and they went quiet for a while. Sometimes there's something to say and sometimes there isn't. At least he and Larry could sit with each other in silence. That was something. But silence was difficult in its own way now. Silence and *not-doing* meant that images of Mary came to him. He saw the two symmetric circles of blood in her chest, circles which expanded as Mary's dying self still contained enough inward pressure to force the darkening liquid from these newly formed holes. He saw her body spasm in sudden small jerks as if her shocked and confused physiology was making one last frenzied attempt to repair itself. Worst of all, he saw her eyes and knew she was beyond his reach, and he hated that.

"You think I've got chances left?" said Michael, shaking his head. His voice was barely a whisper. "To tell the truth, I can't imagine life without Mary. I can't imagine not being able to see her, to talk with her..." (Michael held up his hands in the morning light) "...never touching her again."

Michael searched Larry's beaten and flaccid face. "Larry, I'm fucking cracking up here. I was cracking up before they shot Mary. Larry, tell me what to do. No more Charles Kidding, OK?"

Larry offered him a grin. "Michael, I was a logician, and then I became a cynical logician, and then I became a disillusioned and cynical logician, and eventually I became this man whose only pleasure in life consists in getting drunk and finding evidence to substantiate the absurdity of his own existence. Any advice I can offer isn't likely to give you a warm fuzzy, is it?"

"I don't care Larry," said Michael, a tone of frustration in his voice. "Just tell me what you think."

Larry sighed and took a deep swig of Michael's bitter coffee. "Michael, I need to explain something. The Board of Directors at the University will tell you that I got fired because I became an unreliable drunk, which is certainly true. But there was another reason, a more important reason." Larry looked at him closely, and Michael saw in the philosopher's glassy blue eyes a reservoir of vulnerability he hadn't noticed before. "I had to stop teaching because I couldn't trust myself to say or do anything. I'd ruined enough lives. Do you understand?"

Larry looked away and Michael followed his line of sight into High Falls. A clean line separating shadow from light cut obliquely through the falling water, the sunlight glinting off the green water as it fell over the edge and dropped into shadow below.

"I'm sorry," said Michael, "about what happened to your daughter." Larry looked over and their eyes met. Larry nodded slowly and then looked back into the falling water. "Larry," continued Michael, "I lost people I loved too, a long time ago."

"Family?" asked Larry.

"Yea."

"It's hard, isn't it," said Larry.

Michael nodded and they fell into silence. Michael didn't know how long they remained silent, but it certainly felt like a long time. He watched Larry from the corners of his eyes now and again, wondering what he was thinking about, wondering if he was okay. Larry drank coffee, rubbed his eyes hard with the balls of his hands, and gazed at the falls. Eventually, Larry turned to him and spoke, his voice low, his tone serious.

"Human beings are built for relationships. I can't know myself in isolation – I can only understand myself in relation to others. So without relationships we eventually become insane. Sitting alone in a cave for years and trying to purify your mind is nonsense. Adopting elaborate metaphysical systems designed to tidy up the cosmic mess doesn't help either. Material wealth and status will only get you so far." Larry gazed at the waterfall for a moment, reflecting, and then looked at Michael again before continuing. "It's probably important that human beings discover something vital to do, something meaningful, the sort of thing Sartre called a 'life-project', but even that has its limits. The thing is, I become myself through relationship, and it is only by having a self that I exist at all. So we need relationships, and the strongest type of bond in a relationship is love. I know because I've felt it. But..." Larry paused to consider his next thought. "… Love will destroy you. In the end, it's not death that wipes us out. Some sad cases are never fit for relationships and they usually find a way to *check-out* before middle age. The rest of us? Well, the object of our love gets taken from us, or at some point we become unfit for love – it's then that we're dead." Larry looked out at the crashing water before continuing, his voice softer, far away. "Love is the best we've got, and it won't be enough. It's that which can be won and that which is lost. It's a balm to the soul and the primordial thorn in our hearts. It's the art of impossibility."

Larry took another drink of coffee and rubbed his forehead hard with his hands. He cleared his throat, spat a thick viscous wad of greenish-yellow phlegm over the railing and into the river, and wiped his mouth with his sleeve. "And yet," he continued, "some of us are better at relationships than others, some have a better ride before the ride eventually crashes." Larry looked over and held Michael's eye before continuing. "Your identity, who you are – it's not something printed on plastic cards which go in your wallet."

Michael gazed into the falls, thinking Larry's ideas over. "I cared deeply about Mary," he said eventually. "She was incredibly important to me, but I never told her." He reached over and touched Larry's arm, a gesture ensuring his attention. "And there was something else. I know that Mary cared about me, but she was… there was something not right about her. Something I didn't understand. She was an amazing person, but I don't know if she could be in love with me, or any man."

"There's so much we don't know about people," said Larry. "So much which is kept private."

They sat together in silence for a while, Michael thinking over Larry's words, Larry wondering what the hell had happened last night. Eventually, it was Michael who spoke.

"Larry, what should I do?"

Larry shrugged. A few moments passed and then the philosopher-bum pulled himself up using the bridge railing for support. "Now how did that go?" he whispered to himself. Larry raised a hand, palm open to the elements, closed his eyes, faced the morning glare, and spoke, his tone reverential. "Ah, love, let us be true to one another! For the world, which seems to lie before us like a land of dreams, so various, so beautiful, so new, hath really neither joy, nor light, nor certitude, nor peace, nor help for pain; and we are here as on a darkling plain swept with confused alarms of struggle and flight, where ignorant armies clash by night."

Larry's hand remained raised, his posture frozen like some disheveled statue, as if the words of the poem were still reverberating somewhere inside him. Michael saw wetness forcing itself at the edges of his closed eyes, but Larry quickly wiped his face with his sleeve, and began to shake and laugh in a maniacal fashion.

"Can you believe that?" asked Larry. "*Ah, Love, let us be true to one another.* Matthew Arnold wrote that. He was a schools inspector for thirty-five years. Thirty-five years! And a really good agnostic." Larry looked away now, and Michael found himself smiling.

"Larry," he said, "you're an idealist."

Larry groaned. "You caught me in a moment of weakness, okay?" Larry leaned against the railing, unzipped his fly, and pissed a dark stream of urine one hundred feet into the gorge.

Larry rejoined Michael on the bench and they stared for a while into the crashing falls and the gorge of green water below, each alone with his thoughts and memories. Michael again noticed the bit of paper stuck to the shoulder of Larry's sports coat.

"You've got something stuck on your jacket," said Michael as he reached over and pealed the paper off. He was about to stuff the paper in his pocket when he noticed the handwritten note. Michael read the first line aloud. "Dear Larry." Larry looked over, an expression of confusion on his face. "Looks like someone wrote you a note," said Michael. Larry stared into space, reflecting. A moment later he shook his head and laughed. "Oh Christ," he said.

"What is it?" asked Michael.

"I think I may have had a moment of clarity yesterday evening," he said, his tone sarcastic.

"You mean you wrote this note… to yourself?"

"I think so."

"Should I read it?" asked Michael encouragingly.

"Why not?"

"Dear Larry, you are a coward." Michael looked over, his brows pulled together as if he himself had been insulted. Larry waved his hand dismissively. "Carry on," he said.

"Purgatory means not having enough courage to live or to die, and there are only cowards in purgatory. So…"

"That's it," said Michael. "You didn't finish the note – how did the rest go?"

Larry stared into space, looking inward, searching. "Nope," he said eventually. "I haven't the slightest idea."

"But there was something else you were going to say," said Michael, "something positive, like something you needed to do. It says *so*…." Larry stared at his hands for a moment, his expression screwing up into a bout of effort as he tried to remember yesterday evening. Eventually, he rested a hand on Michael's shoulder. "I'm sorry; I can barely remember writing the note."

Michael raised an index finger. "Well, I'm gonna keep the note for you."

Larry nodded. "Okay, you do that."

CHAPTER 5

Two weeks past, though Michael's experience of time had altered. He noticed that he was no longer aware of time as a matter of numbered squares on a calendar, as tasks to be managed, or a routine to be kept. Rather, he recognized occasional changes in the environment which seemed to *signal* the passage of time. He was aware, for example, that the high school students had returned to their classes. He noticed that unseasonably cool weather had produced a few pale yellow leaves on the neighborhood oaks and maples. He reflected obliquely one morning that his fingernails had grown.

He would stop into a Starbucks and drink coffee if he felt the impulse, but he had lost any inclination to study the financial markets. Michael didn't care which Starbucks he went to anymore. He discovered an extra queen-sized mattress in the Deveroix's basement, dragged it to his rooms, and dropped it carelessly onto the middle of his hardwood living room floor. He borrowed one plate, one bowl, one cup, and a single set of cutlery from Mrs. Deveroix. He kept a bottle of milk in her fridge, some cereal and cans of food in her cupboards. Very occasionally he felt a moment of slight irritation at his minimalist existence, but in truth, he wanted for nothing more.

He hardly slept, and if he did it was a fitful, obnoxious slumber. Most days he spent time sitting on his mattress and trying to read some books he'd got from the library, but without much success. One day, he had a sudden perception that the German soldier Burt told him about was standing quietly in the corner of his living room. When Michael looked up from his mattress, he was sure that he saw him for a fleeting instant, standing there in his tattered army uniform. He wondered if he was becoming mentally ill, felt anxious for a moment, and then decided that he didn't care.

Michael visited Larry at the park a few times over those weeks. They didn't talk much about Mary or Larry's daughter. They seemed to know that these topics could only be broached in small doses. Larry continued to record examples of human absurdity in his notebook, and he would sometimes share his latest discovery with Michael. Their conversations were more or less sensible depending on how drunk Larry was.

He felt Mary's absence as a dull and heavy ache in the centre of his chest. One night he woke with a feverish start, sure that he felt Mary's breath on his neck, her warm slim palm on his bare thigh. Sometimes he replayed conversations they'd had. A few times he even invented conversations they'd never had.

Michael made a visit to *Tasco's Odds and Ends.* He found Burt at his battered desk in the rear of the shop, staring into space, a finger holding his place in a book. The old man was so still, so inert, that he looked like he'd been shot and stuffed. Burt nodded slowly when he noticed Michael and retrieved two coffees from the back room.

"The police had me down at the station for five hours before they released me," said Burt. "It took me that long to convince them that Mary and I weren't involved in some sort of assassination attempt. The problem is that the average copper's idea of art is a Bart Simpson poster thumb-tacked to a wall. Every time I told them that Mary was using the gun for artistic purposes they just stared at me like I was psychotic. I even had an interview with a forensic psychologist at one point."

Neither of them could find it in themselves to laugh at Burt's attempt at humor. He told Michael twice that he blamed himself for loaning Mary the shotgun. Michael tried to reassure him, but without much success. Burt looked awful, and Michael knew without asking that Burt wasn't sleeping much either. Michael found they couldn't say much about Mary, but he imagined that they would in time. Michael realized how much he liked the old man. In a way, he was the closest thing he had to Mary. He suggested they get a beer together some time.

Sam was preoccupied with *his listener,* Rose from shit-kicker Idaho. Communication had graduated from email to telephone, and there were some pretty loud arguments at the moment between Mrs. Deveroix and Sam about how much time he was spending on the phone. Sam still dropped into his rooms occasionally.

"Whoooo Mr. W. – where's all your shit?"

"Gone to the Salvation Army?"

"You gave all your shit away to the Salvation Army?"

He told Sam that a good friend of his had died and that he was making some changes in his life, and *no*, he didn't exactly understand why he had got rid of all his stuff. He came back to his rooms one day to discover that Sam had left him four bottles of good British ale, one bottle which was new to him.

Michael spent a surprising amount of time riding around on the moped, often with no particular destination in mind. One day, Michael puttered towards the east side of the city. Though the shadows of early evening had begun to fall, the day was still bright and clear. And yet, he absorbed store fronts and intersections obliquely, as if he drove through a heavy fog. One particular building, however, did pierce his consciousness. He was approaching the Firebrand Plant and its large employee parking lot. Michael recalled Mary's enthusiasm for watching *the manhole people*. He pulled to the side of the road and walked to the metal fencing bordering the plant. There they were, just as Burt had said. Six employees in matching corporate overalls standing on their own manhole cover. Must be break time. Each manhole was about fifty feet from the next, and these solitary and yet intimately connected figures looked strangely serene as they smoked their cigarettes. The arrangement of smokers and manholes was eerily symmetrical. What was it Burt had said? Something about how an employee had discovered that the manhole cover was city property, and therefore the corporate smoking ban didn't apply when standing on this small metal island. Michael felt a fresh wave of sadness flow through him.

Michael decided to walk for a while. He passed a convenient store, a liquor store, a laundromat. Pedestrians drifted by and seemed to look straight through him. I'm a ghost, he thought, an immaterial apparition floating through this corporeal world. He felt himself to have no substance, and he realized that he'd been feeling like this since Mary died. But then Michael decided that he hadn't felt like a ghost since Mary died; he had felt like a ghost for a very, very long time. The sensation had simply grown stronger with Mary's absence.

At one point he discovered that he was staring into something vaguely resembling an antique shop. Looking through the plate glass window, he noticed a revolver resting on a stand, the sort of handgun you might see in a Western film.

Michael entered the store and picked up the revolver. The cold blue-black metal was surprisingly heavy, or maybe it was just heavy for a ghost. He turned and slowly approached the sales counter, behind which sat an Hispanic man who read a tabloid. Michael stood directly in front of the counter, cradling the gun in both hands, a mere two feet from the man, waiting. But the Hispanic man took no notice of him. Perhaps he really didn't exist anymore. A strange impulse grew up in Michael and he gripped the gun handle and put his finger over the trigger. He slowly raised the revolver and pointed the barrel at the side of his own head. The man turned the page of his magazine and continued to read. Michael stood perfectly still, aware of Latino music coming from a cheap radio. He could sense a circular coolness where the barrel pressed against his temple, and his vision settled on some batteries hanging behind the counter. *Gold's Universal, AAA, Ultra Plus Formula, Mercury and Cadmium Free.* He wondered what Cadmium was. The man raised his head and stared impassively at Michael, as if he looked up everyday to see a man standing before him with a handgun pointed at his head.

"It's a replica," the man said, an expression of bored indifference on his face.

"Oh," replied Michael. "So I wouldn't be able to kill myself with the gun?"

"Not unless you beat yourself to death with it."

Michael sighed heavily and lowered the revolver. They gazed evenly at one another for a moment longer, until it became clear that there was nothing further which could be said. He turned and walked slowly through the store. Michael replaced the gun on its stand and made his way into the street.

He got as close to home as the corner of Jefferson Avenue and Main Street before the roads got tangled up in his mind. A grey sky heavy with rain and wind hung low about him as he considered his geographical options from the seat of his moped. Yes, he was certainly misplaced again. Michael was angry at being lost, angry at the weather, angry at a new and troubling sound the moped was making, angry at everything... and nothing. It was the newspaper boy who helped him get home this time.

He found he was alone in the house. Michael hung the riding leathers over the bathtub, entered his rooms, and sat down on the mattress in the centre of his bare living room. He stared into empty space for a while, aware of a gusty wind which beat rain against his window and a *dark emptiness* he felt in the pit of his chest. His wallet pushed uncomfortably into his ass, and he removed it. He gazed dumbly at the leather object he held in his hand, feeling an extraordinary weariness throughout his body. Michael opened the wallet and looked inside. Seventy dollars, a debit card, and Julie Miller's business card. Michael made his way to Mrs. Deveroix's phone and dialed Julie's number slowly, his tired brain working hard to complete the task. He wondered why he was calling.

"Hello, this is Julie Miller."

Michael opened his mouth to speak, but nothing came.

"Hello… is there any one there?" said Julie.

What could he say? There was nothing to say and yet he did not have the inclination to hang up, to break the connection. He was numb with indecision, or maybe he was just numb.

"Michael… is that you?" How strange that this soft voice should be using his name and asking if it was him.

"Yes…" he replied.

"Are you all right?" Julie asked.

"No, I don't think so."

Michael heard the knock on his door, and then Mrs. Deveroix's voice.

"Michael, there's someone here to see you – a Julie Miller."

Michael opened the door and thanked Mrs. Deveroix. Julie stepped inside and he closed the door. They faced each other, quiet for a moment. It was only 6:30 PM, but the sky was so heavy that they stood in half-light. The room was lit momentarily by lightening strikes, and violent gusts of wind threw heavy rain against the window. Julie stepped closer.

"Michael, what's wrong?"

He looked closely at her, noticing that she had been caught by the rain. She hadn't bothered to put a raincoat on and her blue Department of Heath blazer was soaked. A water droplet fell from her nose. How could he possibly explain?

"I don't feel… real," said Michael. "I get lost sometimes." Michael searched her face, wondering if she thought he was insane. She looked straight into his eyes, waiting. He took a deep breath and blew it out before continuing. "I don't know if I exist anymore."

Julie stepped forward and placed her hands on his upper arms. She spoke, her voice a whisper, her tone serious. "*I* know you exist."

"How?" asked Michael. He was genuinely curious.

"Because I love you."

He hadn't expected that. Julie's hands felt impossibly warm. "You do?" he asked.

"Yes," she said.

She seemed serious. "But how… I mean why?" Michael asked.

"I just do," she said.

Michael was at a complete loss for words. He searched her face and realized that he could look straight into her eyes. She was smiling at him, a nervous, shy smile. The room had grown noticeably darker in the past few minutes. He felt indescribably weary and he wondered if he could stand up for much longer.

"A close friend of mine died recently," he said. "Her name was Mary."

"Oh," said Julie. "Was she a girlfriend?"

"Not exactly. But she was very important to me."

"I'm sorry Michael."

They were quiet for a while, and Michael sensed that the silence was okay – like the way he and Larry could be silent. He felt his eyes begin to close. "I'm just so tired…" he said. "I haven't been able to sleep."

"Then you need to go to bed," said Julie.

"Yes," said Michael, though he didn't seem to be able to move for some odd reason. Julie began to unbutton his shirt. The manager of the Vital Records Department makes a house call, expresses her love for him, and begins to unbutton his shirt. It should have been quite outrageous, but Michael seemed to observe it all with a curious and exhausted detachment. Julie removed his shirt, folded it neatly, and placed it on the floor. She took her soaking blazer off, folded it, and placed it on top of Michael's shirt. She removed her shoes, took off her skirt, and stripped her pantyhose off. She unbuttoned Michael's trousers and removed them. Julie unbuttoned and removed her Department of Health shirt, and unclasped her bra which she dropped to the ground. Michael gazed unselfconsciously at Julie's large breasts, noticing abstractly that they were perfectly formed with big, circular nipples. She pulled herself into

Michael and wrapped her arms around him, and Michael absorbed a scent of soft femininity.

Michael and Julie moved in silent unison to the mattress. He lay down on the mattress and curled up on his side. Julie pulled the thick duvet over them and curled up behind him. Michael felt Julie's warm soft form pull in close to him, her breasts against his back, her knees tucked in behind his legs. Julie found his hand and held it. Michael let out a long gasp of air, like a dying man, and fell into a deep sleep.

The first thing which struck Michael on waking was how light it was in the room. He assumed that the overhead light was on, but then he realized that the room was illuminated by *sunlight*. Michael sat up, confused. He looked down at Julie, who opened sleepy eyes. Michael tilted his left wrist, as if to view his watch. His watch, of course, was now on the wrist of a Salvation Army truck driver.

"Julie – what time is it?"

Julie checked her watch. "Eight-thirty."

"My God," said Michael. "I slept all night – I never sleep through the night."

Julie smiled. "That's good."

Michael realized that he wanted to know what day it was. It was the first time since Mary's death that he cared to wonder about something so mundane. "What day is it?"

"Saturday," Julie said.

They looked at each other for a few moments, and then Michael reached out and put his hand on her bare shoulder. "You're here," he said.

"Yes, I am," said Julie.

They heard a thunderous crashing on the stairs, and Michael wondered if he should offer Julie any warning. There was a rowdy knocking on the door, and Sam entered the room.

"Whhoooooaa, Mr. W. Sorry 'bout that. Didn't realize you were with..."

"It's okay Sam." Michael glanced at Julie, but she didn't seem phased as she watched the short, round man standing in the door frame.

"This is Julie," said Michael. "Julie... meet Sam." Julie waved and smiled.

"What's up Sam?" Michael asked.

"Oh, I'm leaving for Idaho this morning and I wanted to say goodbye."

"You're leaving to visit Rose, then?" asked Michael.

"Naw," said Sam. "More than visit. I'm moving there. I'm gonna move in with Rose. She's going to school for graphic design and she's gonna help me develop Dark Star Radio. It was her idea that I move out there."

Michael wanted to see Sam off, so he and Julie got dressed and met Sam and Mrs. Deveroix in the driveway. Sam's motorcycle rack was piled pretty high with bags and a tent, and Michael wondered whether he'd make it. Still, he didn't want to say anything to dampen Sam's obvious buoyancy. Mrs. Deveroix looked pretty buoyant herself, which, all things considered, wasn't surprising. Everything was soaked from the storm the previous night, though the rain had stopped and the sun was making abortive attempts to break through thick racing cloud. Mrs. Deveroix and Julie were discussing something in that easy style that only women seem to be able to manage, and Sam leaned closer to Michael's ear.

"Nice work," he said, his tone solicitous. "Great tits."

"Thanks Sam," said Michael.

Sam lowered his tone even further. "You should hear the things Rose says she wants to *do to me* when I get to Idaho. Some of them may even be illegal in that state." Sam raised his eyebrows.

Michael smiled at him. They went quiet for a minute, waiting for the women to complete their conversation. Michael looked at Sam closely, the big man straddling his motor cycle. Despite his appearance, despite the juvenile crassness, he felt a real warmth towards him. He was happy for Sam. They promised to stay in touch, and Michael hoped they would.

When the sound of Sam's cycle faded, Mrs. Deveroix offered to make them breakfast. Michael objected, but she was in such a good mood that she was determined to cook them a *proper* breakfast. She served them eggs easy-over, cooked tomatoes, and bacon, and then disappeared into the living room. Michael and Julie were just finishing when they heard the doorbell. Michael was startled when a moment later Mrs. Deveroix appeared in the kitchen, followed by a policeman. He looked familiar, and Michael realized that this was the cop he had reported his stolen car to. That event seemed a lifetime ago, though it couldn't have been more than a few months.

Michael pushed back his chair. "It's okay Mr. Wilson," the officer said. "You don't need to get up. I've just come by to deliver some good news. One of our officers pulled a group of youths over yesterday, and it turns out they were driving your car. It's got a few scrapes on it and needs a wash, but it seems intact. You can pick it up at the police impound downtown whenever you want."

"Well thank you officer," said Michael. "It was good of you to come by."

The officer held up a large plastic envelope and Michael saw his multi-file and wallet. "And," the policeman said, "the personal documents and wallet you reported missing were also found in the car. No cash in the wallet of course." He handed the envelope to Michael, who placed it on the table.

"Thanks," said Michael.

"Don't you want to check the documents," said the officer. "Just to make sure everything is there."

Michael looked over at Julie, and they shared a grin. "No, that's not really necessary," said Michael.

The officer looked perplexed. "Are you sure? Checking your documents is the only way to ensure you've got all the ID you lost."

"I appreciate your concern," said Michael, "but I'm not worried about it."

"Suit yourself," the officer replied, his face marked by curiosity and disbelief.

Michael and Julie finished breakfast and decided to walk to Starbucks and get some coffee. As they emerged from the back door of the house the sun broke free for a brief and dazzling moment, and then was lost again in swift moving cloud. They turned right onto Sutherland Street and Michael took Julie's hand in his. The soft feminine shape felt good in his palm, but he thought of Mary just then. For reasons he could not understand, the clearest image of Mary formed in his mind. He saw her standing before him, pure and naked. The image was certainly Mary, but different for some reason. Her skin seemed impossibly white, almost translucent, and Michael noticed that the scars on her legs were absent, as if healed. Mary smiled at him, serenely, as if beyond the reaches of this world. He was pleased to imagine Mary this way, but her memory also cut into him with a sadness which had the force of physical pain. For a moment, the pain of Mary's absence mingled with the pleasurable warmth of Julie's hand. Maybe it would be like this for a while. Maybe it would be like this forever. He couldn't be sure.

They continued down Sutherland Street, the wind rattling the leaves overhead. Michael put his free hand into his trouser pocket and discovered a slip of paper there. Curious, he pulled the sticky piece of paper out. Michael recognized the hand written note immediately. He read aloud, "*Dear Larry, you are a coward….*"

"What's that?" asked Julie.

"It's a long story, but I'll tell it to you some time."

"OK," said Julie.

The wind continued to press hard against them, but the storm had blown itself out. Quite suddenly, the sun broke into a bright patch of blue, and the light played upon the soaked tarmac, grass, and trees.

"Have you got any plans after coffee?" asked Michael.

"Not a thing."

"There's a friend I'd like to visit. Can you come with me?"

END

AUTHOR'S NOTE

Certain ideas in this novel have been influenced by other thinkers/writers, and it is important to give credit to them.

At one point, Larry compares himself to lichen. The ideas concerning lichen were influenced by Bill Bryson's fascinating and entertaining book, *A Short History of Nearly Everything.*

During the initial library scene with Larry, Larry discusses hotels. This viewpoint was taken from an album sleeve by the musical artist Moby.

Concerning the man who has sexual difficulties related to white high heels, this was based in a case study the author read many years ago, but he cannot recall or find the reference.

Larry references something "Woody Allen might have said". This joke was in fact part of a stand-up routine Allen did.

Many of the ideas Larry presents during his drunken speech in the park are related to ideas Pascal originally wrote about, and which were further developed by Camus and other existentialist writers. During this same speech, Larry refers to the shadow of a hawk crossing over the crop rows. This image was influenced by a poem by Richard Wilber.

'Larry's law of uncertainty' was influenced by ideas presented in Irvin Yalom's book, Existential Psychotherapy, published in 1980.

The quote at the beginning of the novel (i.e "the saint of yesterday…") is similar to an idea the author read many years ago, but the author cannot find any reference to who may have expressed this idea.

The references to the Henry Metelmann sub-story are genuine, and based on the autobiography, *Through Hell for Hitler*, published in 2002.

References are made in the novel to research conducted on the 'ideal female form'. This research actually exists and the novel's presentation of research findings is accurate. See *D. Singh (1993). Adaptive significance of female attractiveness: Role of waist-to-hip ratio. Journal of Personality and Social*

Psychology, 65, 293-307. However, references in the novel to the authors of this research are entirely fictional.

If you enjoyed reading *The Art of Impossibility*, please post a review at Amazon and let your friends know.

CONTACT DETAILS

Visit the author's website: http://bwahl.ravencrestbooks.com/

Cover art by Silvia Kuro: http://www.kurosilvia.com

Published by: Raven Crest Books: http://www.ravencrestbooks.com
Follow us on Twitter: http://www.twitter.com/lyons_dave

19680353R00180

Made in the USA
Lexington, KY
02 January 2013